PROJECT DARKHEART

A BLACK SPEAR NOVEL

I0846855

BENJAMIN SPADA

FROM THE TINY ACORN…
GROWS THE MIGHTY OAK

This is a work of fiction. References to real people, events, establishments, organizations, or locales are intended only to provide a sense of authenticity and are used fictiously. All other characters, and all incidents and dialogue are drawn from the author's imagination and are not to be construed as real.

Project Darkheart | A Black Spear Novel
Copyright © 2025 Benjamin Spada

Printed in the United States of America

For information, address: Acorn Publishing LLC
3943 Irvine Blvd. Ste. 218, Irvine, CA 92602

www.AcornPublishingLLC.com

Cover Design by Damonza
Interior design and formatting by Debra Cranfield Kennedy

Anti-Piracy Warning: The unauthorized reproduction or distribution of a copyrighted work is illegal. Criminal copyright infringement, including infringement without monetary gain, is investigated by the FBI and is punishable by up to five years in federal prison and a fine of $250,000.

All rights reserved: No part of this book may be used or reproduced in any manner whatsoever, including Internet usage, without written permission from the author.

AI Use Restriction: Without limiting the author's exclusive copyright, any use of this publication to train, develop, or improve generative artificial intelligence (AI) technologies, machine learning systems, or large language models is expressly prohibited. The author and Acorn Publishing LLC as the licensed publisher reserve all rights to license use of this work for such purposes.

ISBN-13: 979-8-88528-143-0 (hardcover)
ISBN-13: 979-8-88528-143-0 (paperback)

"Lovers of action, technology, and heart will find it hard to put *The Warmaker* down. It's a worthy sequel to *FNG* and bodes well for the next exciting Black Spear mission and our relationship with Cole West."

—Steve Stratton, author of *Shadow Tier* on *The Warmaker*

"*The Warmaker* will surprise and shock you as the layers of evil are peeled back. A bona fide, edge of your seat thriller!"

—Thomas M. Wing, CDR US Navy (Ret.),
award-winning author of *Against All Odds* on *The Warmaker*

"Spada has expertly woven a tapestry of action, mystery, and suspense, complete with plenty of next-generation weapons technology, in a race to prevent World War Three."

—Isaac Lee, LtCol USMC (Ret.),
award-winning author of *Hangar 4* on *The Warmaker*

"A remarkable action-packed breath-taking narrative that guarantees a concentrated dose of adrenaline shot straight to the heart."

—Best Thriller Books on *The Warmaker*

"Benjamin Spada knocks it out of the park with *Project Darkheart!* Cole West and Black Spear stands shoulder-to-shoulder with Joe ledger and Jack Reacher. Wicked fun!"

—Jonathan Maberry, NYT bestselling author on *Project Darkheart*

"*Project Darkheart* is a brutal, pulse-pounding masterclass in modern action-thriller storytelling. From its razor-sharp plotting to its bone-crunching violence, Benjamin Spada delivers a tale that grips like a chokehold and doesn't let go."

—Nick Horvath, author of *Sledge vs. The Labyrinth*

This book is dedicated to my mother,
who taught me to never stop fighting for my dreams.
To my father, who taught me to
stand and face all my nightmares.
And for Jackie, always.
To the moon and back.

PROLOGUE

She wanted to know about my nightmares, and I feared what the truth would bring.

For months now I'd been going through mandated psyche evals and counseling. Normally, I'd complain about the time wasted on the shrink's couch and not out in the fight, but I suppose when you're single handedly responsible for the deaths of over two thousand people, it raises some valid concerns over your mental health.

Still, I have an unhealthy sense of responsibility for a lot of matters in the world. A terrorist cell in Dhaka engineered a hyper-infectious strain of anthrax spores? I should've been there. A death cult out of Yellowstone simultaneously got their hands on next-gen Novichok? That's my fault. Inflation rates in this country still skyrocketing? My bad.

That's why I only dragged my feet so much when it came to going through with these sessions. My boss, Mr. Rourke, agreed not to bench me as long as I kept up with the visits. I had some unspent brownie points with him so he'd reluctantly okayed field work last week, which meant today's counseling was an appointment by phone. Said brownie points were earned from a few months ago when we'd been pulled to the very brink of global war. That wasn't anything out of the norm for this outfit, but what set this instance apart was that it was all based on a lie from within Black Spear's circle of trust.

Nothing like finding out Samuel Cain, the man who supplied us with all of our cutting edge tech, was an utter psychopath to make our entire black-ops unit even more paranoid. Yours truly had put the kibosh on all that nonsense, Cain got himself barbecued in a rather grand funeral pyre, I walked away with some serious trauma, and the world kept trotting along as if nothing had changed.

"Are they getting worse?" my counselor, Dr. Bernice Candy, asked.

With a name like that you'd think she'd have a sweeter disposition, but I'd discovered early on that she was pretty much allergic to my sarcasm. She'd been doing this job with guys like me for decades. It meant she was familiar with most shooters' terrible coping mechanisms, had no reservations at calling us out on our bullshit, and wasn't easily rattled when we finally decided to spill the dark truths taking up real estate in our minds. She was a stout little woman you'd think would be right at home behind a nursing station desk or being a principal of some elementary school rather than having Black Spear operators in her office.

"I never said I was having nightmares, Doc."

"Boy, I imagine someone like you is quite skilled at lying. Problem is, each and every time you've actually *made* it into my office and sat on my couch you've sported some serious bags under your eyes. You haven't been sleeping."

I checked my watch. "Occupational hazard. We tend to keep odd hours."

"I think we've been making good progress, but having a session over the phone just isn't the same. I can clear my afternoon, why don't you come by my office?"

"No can do, Doc. I took your advice, and I'm trying to put

myself back into the world, you know? I took a short trip out of town."

I stifled a scoff, the frigid air frosting around my face. I'd grown a beard over the last couple of months and was grateful for the added warmth, but now ice crystals rimed my cheeks and had me second guessing that decision.

"I know you're being a smartass, but it's not an exaggeration to say that you personally *saved* this world from catastrophe. What good is saving it if you don't let yourself be a part of it once the fires are out?"

"Exactly!" I said as I adjusted the stock of the high-powered rifle tucked in my shoulder. "I think I just needed to get out of San Diego."

"Cole . . ." she said more cautiously. "Where are you right now?"

I surveyed the Siberian snowscape before me. The vast white tundra stretched for miles in every direction, broken only by the small cluster of military buildings and the helipad on the horizon. Were it not for that, and my reason for being here, this place might be comforting in the strange way that only solitude can be.

"Tahoe," I lied. "Thought I'd take a skiing trip."

"Skiing and sleep deprivation? Knowing you, I'm sure there's some tequila mixed in there, too. Please tell me I'm wrong. I'm not sure if it's safe for you to be doing that right now."

"Doc, really, you don't need to worry. I'm not *that* stupid; it's not like I came here alone. I've got a friend to spot me."

Prone in the snow next to me lay Daniel Kelly. Nicest guy I've ever met, and without a doubt the most skilled marksman you could possibly find. Luckily for me, he was gracious enough to take me under his wing. I've always been a crack shot, but comparing skillsets between us had at first been like comparing your local Subway sandwich artist with Gordon Ramsay.

Kelly pulled his eyes away from his binoculars and held up four fingers. Four minutes until our opportunity presented itself.

"I'm glad you're getting back to the world," said Bernice. "And it's good you're not pushing everyone away like you try to do to me. But a part of me is worried that you're avoiding things."

A helicopter screamed by overhead. The snow buffeted us. Kelly and I went still as statues, letting the swirling powder fall atop us to further hide from curious eyes. The moment passed, and I once again peered through the scope.

"Do I have to ask if you remembered to bring your medication?" she asked.

Rather than answer, I mentally went to my pack in the snow beside me. My various prescriptions were tucked away in the front pouch and stuffed with some cotton balls so that I wouldn't rattle like maracas with every step.

"Yes, Mom, I brought the pills."

"In our first sessions you admitted to experiencing certain auditory and visual hallucinations. Fire and the burned bodies, in particular. Skipping your meds is a really stupid way to have another episode."

Bernice was always direct with me. It was one of the reasons I liked her and why I didn't piss and moan too much about these sessions. My being difficult had nothing to do with machismo bullshit like ignoring my trauma. It was much simpler than that. I did what I had to do to stop Samuel Cain and no amount of talking about it would change anything. I carried it, fully aware of how bad the weight was, because it was my weight to bear.

Kelly tapped me on the shoulder. The helicopter lowered for a landing and the target would shortly be in sight. Those terrorists out of Dhaka getting up to no good with anthrax? They'd bought their research from a Russian bioengineer. Obligatory nefarious bioengineer was now returning to this installation. In another moment, I would unceremoniously return him to the earth. The rest of our team would retrieve his computer to see who else he'd shared his work with.

"We can up your prescription if we need to. Are you still seeing things?" she asked. I realized I'd been silent just a moment too long.

Flames lit up on the snow in my peripherals as I looked through my scope. The crackling fire found its way to Kelly's body, and he looked towards me. The skin on his face peeled away from his skull as the fires spread across the sprawling tundra. The stench of scorched flesh and burnt hair stung at my nose. A gag fought its way to the top of my throat as the blackened skeleton before me was consumed by the flames. All around me the snowscape turned to an inferno. The helipad in the distance was a roaring pyre, the guards awaiting the helicopter nothing but scorched bones.

I blinked. And the snow-capped tundra of Siberia returned to normal.

"Of course not."

I hadn't had an episode like that in a while, and no I was sure as shit not about to tell Kelly or Bernice or anyone else.

"Do you still blame yourself?"

Again, always direct.

"We've been over this already," I answered.

"Things can change over time. Attitudes, and how we see ourselves."

I needed to wrap this up. My window was coming up and I didn't need her to hear the gunshot.

"I've told you before: I don't blame myself for what I had to do. I'm responsible for their deaths, sure, but I place the blame on Cain. I might've pulled the trigger, but he loaded the gun so to speak. There's a difference."

Her silence was oppressive as she listened for some sort of tell. But in this case, I was being truthful.

"That's a very logical way to think about it, Cole," Bernice said. "But our feelings and logic very rarely go hand in hand. Sometimes it takes constant reminding of the truth before we can accept it as reality."

"And what truth are you getting at?"

"That you were faced with an impossible moral situation, and you made the best decision possible. The number of people you saved is tenfold who died. A hundredfold. Objectively, the scales were weighed in your decision."

I shifted uncomfortably, and it didn't have anything to do with the icy snow. Nothing like being patted on the back for offing thousands to make you feel like you had ants under your skin.

"Cole, in person or over the phone, you get from these sessions what you give. I can work around your guard all day, but we'd make better progress if you let that shield down. Give me an opening, boy."

I frowned. Letting your guard down was hardly a trait characteristic of people in my profession. She sighed at length. I heard the telltale sound of her penning down her observations in that notebook of hers. I adjusted myself one final time and gave the signal to Kelly to radio the others to make ready.

Bernice was about to start another round of questions when I cut her off.

"Let me ask you something, Doc. You're one of the most rational people I know. I mean, you have to be in order to do something like this, right? Logic. Facts. Stoic reasoning. It's got to be your bread and butter in order to survive hearing all the dark crap that comes with cracking open heads like mine. So, tell me, would you have done it?"

I narrowed my eyes. Tunnel vision set in as I focused on the rifle's scope. I put a hard edge to my tone.

"Would you have pushed that button?"

The bioengineer stepped from the helicopter. Kelly used an instrument to check wind speed and direction, then signed it to me. I adjusted my hold so that my reticle hovered over the scientist's shoulder.

"I don't think I'll ever be in a position like you were in."

"I'm asking if you were. What good are those objective scales when it's your hand on the button? Would you have found comfort in them then?"

She didn't give me an answer. I pressed her anyway.

"Would you have pushed the damned button?"

I could hear her notebook closing with impossible delicacy, "I think that's all the time we have today, Cole."

Yeah, I thought to myself, *I didn't think so.*

I pulled the trigger.

PART 1
NEMESIS

*"Show me a hero and
I'll write you a tragedy."*

—F. Scott Fitzgerald

CHAPTER 1

It had taken months to find him. When they did, they initially had thought to surprise him in his Bangkok hotel room. They had intended for it to be a display of force by arriving twelve strong in his room. Twelve of their very best. Some of the deadliest killers they had. Alone, each of those killers had been responsible for scores of successful hits. Together in one room, what could the man in black do?

He'd killed six of them in less than five seconds.

His name was Black. Mister Damien Black. And he wasn't the sort of individual who took kindly to unexpected visitors.

The one in charge had stayed the slaughter by ordering his survivors to stand down. They weren't there to do him harm—as if that was even a possibility—rather they were there to deliver a message.

"Lady Holt would like to meet you."

A man as hard to track down as Black made it awfully difficult for something as simple as that. The offer intrigued him. He smiled, a smile so cold it chilled the hearts of all six of those extant killers, and he handed his blood-soaked knife over to the leader.

"Take me to her."

The following morning, he was halfway across the world, being chauffeured in the back of a Rolls-Royce. The only other occupant besides the driver was the leader of the failed ambush. He'd since introduced himself as Simon Ellis, but beyond that there were no other pleasantries. Ellis wasn't the one truly in charge. He was merely a messenger, so Black saw no need to learn any more of him than he already knew.

What he knew was useful enough. There was a telltale bulge of a pistol at his hip, and most men wouldn't have noticed the concealed blade Ellis had just inside the wrist of his jacket sleeve. Black wasn't most men.

The Rolls-Royce traveled on a private road lined with tall pine trees. The early sunrise cut through between them in blades of narrow light, casting down upon the thick morning fog that hung low in the air. They came to a great wrought iron gate where several armed sentries waved them through. The sentries were sharply dressed, and Black noted that each held automatic weapons.

Their destination, hidden away behind acres of undisturbed forest in the middle of nowhere, was Willowmist Manor. It was breathtaking in a way that Black found only very old architecture could be. The sort of building that emanated power and influence just by looking upon it. That thought brought another cold smile to Black's face. It told him that these people were as serious as he'd hoped.

The Rolls-Royce pulled up to the front of the manor and Ellis escorted him inside. There were more and more guards walking the grounds, trying to remain out of sight while still keeping a close eye on their guest. Black was fully aware of exactly where they were. Ellis guided him through the winding hallways until they found themselves outside a large set of double doors. Ellis knocked thrice before entering.

As Black entered a large dining room within, he was accosted from the side by a true giant of a man. He was well over seven feet tall, black of skin, and wore a deep-blue notch collared trench coat with a felt bowler cap held in one hand.

"This is Mr. Dorian Rinx," Ellis explained. "Rinx takes the safety of Lady Holt quite seriously."

Rinx patted Black down with hands as sturdy as granite. He was thorough in ways that Black admired.

"He's unarmed . . . ?" Rinx asked, somewhat surprised. The whole time Rinx stared death at Black.

Ellis gave a curt nod. Black noted that however the tiers of leadership worked, clearly this Rinx was above Ellis. Satisfied, Rinx gestured towards one of the chairs at the table.

Rinx dismissed Ellis and walked to the far side of the room. Black examined the table before him and couldn't help but wonder how many meetings like this had occurred in the past. How many decisions had been made here that went on to affect thousands? Millions? The whole world?

The door Rinx stood by boomed open, several more guards entered, and Rinx pushed in an older woman in a wheelchair.

She was thin to the point of being nearly skeletal, but there was a hardness to her face that said it was a mistake to think her frail. Pale blonde hair was cut to a short bob that just reached her neck. Her bony fingertips were clasped together and her head tilted with curiosity at Black. There was something almost predatory to that tilt. Like a praying mantis, or some bird of prey.

Rinx carefully wheeled her to the table. For a man so large, he guided her wheelchair as delicately as a figure skater.

The reason for Rinx's care, beyond devotion to his duty, was a medical condition Lady Holt had suffered through her entire life. *Osteogenesis imperfecta* type 2. Commonly known as brittle bone disease. Most people born with her particular form of the disorder didn't live long after birth. She herself had been born with both legs fractured. Though she of course had no memory of it, it had set the tone for what life was: pain. And she had spent her entire lifetime suffering it, surviving it, and being strengthened by it. Every time she broke something, and over the course of her life there had been countless breaks, she had come back harder in spirit. She was fragile in the same way that shards of glass were. Easy to break, easier still to cut yourself on it if you weren't careful. Brittle, but no less dangerous than a viper.

"Lady Holt," Rinx stated, "your guest as promised. Mister Black."

"Thank you, Dorian."

Rinx positioned himself to stand behind her, absolutely towering over her and looking down at Black as if to dissuade any undue violent behavior. The two of them sat at the table for a moment; her in a soft white pantsuit and him dressed all in black as he always did.

"You were bloody difficult to find," she said and reached out to carefully drink from a cup of tea. "My name is Margot Holt, and I believe we have use for you."

"Your reputation precedes you, ma'am," Black said simply.

Holt put the cup down. "Good. Your own reputation is quite . . . *colorful*. I'm told you came unarmed. We all found that very surprising. No weapon?"

Black's face was a blank mask. "I will take one from one of your men's bodies should I need it."

The nearest guard flinched. A sharp look from Rinx and the man straightened, his grip upon his weapon renewed.

She scoffed, "You're amusing. That's lucky for you. If you were boring, I would have Dorian pull out your spine for killing six of our men."

Rinx rolled his shoulders back, the tremendous muscle beneath his coat bulging for a split-second as if to show Black that Holt's threat wasn't hyperbole.

"Those were some of our best."

This time it was Black's turn to scoff, "If they were your best, ma'am, then you truly do have a use for me."

She didn't frown. She didn't smile. Either would have caused an ache to form across her cheekbones. Instead, she cut right to the point of the meeting.

"We seek to acquire a piece of technology I've been led to believe you are familiar with." She signaled Rinx, who handed a document folder over to Black. He looked it over, reading the top sheet in an instant and chuckling to himself as he recognized it.

Morpheus.

"Oh, this old thing? Quite dangerous in the wrong hands."

"My boy, our hands are the only ones that would see it put to effective use." Her eyes narrowed, and she rested her chin upon her clasped fingertips. "That is, if it exists. Despite our reach—which I don't need to tell you is quite extensive—all we have come across is rumors and fractured intel."

"It's real," Black said bluntly.

"How do you know?"

He smiled, ear to ear. When he did, he was pleased to see that Rinx frowned. "Because, ma'am, I've seen it in person."

Holt looked over her shoulder and gave Rinx a silent signal. His own eyes flicked from her, to Black, and back to her again as he measured the truth to Black's words.

"Very well. We're willing to double your regular fee. Sixty-percent upfront and the remaining forty—"

"Pay me my regular fee in full upon completion," Black cut in.

For a moment Rinx thought of breaking him for daring to interrupt her, and Holt must have heard his gloves scrunch up into fists, but she held one of her withered hands up to dismiss the thought. Just like that, Rinx's posture softened.

Black slid the Morpheus documents back across the table.

"I'm not a greedy man."

"There is another element in this matter we should mention," Holt said as Black stood to leave. He paused. "They've become inconvenient for us in the past. Certain endeavors of ours have had less than desirable outcomes thanks to them." Holt leaned forward to the very edge of her chair, managing to somehow appear a giant despite her decrepit form. "You know who *we* are. You know why we can't afford for them to interfere again. You do this for us, consider yourself welcomed into our world. We're talking power here, boy. *Real* power."

Mr. Black's eyes narrowed in interest. "And who are they?"

Lady Margot Holt couldn't fight the snarl that twitched at the corner of her nose. "A band of soldiers playing in the shadows. Trying to convince themselves they aren't scared of the dark. *We* are the dark, dear boy. They need to be reminded why they are meant to fear it." For a moment she avoided looking at him, as if speaking the name of the group that annoyed her so would be like validating a housefly as an enemy. "They call themselves the Black Spear initiative."

That smile found its way to his face once more, this time so wicked with its promises of bloodshed that it gave even Holt pause.

"Ma'am, I've killed Black Spears before. This time will be no different."

CHAPTER 2

Cole West. 2:15 a.m.
Home Site
San Diego, California

Whenever I have trouble sleeping, I go to the dojo to train. I'd hit the speed bag until my shoulders were made of fire, work the free weights to keep the blood flowing, then assault the heavy bag until I was too tired to even lift my arms. After that I'd force my hands up and do it all again. And again. And again and again and again until I was so broken off that I couldn't pull myself off the mat. If it wasn't hand-to-hand, then I was using a dull knife to run drills against one of the practice dummies.

I've always been good with a knife, but lately I wasn't sleeping at all, which meant I was getting plenty of time in to train. Which meant I was getting *really* good.

On a lucky night, my good pal Billy would be here to go a few rounds with me in the ring. I had a solid ten inches of height and sixty pounds on the wiry bastard, but he was a born fighter. Combat was in his blood. And he was fast. Damn fast. He had this annoyingly effective habit of battering me with Wing Chun-style chain punches just to show me how much faster he was. If you're familiar with the movie *Ip Man*, chain punches were Donnie Yen's blurringly fast signature move. Call me biased, I'm willing to bet Billy could give

Donnie a run for his money.

As it turned out, Billy was unavailable tonight, but Kelly was more than happy to spar with me for a few rounds. Beyond being a student of his marksmanship, and occasional sparring partner, Kelly was also my de facto second in command. I was just thinking about how grateful I was to have his support when his boxing glove slipped my guard, and he landed a devastating cross.

Stardust and floating embers exploded in my vision. Before I could counterpunch, his other hand followed up with a brutal shovel hook to my floating ribs that had me sputtering for breath. I found myself down to one knee, my mouthguard spat upon the mat. Blood welled up inside my cheek.

"So, you just gonna lay there bleeding?" Kelly asked. "Or you gonna stand?"

It was a favorite question of Kelly's. Whenever we sparred things tended to go 50/50, yet every time Kelly managed to knock me on my ass, he'd ask the same two questions. And every time, I would answer the same way.

"Standing," I said as I shook the glimmering stardust and floating diamonds from my vision.

"Sorry, couldn't quite hear you?" teased Kelly, cupping one of his gloves against his ear.

"Standing."

I stuck my mouthguard back in, swallowed back blood and spit, and put my fists back up.

"You keep letting me knock you around like this and you'll never take the title from Billy," Kelly said as we circled each other.

An overly exaggerated and painfully sarcastic laugh echoed from the hallway.

"Don't get his hopes up," an approaching voice said.

Speak of the devil. Billy walked in with a sleepy yawn and stretched out his arms. He approached the ring, snapped to attention, and addressed me with the most over the top salute I'd seen yet. "Good evening, sir. The front desk has been receiving some noise complaints, seems to be coming from this area. I came to ensure my captain wasn't getting jumped."

My promotion to captain was still new and strange to me. My predecessor left behind some very big shoes, and I wasn't comfortable wearing them. So far Billy had been the only one on the squad who appeared put off by it. The rank of captain was passed to me and not him or Kelly, despite their seniority, so I could see why he was annoyed. Kelly on the other hand was too friendly to have something like that break his shine. There were times I still wondered if I was good enough for Black Spear, and then all of a sudden here I am *leading* in Black Spear. But if there was one thing I knew about leadership, it's that nobody wants to follow anyone who doesn't want the job. So, I've been running with it ever since.

"Trouble sleeping?" I asked.

"Join the club," said Kelly.

"Lately you've gotten dangerously close to *almost* being able to take me," Billy answered. His hands blurred as he throttled the bag with a quick six hits, following with an upward backhand and then finishing with a sudden elbow strike. "Can't have you thinking you're actually better than me. Sir."

Another one of his barbed comments. They'd been coming a little more frequently as of late.

"I wear the captain's bars but cut the 'sir' shit, Billy." Less humor in my tone lest I invite more of his ire. "We both know that's not how I roll."

Billy shrugged. "It's your team."

I really couldn't fault him for being sore. But I could fault him on his attitude affecting how tight-knit our squad was. I crossed my arms and, despite how spent I was from training, forced steel into every fiber of my body. "Yeah. It's my team."

That gave Billy pause. He frowned, the moment passed, and the animosity seemingly evaporated. Hopefully this wouldn't be a lasting thing and he was just challenging the pack's new alpha to see if he deserved it. A smile found its way on Billy's face once he saw I wasn't going to show my belly so soon. "So, you up for another lesson?"

The way he gestured towards the ring seemed more like a friendly invitation to the guillotine. I rolled my shoulders around a bit and cracked my neck.

Before he could step in and I could get my next round of licks in, I heard a buzzing coming from my gym bag. Billy stood closest to it. He reached down and retrieved my phone. His smile disappeared once he saw who was on the other end. Our lovely boss, Mr. Rourke.

"Saved by the bell," Billy said as he tossed it over to me.

I caught it one-handed without looking, without breaking the stare I'd been giving Billy. "One of us was."

CHAPTER 3

Cole West. 2:45 a.m.
Home Site
San Diego

You know that feeling you get when there's an answer you've been after and you don't know what it is yet, but it just pulls at you? A forensics instructor I recently trained under called that 'the gravity'. When you're onto something, something huge, and it seems so massive that its draw grows stronger the closer you get. The gravity of it. That's what I felt right now.

For nearly a year we had been chasing shadows in the dark. That whole mess with Samuel Cain, his psychotic conspiracy, and the world teetering on war didn't exactly wrap up neatly with a bow by mission's end. Everything pointed to there being someone higher up the food chain orchestrating it all. Or maybe there wasn't. Every time we had a lead or even some semblance of a clue, it would either dead-end or prove to be nothing. No connection. Nothing concrete. Eventually all trails went cold, and there was nothing to go on but that pull towards a greater truth.

My own mentor and Cerberus's previous captain, Vaun, had left Black Spear determined to bring them to light. Yet in six months' time, we'd yet to receive so much as a phone call from him. That had only thrown fuel to the fire. Had Vaun gotten too close to uncovering something more? The sad truth was, Vaun had left Black Spear a broken man. It seemed likelier that upon failing to find any trail to follow, Vaun was now quietly nursing a drink and surviving his retirement one day at a time.

Still, there was that feeling. The feeling of more. The feeling of a great mysterious 'them'.

That's what we started calling them. *Them*. We spoke of Them only in brief mentions. It was like we were all afraid of how big it all might really be, or maybe we were afraid that years of black-ops spook work had finally made us paranoid to the point of crazy. Either way you looked at it, when guys like us spoke in hushed whispers, something was wrong. *We* were supposed to be the ones everyone feared.

We kept odd hours, but it still takes a damn good reason for me to be happy about a mission briefing at two-thirty in the morning. And Rourke had given me that reason in a single sentence when he'd called me in the dojo.

"West, we have a lead on them."

Ten minutes later, my crew eagerly waited in the briefing room with Rourke. Billy and I arrived first. Moments later Kelly, and the designated big-guy, Brandon "Tag" Taggart, entered. Kelly, ever the nicest guy in the room, was kind enough to bring coffee for everyone. How he managed to shower, get changed, and still get coffee was beyond me.

We were joined by our White Shield liaison, Lorraine Harper, or Rain as she preferred. Rain had been a career analyst for the CIA before her skillset had caught the eye of White Shield, the intelligence counterpart to Black Spear's operations side. As our liaison she was our go-to for live mission intel; on more than one occasion her fast fingers on a keyboard (and skill at bypassing firewalls) had made the difference between success and failure.

Part of me felt like half of Rain's reason for jumping ship over to

White Shield was her insatiable curiosity; the other half thought it was the laxer grooming standards she was afforded. She dyed her hair a different color and cut it a different style more often than I changed my socks. This month's flavor was an electric blue shoulder-length ponyhawk. If she wasn't damned good at what she did Rourke would have a conniption. As it stood, he didn't so much as mention it.

Rain cracked open a small can of sugar-free Red Bull and downed half of it. "We finally have a lead, boys." Images loaded onto a display projector on the far wall. If I was hoping for mugshots revealing a sinister cabal with each member sporting a nefarious moustache or facial scarring, I was sorely disappointed. Instead, the screen had what looked like banking data. Far less sexy, but arguably a more tangible lead.

"In the aftermath of Cain's Warmaker plot, we arrested nearly fifty Common Defense Industries employees or associates," Rourke explained. "Information they eventually provided didn't lead to much. We might've had more to go off had West not been forced to torch most of the bastards."

Yeah, fuck you, too.

"An aide to Cain's CFO gave us quite a long list of offshore accounts that we've been monitoring for activity. White Shield assisted in seizing most of the funds, but we left twelve untouched as a lure," Rourke explained. "We figured if we followed the money, it would lead to them. Unfortunately, there was zero activity in any of the remaining funds. We're talking millions just sitting, stagnant."

"That's troubling. If they can afford to let money like that just sit around, then it means they've got pockets," I said. "Really damn deep ones, too."

"But not *that* deep," Rain jumped in. She blew up one of the accounts so we could see a recent sizable transfer. "Call it greedy, call it risky: they took the bait."

Billy leaned back in his chair and propped his boots up on the table. "Sweet. What are they funding this time, another pandemic? Crash the stock market? Arming a resurgent Third Reich?"

"It would be the Fourth Reich, wouldn't it?" Kelly corrected.

Billy flipped him the bird, but his grin faded when he saw the look on both Rain and Rourke's faces.

"They transferred three hundred and thirty-three thousand dollars to a Mr. Penn Umbra of Baden-Württemberg, Germany," Rourke declared. If he was getting at something, I was missing it. I looked at my team, and they all looked nervous. Rourke picked up on my ignorance and elaborated. "The name is a previously known alias, but one he hasn't bothered using in a long time. They hired Mr. Black, captain. The amount transferred is half of his standard pay."

You don't walk around with a name like Mr. Black, use a painfully obvious alias like 'Penn Umbra', or make an entire room of seasoned shooters nervous, unless you have a really, *really* good reason to do so.

"Okay I'll bite. Who's Mr. Black?"

"You remember the Marstelli twins from last year?" Rain asked.

"Freelance enforcers for Cain. One bald and creepy, the other talkative and creepy. Numbers three and four on our most wanted list. Yeah, what of them?"

"Who do you think number one is?"

"*Was*," Rourke corrected. "Technically, he's number zero. The number of casualties he's single handedly caused deemed it necessary to remove him from the list entirely, otherwise we'd be feeding FBI agents and random patrolmen to his already mountainous kill tally."

I arched an eyebrow at that train of thought, certain there was more to it. With Rourke, there always was. Before I could dwell further on it, Rourke lifted his chin at Rain. She took a sip from her Red Bull, then gave me the CliffsNotes.

"Black is a terrorist for hire. Assassin. Mafia enforcer. Industrial saboteur. He doesn't restrict himself to one occupation as long as the check clears," Rain said.

A blurry face shot went up on the screen. He couldn't have been that much older than me. Despite the low resolution of the photo, I could make out sharp features, high cheekbones, and slicked back jet-black hair.

"He's a true ghost. INTERPOL pulled this from a closed-circuit video camera across the street from the British embassy in Rome. The ambassador and his entire security detail got whacked in an elevator. Nobody sees him coming, and these are the only shots we currently have."

A few more pictures populated the screen. None were clear, all were made even fuzzier when blown up, which told me that they were taken from a long distance.

I studied Black's eyes. The pixelated distortion cast a strange effect on them. Inhuman.

"If he's this elusive, it'll be hard to pin him down and get him to talk about Them."

Rain slurped the remainder of her Red Bull, then pointed her clicker over her shoulder while smiling wide. A final image appeared. It looked like a waiting area. When I looked closer, I realized it was an airport terminal. And there in the lower right corner approaching the gate, clear as day, was Mr. Black.

"Captain, this picture was taken today. He boarded a flight from Moscow three hours ago."

"Son of a bitch . . ." Tag murmured, nearly rising from his seat in anticipation.

"That's a seventeen-hour flight," Rain added. "We may have just been gift wrapped the one opportunity we'll ever get at snatching him when he's most vulnerable."

I nodded in agreement, "Coming off the flight. A lot of potential for collateral damage in the area, but I like the idea of hitting him when I know he won't have a gun or knife on him. Assuming Moscow's version of TSA did their job."

"Don't underestimate him, West," Rourke said sharply. I noticed that, so far, he had not once referred to me as 'Captain'. Even after all I'd done, I still wasn't his favorite horse to bet on. "Even without a gun or a blade, he's dangerous. I cannot stress that enough."

"What are we packing for this? As much as I'd enjoy hauling a bazooka through the terminal, we'll have to carry light. If he's unarmed, it won't need to be much. But that's assuming he couldn't find a way to sneak something sharp and metal past the detectors," Billy said. "Not exactly an impossible task."

"As far as armaments go, it's pretty standard affair. I'll let West make the call on that," Rourke answered. "Now as to whether or not Black is armed, I've called someone in to help with that side of the situation."

As if on cue the door to the conference room opened. In walked Dr. Madison Archer, our very own James Bond style Quartermaster. Madison was what most guys refer to as the full package. It wasn't just that she had the body and curves of a goddess, or the reddish chestnut hair that would've been more at home in a shampoo commercial than on an actual flesh and blood human being. The truth was she was brilliant and took no shit from anyone who thought there was any reason other than her brain that had gotten her to her current position. It takes power to walk into a room full of killers like us and still possess the kind of confidence that dominated the room.

I'm pretty sure everyone knew I'd had a thing for her since first setting eyes on her. Rourke fixed a hard look at me to see how I reacted to her entrance. I disappointed him by not so much as glancing in her direction. Madison had worked for Samuel Cain. In order to pay her debt for the part she'd unknowingly played in developing his weapons, she'd agreed to develop tech for Rourke.

Since then, she'd far exceeded his expectations.

Madison wore a long pale-tan coat cinched with a belt and tall riding boots. She'd once confided in me that she spent so much time in sterile research environments, wearing bland splash-proof lab coats, that when the occasion presented itself to wear anything else she leapt for the opportunity to dress a bit more stylish and provocative. I guess that still stood true at this early hour. However beautiful she was, I was genuinely more interested in whatever was contained in the two hardback cases she held in each hand.

She plopped one on the table in front of Kelly and me and carried the second to the front of the room. "These should alleviate any concerns on Black having any aces up his sleeve," Madison said, undoing the latches on the second case and lifting the lid. From it she retrieved what looked like an interesting camera. I use the word 'interesting' because it was the only way I could think to describe something that simultaneously resembled an oversized camera from the 1800's while also looking futuristic enough to have come from the local Apple Store.

"A camera? A little low-tech from the designer who gave us corrosive nanites," Billy said.

Madison responded by pointing the weird camera in our direction and pressing a button. I flinched back, expecting a bright flash, but instead there was just a brief ping and a low hum. After a moment a small slip of paper fed out from the bottom of the camera. Madison slid it across the tabletop towards me. "One x-ray camera; two charges."

The photograph she'd passed me showed skeletonized versions of my squad. More importantly, the photo revealed the firearms and steel-bladed knives we each had on our persons. My attention was drawn to our bones glowing bluish white, nearly the opposite of the charred black ones that stained my memories of late.

The stench of burnt hair. The screams as they begged for their lives . . .

It gave me pause for a moment. I felt anger rising in my gut as my fingers gripped the photo tighter and tighter.

Tag caught me getting lost in my thoughts as the skeletons stared back at me in the photo. He pulled it out of my hands and gave it a quick look before handing it to Kelly, glancing at me out of the corner of his eye to consider what he'd seen on my face.

"It's a tad underwhelming," Kelly admitted as he looked at the photo. "I seem to recall using a next-gen x-ray scope on a rifle that puts these doodads to shame."

"And I seem to recall that prototype not making it to production for a reason," Madison countered. "It wasn't exactly safe. Matter of fact, you might want to get yourself checked and make sure you don't have a tumor growing behind your eye."

Kelly gaped at her dark humor, but I could tell it was just a jab for not appreciating the equipment she was providing.

"His flight arrives at LAX in fourteen hours," Rourke said, snapping me fully back to reality.

"One man snatch and grab? Should be simple enough," I said, speaking to myself as much as my team.

"Nothing's ever simple with him," Rourke said deliberately. "I'm bringing in Valkyrie Squad to assist you."

"Two squads for one man? You don't think that's a little overkill?" I asked. When I looked to my squad, nobody shared my optimism. "Okay, what the hell? I get I'm the only one who hasn't heard of him before, but if he's this dangerous why hasn't Black Spear already tried to take him out?"

For some reason my entire team averted their eyes from my own. Unsurprisingly, it was Rourke who finally broke the silence. "We already have, West. Many times," he said through pursed lips. "Your predecessor Vaun was the latest to try three years ago."

"That doesn't track. Vaun was the best. How did Black get away?"

"West . . . three years ago Black killed John Crow. You could say he's the very reason you sit in this room today."

CHAPTER 4

He finished reading the names on his list, cramped within the confines of the plane's lavatory, before stowing the piece of parchment within his inside jacket pocket. Black began washing his hands meticulously, the blank face of his reflection staring back at him from the ruddy mirror. Both eyes showed nothing. Merely bottomless pools. He stared for a moment, watching and waiting for some flicker, but there was none. No spark. No glimpse of light fighting just beneath the surface. Only blackness. Only him.

He didn't need to re-read the names to remember them, but it was a force of habit. Black's memory was unparalleled. Pulling the names from memory was as effortless as remembering that there were exactly nine rows to pass before he'd get to his seat in coach, and that his seat was right next to the frail elderly man who'd used the golden-topped cane to hobble aboard.

One row behind his seat was the young couple who'd squabbled while boarding about not upgrading their seats to first class. An off-hand remark had been thrown out about the man's current salary. Black had noted that the exquisite silver chain necklace the embittered woman wore was precisely twenty inches long; he'd measured it visually by comparing it to the width of the water bottle that she'd been drinking from.

A businessman in a knockoff Armani suit sat in the row in front of Black's seat. Evidently a nervous flyer, he had already guzzled six travel-sized vodka bottles and fidgeted opening a seventh.

The old man's gold-topped cane would make an effective club. The woman's silver necklace was the proper length for him to fashion into an expedient garotte. And the businessman's vodka bottles, when held between his knuckles and broken off, would cut as well as any knife. Lesser people were so blind to the inherent danger of their surroundings.

All this information, catalogued in his mind with laser precision, flashed through his thoughts in an instant as he turned off the lavatory faucet. To say that Black had incredible situational awareness was an understatement. He wasn't just "aware", he knew details about the cabin that even the people that were sitting in it right now were ignorant to. It was why he was so good at what he did.

Black tightened his tie, exited the lavatory, and passed the nine rows before his own. The old man with the cane was fast asleep, as were sixty-four of the sixty-eight other passengers in the cabin. Black slid past the old man and eased himself into his assigned seat.

Once more he pulled the parchment from his jacket, entranced by a strange desire to read off his targets' names again. Five people. An easy enough task. That, and Morpheus . . .

Black was well versed in just about every weapon the world offered. But Morpheus? What Lady Holt desired was nothing less than chaos itself. Black was a professional, and had as much emotion as a Mako shark, but even he was interested in seeing what she intended to use it for.

"Business or pleasure?" asked a passing flight attendant, eager for conversation in the otherwise silent cabin.

Black smiled as he folded the parchment and placed it once more in his pocket. "Business," he answered. "Unfinished business."

INTERLUDE 1

"Subject's name is Private Edmond Carson," the voice blared through the speaker system. Ed was escorted into the clean room by two armed guards and handcuffed to the table. "Private Carson is currently serving life imprisonment for the murder of two of his fellow soldiers. Tell me, Private, how do you feel?"

Ed looked at his palms, pulling slightly against his restraints to feel how secure the anchor on the table was. "Cold. Why do you keep the room so cold?"

"No, Private Carson," the unseen voice responded, "tell me how you feel. Your state of mind, please. Are you at all anxious? Uneasy?"

"Bored." He shook his handcuffs just to hear the chain links rattle. "What does it matter how I feel?"

"We need to establish a baseline."

"Eighteen months of staring at a prison wall, I'd say I'm just about as baseline as can be."

A technician in a silver clean-suit with a mirror face-shield entered the room. He connected EKG leads to Ed's body. Ed made a show of lunging at him to see how bad he would jump but was disappointed when the tech didn't so much as flinch.

"Private Carson, we require verbal confirmation that you are here of your own voluntary free will before we can proceed. Are you here of your own voluntary free will?"

The sight of the clean-suit was a bit unsettling, but so far none of this program *hadn't* been weird in Ed's eyes. If whatever they were researching was one-hundred percent safe, they wouldn't be pulling their subjects from Leavenworth. Their use of the military's most desperate and hopeless prisoners spoke volumes.

"Yep, I volunteered," Ed said. "Beats the alternative."

The voice went silent, leaving Ed alone in his thoughts. His mind had been all he had left to keep him from falling to insanity, and he'd grown used to the routine pattern he found his thoughts circling. Celebrities he'd fuck if he wasn't locked up, the food he'd scarf instead of the shitty prison rations, the cars he'd love to drive. Those trains of thoughts ran on well-traveled tracks.

He'd barely begun his familiar mental list when he felt a tingle. It was like a static charge, except instead of feeling it along his fingertip it was tickling on the end of his tongue. A few beads of sweat gathered along his forehead. Ed expected to hear some kind of beep or at least for the voice to let him know they'd begun.

"I guess we started then?" He forced a smile, then stopped and shook his head when a sudden wave of dizziness hit him. There was a taste in the air, too. A taste like . . . metal?

The window across from him doubled as a one-way mirror. Ed stared at his own eyes and tried to steel himself, letting these Docs know who was boss. They weren't going to shake him. He'd get through this little test. Shave *decades* off his sentence. Yeah, he had this in the bag.

"Private Carson, what do you see?" the voice asked.

"I see a buck-sixty of American badass."

Ed's forehead dripped with sweat. He felt his armpits grow damp and the tickle of cold drops as they slid down his flanks. That charged metal taste in the air intensified. Ed thought that if he stuck a lightbulb in his mouth it would light up bright.

"Private Carson, what do you see?"

"I see a guy getting sick of stupid questions."

He kept staring at himself. Tight-lipped and sweating. And then the sweat changed color. It grew pink, then red. Dark red. Blood red. It dripped from his pores and ran down his eyes. He tried to wipe it away but his hands, still shackled to the table, couldn't reach.

"Private Carson, what do you see?"

"What—what the fuck is this?!"

His bleeding face drenched the front of his shirt. Ed wrenched against his handcuffs again and again. He bucked in his chair, but it was welded to the floor. A scream ripped forth from his throat as the handcuffs pulled harder against his wrists.

And then the skin broke. More blood spilled forth, and something more. Something white and wriggling amongst the blood. Ed's scream hit a crescendo as plump maggots burst forth from both wrists. They spread out, squirming up his arms and splashing onto the bloody floor.

"Private Carson, what do you see?"

"Oh, Jesus, Mary, and Joseph! Cut it off! Somebody help me!"

A tickle twitched at the corners of his lips. Ed looked in the mirror and watched as a swarm of maggots began to spill forth out of his mouth. He gagged and choked, unable to breathe through the blood and larva filling his throat. The bright lights of the clean room were swallowed by a deep shadow that left nothing but Ed, Ed and that damned mirror showing him everything that was happening.

Ed felt a sharp stab in his chest, his back arched as his pain mounted, and then something deep within him burst as he died.

On the other side of the wall the research team jotted their notes down. "Subject expired after two minutes of exposure to Morpheus, level five," their leader noted. "Prep the next subject, we will begin at level three this time."

CHAPTER 5

Cole West. 3:20 a.m.
Home Site
San Diego, California

Less than fourteen hours to go. But it would be a wonder if I'd make it the next twenty minutes before putting my fist through a wall. You don't sign up to do military black-ops without first accepting that there's going to be dirty secrets everywhere. Some you know, but even more you're kept in the dark on. I guess I'd just expected that I'd be privier to them after all the good I'd done. Nothing like a last-minute reveal to make you remember how little faith and confidence your boss had in you.

I stormed out of the room as soon as our mission brief had concluded, wanting to be as far from Rourke and his secrets as possible. Kelly, still my acting lieutenant on Cerberus Squad, had caught me by the elbow on my way out.

"This isn't the type of mission to go in angry on."

"Yeah," I said and pulled my arm free of his. "Tell them to take a nap, grab some chow, drink some coffee. Whatever. I don't give a shit. Then get the gear loaded up, and I'll meet you at the helipad. Black's plane lands at eighteen-hundred, I want to be there well in advance."

I needed to get my head on right before I showed my face to my team again. My simmering anger issues were a poorly kept secret at this point, but as Cerberus's leader I had a responsibility to keep it together for them. The last thing they needed before punching out and going to work was to see me come apart at the seams. As a precaution, I took my regimented dose of meds Bernice prescribed. Then I paced around my room, going through the full gamut of calming skills she had forced me to learn. Eight count breathing. Positive visualizations. Words of self-affirmation. Grounding techniques.

None of it worked.

Black had killed John Crow. A long time ago, before Black Spear and all the bullets and all the blood, John had been my best friend. I'd looked up to him. Wanted to be as good as him. He was one of those rare guys you meet who's just genuinely good people. Which is why I'd been destroyed when he'd taken his own life. Except, I'd found out years later that his suicide was merely a cover story for his recruitment into the Black Spear initiative. He was Vaun's right hand, and it was only his dying promise that *I* of all people could fill his shoes that had brought me right here.

Ever since Vaun had told me the truth, I'd felt sort of touched by it. Me having a place on Cerberus was because of John. Because of the respect and faith he had in me. But that wasn't the full truth anymore. Me being here because of John's faith was secondary: I was here because Mr. Black killed my friend.

I stopped trying to swallow down all my anger. Instead, I needed to let it be. If it couldn't be made to go away, then at least I could keep it from getting out. Let it fill me. Radiate out from my heart all the way to my fingertips. Building as some terrible energy, like a mad dog's bark just waiting within its jaws. The smell of burning bodies tickled at the edge of my nostrils as that fire inside grew. Growing, but contained. Held back. Kept in check by sheer force of will and necessity.

Yeah, that could work.

A knock at the door ripped me back to reality. In an instant my pulse slowed, my hand unclenched, and a long-held breath slowly escaped my chest. It felt like easing a nocked arrow off a drawn bowstring. I took just a second to compose myself more and then went to answer. I'd be glad if it was Kelly. Despite my highest reluctance, his infectious optimism is damned near impossible to resist.

Instead, I found Madison waiting outside. Arms crossed. Face pulled into a displeased frown.

"Evening, Doctor," I said, craning my neck out into the hallway to see who else was with her. She was alone.

"It's technically morning, West." She pushed past me into the room.

The door had just closed behind her before she pulled me in and pressed her lips against mine.

We stayed like that for a breath. Just feeling that connection, that electricity.

"You were supposed to tell me when you got back from Russia," she said when she finally broke the kiss off.

"I thought it'd be better to let you sleep until morning. Not that you need the beauty sleep," I said with a sly smile.

"And I thought there'd be more time before you had to go out again."

Her long coat fell from her shoulders, my hands had her silk blouse and short skirt following it half a heartbeat later. I wanted to tell her that there would always be another mission, that there would never be a right time for us, that we would forever be stealing little moments like this. We'd be forced into hiding it from Rourke and everyone else for as long as this could last. I wanted to say all those things. Instead, I carried her towards the bed as she kissed me.

Her hot breath against me drove my blood wild. The way she bit her lip urged me to take things slow and that we had all the time in the world. But her hands against my back pulling me into her spoke her true desires. There were no illusions between us as to what this was. I was a killer with too many notches on my gun, she was a scientist with a guilt-ridden conscience. We both shared the scores of dead left in the wake of Cain's plot. She designed the weapon that took their lives, but I pushed the button. We were both looking for a reprieve from that pain and had secretly been finding it in each other for a few months now.

It never went away for good, but by God did we give it the old college try. A voice in the back of my head scolded me for being selfish, warned me that I should've been prepping with my men, but Madison's hushed gasps in my ear quieted everything else. There was no mission in that room, only her arms around me. There was no team to be concerned with, only that primal cliff we found ourselves hurtling towards. There wasn't even any thought lost on the enigmatic Mr. Black.

Just her, and just me.

Her gasps quickened as did the pace of our intimacy. Nails dug into my back, mixing together that intoxicating cocktail of pain and ecstasy. And like an addict, I took to it. Wanting more, wanting the high to last, wanting more than anything to ignore that upcoming cliff racing for us. That ultimate release when this moment would reach its climax, and we'd have to go back to the reality of the world after.

But then it was there, and I was falling into her. It washed over both of us. I let go, allowing it to take the two of us away from the pain.

I didn't sleep. Not that I remember, at least. It was more of a state of blissful nonexistence. I just lay there for as long as possible, not thinking of anything. Funny how the best moments lately are when I don't have a single fucking thing on my mind. The problem with realizing that truth is that it is itself a thought, and then all the rest comes rushing back.

That rush of thoughts must have been too loud, because Madison stirred from her sleep. She held my hand in hers and squeezed.

"I know you won't stay," she whispered.

"And what if I did . . . ?"

The question hung in the air. It was a lie to even ask it. I am who I am. Maybe once upon a time I could've walked away, but that fork in the road was too far gone.

"He's different," she said.

Black. The killer of my best friend. Arguably the one responsible for the chain of events that led to me joining this team. He was the one loose end Captain Vaun had left behind for me. I looked forward to tying it up on his behalf.

"He's dangerous, Cole."

I gave her hand one last squeeze. "So am I."

CHAPTER 6

The way of men is the way of the blade. The gang. The fighter. It's hardened knuckles against the cracked skull. It's the will to survive that's carried every generation from the primitive caveman to the soldier on the beaches of Normandy. It's about getting up just one more goddamn time, no matter how bad it hurts. It's choosing to stand, refusing to lay down and bleed. Always, *stand*. It's looking the reaper in the eye, spitting out a mouthful of blood, and saying, "Is that it? Is that all you've got?"

Ideals and laws are honorable goals to strive for, but they don't keep you safe at night. It's people like me and my friends, holding the line, with a knife in hand.

Thoughts like that put it all in perspective for me. Right now, I was on the clock, and that meant that my entire mountain of internal shit and current mental issues could sit comfortably on the sideline. I took the pills Bernice gave me to make the bad thoughts go away and waited for them all to go quiet. The thoughts died down, and I went cold. Goddamn arctic.

Black's flight was ahead of schedule. It didn't matter. We were ready. In fifteen minutes, his plane would arrive at the terminal.

Maybe five minutes after that he would be walking out of the gate, and two minutes later Cerberus Squad would drag him through a TSA side exit sedated and with a bag over his head. I may be quite an accomplished killer, but if everything went according to plan there wouldn't be a single drop of blood shed. My team didn't make mistakes.

My team was, however, undermanned. We were down to four men, which as a rule we should *not* be doing, and that was the only reason I stopped arguing against Valkyrie Squad tagging along. There were a couple possible recruits with promising backgrounds we were thinking of adding to Cerberus, but I hadn't gotten around to assessing them and this wasn't the mission to throw new blood into the fire. Add it to my growing list of shit to do.

"I still think we should've brought the new guys," Billy said, reading my mind.

I slid one of the x-ray camera cases towards him, not bothering to respond.

"What about you, Tag? Feeling a little outnumbered?" Billy asked.

Tag stood across the terminal, his camera ready in hand. He gave an uneasy grunt, which came through loud and clear through our comm channel. The big man could fill whole dictionaries with the various grunts and murmured noises he used to eloquently capture his feelings.

"Kelly, what do you think?"

"I think it was the captain's call," Kelly answered. "Besides, Valkyrie Squad's got our backs."

A feminine chuckle came through the line. "Don't worry, boys. We won't let you get caught with your pants down."

That would be Major Magdalena "Magnum" Cruz, Valkyrie's leader. Our backup was staged just past the terminal in a secondary ambush point, just in case Black somehow snuck by us. I tried not to question Magnum's choice in staging at Starbucks and grabbing a coffee while we all waited.

"This is Toxin. Cut the chatter," I said, using my combat callsign and erasing all humor from the channel. "Mission is a go. Callsigns only."

Kelly, the only one standing closest to me, clapped me on the shoulder. "We've got this, bud."

He held a folded magazine in hand, concealed within was a single shot dart gun. Kelly didn't miss. One shot was all he would need. The dart was loaded with Sandman, Black Spear's proprietary tranquilizer. It worked faster than nerves could process. It wouldn't matter how lethal a killer Black was: one dose of Sandman and everything but his heart rate and breathing would be gone. A little hard to be a deadly assassin when you're too busy drooling on the floor.

I tapped the button on my earbud to mute it so I could speak privately for a moment. "You think I made the right call?" I quietly asked Kelly.

Kelly worked the slide on the dart gun. "Don't question yourself. This is your team."

I nodded. "You're a good friend, man."

He fought back a smile, and per the usual he failed. "And you're a good leader, bud. They'll see it too. Just gotta let them."

And then the first passengers started walking off the plane. People, just going about their lives. Some must have been coming home after finishing business overseas, others perhaps seeing American soil for the first time. Each of them ignorant of the underlying danger they were walking through. The viper in their midst. I tried assuring myself that there wouldn't be any danger, because my team was too good to *let* it happen. It was a cocky boast, one that even I wasn't comfortable swallowing.

I watched the flow of outgoing flyers through my peripherals, careful not to look directly at them. If I spotted Black, and then made the mistake of making direct eye contact, it might spook him. A spooked killer is a rash killer. A rash killer can be an extremely dangerous thing.

Just as I was wondering if Black would ever walk out, and a strangely hopeful part of my mind was thinking maybe he hadn't been on the flight after all, I spotted him.

"This is Toxin. I've got eyes on Kodiak."

Kodiak, as in the apex predator.

There he was. His hair was slicked back and so dark you'd think it was made of crude oil. Sharp features on his face from cheekbones to jaw line. I'd go as far as to say the guy could have the looks of a model if not for his eyes. Even looking from my peripherals, I could see they were just... off. Other people's eyes glint and reflect, the pupils react and expand or contract as they look around the room. Black's did neither. It was like those narrow pinpricks were unable to register his surroundings. His irises were such a shadowy brown, I honestly couldn't gauge whether they were reacting to anything at all.

Everyone has a distinctive gait. I've been told I walk purposefully, as if every footfall and shoulder motion is deliberate. Tag walks sort of like a wrecking ball on an ice rink, all that mass moving gracefully. Billy tended to strut about as if he was on the catwalk, all chest out swagger. Black? He walked like a knife. He cut through the crowd, weaving through them effortlessly. Finding the gaps between and sliding through without so much as quickening and shortening his pace.

He was twelve feet from me and our window was closing.

"Kage," I said to Billy, using his callsign. "Take your peek."

I looked across the room, saw Billy fake an obnoxious selfie and angle the camera to focus on Black instead.

"Say cheese, asshole," Billy whispered, and he took the x-ray snap.

The moment dragged as Black walked in my direction and Billy's photo developed. Tag adjusted his own camera, waited until Black passed him, and then took the second photo of his backside.

"Window's closing, talk to me," I said.

Kelly's fingers rattled along the spine of the magazine concealing his tranq gun, each tap of his finger in rhythm with Black's steps. Black was a mere five feet away now. But we needed the picture first. He could have a bulletproof vest that would block the dart, or a damn faulty suicide vest that could blow if he took his hands off a dead man's switch.

But then Billy's voice was in my earbud. "He's clean. Only metal on him is the belt buckle. Take the shot, Forty-Seven."

Forty-Seven, Kelly's callsign in honor of an infamous video game hitman. Said character's feats of accuracy were the stuff of fiction; Kelly's were real.

Kelly's hand moved to the grip of his tranq gun.

"Hold for Boomerang's word," I instructed. He nodded, keeping his hand hidden within the pages of the folded magazine.

"Wait, he's got something in his back left pocket," Tag said in a hushed growl. "Hmm. Looks like a cell phone."

Cell phones have call history. Cell phones have GPS. Both are invaluable in finding a group that doesn't want to be found.

"Take him," I whispered to Kelly. "Boomerang, you're up."

Kelly walked towards Black at a perpendicular angle, and right as he crossed in front of him, he nudged the magazine just out of the crook of his folded arm and snapped Black dead-center in the chest. The reaction was instantaneous. His shoulders slumped, those dark eyes of his closed, and right as he became dead weight Tag came behind and pulled him around a corner.

I already had the service door open to a maintenance hallway. Tag hauled him in quicker than anyone would notice and tossed him unceremoniously on the ground. I cut a look back outside. No one even glanced in our direction. In all, it had taken just about four seconds. Our squad was lethally efficient even when we were working with the bare bones manning.

Kelly sat down at a seat across the walkway from our doorway.

"I told you," Kelly said with a wide grin as he began to genuinely read his magazine. *Vanity Fair* of all things. He looked over the top of the page to give me a wink. "We've got this in the bag."

I looked down at our captive. Tag searched him and pilfered through his pockets. From his inside jacket pocket Tag retrieved a folded piece of parchment. He opened it and read it, then nodded to himself and handed it over to me.

"Looks like we've got his hit list," Tag said as he continued his search.

The parchment held a list, scrawled in gold ink. I read the names of five complete strangers and then committed them to memory.

Evan Uric, Milo Whail, Stew Cleo, Grant T. Dragonab, and Allen Diekly.

Absolute nobodies to me. Whoever and wherever they were, they owed Cerberus Squad a round of drinks and a serious thank you letter right now.

"It's not a cell phone," Tag grunted as he pulled a small device from Black's back pocket. "Looks like a car alarm?" He set the small two-button remote on the floor next to him. It couldn't be larger than a case of TicTacs.

"What else does he have?" I asked. I took another glance out of the service door to see if we'd drawn any attention yet. So far, so good. "What do you think that does?"

Tag shrugged, "No idea."

"It does this," Black said, his head snapping upright as his hand shot out and pressed one of the buttons. My stomach leapt up into my throat as I saw what Black held in his other hand. Kelly's dart.

"I caught it."

CHAPTER 7

Cole West. 4:15 p.m.
LAX
Los Angeles, California

I was screaming something. Maybe an order to Tag to step back so I could just put two bullets through Black's head then and there. Maybe I was yelling for Tag to restrain him. I never got a chance to finish screaming whatever it was before the explosions went off behind me.

"Hold him!" I bellowed to Tag as I leaned out of the doorway. Three, no *four*, small bangs echoed off the walls of the terminal. I looked around and saw several injured civilians. And then a fifth bang sounded off. I watched in horror as a young woman's shoe exploded with the force of an M-67 frag grenade, taking the entire lower half of her body with it. All throughout the terminal were the bodies of the dead and the mangled. I'd seen people turned into red chunk, and it was never a pretty sight, but this was downtown Los Angeles, for God's sake.

It occurred to me that, despite the carnage, I wasn't getting any flashbacks. My brain was doing a pretty good job of keeping me in the here and present rather than taking me to my own nightmares. Maybe Bernice's pills were helping after all. Fire leaves the same signature charred scent on everything, but explosions? Bodies that are blown up leave a foulness in the air altogether different than burned ones. It's as if your tongue can taste the remnants of the parts that were vaporized.

Two more bombs went off while I tried to swallow reality down. One detonated at the back of some poor soul's head and showered everyone nearby with bits of skull and charred brain matter. The second blew around the corner. All I saw was smoke and meat flying from out of sight.

I don't know how he did it, but I knew what he'd done. Black had somehow boobytrapped his fellow flight passengers.

"What the hell just happened?" Magnum screamed into the comm link.

"Civilians … they …" Kelly started to say, the words fumbling from his tongue. "They just exploded."

"Where's the target?" she demanded.

"We got him," I answered. "Valkyrie, we've got twenty-plus injured civilians here."

"Roger, en route."

"Jesus Christ," I breathed. "Tag, hold that motherfucker still."

Tag pulled Black onto his feet and shoved a giant fist against Black's chest, pinning him against the wall.

"Flinch," he barked. "Give me one goddamn reason to put you in a body bag."

Black's head tilted slightly, as if he was measuring the giant that stood before him. And then out of nowhere a black-bladed knife flashed in his hand and left a huge slash across Tag's inner arm. In a blink he cut Tag's forearm and bicep twice more, then buried the point down deep into the flesh between Tag's shoulder and neck.

Tag screamed out and clamped his hands around Black's own as the assassin tried to push the knife in deeper. Impossibly, the smaller man was giving Tag a struggle.

"Where the hell did you get that?" he asked in utter disbelief.

Tag reached for the snub-nosed .44 magnum he kept in the small of his back, but he had to stop when it took both of his hands to keep Black from driving his blade all the way to the hilt.

"Sleight of hand," Black answered. "Just like how I got this."

He stuck something against Tag's chest with his free hand, and Tag glanced down with eyes widening in horror. His very own snub-nose .44 was pointed at him.

"Bang, you're dead."

CHAPTER 8

The revolver didn't sound like a gunshot as much as it did an audible act of God. A deafeningly powerful roar that sent the .44 hollow point hurtling at well over a thousand feet per second to close the point-blank distance of mere inches. The big man flew back against the wall as the heavy round hit him in the chest.

"Nice gun," Black said, stowing the revolver inside his jacket. No blood came from the entry wound. Black prodded at the soldier's shirt and felt the armor underneath. "Hmmm, even nicer vest."

He stepped to the doorway where the other man, the leader, was just now turning around to see what had happened. Black waved at him playfully with one hand, while holding up a security keycard with the other. The very keycard that granted access to this service corridor. Black had swiped it from the leader's jacket when they carried him in. The man made a move, but Black used the toe of his shoe to slam the door in his face.

Black gave a second's pause at the door just to hear the man scream in anger on the other side. The door thumped in its frame as he beat his fist against it. Satisfied, Black turned heel and walked down the hallway. He stopped at the crumpled giant on the floor, then leaned over casually.

"I'm going to need this back," he said politely. Black wrenched his knife out of the man. There was an immediate arterial spurt, and the giant winced, turning a shade paler in an instant.

The knife was made from single piece of hand-knapped obsidian, the handle wrapped in off the shelf paracord. Utterly invisible to metal detectors and sharp as a razor. It wasn't lost on Black that for all man's advancements in technology, a simple piece of sharpened rock was as deadly and useful today as it was thousands of years ago. In a modern world of carbon steel alloys, injection molded plastic handles, and ever more advanced 3D printing, there was something profound that came with obsidian. For Black, it took him back to a more primal time. Pure. A time free of finery, a place with no room for anything other than death or survival.

He kept a dozen identical knives hidden on his persons. Up either sleeve, concealed in secret vest pockets, tucked in the small of his back. Even though he himself had personally knapped each one, there was no sentimental attachment to them. He was not pathological; he did not feel an uncontrollable compulsion to use them as some sort of signature. They were purpose built. He used paracord to wrap the handles because paracord is readily available. The knives were untraceable, undetectable, and utterly replaceable. His twelve blades were as disposable as the lives he took with them.

The thirteenth blade was different.

The thirteenth blade was special. It was a tool reserved for only the most exquisite of uses. Special kills deserving of a special death. Rather than using meaningless paracord for a wrap handle, this one was fashioned with fine black Portoro marble. White swirls veined through the material like lightning frozen in stone. Or, more appropriately, like souls forever trapped in the handle. It's eight-inch tapered stiletto style blade was chipped out of obsidian sourced from Jalisco, Mexico. That stone was utterly flawless. A black glass so pure it was as if it was made from the void itself. There was something about the marble and obsidian he loved: two stones from two continents away brought together as one. The black of the blade and the whisps of white within the marble reminded him of life and death, and the thirteenth blade was but a key that ushered souls from one side to the other.

"We'll find you," the giant muttered, his voice barely above a whisper.

Black shook his head, "For your sake, you should seriously reconsider that."

He knelt and picked up his detonator from the floor. Such a useful little tool. The sticky-bombs he'd tagged several of his fellow passengers with were roughly the size of a quarter but as thin as a band-aid. If you were sleeping when one was placed on you, which they all had been when he'd returned from the lavatory, it would be nigh impossible for you to know until it was too late. Each of the stickies carried half a gram of PX-2, a next-generation plastic explosive. The stickies weren't powerful enough to blow up a plane, but if you were unfortunate enough to have one on the sole of your shoe then it would take the whole foot with it. Just enough explosive force and bloodshed to cause sufficient distraction.

With one hand he gently turned the giant's face away to expose his ear. And there it was. Black plucked the earbud communicator from the big man's ear and tossed it in the air before catching it with his other hand.

He thought of his list, considered if it mattered that his enemies had taken it, and thought amusingly that it would all still work out according to plan. These operatives could send as much help as they wanted, and Black's names would die all the same. The targets could no more evade his blade than they could their own shadow. Of all the things Black was, he was above all focused. As singular in his purpose as a plague. There were countless killers for hire on the market, but not one of them was as unflinchingly deadly as him. Ending life was what he was made for. You strip away many people's layers, be they policemen or soldiers, and you see that they are killers at their core. But Black took great satisfaction in the purity of who he was. He had no layers. There was no high-ranking general somewhere he could pass the blame for his kills. No law to restrain his purpose, no code of ethics to stay his hand.

A hunter was only as good as the prey he sought, and in recent years his targets had utterly failed to please him. Easy kills. Vulnerable men with bad habits of being out in large crowds or sleeping in homes with sub-par security systems. Taking their lives was no more satisfying to him than a shark would be from feasting on krill. He longed for a challenge in a way that no one could ever understand. He longed to unsheathe the thirteenth blade and add another soul to its collection. It was why he'd taken Lady Holt up on her offer: for the thrill he had been too long without.

When he thought back on his life's work, there were many moments he was proud of. The jobs that were supposed to be impossible, the targets that were meant to be untouchable. And then, high above all on that list of moments, there was his greatest kill. The one that never strayed far from his thoughts no matter how many years it had been.

Adrian Rasp.

Oh, how they had fought. It was exquisite. Black had fought with Adrian for years until he'd killed him once and for all. Even now, Black could hear his last pathetic scream. The way that it had abruptly stopped once Black delivered the final blow. It had been nearly ten years since then, and to this day Adrian had been the one person no other challenge could top.

Recently, Black had even allowed others to climb the ladder of notoriety in hopes that they could be cultivated into a threat for him to take out. Like crops of killers being farmed and groomed just so he could harvest them when they were ripe. Phobos Marstelli had been one, the dreaded Yakuza headsman *Mamushi* another, and the one they simply called the Ghost. But Phobos was gone, the *Mamushi* had made his first mistake and was taken off the game board, and the Ghost had vanished and was most likely long-since dead.

No one else was worthy.

But this assignment would give him what he wanted. A *new* greatest kill. A fresh name to etch into his memory. Black could hardly wait to stain his thirteenth blade with their blood.

CHAPTER 9

Cole West. 4:20 p.m.
LAX
Los Angeles, California

The screams of the dying behind me. The horrified shouts of the terrified mixed in. Alarms throughout the terminal blared and completed the chaotic abattoir.

Valkyrie arrived and triaged as many of the casualties as they could. Any second now airport first responders would be on the scene, and we could disappear. Right now, it was up to us to keep as many people alive as we could.

"The target?" Magnum asked me.

"Other side of the door."

"What?!"

"I didn't stutter, damn it."

Kelly pushed both of us aside, weapon at the ready, and used the second access card we had to swipe open the security door. From Tag's .44 firing to now had been the span of seven seconds, and I knew too well how little time that could leave us to save him.

But Tag was alive. For now. His darker olive skin was paler than I was comfortable with, and the splashes of red staining the walls and his clothes were just as bad. Kelly was already on him. Thin lacerations lined Tag's arm, but they weren't the source of the worst of the blood.

I surveyed him in an instant and found it: the downward puncture between his neck and shoulder. Kelly pulled a small pouch of clotting powder and sprinkled it into the stab wound.

Since assuming command of Cerberus, I had yet to lose a man. Today would not be that day.

"Holy Santa Claus shit this is a fustercluck," said Billy as he entered the hallway. His arms were soaked to the elbow with blood from helping the other injured. Normally quick of wit and the first to crack a joke, he suddenly found himself at a loss for words when he saw Tag's state. Instead, he crouched down next to Kelly and handed him a roll of bandages while nodding to the neck wound.

"Artery?"

"Bright red," I said, pointing to the splatter on the wall. Arterial blood is brighter in color than blood shed from the veins or capillaries.

"What the hell did he cut him with?" Billy asked.

"Obsidian," Tag mumbled, his eyes fluttering. "Volcanic stone."

Billy's eyebrows arched. "You're telling me you got stuck with goddamn *Dragonglass*?"

Tag nodded slowly, the small motion visibly paining him.

"Well, shit, I mean it's a good thing you're human, you know, and not a zombie. Otherwise . . . *tsssh*!" He mimicked the sound of ice shattering, which earned him a smirk from Tag.

"Toxin to Yellow Pages," I said into the comm channel.

"I never agreed to that callsign . . ." Rain's voice replied disdainfully.

"Kodiak is loose. I say again, Kodiak is loose."

"Jesus, what happened? Reports are flying in of a terrorist attack. Multiple suicide bombers."

"Fake news," I said. "Check the security footage. He booby-trapped them and waited until we made our move."

"Yeah, about that. The security cameras cut out for two minutes, I had nothing but static, and then this. What do you need?"

I looked outside the access corridor to the terminal strewn with little chunks that used to be limbs. Nearly fifty civilians still tried to crawl or shamble away to safety. Others made the cold linoleum floor beneath them their deathbeds as they succumbed to wounds before either we or Valkyrie Squad could provide aid. Many more would die if we didn't stay to help until the rescue crews could get here.

My jaw clenched so tight it was hard to get the words out. I was on the verge of grinding a crack into a molar. "The target is the priority. All this is to slow us down. Access all footage available and track him, we're reengaging."

Kelly gave me a sharp look, as if to ask if I knew what I was saying, but then saw my mind was made up and nodded solemnly. It took both Kelly and I to haul Tag up on his feet; Billy ran off ahead to get our ride ready. We knew nobody would think to look twice at yet another injured bystander being pulled away.

"Valkyrie, on me," I ordered.

"We can't just—" Magnum started.

"If we don't nail him down, then this will be just the beginning."

Valkyrie's leader took one last look at the terminal, then reluctantly nodded at her team to fall into the access corridor. "You're a cold son of a bitch, West. You know that?"

I didn't have anything smart to say. There was too much truth to her words.

CHAPTER 10

Darren Rourke. 4:23 p.m.
Home Site
San Diego, California

A tremor ran through his hand as he popped the little white pill into his mouth. He swallowed it dry, impatient for the medicine to take effect and numb the fire that danced across the nerves in his jaw. Rourke was not one prone to worrying. It just wasn't in his nature. But what just happened in the past ten minutes? The shit hadn't just hit the fan. It had hit a four-megaton bomb and was in a quickly spreading mushroom cloud of crap. Yes, he was very worried.

No amount of digital wizardry and cover-up would be able to control this. The scene had been filmed and captured by dozens of cell phones, the standard federal response had already been triggered, and feds would be taking on the investigation. Reporters would be on the scene any minute now, the ensuing interviews would be played and replayed again and again in the coming weeks. None of which made it any easier for Rourke's men to covertly handle the *real* problem.

Cerberus and Valkyrie Squads would be able to egress without obstruction, but that wasn't the issue. The problem was that Black Spear's anonymity and autonomous nature was key to their success. They handled the problems others couldn't because there was never any outside involvement. A terrorist attack in one of the nation's busiest airports would draw unwanted attention and involvement from nearly a dozen federal entities.

"This is going to cause problems," the woman behind Rourke said as he watched the madness unravel on the projector screen. The woman was Kara Mason, formerly one of Black Spear's best operators and currently Rourke's assistant and bodyguard. Even in her conservative pantsuit and modest heels, she was lethal. In fact, he'd once witnessed her quite literally use a heel to lethal effect.

"Casualties were inevitable. Did you forget how dangerous he is?"

"No," Mason said, a finger absentmindedly tracing the hook-shaped scar on her face. "I remember quite vividly, sir."

"As do I," said Rourke, the pain in his jaw flaring once more.

The two of them had already faced Black years prior, and he'd left his mark on both of them. A scarred reminder that he was still out there. That the living nightmare could still be among them.

"You signed their death warrants the second you tasked them to bring him in alive."

"It's been years since we've had a legitimate chance at him. We *needed* to take it."

"Have you considered that it was his trap and not ours? Why would he make it so easy to find him now? Him using an old alias wasn't a sloppy mistake. He doesn't *get* sloppy, and you know that."

Rourke bit his tongue. Simply doing that caused his jaw untold agony. Mason never minced her words. That—and her skillset and track record—was why Rourke kept her by his side. But her assessment now was uncharacteristically charged with emotion. With anger.

"It's not too late to pull the teams back, sir."

"He's one man," Rourke replied. "He's on the run, all on his own, with two squads in pursuit. He's a lone wolf, always has been, and there will be no back-up for him. As dangerous as he is, we still have the advantage. Cerberus Squad has faced far graver threats, and Valkyrie's Major Magdalena Cruz is one of the best."

"Maggie is, dare I say, a friend," said Mason. Her eyes narrowed. "I'd hate to think you're making a rash decision that could put her at unnecessary risk."

"It's been a long time since Major Cruz was your Lieutenant, Miss Mason. Frankly, it's a discredit to her abilities that you don't have more faith in her."

"I have utter faith in her," Mason hissed. "West, on the other hand, has a far shorter history. I was making sure you factored that into your equation."

As a matter of fact, it had. Captain Eric Vaun, West's predecessor as Cerberus's leader, had left such a large shadow behind that Rourke thought it impossible for West to escape it. Of the numerous teams Rourke commanded, West was one of the most junior. That wasn't to say he was inexperienced. In the few years since his recruitment into the Black Spear initiative, West had been instrumental in turning the tide in more than one incident that would have destroyed the nation. But being a capable soldier and being an effective leader were not the same thing.

"We have his target list," Rourke murmured. "Get White Shield on locating them, I want teams shadowing each one. Find the connection between them. Whatever it is must be severe enough that they called in such big guns."

Mason gave a curt nod and dismissed herself.

Rourke delved back into the files on his computer. He'd been reviewing everything they had on Black. Once he was sure Mason was out of his office, he hit a key and accessed an entirely different drive. This one held files that no one else, not even White Shield, knew of. It was Rourke's, and Rourke's alone.

Within the hidden drive were files detailing every kill, both confirmed and unconfirmed, that Rourke had personally been able to link to Black. To say the list was extensive was an understatement. The breakdown had everyone from politicians, mafioso, to Black Spear's own operatives, and even unsanctioned hit teams. When he'd caught wind of traces of the man somewhere in the world, but those traces weren't solid enough to act on himself, he'd sent others. Unknown to all, over the years Rourke had pursued unconventional avenues and hired other hitmen and criminals to take out Black. The money was not well spent.

Rourke justified it to himself that Black Spear was outside the realm of ordinary rules, anyway, bending what was 'allowed' went hand in hand with their line of work. But somewhere, hidden within all the corpses he left in his wake, was the clue Rourke was after. A weakness. Some chink in this killer's armor that they could exploit. It was there, and Rourke would find it or die trying.

INTERLUDE 2

Their study was slowed by the numerous variables between subjects. Age, ethnicity, gender, mental aptitude, and even the crimes they were incarcerated for were just a few of the many factors that could alter the results of Morpheus exposure. That, and they could only secure so many volunteers at a time.

"Who do we have today?" asked Doctor Erin Childs. Of all the staff on the project, she remained the most enthusiastic. Between people cracking under the demanding schedule of their work, and those who could only stomach its nature for so long, their team had a fairly regular rate of turnover. Yet, two years in, Childs was as eager as ever.

"Subject's name is Airman Tyler Lodge," stated the leader of the project, Doctor Hertz.

Hertz had been head of Morpheus research for nearly a decade. It was his length of service that others found very off-putting. Ten years saw what little hair he still had turn silvery gray, while his charming boyish looks that had caught the eye of so many coeds at Stanford had grown gaunt and grim. His eyes held none of the optimism of Childs, but everyone knew his dedication to the research bordered on obsession. "Airman Lodge is currently incarcerated for the rape of a minor."

One of the newer team members, Andrew Wynn, examined Lodge through the monitor as the guards escorted him into the clean room. "Charming. I was getting tired of processing nothing but killers."

"He's pretty for such a pig," Childs whispered.

Before Lodge's crime he had been an avid fitness enthusiast. Even in his confinement he'd maintained his impeccable shape with a strict regimen of bodyweight exercises in his cell. Hundreds of pushups, crunches, and squats were a great way to pass the hours of isolation.

"Ten bucks says he whimpers," Wynn laughed. "Guys like that? All show. He's a quiet one, he'll fade without a peep like a fart in the wind."

"Quiet? Hell no, that's a screamer if I've ever seen one. You're on," Childs said.

They shook on it. One of the technicians, having returned from attaching the EKG leads to Lodge's muscled body, removed the hood from his clean suit and cocked his head towards the monitor.

"You never know," the technician said, "he could go full Krueger."

Both Childs and Wynn looked at each other.

"Don't even joke about that, man," Wynn said, fighting back a shudder.

Childs focused back on her workstation, choosing to ignore the goosebumps that rippled across her arms. She took a moment to review Lodge's file before turning to Hertz. "Sir, was he picked for his physical characteristics, or for his crime?"

The leader pushed the microphone away so as not to accidentally speak through it. "Both," Hertz said. "There's an undeniable connection between this man's vanity and his crime. I'm curious how that will affect his exposure reaction."

Childs nodded and Hertz returned to the microphone.

"Airman Lodge, we require verbal confirmation that you are here of your own voluntary free will before we can proceed. Are you here of your own voluntary free will?"

Lodge flexed his muscles at the mirror in front of him and shrugged, "Ready when you are, doc."

There was a sound, muffled by the walls, but Lodge's keen ears perked up all the same. It was like when you switched on an old tv, and the picture hadn't yet popped onto the screen. The air felt energized, gaseous. Lodge was sure he was breathing something in. Once aware of it, he found himself breathing shorter shallower breaths.

"Please breathe deeply," Hertz's voice said through the speakers. "It can affect our readings. Now tell me, Airman Lodge, what do you see?"

Lodge sat up straight and squared his jaw, admiring his reflection's cheekbones. "An innocent man wrongfully convicted. Handsome one, too."

Hertz checked the instruments near him. Lodge's vitals were solid, and he'd been exposed for two minutes thirty seconds now. On the other side of the wall, Lodge continued to watch himself in the mirror. Lodge thought to himself that he was more tired than he'd realized, but serving hard time in advance of the likely life sentence he faced would do that to anyone. The bags under his eyes were bothersome, but not unexplainable.

"Airman Lodge, how do you feel?"

Lodge took a deep breath and sighed. "I feel like so far this is the easiest pardon a guy could earn."

Hertz turned to Wynn. "Turn it up. Level five."

Wynn adjusted the controls.

Lodge's nostrils flared. He sucked in a deep lungful of air, still uncertain of what they were exposing him to but not willing to let them see him scared. His pulse quickened; his chest grew hot. Once more he caught himself looking into his reflection's eyes. Captivated at first, but then his gaze was drawn to a line on his cheek. A wrinkle. He could have sworn it wasn't there before.

"Airman Lodge, what do you see?"

He gave no answer. He was too busy staring at the other side of his face where additional wrinkles appeared. His cheekbones, moments ago sharp and prominent, were becoming sunken, sickly.

"What the hell did you . . ." he began to ask but found himself short of breath. Lodge's head dropped down as he had to fight to catch his breath. "What the hell did you to me?" Lodge snarled and looked back into the mirror, his anger instantly shifting to fear as he gazed upon the face of a rapidly aging man. His perfectly golden hair now ran gray and thin. Muscles, built through years of dedication, shriveled in seconds. In the span of five wheezing breaths, Lodge withered away to a husk.

It took all his strength just to keep his shaking wrinkled head aloft. The metal handcuffs around his wrists ached horribly. Worse yet, he heard the clattering sound of his rotting teeth falling from his leathery gums to the linoleum tile below. He felt weak now, so weak it grew impossible to stay upright or even breathe.

"Airman Lodge, what do you see?" Hertz asked one last time.

It was no use. Tyler Lodge's ears no longer worked. After a moment, his chest fell once more and did not rise again.

Childs jumped when she found Wynn leaning over her shoulder. "Told you he was a quiet one."

CHAPTER 11

Dorian Rinx held the car door open for her as she delicately slid inside, then hunkered down and sat next to her. The Rolls-Royce lowered two inches from his considerable weight.

"He's putting on quite a spectacle," said Rinx, turning the screen of his phone in her direction so that she could see the news articles.

"The biggest fire creates the largest shadows," she answered. "He could have blown up the entire airport, and all it would do is hide us more. Our entire world lives in darkness, Dorian."

"You're not concerned his light might reveal us?"

Holt stifled a dainty snicker. "You could cut into that boy and he wouldn't say a word, even when he was nothing but pieces unfit for mice."

Rinx pursed his lips.

"Oh, speak your mind, dear. You're pouting like a bloody schoolgirl."

"He's not a boy, ma'am. He's a mad dog that we let off the chain. I don't want it coming back to bite us."

Their car lurched as the driver steered over a bump exiting the manor's wrought iron gates. It jostled Holt slightly, and she winced.

Rinx shot out a powerful yet gentle hand to help keep her still before shooting an angry look at their driver. His eyes flicked from Rinx's to the road, adjusting their speed ever so slightly and carefully maneuvering the car to the road. Still, Rinx motioned for him to pull the vehicle over.

"You worry too much, Dorian."

"It's my job to worry."

"We need Morpheus for our next phase," she said curtly. "Unless you have a crystal ball to locate old Cold War relics long-since shelved, we have no recourse but to employ his services. For the time being."

The driver carefully slowed their vehicle to a stop just outside the gate. Rinx stepped out and signaled both the driver and guard on the passenger side to get out.

"Bloody hell, Dorian. I would hate for my own plane to leave me behind should we delay further."

Rinx sized up the driver. He towered over the man by nearly ten inches. He handed his bowler cap over to the guard, who graciously accepted it, and then punched the driver low in the side. The wind blew out of him instantly, followed shortly by a cough of blood as the driver collapsed to one knee. One broken rib, his liver most likely bruised as well. It would serve as an adequate reminder of how sensitive their passenger was. In Rinx's opinion, he was being let off lightly.

The driver wheezed his apologies while rising to his feet and placing his hands plaintively behind him. His grimace was barely restrained, and the driver was unable to stand without leaning to one side. Rinx gave the other guard a nod and jerked his hat away from him.

"You're driving now."

Rinx hauled himself back inside the vehicle and offered his condolences to his charge.

"We will suffer Mr. Black's services only as long as it is necessary," Holt assured him. "Besides, if he proves to be any trouble, I trust you to handle it. Until then, try to lighten up."

Rinx's leather gloves stretched across his hard knuckles as his hands balled into fists. "At your command, ma'am."

CHAPTER 12

Black Spear's primary facility in Los Angeles was still under construction after the previous one had been unceremoniously destroyed in my first mission. For the time being, the best we had were a collection of safehouses. The safehouses held weapons, equipment, beds, food, and offered medical on-call. Said medical was currently bandaging Tag up and prepping him for a nice little helicopter ride back to more adequate facilities closer to Home Site. But us? We were gearing up to carve out someone's heart.

The slow trickle of adrenaline in my veins did a solid job of staving off the effects of sleep deprivation. I was nearing the thirty-hour mark but felt sharp as ever. I promised myself I would rest once we nailed Black and not a second sooner.

My thoughts scattered briefly. For some reason they turned towards Madison, and I wondered how much of the news she'd already caught. She knew how important it was for us to keep our relationship low-key and that, especially when I was on the clock, I couldn't take any calls.

I stopped in my tracks upon realizing what my last conscious thought was.

Shit.

I'd used the R word. Relationship. And like opening Pandora's box, it became kind of hard to unthink something once it took root. I shook my head to send the thoughts from my mind.

"How long since you've slept?" Kelly asked me.

I checked the sight on my rifle, then worked the charging handle to make sure it was well oiled. "I'm overdue."

Kelly took a long look at me, no doubt taking inventory of the tired crow's feet on my eyes that were evolving into damn ostrich feet. He looked over his shoulder to see if anyone else was nearby. Billy was too busy making sure he told the helicopter pilots how to do their job and get Tag to safety, Maggie and Valkyrie Squad were downstairs loading gear up into the vehicles. We were alone.

"Everyone's got a limit, Cole," he said.

"Yeah? Well, I haven't found mine yet."

"That's the thing: it tends to find you."

I stopped thumbing rounds into the magazine I was loading, "What would you have me do? Take a nap while Black gets away? Should I just pack it up and go home?"

"Why do I feel like you want to?"

"Right now, the only thing I want to do is stick a knife in that bastard's heart."

"No not that," Kelly said and stepped closer. "Like you want to leave Black Spear. I've seen it in your eye and don't tell me I haven't. Nothing's been the same since Cain."

There were a thousand things I wanted to scream at him then. I wanted to tell him how wrong he was. I wanted to admit how right he was. I wanted to tell him I barely knew what the fuck I was doing right now.

"You know I wanted out, right?" I said, forcing a smile. "After that first time when Vaun brought me in. I told myself 'Hey, we'll do this for a little while, but we can't do this forever.' I mean who could, right? This job. What kind of man would *want* to do it forever? So, I'd just pack it up one day. Preferably when I was still alive."

Kelly found a chair and sat in it, his eyes falling to the floor. I wondered if that meant he'd had similar thoughts before.

"But then Cain happened," I continued. "And it came down to me. Again. And it was my hand on the button. And I killed everyone, and the day was saved. Again. But all that shit?" I pointed to my head. "It's all up here. I've barely been with Black Spear for two years, and I have more kills than all of you combined. That'll never leave. And now I'm in charge of Cerberus, which means I can't walk away. So, I'm *here*, Kelly. I'm shackled to this life because this is who I am now."

He was smart enough to hold off on offering encouragement just yet. I guess he could see how much pain I was in. But after a moment he finally spoke.

"There's honor to it," he said. "Shouldering your duty though you don't want it. Vaun saw something in you the whole time. It's why he chose you. With him gone, he knew you'd be the leader Cerberus needed. And you're on your way, Cole. I don't know how you carry what you're carrying, but you gotta keep going."

I heard what he was saying and impossibly felt some of my anger ebb. I looked at him and wondered if he was expecting a bro-hug to close out the moment. Instead, he passed a loaded .45 caliber magazine over to me. I caught it one handed and examined the bullets; they were tipped with red. Hades bullets. Black Spear's proprietary armor-piercing incendiary rounds. They burned through pretty much anything and fragmented once inside. Every Hades round was essentially a miniature frag grenade that went off inside whoever was unlucky enough to get hit by one.

"Just for you," he said with a shrug. "In case Black has some more tricks up his sleeve and found himself some body armor, figured we'd give him a little surprise of our own."

"Always looking out for me," I said with a smile.

"Eh, it's what I do best."

We settled for a macho handshake and pulled it in for a short brotherly embrace.

"You know we're still supposed to bring him in alive?" I said as we left the safehouse armory for the garage downstairs.

"Alive and in one piece are two different things."

"If I miss his leg and sink a Hades through his heart, I'm going to tell everyone it was your idea."

"Fair enough," he said with a laugh.

I tapped the button on my earbud to open a line to Rain as we descended the stairs. Billy was already waiting for us with Valkyrie Squad. I gave him a look while waiting for Rain to respond, a silent way of asking if Tag was good, Billy responded with an unenthusiastic Shaka hang-loose sign and a nod.

"Yellow Pages, you alive?" I asked once the line was secure.

"I'm just peachy over here. I still hate that moniker, by the way."

"I'll let you brainstorm better ones after you give me some good news. Please tell me you know where this rat is hiding?"

There was a pause, and I worried for a second that Black had well and truly ghosted us. But then Rain's droll voice was back.

"Well, Mister Toxin, it's a good thing I was monitoring all local traffic cams on the off chance you all screwed the pooch on this thing. He slipped into a curbside Police Cruiser when the officer rushed into the airport, I tracked its LoJack. He took it for a pleasant drive before switching cars outside a gas station."

"Any civilian casualties?"

"Surprisingly none. The car was unoccupied, some old lady parked it there this morning then took a bus. I did a quick background check on her just to be sure. She's clean."

"He works alone," Maggie reminded.

"Black found an old foundry warehouse to hole up in," Rain continued. "I've been watching all exits since he went inside."

"Copy. Any word on that hit list?" I asked. We'd sent the physical list back with Tag in case it held any clues, but we'd already relayed the names to Rain so she could start digging.

"Yes and no. Three of the names we've found, unfortunately Stew Cleo has a few dozen matches we're trying to narrow down. We're including all variations i.e. Stewart, Stuart with a 'U', and both spellings of Cleo. With and without the 'H'. Trying to find which of these Mr. Cleo's is the right one is proving difficult. There's six in California alone."

"Tell me about the others. I want to know who Black's after."

"That's the weird thing, boss. I can't see anything viable linking them. Uric is a retired schoolteacher out in Wyoming. Whail is the closest to us, he's a junior agent with the FBI. I thought there might be something there, but there's nothing significant about him. He just graduated from Quantico a year ago and has been working out of the San Diego field office. No cases on his desk or under his belt that screams worthy enough of being whacked. Nothing connects these names; they're not even in the same area of the country. I mean, for crying out loud, this guy Diekly owns a floral shop out in Boston. Not exactly hitting me as a significant threats worth paying six-hundred large to take out."

"There's got to be something. What about the fifth guy, Dragunov?"

"It's Dragonab, with a 'B'. A far less common Serbian variation on the spelling, but there is no record of a Grant Dragonab anywhere in the country."

"Expand the search. I don't care if he's ex-KGB spending his golden years in Siberia, I want to know who he is and where."

Billy leaned over to whisper in my ear, "Is it really our problem if Black wants to off Russian citizens on foreign soil? Not exactly our jurisdiction."

"If they and Black are interested in him, then so are we," I answered. "Yellow Pages, I want as many teams as we have available guarding the targets we've found so far. Figure out which Stewart seems the most likely and do the same. When they realize we've taken Black out, I have a feeling they're going to send other shooters."

"Already on it, Toxin," Rain answered. "The big boss issued orders as soon as we had the list. We're stretched thin as it is, and these targets are all over the map. Mr. Rourke has called in reserve squads to help cover down." That was a little surprising but reassuring nonetheless to know that Rourke was in full support of this mission still.

"Now, where's Black?" I asked.

"That's just it, Toxin. I've been watching him since he sheltered in that warehouse, and he hasn't left. He isn't doing anything."

"What the hell you think he's up to?" Billy whispered. "Standing around idly doesn't fit his profile."

I looked over the footage Rain transmitted to my wrist-computer screen. It all looked calm and quiet from the outside.

"He is doing something," I said. "He's waiting for us."

CHAPTER 13

Rain clouds brewed above. They made me that much more eager to get inside Black's refuge before we all got soaking wet and miserable. I was already pissed and miserable. But being soaking wet would've been sprinkles on the shit cupcake the day had been. Officially we were still supposed to bring him in alive. Unofficially, I didn't exactly plan on things turning out that way.

I did one last hasty gear check. My rifle was an AWS by Alexander Arms; to the layman it would look like a standard military M-16, but it was chambered in the beefier .50 Beowulf instead of 5.56mm. The difference being that, compared to 5.56mm, a .50 Beowulf round was over twice the size, had three times the power, and four and a half times the momentum. Its stopping power was a selling point for many big game hunters. If it could take down a seven-hundred-pound Grizzly then I had faith it was more than sufficient for Rourke's "number zero" killer. With larger caliber came larger recoil, but I'm a big guy. I can take it. As a backup I carried a Para Black Ops .45. I'd been using the same handgun since day one with Black Spear, and it hadn't failed me yet.

I always brought something sharp and pointy in case things got up close and personal. Most days I went by with an automatic switch-blade. On a mission like this, even the half-second it would take to open the blade could cost me my life. Fixed blades were less prone to breaking, and they never failed to open. Just draw and cut. For that I had a large Pohl Force tactical MK-9 combat knife. Its design sported an intimidating curved blade that narrowed into a spear-point, and its reverse edge was just as sharp. I honestly gave it more TLC with a whetstone than I ever did my own mental health. I kept it ready, attached to the front of my vest near my shoulder. Pinned lower on my vest near all my spare magazines were a few flashbangs for good measure. I wasn't leaving anything to chance this time.

I finished my check just in time to see that the others had done theirs as well. There was a coldness to us all. Normally someone would be cracking a joke to lighten the mood but today was different. My squad was down to just three men now. None of us were in a very humorous mood.

"You sure you don't want to go up with them?" I asked Kelly, nodding towards Valkyrie Squad. They were moving towards the rooftop across from Black's warehouse to take up snipers' positions and act as our personal guardian angels. "You with a sniper scope might come in handy."

"Black hurt one of our own," Kelly answered. "I'm with you to the end on this one."

I didn't need him to say anything to know that he was shouldering some of the blame for the airport. His tranq dart shot was supposed to take Black down. If he'd made the shot, those people wouldn't have died, and Tag wouldn't be in a hospital. Trying to convince him that Black catching the dart out of midair was next to impossible would've been pointless.

"We're good up here, Toxin," Maggie said through the comm channel. "We've got a clear view from the north side here; Wizard and Matchbox have the west."

"Copy."

I puffed out my cheeks, then looked at Kelly and Billy. "Any reservations before we do this?"

"We could say a prayer first if you'd like?" Kelly offered.

Billy scoffed, "Oh, please. I'd prefer if the big man upstairs just turned a blind eye to what we're about to do to this son of a bitch."

I looked up to the sky for a second. It was odd, and I wasn't even sure why I did it. Then I squared my jaw, my teammates saw it and their own faces went like stone. Time to go to work.

"All points, this is Toxin," I said. "Orders are he comes in alive. That being said, I'm looking to carve a few pounds of flesh. I'm not taking any chances with Sandman darts this time. He can't catch bullets. Go for his kneecaps if we can, aim for the head if you have to. Magnum, if he gets the drop on us again, don't wait for the go ahead before you take the shot."

"Roger that."

"Any questions?"

"Just one, actually," someone remarked. Then there was a low chuckle. One that was void of all mirth. It was Black's voice. "What took you so long?"

If the world's deadliest assassin intruding on our secure comm channel worried my team, they did a damn good job of not letting it show.

"I hope you don't mind I borrowed the big guy's little earbud?"

"Don't worry, we'll come get it back in a minute."

"Oh, good, that's so good. I was honestly beginning to worry you were as bad at tracking me as you've been at stopping me."

Kelly motioned for me not to play his game. I did anyway.

"Just wanted to give you a head start and get comfortable, that's all. You need anything before we come drag you out? We could grab coffee first. How do assassins take it, two cream, one sugar?"

"Assassin . . . see I never liked that word." Black had an unsettling tendency to hiss his s's like a snake.

I signaled Billy and Kelly to approach the large foundry. I took the point.

"To me it's just like connoisseur," said Black. "Or aficionado. It sounds so exotic and pretentious. As if there's something more complicated to what I am."

"How about hitman?"

We reached the other side of the street and hugged the wall outside the warehouse. There were large shutter doors around the corner that we'd use to get inside. The entire second floor sported windows that would give Valkyrie's snipers a perfect view of the interior.

"Hitman? For some reason I always thought it sounded thuggish. Imprecise."

"And I guess you're more complicated than that?"

"Me? Oh, no. What I am is really rather simple."

We approached the shutter doors in a slow stalk. It was less of taking steps as much as it was continually rolling forward along the arch to the balls of your feet. Weapons sway less this way.

"And what is that?"

We stacked up outside the doorway.

"I'm a servant of death," Black answered. His response gave me pause; my two teammates similarly hesitated outside the warehouse entrance. "Death is the only true god in this world, and I am his greatest prophet. I've spread his gospel to every corner of this wretched world. Old and young, rich and poor, I've brought them all to kneel before him. Come and see . . . come and pray with me."

Billy gave me one last look, and I nodded. We pushed past the shutter doors, guns up and aimed in every direction. There was no sign of Black. The room we entered was the foundry floor. Conveyer belts before us, years without use, had a thick layer of dust and industrial grime atop them. Huge machines of unknown purpose were here and there. A metal catwalk that made up the second floor was above, its support columns descended around us. The far wall was made of small square windows, behind which was what looked like a patio break area. Plenty of places for him to be hiding behind.

"Why don't you come out, and we'll write a gospel together?" I shouted, no longer bothering with the earbud comm. My voice bounced off the concrete walls around us. The echoes slowly died. "For some legendary killer, you sure seem scared to show yourself."

"Not scared," he whispered. It seemed to come from above, but when I aimed high on the catwalk there was nothing there. "I just thought we could use a little privacy."

There was a loud mechanical blaring. And then the shutters slammed shut behind us. I spun, realizing too late that while this decrepit factory was long-since closed the shutters looked brand new. More than that they were made of heavy-gauge steel half an inch thick. The alarm continued. Maggie was in my ear, asking what the hell was going on. The light from the windows faded as large metal panels slid into place over them.

Then there was darkness. Us, alone, in the black.

It had been six months since Doctor Hertz was relieved of his position as the director of the project. At first, people simply thought that years of managing the project had finally gotten the better of his nerves, but the truth became clear when files indicated he'd been transferred to the basement. Sub-level seven. It was known by a different name amongst the research team: the Seventh Circle of Hell. It was where the rest of the so-called Kruegers were confined. Locked away in darkness to be studied, but years of research had thus far shown there was nothing to be gained from observing their madness.

Hertz's psychotic break had proven that years of indirect exposure to Morpheus was just as dangerous as a direct high-level dose. Since then, further safeguard protocols were put into place. Mandated regular off-site leave rotation, a regimen of preventative medications for every member of the project, and finally everyone on the floor was required to wear the insulated suits when Morpheus was being used regardless of which side of the glass they were on. It worried Childs that, decades later, they were still just breaking the surface of understanding what it was they worked on.

In the six months since she'd taken over as the director of the project, Childs had not once tested Morpheus above level four exposure. Some very important people very high up the chain of command wanted them to move forward and work with level ten, but after going through the research logs Childs found that not even Hertz had gone over eight the entire time he'd worked here. He'd only gone to eight once, and the resulting fiasco had cost the lives of two researchers. But the people prodding them towards pushing the levels were ones who made it difficult to say no. They were the types of people who quite literally determined whether funding continued and if the lights would stay on.

Childs exhaled slowly, her breath fogging up the face-shield of her protective suit. "Okay, Wynn, bring it up to seven."

Wynn's hands hesitated for a second above the instruments before him. He looked to Childs one last time for confirmation and then proceeded. The test-subject in the observation room tensed as suddenly as a bowstring pulled taut. Childs didn't bother to learn their personal information anymore. Her nightmares were crowded enough as it was. She did her best to remind herself that he, like all the others, had been a volunteer. He'd signed the waivers and knew what he was risking.

But that was a lie. None of them did. Not fully, at least. And yet they exploited the desperation and ignorance of prisoners with nothing to lose again and again.

The man's pupils tightened to pinpricks. Veins bulged on his face and neck. His breathing turned to ragged animal-like panting.

"We shouldn't have gone past six," Wynn said. His hand remained on the controls, but they knew it was too late to change anything.

"Command wanted eight this week," said Childs.

Wynn looked at her as if she'd gone mad, and through his face-shield she could see that he was sweating profusely.

"I think we should—"

"Just do it."

Wynn reluctantly pushed the settings to the eighth level, and the man in the testing room was gone. He was replaced by a feral beast that pulled against his restraints until they made his wrists bleed. The chair was welded to the floor, but he thrashed at it with everything he had. The handcuffs held. The chair held. This wasn't their first rodeo and the controls set in place were more than adequate.

"Jesus, another Krueger. Third this quarter," Wynn said. He waited for Childs to nod at him before he set the systems to zero.

A deep hum sounded as the Morpheus exposure vents in the ceiling sealed and the weapon deactivated.

"What exactly are they wanting from us here?"

Need-to-know basis was such a fickle thing for her. There were no illusions about the consequences should anyone leak anything, so what would it matter if she told Wynn more things that could get him killed for talking about?

"They want precision," she said. "Not area of affect."

Wynn stared at the animal on the other side of the glass. It had since given up on freeing itself and instead was biting chunks of flesh out of its own shoulder and spitting them onto the floor. Already it had gnawed deep into the flesh and hooked a canine into the bone.

"I don't know how much longer I can do this, Erin."

"You may not have to," she said. The rest of the staff and technicians were finishing their notes, security came in to subdue the test subject and bring him down to level seven. Childs walked Wynn over to the glass and spoke very quietly.

"Command is initiating phase two."

"I thought that was just a rumor?"

"We're going to be breaking down into a few sub-projects soon. They want to see focused applications for Morpheus on a surgical level."

The test-subject's face slammed against the glass as the security team restrained him. Bloody teeth gnashed at them, and he began to beat his skull against the window until the glass cracked.

"Morpheus is more than capable of shattering minds, but we just need to split them a little."

She leaned closer to Wynn's ear and whispered, her words snagging him deep as butcher's hooks. "Welcome to the Darkheart Project."

CHAPTER 14

I flicked on the flashlight on my rifle without a moment's hesitation. Billy and Kelly did the same. Our three beams of light scanned up and down, left to right, slicing away through the shadows in triangles like cutting pie. But the darkness was ever hungry, swallowing up the lit areas once more as soon as the beams passed. If Black was hiding in the darkness, then the darkness wasn't keen to give him up yet.

A rattle came towards our left and I sighted in on it. I found myself looking at nothing but a length of heavy chain hanging down and swaying slightly back and forth.

"I've been very curious to meet you," said a voice as quiet as a graveyard wind. It came from Billy's right, but the speaker vanished.

"Cerberus Squad." He drew the name out, making our team sound like some curse. "Your team is the talk of legends. But that was another time, another . . . *Captain*."

A scrape of a sharp edge against concrete sounded behind us.

Kelly whirled, catching a blur of movement just outside the circle of his flashlight beam. He fired three rounds. The gunshots sounded a thousand times louder in the vast empty room.

He missed.

I tapped the button on my earbud, "Valkyrie: switch to thermals. Put some fifty cal through the damn wall if you have to."

There was no response. There wasn't even static it was just . . . dead. Black was hunting us, trying to keep us on our heels and waiting for the first opening to cut into us.

"Back to back!" I ordered.

The three of us huddled tightly. Each of our weapons and lights pointed in a different direction as we slowly turned in a circle.

"Comm is being jammed," Billy muttered.

"Yeah."

"That's not supposed to be possible."

"Yeah."

A loud clatter sounded and when I looked, I saw the heavy chain falling to the floor. I found myself breathing heavy and tried to steady my nerves, trying to take comfort that this was just one man we were up against. We still had the advantage.

"You. The leader," whispered Black, his voice seemingly from nowhere and everywhere all at once. "You're special. *So* special. The man whose story began by stopping an entire army from unleashing a virus. Who single handedly prevented a global war from starting. That last one drew my attention. Saved millions by killing thousands."

"Yup, I've got a few notches on my belt," I said. "Still room on it for you, though."

"Someone like you who's survived against the shadows for so long," he continued, "you must have wondered. Whether there would be a reckoning. Whether the shadows may be hiding something. Something *worse*. Something you couldn't beat. Well, here I am at last."

Then he was there right in the center of my flashlight. Standing with arms outstretched in stigmata pose, an obsidian blade in each hand. He still wore the same black three-piece suit from earlier and his hair, dark as crude oil, was slicked back without a strand out of place.

My rifle thundered twice as I sent two .50 Beowulf rounds his way. But he pivoted so gracefully that it was nearly inhuman, and he was gone. Blended back into the darkness. Billy moved to cut off his escape, breaking the circle despite my protests.

The assassin was silent as a damned ghost and disappeared just as easily. Billy dared to fire off a short burst into the shadows. It illuminated Black like a strobe light. Three snapshot freeze frames of him five feet away from us, then one, and then gone entirely.

"And you, the fighter turned the obedient dog," Black said. "I would have enjoyed facing you in your prime."

Billy turned slowly, practically shaking. The man had gotten under his skin.

"Such a shame."

Something whistled through the air and then a knife was sticking out of Billy's shoulder. It sank two inches deep into the flesh, perfectly penetrating the unprotected section of his shoulder outside his vest. Billy's rifle fell to the ground. I saw the blur of a black coat and the rifle disappeared.

I risked a shot in the direction I thought Black was running towards. The Beowulf roared like its monstrous namesake. Instead of hitting the slippery bastard, I punched two holes in the panels covering the far windows. Sunlight, barely making it through the rain clouds outside, shot back through the holes.

Kelly moved towards Billy. He helped him to his feet while I stupidly aimed in the direction the knife had been thrown from. Once more I found myself looking at nothing.

I felt something brush against my leg. I risked a glance down, and strangely saw my own rifle sling dangling down by my feet. He'd gotten close enough to cut it from my shoulder and I hadn't even seen him.

I turned about to face behind me. It was the only direction he could have come from. Before I could see what my flashlight illuminated, someone kicked at the back of my knee. I staggered, spun, then started to raise my weapon-

Only my rifle was gone. Snatched from my hands as I turned. I heard a clinking sound. Then my own flashlight rolled towards me along the floor, slowing and spinning its light in circles. I knelt to retrieve it. When I cast its beam back to the floor, I found myself looking at my rifle, disassembled and its parts neatly separated before me.

"Now then, where were we?" Black asked.

A speaker blared and the panels by the windows instantly opened. The sudden change in light made me squint. I drew my sidearm with one hand while pulling my MK-9 knife with the other. Things were about to get *real* dirty.

Black came out of nowhere. One second there was nothing and the next he was right behind Kelly. Our marksman tried to raise his rifle but Black's hands flashed out and jabbed him twice in the knuckles. Kelly's hands went limp. His weapon fell to the ground. Even as I aimed my pistol for Black's face, I pieced together what had happened. The dart. Black had used the same Sandman-laced dart Kelly had tried to shoot him with to stick both of his hands. It was just enough of the tranquilizer to make his hands completely useless.

I sighted up a shot. My .45 had a four-pound trigger weight and I was squeezing with three and a half. Black ducked and weaved, placing Kelly in between my shot and him.

"Take the shot," Kelly urged, eyes wide with panic.

One muscle twitch in the wrong direction and a .45 caliber Hades round would hit Kelly instead. I sidestepped to get a different angle as Black's hand leapt out once more, this time sticking the dart in the back of Kelly's neck. He went limp and dropped. I added another half-pound of pressure and my gun bucked in my grip.

The incendiary bullet struck dead-center in his chest, flattened, sizzled, and fell to the ground. Son of a bitch was wearing body armor after all, and for it to stand up to *our* armor-piercing rounds was no small feat.

Black closed the distance between us in the heartbeat it took for me to adjust my aim for his face. His vice-like grip latched onto my .45's slide and pushed it to the side as another bullet rang out. I watched in near fascination as he turned into a perfectly placed elbow strike that knocked my sidearm clear from my hand while his other hand slipped my knife from my grip.

Jesus, he was fast. I'd never seen anyone move like him. But speed was never my only strong point. My best strength? Precisely applied brute force.

I attacked with a three-hit combination that drew from three different martial arts. Each one favored raw power and damage over anything flashy. First was a Muay Thai flying knee, I followed it with a straight punch that was pure American boxing, and finished with a devastating roundhouse kick pulled from Tae Kwon Do. Three strikes, three styles.

Except there was a combination of more than six styles in the way he dodged and countered. For him it was effortless, as if he already knew what I was going to throw his way before I did. I hit nothing but air. By the time I realized he was going to slip my kick it was already in motion. The train had left the station, and he was fully prepared. Black caught my leg before using my own weight and momentum to throw me over his shoulder.

I tried to get back on my feet but had taken the fall badly. All the air in my lungs was expelled and my diaphragm refused to let any more in. I fought myself not to curl into a ball and pass out. Kelly lay face-down less than three feet from me. Everything was paralyzed but his eyes, which darted around frantically. Black looked down at the two of us like we were insignificant prey. Not even worthy of killing.

And then Billy was on him, screaming in fury and throwing a flurry of punches his way. Black caught one of Billy's fists in the palm of his hand. His head tilted with amusement.

"Hello, *Mamushi*."

Black was fast, but Billy had the fastest hands I'd ever seen. They exchanged fists. They traded kicks. Not one hit landed on the other. Two masters of hand-to-hand locked together in a dance of combat where neither had an edge.

"Get him . . . Billy . . ." I wheezed, finding the strength to get up to one knee but unable to stand.

Their fight carried them to the far side of the room where they became nothing but silhouettes against the backdrop of the windows behind them. At any moment Black could have pulled one of his obsidian blades, and Billy could just as easily draw one of the Tanto knives he favored. But this was a test of wills where both would stop at nothing to show the other that they were better.

And then I saw something not possible. Black started moving faster. They would both counter each other's string of punches, an exchange of evenly timed back and forth, and then Black snuck a quick jab into Billy's injured shoulder. There was a rhythm to their duel and Black was finding a half-note in between the tempo. Counter, counter, poke. Counter, counter, poke. Each time Black struck Billy's wound, his arm moved slower.

On the fourth hit Billy's arm fell limply. He pushed the attack. As if taunting him, Black put one hand behind his back and continued to dismantle him. The fun ran out, the slight smirk on Black's face vanished, and the assassin's eyes went dark. Black snarled and tripped him down to his knees. He twisted Billy's wrist and locked the arm out with one hand while he battered Billy's shoulder again and again with the other. Blood flung out from his knuckles with every blow.

From the corner of my eyes, I saw my lost sidearm. I finally managed to suck in a new lungful of air and ran towards it. I fell into a slide, picking up the .45 as Black continued to brutalize my friend.

"You're *nothing*," Black spat. He pulled his fist back once more and this time slammed it into Billy's jaw. A single punch. A sickening crack like old wood and then Billy's jaw canted unnaturally off its hinge. I leapt at Black from behind, roaring like a beast as I placed the pistol's barrel against his temple.

"I've got you now, you slippery son of a bitch. Let's see you catch this," I said through gritted teeth.

"Someday someone may beat me," Black sighed. He was completely calm despite the loaded gun pressed to his skull. Bored, even. "But it won't be today. And it *won't* be you."

Fuck him if he couldn't take a hint. I pulled the trigger.

Click.

I'd only fired two rounds, there should have been five left in the magazine. I wasn't empty. It wasn't possible. Too late I realized my mistake. Just moments ago, when Black had grabbed my .45's slide and disarmed me as I fired, he'd held the slide in place. The weapon hadn't cycled properly. Which meant the casing from my second shot was still stuck in the chamber.

His head whipped back and caught me in the chin. He spun towards me and delivered a heavy open-palm strike into my throat that pushed me back. Creating distance was a mistake, though. I recovered from his blow, worked the slide to feed a fresh round into the chamber, and aimed right between his eyes.

Black stood there, smiling. Because he held Billy's broken body up like a human meat shield between us. I shifted my weight, looking for my window, as Black drew closer. His face bobbed back and forth. A psychotic white smile flashed in the dark. I tried to fall back on the marksmanship lessons Kelly had tutored me with. Find the shot. Take it. But the only thing I could think of was that this madman would move Billy's head in the way of my bullet.

"Go ahead," teased Black. "Take it. *Take* it! End it here. Now. I promise you won't get another chance."

Billy was barely conscious. He stood on shaking legs, and Black shifted him this way and that to make it difficult for me to draw a bead. I should've taken the shot, but instead in that single heartbeat span of hesitation I lost the opportunity.

He threw Billy at me, nearly two hundred pounds of dead weight and battle rattle equipment, and I had to lift my gun barrel up to avoid punching it through his eye socket. Black was there in that half-second. His hands latched upon my weapon and ejected the magazine, kicked it far out of sight, then worked the slide to send the last round clattering to the floor.

I swung my empty weapon like a hammer with one hand while throwing a jab with the other. Black backpedaled away. My knuckles punched through nothing but empty air. I spared a look at the ground and the one bullet there. The magazine was gone, but the last round remained. I wondered if I could load it fast enough.

"Come on then!" I bellowed, shaking both my pistol and fist like a battle-ready Viking. But Black kept his distance. Then, he scoffed.

"Sleight of hand, eh?"

He dropped something to the ground and plugged his ears.

I looked to see what he'd dropped. I found myself staring with wide eyes at the pin to one of my own flashbangs. A flashbang that was still on my vest. I only had a second to remove it from the pouch and throw it away. It wasn't enough, and the grenade detonated.

Morpheus Research
15 years ago . . .

"Things are progressing. Finally," Childs said. "Sorry, that sounded like I'm bragging. I promise I'm not. The fruits of our labors would've never been possible without you. What's that saying? Standing on the shoulders of giants? Well, I guess it's especially true now that you're down here."

Doctor Hertz's breath fogged up the small window from the other side of the door. In the five years he'd been locked away in the Seventh Circle, he'd deteriorated more rapidly than all the others. The thing in the cell had no trace of humanity left. It was a phenomenon they had yet to fully understand, which was yet another reason they couldn't simply dispose of the Kruegers.

"I sometimes wonder if there's a part of you locked away in there," she said. "Some semblance of that brilliant spark still hiding in the shadows. Maybe that's why I'm devoting my focus towards the Darkheart subdivision. If we can master the ability to crack the mind, then perhaps we can crack away broken parts and reverse . . . this."

As if on cue Hertz gnashed his teeth at the door. The ones he still had were broken and yellowed. Some had rotted out; a few others were fractured from when Hertz had thrashed his face into the wall in a fit of rage his first week down here.

Childs had to crack this. After all they'd done, after all the sacrifices their research had devoured, there had to be something on the other side. Something that made it worth it. She looked into the crazed eyes of her former mentor and forced herself not to fall prey to her own despair.

"Wynn will be transferring down here soon," she said sadly. "He'll be in the room next to you. You two will have plenty of things to talk about, I guess."

Hertz's only response was a pained howl.

The elevator at the end of the hall dinged, signaling that the security escort had arrived with the deranged Wynn in tow. Childs couldn't bear to look as they dragged him, sedated, into his cell. She took one last glance at Hertz through the glass before walking away. A thought that had been clawing its way around her head recently reared into her mind once more: if everyone who worked here was cursed to lose their minds, just how much time did she have left?

CHAPTER 15

Even from the rooftop across the street they could hear the pop of the flashbang. She watched through her magnified scope as Captain West was blasted through a wall of tall windows.

"I've got eyes on Toxin," she said. "East side balcony area."

"Jesus, what's going on in there?" her squad marksman, Wizard, shouted.

"No idea. This is fucked."

From the second Cerberus Squad made their entry, things had gone wrong. Scratch that, from the second Cerberus had *decided* to enter. Maybe even earlier. Since Cerberus was only a trio now, it didn't even feel right to call it a squad. Their comm had gone dark, which was just as unsettling as finding out that Black had been listening in the whole time. She'd had her men switch to a separate channel, but the thought still made her skin crawl. Magnum would have liked nothing more than to be the one to turn Black's skull into pink mist. The only problem was once those security shutters had dropped, they had no shot. Not even their thermal scopes could penetrate and see inside. Like she'd said: fucked.

Now, seeing West blown out of the building and crisscrossed

with glass cuts, Magnum was even more sure that things were going to end disastrously for all parties involved.

"Anyone have eyes on Kage or Forty-Seven?" she asked.

West looked to be in bad shape. She had a gut feeling the others were even worse.

"Oh shit," Wizard said. "Not good, Mags. Not good at all."

Before she had time to ask, she watched as another body was thrown through the window. Daniel Kelly. He fell like dead weight, and she didn't want to know how true a description that was. And then she saw their target. Black eased through the broken window, dragging Billy Ho out with him by the ankle.

"Kodiak is in the open."

Her breathing slowed as her target reticle centered on Black's head.

"Is this asshole *whistling*?" her demo-man, Matchbox, asked.

"I've got a shot," she said.

"We all do, Mags. You want to do the honors?" asked Wizard.

She did. She really fucking did.

"This one's a long time coming, boys," she said. "Mama's got him."

Her face pulled into a smile as her finger curled along the trigger. Black had hurt too many people over the years—too many friends—and she wasn't about to let him get one more damn day on this planet. She had been so focused on the moment, on her shot, that she never saw the hooded figures climbing to the rooftop behind her. Didn't notice as one crept behind her in utter silence.

Neither did the rest of her team.

CHAPTER 16

"Rise and shine, West. Rise and shine."

The voice was the first thing my mind processed. The second was the length of heavy chain, the very one I'd seen earlier inside the foundry, now trapping my wrists behind my back. More of it bound my ankles together. Once I had taken into account how helpless I was, half my face decided to let me know that it had gotten a bit of flash burn from the blast.

My eyes fluttered. I had trouble adjusting to the dwindling sunlight of the early evening. Black turned his back on me as he stared out at the surrounding buildings' rooftops visible from the patio area. Dark clouds thick with rain brewed above us. Thunder lightly rumbled in the distance, threatening to spill forth their showers.

Valkyrie Squad would have taken the shot by now. As disoriented as I was, I was still conscious enough to do the math on what Black being alive meant. It meant our friends were not.

The only friends of mine I knew for sure were still among the living were Billy and Kelly. The three of us were on our knees, each chained at wrists and ankles, facing one another in a triangular huddle. Billy tried to say something, but his unhinged jaw wouldn't form the words. The tranquilizer had run its course through Kelly. He couldn't seem to pick his eyes up from the ground. There's helpless, there's hopeless, and then there was this.

"If one of you moves, I kill the other two first," Black said.

He turned around, and I saw that he held Tag's revolver, examining it closely as he stalked in a circle around us. Billy's battered eyes looked at me. There was something angry in them. Not at Black, though. At me. His broken jaw might not let him speak, but his eyes alone spoke volumes. We were here because of me. *My* call. My team.

Black spun the revolver around his finger. "Somewhere out there, we all have a bullet. It's funny to think about, isn't it? Molten metal cooled within the earth for millennia, waiting to be made. Mined from the ground, cast into a bullet. Waiting to be fired. All that time it's been out there, and now? It's here."

He aimed the snub-nosed magnum at me with one hand.

"What'd you do with the others?" I asked.

"Me? Nothing. I assume some acquaintances of mine made quick work of them, however."

Acquaintances. We'd been operating under the impression that Black was ever the lone wolf type, and that the concept of back-up was entirely beneath him. The amused look on his face told me that he was reading my thoughts.

"Things change," he said with a shrug. "A job like this, a chance to *really* make Black Spear bleed? It was too good to pass up, even if I had to take on some extra help."

"You seem to know a lot about us." I worked at the chain around my wrists. It was tight, but I felt it give just a little. A subtle look to the other two confirmed that they were already doing the same.

"You interest me."

"Enough to pull you out of retirement and into the light?" I asked.

As he patrolled around the three of us, he put the gun to the back of each of our heads. Taunting us with his finger on the trigger.

"Retirement is boring," he said.

"Who hired you?"

"I told you before," he said and knelt behind Billy. He jammed the barrel of the revolver behind Billy's ear as he spoke to me. Billy refused to shy from it. "You made so many dangerous enemies, West. They are everywhere. They are *legion*."

Something about his words made my stomach sick. Something familiar.

"There's a bullet for everyone," he said again, lowering the revolver's hammer. "The only question is whose is it? The fighter? The marksman? The leader?"

He waved the gun back and forth, giving each of us a chance to look down the barrel.

"Decisions, decisions."

"It's mine," Kelly said, rising to stare Black down.

"Shut up, Kelly," I ordered. "This is on me. I brought us here."

Black switched to aim at me.

"Frkng jsst shtt mmm," Billy mumbled.

Fucking just shoot me.

He pushed the barrel against the hinge of Billy's cracked jaw, and Billy moaned in pain.

"Me," Kelly said with genuine fear in his eyes. Not for himself, though. He was afraid he was going to have to watch one of us die.

"Shoot *me*, damn it!" I screamed. I strained against my bindings. I could get loose if only I had more time. It was something Black showed no sign of permitting me. "You better shoot me, asshole. Because if you don't, and you take one of them? There aren't words for what I'm going to do to you."

I stared him down, eyes overflowing with grim promise.

Instead of flinching, he smiled. Wide. It was absent anything joyful, it was a smile filled with dark pleasure.

"There it is," he said, squatting down on his haunches next to me and placing the revolver barrel under my chin. "I was wondering when it would show. I know that within that chest beats a darker heart. Every time you pull the trigger it gets just a little bit blacker and beats a little bit louder. Little by little, making you more like me. One trigger at a time."

"I'm nothing like you."

"No?" his finger tapped playfully along the trigger. "You've taken over two *thousand* souls, yes? That's more than I ever have, maybe more than I ever will. That's beautiful. We're both servants of death. You just don't know it yet."

His trigger finger danced with a light tap, tap, tap. I wanted him to do it. A .44 through the skull would be painless, and far better than having to watch one of my friends bleed out in front of me. It'd be quick. And it would be one surefire way to not have any more sleepless nights.

"Look to him, gentlemen," Black said softly. "Watch as I take your captain from you."

I pressed the bottom of my head flush against the barrel. "Pull the fucking trigger already."

"Okay."

Black pointed the revolver at Kelly's throat and fired. Thunder cracked in the sky at the same exact moment. Blood shot forth from Kelly's neck as the bullet knocked him onto his back. Rain fell from the sky as the first drops of blood fell to the rooftop.

"No!" I screamed, feeling the chains around my wrists finally shaking loose. Loose, but not loose enough. I thrashed towards Kelly as my still shackled feet knocked me down again, forcing me to worm over to him on knees and elbows.

"I can't wait to see what you'll become now, to see how dark that heart can be," Black said as he stowed the revolver away. "You've escaped death too many times. Walked away thinking there was no one to best you. But that dream is over, West. I shall become your nightmare. Know this: everyone that dies, every soul I claim, and every step I get closer to Morpheus is because of your failure."

Black looked down over his nose at Kelly who writhed on the floor, drowning in his own blood.

"He is only the first."

I shook my bindings off and crawled towards my friend, absently aware that Black was already gone.

Kelly's boot soles tapped against the rooftop as the blood poured out of his neck. I knelt next to him and held his head in my hands, wishing that I could just undo his chains and give him a bit of comfort.

"Don't stop breathing," I said. A spurt of blood coughed up from the entry wound in his Adam's Apple. "Don't you stop fighting, goddamn it!"

Kelly's life gushed out the back of his throat. No rhythmic arterial flow, just a continuous stream. His eyes flickered. Any moment now, they'd roll over dead. It was a truth that I knew the second Black fired, and it was a truth I still refused to accept.

'So, you just gonna lay there bleeding? Or you gonna stand?'

The memory twisted in my stomach worse than a thousand blades.

"He's gone," Billy managed to say through his ruined jaw. He'd escaped his chains and now sat on the other side of Kelly's still body. His boots had stopped twitching in shock against the rooftop. I forced myself to look into Kelly's eyes and accept what Billy had said, see the pupils expanded in that final moment of nerve release. And it was true, just as I'd known it was.

Daniel Kelly was dead. No last words. No deathbed request for vengeance. Just a dead soldier on a rain-soaked rooftop with two comrades, pointlessly wanting to turn back the clock, wishing they could trade places.

Lightning flashed in the sky, and not even the close crack of thunder could drown out my scream.

PART 2

NIGHTMARES

"Believe nothing you hear,
and only one half that you see."
—Edgar Allen Poe

CHAPTER 17

If someone were so inclined to check the names of the owners, they would find that this luxurious top floor penthouse belonged to a Mr. Doug Crawley and his beloved wife, Annette. If anyone cared enough to keep digging beyond that, they would learn that both Mr. and Mrs. Crawley had up to date driver's licenses and paid all their bills promptly. But if anyone was interested in finding either of the Crawley's in-person, they would have to do some literal digging as they had been buried in the Nevada desert five years ago.

This penthouse was just one of many properties like it in this city. Simon had chosen this one purely for the view it provided of the Los Angeles skyline. They had houses everywhere. They had people everywhere. Most of the time acquiring assets for an assignment came down to simply looking up who was nearby.

Black had been less than enthused when Lady Holt insisted that Simon accompany him, even less so when it was instructed that Simon would have his own support team. Even now Black looked them over, entirely unimpressed, even though they had effortlessly slain an entire Black Spear team.

"So, this is them?" Black said as he looked over the five black garbed soldiers. Each wore a Kevlar face mask and identical body-armor that hid their features and made them indistinguishable from the next.

"They certainly look grim."

"They are Immortals," Simon said, full of pride. "They are the very best."

"I seem to recall killing six of your very best when we first met." Black watched them for any reaction and was pleasantly surprised that the five Immortals still stood as statues. Their metallic faces gave nothing away. Emotionless ghosts. Simon could tell that it pleased Black.

"The Immortals are our most capable soldiers, perhaps our first encounter would have gone differently had Lady Holt not asked that we bring you in unharmed."

Black nodded to himself. He walked down the line of the Immortals, then looked to Simon. "Do they have names?"

"Not like this."

Black was confused for only a moment before understanding what Simon meant. Simon had no obligation or desire to spoon feed everything to this assassin. Either he would figure things out, or he wouldn't.

"Take your masks off," Black said. The Immortals refused to move. Simon had to stifle his own smile. It twitched at the corners of his mouth. Black flicked his wrist and suddenly there was a blade in his palm.

"I don't make a habit of asking twice."

"Take them off," Simon instructed.

They obeyed, and then once they removed their masks, they were completely different people. Their postures changed. Softened. Mannerisms and emotion reentered their bodies.

"The mask of an Immortal strips away who they were. It turns them into an idea, and that idea is to be deadly."

"Interesting," Black breathed. "I'm well versed in the concept."

He stepped towards the first Immortal on the left. His mask had concealed a face with a varied collection of scars both thin and ghastly.

"And who are you, O great and deadly killer?"

"Declan," the scarred Immortal replied in a thick Irish accent.

Black moved on to the next. This one was black and had his hair cut to a short military fade.

"Henri," he declared with a French accent.

The third was Hogue, an Australian with a fiery red mustache. Fourth down the line stood Harrison, whose shiny black shoulder length hair didn't have a strand out of place even after being bunched behind his mask and hood. Lastly there was Scaglin, who smiled proudly with a mouth full of crooked teeth when he spoke his name. The smile faltered when Black frowned.

"That's your real name, Scaglin?"

"Yes."

Black mulled it over and his frown deepened, "I don't like it, not at all. It sounds like . . . scabies. Saying your name makes me feel like there's worms on my tongue. From now on you can be . . . Bob." Black smiled, his perfectly white and straight teeth beaming at Scaglin's own yellowed ones. Scaglin opened his mouth to say something, but Simon raised a hand and he stopped.

"And don't smile around me, Bob. Your teeth are hideous."

Simon knew Black was testing them. Seeing how much leash they were allowing him. Simon had no problem letting him have his fun. All you had to do to remind a dog who its master was is give the leash a yank. People like Black, although useful, were so far beneath Simon, he wasn't worth even being frustrated at. To him, Black was not unlike a piece of black pepper stuck to your tooth. Inconvenient, but easy enough to remove.

"Don't mistake your position in all this," Simon said behind

Black's back. He waved his hand and the Immortals left them. "They answer to me, and me alone. This is *my* mission. I cannot accept any failure nor any delays. You are simply here to play a part."

Black gauged him for a breath, then smiled. "And play it I shall, dear Ellis."

He gave an elaborate flourish with his hand and the knife he'd held vanished. If it was meant to intimidate him then Black would be sorely disappointed.

Simon put his hands in his pockets and took two steps closer, completely at ease, "We hired you to do a job. Contract killer. There *are* penalties for voiding a contract."

"Lady Holt will have her weapon."

He spoke in a way that left no room for doubt. Simon gave Black a sly side-eyed look. "You seem so sure of yourself, Black. If you already knew where Morpheus was, you wouldn't be playing your little games."

This time it was Black who smiled. "Don't be afraid, Mr. Ellis. I won't let you down."

CHAPTER 18

I'd sat in this briefing room more times than I could count, but this was the first time it had ever felt so empty. It was just me, Rourke, his right-hand Mason, and Rain with her computer.

Even our on-hand medical staff was ill-equipped to perform certain vascular trauma surgeries, and so Tag had been transferred to Scripps Hospital in La Jolla. Rourke pulled some strings to send Billy to the same place to fix his jaw and patch up his shoulder. And Kelly's body was on a cold table downstairs, waiting to be examined by our medical officer, as if there were any need to determine the cause of death.

"Walk me through it once more," Rourke instructed. The Brooklyn gorilla was as cold as ever.

"I carried Billy Ho and Daniel Kelly out," I said. I could still feel the raindrops pattering my scalp. "The bodies of Valkyrie Squad were waiting for me outside."

I gestured to the pictures on the presentation screen without looking. Seeing them in person was enough for one lifetime. Valkyrie Squad had been lying shoulder to shoulder on the ground right at the foundry entrance. They were displayed neatly with their arms crossed over their chests as if already in caskets for their funeral. The only difference was they had been decapitated and their heads impaled one atop the other on a lone pike behind them.

"They left a video on a memory card," Rain added.

It had been sealed in a soft egg-shell colored envelope below the pike, protected from the rain by the severed heads above it like a macabre umbrella. The image of two drops of blood staining the upper right portion seemed impossible to shake from my mind. All that carnage and just two drops ruining the perfect white of the envelope.

Rourke played the video. Next to him, Mason crossed her arms and lowered her chin. There was an intensity radiating off her that was palpable. The video was filmed from a bodycam one of the killer's wore. The killer scaled a ladder and snuck up behind Magnum. The footage split into five screens to show the scene play out from the perspective of each of the killers. I watched as they approached Valkyrie and commenced the slaughter.

They stabbed hearts. They cut through spines. One of them chopped a large axe of all things deep into Wizard's chest. Another used a hunting knife to stab into Matchbox's neck again and again. He could've ended it quickly by slicing through his throat, but this one wanted him to suffer. Magnum had been the only one quick enough to draw a weapon. She fired three shots, two to the chest and one to the head. Her killer didn't so much as flinch. The one who'd killed Wizard tossed his axe to this one, and he cleaved Magnum's head from her neck with a single swing.

It would've been enough if the memory card's video had ended there. Instead, it continued to show the five assassins brutalize the bodies of Valkyrie Squad.

"What the fuck is that one doing?" asked Mason. The killer with the hunting knife had finished spiking the last head and was cutting something onto each of Valkyrie's heads.

"They, um, cut a message onto their tongues," answered Rain. Her mouth quivered.

I watched her struggle to maintain her composure. We all were to varying levels of success. The video file finally ended and four images popped onto the screen, each a closeup of one of Valkyrie Squad's tongues. Magnum's head was on the bottom. Instead of a word she had a brand mark that resembled a horned skull.

"*Est quiae multi sumus*. It's Latin for—"

"'For we are many,'" Rourke finished. "It's from the *Vulgate*; a Latin transcription of the Bible dating back to the Fourth Century."

Rourke translating the phrase jogged my memory a bit.

"Book of Mark, chapter five, verse nine." I nodded. Rain seemed surprised, I merely shrugged. "Might be a decade or two since I've attended service, but I haven't forgotten everything."

And then something else came to my mind. Something Black had said to me.

You made so many dangerous enemies, West. They are everywhere, and they are legion.

"Fucking hell," I muttered. I ran my fingertips along my head as the thoughts connected. I knew why Black's words had made my stomach sick. It's because Samuel Cain said something eerily similar during the Warmaker case.

"Spit it out already, West," Rourke ordered.

"Something Black said to me, it echoed what Cain said right before he died. He was scared to tell me who was pulling the strings, he said that they were everywhere. That they were legion. Boss, I don't think he was just being dramatic. I think he was telling us who this organization is."

All eyes were on me.

"Legion."

I looked past Rourke, my eyes locked onto the demon brand on Magnum's tongue. I now knew what it was. The mark of our enemy.

The symbol for Legion.

Rourke clicked his tongue. "Sam might've been a treasonous bastard, but he was never one to waste words just for theatricality's sake. We'll get White Shield to cast a wide net and see what they can pull from it. We have a name. That might be enough to narrow our search and finally shed some light on them. Right now, the four of us are at the forefront of this, so what else do we know?"

"They're good," Mason stated. She rewound the video footage to show the five Legion members approaching Valkyrie. "Silent, no hand signals or verbal communication. This goes beyond training and rehearsals. They've done this many, many times before."

Rain pointed to the screen and signaled Mason to pause it just as Magnum had shot one of the killers.

"Well trained *and* well equipped."

"An axe and a couple Buck knives count as well equipped?" I asked.

"How many people do you know that make facemasks and body-armor that our bullets just bounce off of?"

I thought of my own Hades round and how it had simply bounced off Black's chest.

"Point taken. There's something more troubling than that: Legion knows who we are." I saw the muscle along Rourke's jaw tense. "You read the transcript. Black *knew* who Cerberus Squad was. He knew who I was. That Billy was our fighter, and Kelly our marksman. He even hinted at knowing Vaun."

We'd all been so focused on the ones we lost we'd overlooked that alarming detail.

"Not to mention *that*!" I pointed to the pike of heads.

"Transcript didn't list him saying anything about Valkyrie?" Rain said, looking over the mission debrief notes just to be sure. She glanced back at me and found me shaking my head.

"No, not the heads. The spike they're on. It's a spear. Black Spear.

They know exactly who we are, and they want us to know that they aren't the least bit scared."

The room was very quiet then. The only sound was the hum of the fluorescent lights above. Realizing you weren't at the top of the food chain wasn't a common occurrence for this group.

I decided to break the silence.

"Chasing Legion shouldn't be our priority right now. Black is. He's the key to it all, I know he is. And right now, I'm pretty much the first guy to go against him and survive."

"First guy, second person," Mason corrected. One of her fingers traced the scar along her cheek. I hadn't made the connection until just then but made a mental note of it.

"Okay, fine. Point is this: we don't know *anything* about Black. Where he came from. Who trained him. Who he was before he became this. Can't we run facial recognition or something? Track down his birth certificate?"

Rain hissed and shook her head no. "Pros like him are friends with plastic surgery. Facial reconstruction every few years, new identities every so often. Even with what we have now, I doubt anything will come from it. I wouldn't be surprised if this is his third or fourth face by now."

"It's a dead end," Rourke said firmly. "No point digging it. It doesn't matter who he was, what matters is who he is now and how we stop him."

It bothered me that Rourke was so quick to dismiss it. But maybe he had a point. Learning why Black went bad—whether he had a fucked up childhood or had some mental issue caused by adult trauma; nature nurture, chicken egg—was irrelevant. It wouldn't save him from me, nor would it bring Kelly back.

"Fine, did we get any closer to finding Mister Dragonab?"

"We expanded our search, but as of yet there is no Grant Dragonab," Rain answered. "We have a team surveilling a Dragonab family in Manhattan; one Yri Dragonab and Oksana Dragonab. No Grant, but they're the only ones in the country. The other targets have been found. Black won't be getting anywhere near them."

"We're stretched thin, West," Rourke muttered. "We tasked as many of our teams that were available to protect the other potential matches for the names on Black's list, and I cashed in more rainy day favors than I was comfortable using in order to have some adjacent outfits cover the others."

Relocating all of Black's marks to one location to save on manpower wasn't an option. It would give Legion an easy target to single handedly wipe out all of them in one fell swoop. Keeping them far away from one another was the safest option.

"What squad am I being attached to, then?" I asked. "I'm still running point on this."

Rourke's brow furrowed. "You have wax in your ears or something, West? There isn't anyone to reinforce you with. Valkyrie Squad is dead. Your lieutenant is dead. Your squad, which was already undermanned since you *failed* to fill your roster's gaps, is broken. Everyone else is holed up, ensuring Legion can't take the others out. I'm pulling you back."

I was taken aback by him. There was no way in hell I was being benched. I took my time spacing the next three words through clenched teeth.

"Black is mine."

Rourke stood from his chair, and I noticed Mason tense next to him. "Get some rest. Right now, we're squeezing Uric, Whail, all of them. *When* we get a line on Legion, we'll task a team accordingly. Right now, I wouldn't want you anywhere near it. Not now, not like this."

He waved his hands dismissively at me. It took everything I had not to leap across the table and put my elbow through his windpipe.

"You really expect me to sit on the sidelines and watch someone else bring him in after what he did to my team?"

The withering stare Rourke gave me could've degreased an axle. How easy it must be for him to take players out and put new ones in as if we were lightbulbs so easily replaced. The man didn't appear fazed at all.

"You know what gets me?" I asked. "The problem with us being ghosts in the system is nobody gives a shit if any of us die, because nobody knows. How many people do you think Kelly saved in his career? Or all of Valkyrie for that matter? Daniel Kelly gave his life, and you can't even give him a proper military burial, can you? Too messy? No honors. No guests in attendance. No recognition for everything he's done. Just another dead soldier written off."

"They were my men too, West. Stand down. That's an order."

The air felt as taut as a tripwire. I think Mason was wondering whether I was going to lose my temper or not and if she'd have to switch roles from Rourke's assistant to his bodyguard. People still told stories of her in her heyday. But if I wanted to hurt Rourke, she'd be unable to do anything but watch me.

Rourke had always thought little of me. Since day one he'd been very clear that I didn't belong. When Vaun chose me as his successor, Rourke voiced his objections quite loudly. And now after today's failure he could sit there, looking down his nose at me, and thinking about how right he'd been the whole time. No wonder he still refused to acknowledge my rank of captain.

I rose from my seat. That heat in my belly was rising and not even I knew what I was about to do. So, I did nothing. I left, as Rourke had ordered, as peacefully as possible. Walked past the few guys out and about in the hallways without saying a word. Didn't so much as frown or make a mean face. No, I played it cool. Kept it off the surface just like Vaun would've done. My feet took me back to my private quarters on autopilot. I pulled the door shut behind me, half listening for it to latch closed. And once it was, I promptly broke everything in sight with my bare hands.

DARK BEGINNINGS 1

Bullseye. Hitting center mass at this distance was an impressive feat, but hitting *dead* center? There was a reason all the Drill Instructors' attention was on one recruit when the entire Company was qualifying.

They were at the 500-yard mark. At this stage of the shoot, all that was required was for them to hit anywhere on the target. It was one of the many things the Marine Corps liked to brag about: their rifle qualifications went further than any of the other branches. The human-shaped silhouette on the target measured only twenty-inches by forty-inches. Managing to get a hit anywhere—be it the shoulder, leg, or waist—when you're further than four football field lengths away is certainly no small feat.

But every one of this recruit's shots were bullseyes. His grouping was tight, a three-inch circle marker could completely cover them. At one point, they had to ceasefire on the range because they thought he'd missed a shot. After days of perfect marksmanship, it seemed impossible for him to make a mistake. It wasn't until one of the evaluators examined his target that they found out the truth: he'd key-holed a shot. Like Robin Hood's arrow, his aim was so true, he'd shot right through the hole his previous bullet had left behind.

They say Boot Camp has gotten a lot tamer since the days of 'Nam and Full Metal Jacket-style hazing. It's true insofar that recruits aren't murdered or outright beaten if they're incompetent, but the psychological battery and hard guidance made famous by characters like Staff Sergeant Hartman is eternal. Name-calling. Shaming. Punishment for mistakes taking the form of soul-breaking physical training. Drill Instructors were relentless in their mission of grinding recruits down so they could build something stronger amidst the pieces.

Yet none of that was happening now. An awed hush had fallen across the ranks of DIs, and they could do nothing but witness this recruit's skill. It was like watching the quintessential master at work. Bets had been made and lost on how long it would be before he dropped a shot. Today was the last day of qualifications, and his score remained flawless.

Talk of the recruit's prowess had filtered through the command. The CO had heard the story circling the watercooler and made a personal appearance, hoping to see whether this kid was the real deal or more overblown exaggeration. He was quickly convinced it was the former. By the time the recruit took his last shots, the CO had made the call.

Less than an hour later two men in suits escorted the recruit off the range and to the empty Chow Hall. The recruit had, of course, been here many times before but seeing it so empty felt alien. Normally, there were hundreds of others pushing through the cafeteria line as quickly as possible and shoveling food down their throats while Drill Instructors screamed at them. Today it was just the recruit, the two suits, and the large man waiting for them at the table.

"Sit."

The recruit and the large man gave each other a single glance, and they both catalogued every observation that moment held. The recruit noted the swollen knuckles, telltale signs of many fractured fists long since healed. The large man found it surprising that the boy's face was free of scarring since his files noted how frequently he'd gotten into fights as a child.

"How did you do it?" the man asked.

"Do what, sir?"

The man flipped a paper over so the recruit could read it. It showed a breakdown of his perfect score.

"I can assure you my files are extensive," the man said. "But nowhere in there does it say you've handled a weapon before. No hunting. No weekend paintball even. How does someone who has never fired a rifle before miraculously become one of—if not the best—marksmen this range has ever seen?"

The recruit paused. He gauged the man across from him, curious as to what the purpose of this interview was. The suit was telling, as were this man's supposed extensive files.

His answer was simple. "I listened to the Range Coaches' instruction and applied it. That was really all there was."

"All the other recruits received the same instruction on shooting fundamentals. How is it you managed to be the only one reaping the benefits?"

"I'm not too sure? I suppose I was listening better. Or maybe I was just able to remember and apply what they told me better. Maybe the others with prior experience had trouble learning."

The large man nodded knowingly. After a moment, he pulled a few more papers from the folder.

"This rifle qualification is hardly the first test you've aced. Your entry level exam at the time of your enlistment had a perfect score. I went through the trouble of pulling all your school records. Imagine my wonder when I found you had a perfect GPA and off the charts standardized test scores. To be honest, I'm surprised that hadn't flagged you and your name hasn't crossed my desk sooner."

"Some people are just better test takers than others, sir."

He shook his head.

"No. I think it's something a little more unique than that. Something so much rarer. Tell me, have you ever heard of *Hyperthymesia*?"

The recruit pondered it for a second, then gave the interviewer a dismissive shake of his head.

"It's a particularly rare condition; I think to date there's been less than six confirmed cases of it."

"My test scores are because of a disease?"

"Hardly. *Hyperthymesia* is a condition characterized by extremely accurate memory. Perfect recall. The few confirmed cases showed that certain areas of their brains were enlarged; the caudate nucleus, which is essentially the center for procedural memory, and the hippocampus which is believed to store information and facts. I imagine those areas of your own frontal lobe would be the same. Call it a disease or a disorder, I'd argue that it's an advantage that could see you master a great many skill sets."

The Recruit considered everything he'd been told. Remembering things had always just been second nature to him. They were alone in the room now; the other two suits had silently disappeared at some point.

"Sir, who are you? Am I in some sort of trouble?"

The man gave him a hard four-count stare before he spoke.

"Adrian Rasp, my name is Mister Rourke. And I have a position open for someone of your potential skill. I'm here to talk to you about the Black Spear initiative."

CHAPTER 19

Black watched behind Simon, not unlike a lion encircling a water hole, as the other man finished briefing the next phase of the assignment to the Immortals. They asked no questions, they just set about preparing. There was something appreciable to the way they took to task. It was the sheer focus of it. Occasionally one would say something to another, but every one of them went to work, prepping their gear to ensure it was ready with nary a distraction.

"You said they are the best you have?" Black asked, watching curiously as the scar-faced one, Declan, ran a sharpening stone along a large two-handed axe. He did it by feel and sound, listening for the *shing* of the stone along the metal and then drawing a thumb near the edge. Satisfied, Declan nodded to himself knowingly, then tossed the stone to the raven-haired Harrison. Harrison took his turn using the stone to hone the edges on a set of twin double-edged daggers he kept sheathed on either side of his hips.

"They are our most elite soldiers," Simon answered. "Within the ranks of Legion, they are second in respect only to the Praetorian."

Black leaned against a wall and started to roll one of his knives by the blade between his fingers. He judged that Simon was the type to constantly need self-validation, in this case it would take the form of him showing Black how much he knew. Which meant that Black could wait comfortably without asking for Simon to explain more.

"The Praetorians guard those that sit at Legion's innermost ring. Some, like Dorian Rinx, protect the person themselves. Others act directly on their charge's behalf, protecting their interests."

"Is that what you are, then?"

"A Praetorian?" Simon's voice dripped with envy.

There was something else Black heard: ambition. Black's eyes were drawn to a silver ring Simon wore on his finger. The other man twisted it obsessively

"No, I've not been honored with that role yet. Though perhaps soon. They only have two you see, to act as their left and right hands. You understand? It's such a rare title, one my own family proudly held for a time."

Black looked once more to the silver ring and made the connection. Though Simon wore it, it had belonged to someone else. The man kept it now as a memento. A reminder of the supposed highest point of achievement his bloodline had climbed to.

"And this innermost ring, how many seats are at the table next to Lady Holt's?"

Simon paused, then an amused smile crept across his face. He caught himself saying too much. And they both knew it.

"Lady Holt likes you," he said. "But don't forget your place. I don't mind telling you of Legion's workings, because it's just like a pet owner explaining to a dog how the world works. I was born in Legion, third generation, but you merely *exist* in our world. At our discretion."

Black nodded, not giving in to Simon's not so subtle insults. The fact that he didn't get angry only seemed to further get under Simon's skin.

"Is that the lowest tier in Legion then? Dogs?"

He smiled respectfully. Simon's nostrils flared and he bit his tongue. Black managed to push his buttons without so much as a single harsh word.

"Actually, that would be the Branded," answered Scaglin. He looked up from the sniper rifle he had been cleaning and leaned back in his chair. "They aren't soldiers, more like worker bees. The drones. They serve as the eyes and ears across the globe, some willingly. Others, eh, not so much."

"Why do they call them Branded?" Black asked.

Scaglin held up his arm and pulled back his shirt sleeve. It revealed a brand on his wrist of a horned skull. Legion's mark. One of the Immortals had carved the same icon on the tongue of the Valkyrie Squad leader.

"Everyone has to start somewhere," Scaglin said. "Bearing the brand marks them as ours."

"Very well, thank you for the insight, Bob," Black said. Scaglin grimaced and turned back towards cleaning his rifle. "Now, how does one go from being Branded to becoming an Immortal?"

"First they must become a Demon," Simon said, he now sounded annoyed for having to walk Black through Legion's intricacies. "If the Branded are our eyes and ears, then the Demons are the fist. They make up our army, the legions of Legion."

"But only the worthy can be elevated and be made an Immortal," chipped in the red-haired Australian, Hogue. There was a practice dummy made of a rubbery ballistic gel on the far wall, and Hogue had been practicing throwing his large hunting knife at it. The blade sank its full length into the dummy's throat. Hogue paced over to the dummy to retrieve his knife and give it another throw.

Black leaned over Simon's shoulder, "What do you think, Mr. Ellis, do you think I'm worthy of being an Immortal?"

Simon scoffed, "You're barely worthy of speaking my name. Perhaps if you prove your worth, we'll allow you a brand."

Three of Black's obsidian knives *thunked* into the target dummy, barely missing Hogue's fingers by inches. The knives pierced both eyes, the third sank deep into the target's forehead. No one had even seen Black draw them. Their surprise brought a cold smirk to Black's face. Simon's own face soured as he was clearly left wondering just how many of those blades he had hidden up his sleeve.

"I'm not denying your skills, Mr. Black. It is why you were hired. There can be no failure with Black Spear this time."

It was Black's turn to be surprised.

"This time? You're saying they've crossed Legion before?"

Simon walked towards the dummy and pulled one of Black's blades free. He dragged the tip of the knife along the dummy's face as he spoke.

"Not directly, no," he said. "But on two occasions now, they have turned certain business ventures of ours into catastrophic failures. Two years ago, we helped liaise. Introduced a geneticist to a rising militia; he brought along with him a prototype virus. Moses-1. Quite a nasty bug. It certainly wasn't the product we were initially hoping for when we helped bankroll the gen-tech's research, but I suppose even potato chips were an accident. This militia's understanding was that they would use the virus to strike back at the government they felt had failed them."

"And the truth?"

"The truth was their crusade was damned from the start. We sunk a hefty sum into bolstering this militia's coffers. We were never believers in their cause, rather we were very firm believers in the fortune that would be ripe for the taking the moment their viral scare went public. A virus is costly to fight, and the governments of the world would spend fortunes combating it. No one could afford another Covid-19 pandemic, they would spare no expense to nip Moses-1 in the bud. Potential government research grants for vaccines, medicinal costs, payroll for emergency aid workers, and health insurance payments all should have been heading our way. Except all of that was contingent on the outbreak occurring. Black Spear took that from us."

It was a point of professional courtesy that he rarely bothered asking why he was hired, but information was a resource, and so Black was appreciative when a piece of the puzzle landed in his lap. Black Spear's meddling had set them on an inevitable course. They had offended Legion, again and again, and that path led them to him. He was the result. There was a certain beauty to it. Cause and effect, action reaction, and Black would be the final reaction.

"War. War is, well, lucrative," Simon continued.

He said it with such a grandiose air, you would think he was commenting on some unseen scenic landscape rather than one of the most eternal horrors mankind faced.

"Last year we brought the world to the brink of it. The entire global order would have shifted. We were the only ones who would have anticipated it and ended up on top. Governments rise, governments fall. All at our whim. The status quo was overdue for a change. For his part in a plan of such magnitude, Samuel Cain was promised a head at the table. It would not be the first time Legion altered the course of history, but it would be the first time an endeavor of ours of such scale had been stopped. Our war never happened, and now Cain's seat at the table remains unfilled. All because of one man's hand on a button."

"Next time don't make a button, then," Black said slyly.

Simon shot him a look. The Immortals noticed and paused. No doubt, they wondered if Black's offense was cause enough to strike.

"That's it, then?" Black whispered to Simon. "Why you're all taking this so *seriously?* So personally. Cain's empty seat. If you pull this off, succeed where Legion has failed twice in the past, then maybe you're a made man."

Simon scowled. "Ambition, however well placed, is hardly the only reason. The truth is that this ragtag band of soldiers has become quite a thorn in Legion's side in recent years. Black Spear must be made to suffer for it."

Black smiled. "I was beginning to worry that this was all over something so trivial as money and profits. So boring. But it *is* personal, then? That's so much more fun. Death is never really about business, it should be very, very personal."

"On that we can agree, Mister Black," Simon reluctantly admitted. "A bullet is simple enough to end a life. But to send a message? We require something more substantial."

Finally, Black understood. "So that's why Morpheus?"

"Yes," Simon said. "Now all that remains is for us to find it. That is, if you can still hold up your end of the agreement."

He extended the obsidian knife by the handle to Black, who took it and slid it into one of the hidden sheaths upon his vest.

"That's the best part of this. They're going to lead us right to it."

CHAPTER 20

I drove back to the foundry district, I don't even know why I did it. Rourke had temporarily pulled my armory access, which was a smart move on his part. After storming out of the conference room earlier, I had every intent of loading up and going it alone. If there was no back-up to be had, then so be it. I knew Black was the key to everything, and if no one wanted to listen then they could watch from the sidelines while I did it all on my own.

Hard to go it alone against a conspiracy of this size unarmed, though. After letting out some steam trashing my room, I'd grabbed the keys to my Jeep Gladiator and gotten some mileage therapy. I don't think I really knew which direction I'd been heading to until I stopped the vehicle and got out.

Also, to say I was unarmed wasn't exactly true. I still had my sidearm, and hidden in my truck was my trusty Boomstick. The double-barrel had been a trophy from my first mission where I had quite literally taken it from the cold dead fingers of a militia leader. Since then, I'd had the barrels chopped and the stock replaced with a pistol grip. I kept the Boomstick in my private quarters on a shelf on the wall. Rourke knew the value of allowing his soldiers certain privileges, and he had never required me to check it into our armory. An oversight on his part that I took full advantage of.

My phone buzzed as I stepped out of the cab and found myself wandering the empty lot. I took a quick look at it and saw that I'd missed four calls in my fugue state drive. Two from Bernice the ever dutiful therapist, and two more from Madison. I gauged which one would be more pissed at me for not answering my phone and decided to call Madison first.

"Where are you?" she asked, answering after the first ring.

"You think Rourke monitors our calls?" I deflected. "Seems like a thing he would have Rain do. My phone is probably tapped, which means he knows about us, which means he's just seeing how long we *think* we can sneak around."

"Cole, I heard about Kelly."

There was an immediate pulse at my eyes. Tears readied to flow again like bullets loading into a chamber. It physically hurt to force them back.

My sight drew to the inside of the foundry. It was so dark inside. I couldn't see anything in it other than the large windows on the other side that led to the back patio area. The area where Black had chosen which of us would die. The exact place I'd watched him blow a hole through my friend's throat and watch as he'd drowned in his own blood.

'So, you just gonna lay there bleeding? Or you gonna stand?'

The bullet that tore through Kelly's neck meant he'd never gotten a chance to utter any final words. Instead, my mind kept replaying old memories. The familiar catch phrases.

"Cole?" Madison interrupted.

"Yeah, still here."

My feet started carrying me into the foundry. I walked to the spot where Valkyrie's bodies had been displayed, the earlier rain had already washed the ground clean.

"I'm just out clearing my head."

"I'm worried about you," Madison said quietly. "Bernice was trying to find you, too. She said that she needs to see you first thing in the morning."

I was deep within the foundry now. A part of me could swear that Black was still lurking within the shadows, ready to leap out at any moment and finish what he'd started. I came to the large windows, the same spot a flashbang had blown me through just hours ago. A crushing fatigue fell down upon me. I rested my head against one of the untouched glass panes.

"I just need a little time," I said. "I'm okay. I promise."

"It's out of your hands now, Cole."

It would be the easiest thing in the world to accept at this point. I could let somebody else deal with this madness, spend some time bedside with my guys at the hospital. Hell, right now even Bernice's couch and uncomfortable questions sounded more enjoyable than if I stayed on this path.

"You're right," I said. "I just have to get some things in order, first."

Madison tried to protest, but I hung up too quickly. It was a dick move, but I knew that if I stayed on the phone with her for just one more minute, she would convince me to give up this fool's errand. For a long while I sat in that empty building. It was a strange blur where I just stood there feeling the wrongness in the room.

There was an unseen frost in the air that gripped my soul. Defeat. That's what filled this place. This was where I lost.

Eventually I got fed up with wallowing in my own emotions and turned to go back to the truck. I didn't dare to step foot into the patio area where I'd been chained earlier. Even if the rain had washed Kelly's blood away, I wasn't ready to look at the spot where I'd watched him die.

I stopped short when something caught my eye. A metallic glint that reflected the little bit of starlight that had pierced the dark room from the night sky outside. I went to a knee, reaching out for it.

A bullet?

My memory jogged. I realized it was mine. The bullet that had been in the chamber when I'd hesitated earlier. When I couldn't take the shot. When I'd had that *one* moment where I could've taken out Black but had been too afraid of accidentally shooting Billy. The same bullet that Black promptly ejected from the chamber when he'd disarmed me.

I held it between thumb and forefinger, a grim resolve taking hold within me.

Black had told me there was a bullet for everyone out there. I'd just found his. I made a solemn vow in that dark foundry then, a promise that I would not rest until I delivered this bullet upon its rightful place: right in his fucking heart.

I drew my sidearm and locked the slide back to load the bullet in the chamber, but at the last second stopped short. The faint light from the windows showed something on my weapon's slide. A full set of fingerprints was on my gun. My mind flashed back to when Black had grabbed it during our fight and caused it to jam. He'd left more behind than he'd thought.

My teeth clenched like a vice and the muscles all along my jaw tensed.

"Gotcha, you son of a bitch."

DARK BEGINNINGS 2

Rourke administered three tests in the back of the vehicle while enroute to their destination. They were more for his own curiosity than any clinical reason. The first was a list of over forty words, all random, in no particular order. He let Adrian look it over for five seconds, then gave him a blank sheet of paper and instructed him to write down each word he could remember. He, of course, rewrote the entire list perfectly.

The second test was a twenty-by-twenty grid. Each cell had a different number in it. When given a blank grid, Adrian copied the numbers from memory and filled in the blanks within ninety seconds. The last test was purely for Rourke's interest. He handed Adrian a sketchpad, asking him to draw the faces of the two agents who'd escorted him to the cafeteria. Apparently, his hand was just as deft at drawing as it was at pulling triggers. The renderings Adrian composed would be accurate enough for a nationwide manhunt.

"I took an art class last summer," he explained. He seemed surprised by his own drawings. "I guess the lessons stuck with me."

The car lurched to a halt in front of a hotel. They both stepped out. The hotel was upper scale, which was certainly nicer than any place Adrian had ever stayed in.

"What are we doing here?"

"Meeting your team," Rourke said. "Normally, there is extensive in-processing, but with you we'll make an understandable exception. You're going to receive a crash course on how Black Spear works first-hand. Sink or swim, Rasp."

The elevator ride up was slower than Adrian was comfortable with. It wasn't just that Rourke was a massive man and didn't leave much space for him in the car. The entire situation was moving at light speed, and Adrian still hadn't digested his first sit-down with Rourke from yesterday. But he'd wanted to serve for the greater good, and from the things Rourke had told him it sounded like this would be the best opportunity for that.

They walked to the room and the door opened before Rourke had time to knock. The man who ushered them in wore a blood-red vest and tie over a white shirt with the sleeves rolled to the elbows. He was black, had a meticulously maintained goatee, and was built like a fighter. Strong, muscled, but far from bulky.

"Rasp, this is Major Vic Lane," Rourke said. "Callsign: Crimson. He is the commander for Spectrum Squad."

Crimson extended a hand, and Adrian took it. There was not an ounce of softness to it. His skin was like sandpaper, his grip nothing less than mechanical.

"I'll take it from here, sir," said Crimson.

Rourke gave him a pat on the shoulder, handed him Adrian's file, and departed. As Crimson closed the door behind him, his entire posture changed.

"Look here, son. I don't like the idea of some kid being thrown into my ranks, but the boss says there's something special about you. We'll consider this your probationary period. What that means is it'll be callsigns only for the rest of the team. I could give two shits about you knowing *my* name, I've been dead for six years now."

Adrian nodded and Crimson led them into the hotel room

where the other three members of Spectrum Squad waited. Two men, one woman.

"This is Cobalt, Jade, and Gold," said Crimson.

They each gave Adrian appraising glances. Cobalt was blonde-haired and blue-eyed; he looked like he could have walked off the cover of a pamphlet for Nebraska's board of tourism. His eyes appeared cast from fine sapphires. Jade sat in the corner, feet up on a bed, an olive-colored hoodie hiding her face. She played with a strand of hair with one hand, the other flipped a double-edged dagger into the air before the hilt landed perfectly in her open palm. She turned away from Adrian, unimpressed, and continued to toss and catch her blade. The last, Gold, wore horn-rimmed glasses and peaked behind a laptop screen to give Adrian an unenthusiastic thumbs-up. Gold had a five o'clock shadow and dark circles around his eyes, Adrian couldn't help but wonder when he'd last slept.

"Everyone, this is Private Adrian Rasp," said Crimson. "He'll be tagging along on tonight's hunting party."

"Private?" asked Cobalt.

He prepped explosive charges. Although Adrian had never touched anything more explosive than a firecracker, he recognized the charges as some form of plastique. Maybe Semtex or Composition 4.

"Don't worry, he'll be keeping a safe distance. Adrian will be standing in as overwatch."

"He, uh, ever killed before, Crimson?" asked Gold.

"He's really good at killing paper," said Jade.

She'd somehow swiped Adrian's file from Crimson's hand at some point, and he hadn't even noticed her leave the bed. She tossed the file to Gold, who flipped through it. When he got to the part that detailed Adrian's accuracy and Rourke's theory of *Hyperthymesia,* he whistled.

"We're going on a little weekend hunting trip," Crimson said to Adrian.

He indicated a weapons crate on the far table. Adrian walked over and undid the clasps. Within the hard-plastic case was nothing short of a monster. The Barrett XM500 sniper rifle inside was chambered in .50 BMG, a round so devastating the rifle was classified as "anti-materiel" and thus was supposed to be used on enemy equipment not people.

Adrian ran a fingertip along the cold metal of the Barrett. He had no illusions of what type of hunting Crimson had in store for them.

CHAPTER 21

I called Rain while on my way back to the Jeep.

"Boss, while I don't usually enjoy leaving business unfinished, I was sort of looking forward to getting a full night's rest for once," she said.

"You want a more fitting callsign than Yellow Pages then you've got to put in the work," I answered. "Or maybe we can drop you down to Google? Maybe Siri?"

"What've you got for me?" she said, her tone completely changing when she picked up on this not just being a courtesy call.

"Black," I answered.

She groaned, and a sound came through the receiver which could only be her smacking the phone against her forehead.

"You know why they call people like him ghosts, right? Because there's nothing to go off."

"Yeah, about that," I said, dragging it out as I took another look at the fingerprints on my pistol. I set the pistol down on the hood of my truck. "I may have something."

"This isn't exactly authorized, is it?" she asked in a hushed whisper.

I didn't bother to whisper. It's not that I wasn't paranoid enough to think Rourke tapped all of our phones—on the contrary, I wouldn't be the least bit surprised—but I'd just accepted that if he was listening in on my private conversations then it wouldn't matter how quietly I spoke.

"Let Rourke and everyone else worry about finding Legion's trail, you and I can work this angle on our own." I gave the handle of the pistol a little tap and watched it spin on the truck's hood while I thought. "Any word on his targets?"

"None. Am I the only one starting to get the sense that it's a complete goose chase?"

"My thoughts exactly."

"There is one bit of new info about Damien Black you might be interested in," said Rain. I heard her fingers tapping along a keyboard. "Your encounter at the foundry might've actually pieced together a few things."

"Swell. Good to know my friend's throat being blown out wasn't for nothing. 'Things' like what?"

"Well, the obsidian knives he uses, for one. White Shield had a dossier on a private contractor that the Kaneshiro Yakuza have used on occasion, going back about ten years. They called him, and forgive the pronunciation, *Kokuyoseki Kira*: The Obsidian Killer. I took a quick look at some of the autopsy reports of his marks and the cuts look like his handiwork. Precise, lethal. I ran facial-recog off some of the footage your team grabbed of his face, cross-referenced with suspect sketches from other cold cases. One such match came up. This time from a hit on a witness for the Veleno crime family. Records show that Boss Veleno paid to bring in a 'Papa Shadow' to do the job."

I could practically hear the lightbulb above my head ping as I put the pieces together.

"So, you're saying the reason we have so little on him is because he keeps starting new aliases?"

"Sort of. I'd say it's more like when a band member creates a side project? The earliest known report of a Damien Black predates both the Yakuza dossier and the Veleno hit, anyway. I think he was going by different names to stay under the radar."

"Okay, that could explain why nobody's caught him yet," I said. The last part felt rotten on my tongue. There was something more there and I couldn't quite put my finger on it, but I was getting closer. "What's with the obsidian? Is it some type of calling card?"

Rain breathed deep. "I doubt it. He doesn't strike me as the type who would be compelled to leave a signature. It's less of a compulsion and more practicality. Despite a few millennia's worth of advances in metallurgy, obsidian is still arguably the sharpest blade you can get. The edge on an obsidian knife is sharp on a *microscopic* level. Steel sharpens to about five-hundred nanometers wide at its finest point, obsidian sharpens to a single nanometer. I've heard some surgeons reverting to using it for scalpels as the finer cuts leave less scarring."

"Interesting, thanks for the science lesson."

"Being handmade makes it easily replaceable, too. There's no manufacturer to trace it back to, and he can make himself a new one on a whim so long as he's got the material. If you could get your hands on one of his knives, the best we could do is run an analysis and find the source of the rock he used. It's actually fascinating. Obsidian is kind of like a fingerprint, you can pinpoint exactly where on the globe the material came from. Because the magma that cools to make it is unique to each—"

"Rain," I said, cutting her off as politely as I could manage.

"Right. Sorry. Anyway, what've you got for me, Boss?"

I smiled and went to pick up the handgun off the hood.

It was gone.

I froze, turning slowly in a circle and becoming very aware of just how quiet and empty this area was.

"Boss?" Rain asked.

Two men came out from behind my truck, both with guns drawn. They wore ski masks and plainclothes. Though they had the advantage and pressed towards me with clear intent, part of me was thankful. These weren't the guys who'd taken Valkyrie out. They moved much sloppier. Their handling of their weapons and the way they approached me seemed far less practiced. The weapons themselves, a Saturday Night Special .38 snub-nose and a Hi-Point 9mm semiautomatic, further confirmed it. Both guns were on the cheapest end of the spectrum.

A third came from behind me, my own .45 held in his hand. Thankfully it looked like he hadn't smudged the prints on the slide. Not yet at least. He put a finger to his lips and shushed me.

"Let me call you back," I said to Rain and hung up.

The three ski-masked thugs closed the distance without getting too near. They were practiced enough to know that the whole point of a gun was that your target didn't need to be close. If they got too close, I could disarm one, use him as a shield, and take out the other two. I was reminded of how Black had done that very thing with Billy against me.

They kept me at a respectable distance, each one facing me from a different angle.

I put my back to the hood of the truck and held my hands up. "Nice night for a walk, eh?"

"Stupid of you to come back," the one with my gun said. "And here I thought freezing our asses off out here was a waste of time. Alright then, I'm sure you know the drill."

He gestured for me to remove whatever else I was hiding. If he'd decided to pat me down himself, I knew ten different ways I could've turned it to my advantage. Even if these guys weren't Legion's A-listers, they were no rookies.

I carefully removed my jacket and set it on the hood. My MK-9 knife was sheathed in a shoulder rig that they could now plainly see, a back-up Marfione Apex knife with a broad spear-point blade was tucked into the back of my belt.

"Slip the belt," the masked man instructed.

Smart, if he had told me to set the knife itself on the ground, I could have closed the distance and killed him. Throwing it wasn't an option. That was a skill that I didn't have, nor would I want to try while two men had guns on me. I undid my belt and let it fall to the ground. Next, I gestured to the large MK-9 still strapped by my shoulder.

"Easy now," he said. "Real slow. Set it on the hood."

I did as I was told. I held the knife by the blade rather than the handle just to make sure they knew I had no intention of using it. Not how they thought at least. I smiled, which even with their faces hidden by their ski masks I could see unsettled them, and then banged the pommel of my knife against the hood hard.

BANG. BANG.

"If no one is around to hear our gunshots then they sure as shit won't hear you banging around with that." The leader laughed. "Trust me, this is a private meeting. We checked."

"Didn't check everywhere," I said, and slammed the knife against the hood twice more.

BANG. BANG.

Then, I screamed.

"Sic 'em, boy!"

A dark wrecking ball on four legs flew from the bed of the truck and slammed into the shooter with the .38 from behind. This blur of fangs and fur went by the name of Dante, and he absolutely did not appreciate when people threatened me. Dante was a hundred and fifty pounds of jet-black Canary Mastiff, and his bite was definitely as bad as his bark. There's a primal level of fear that even the most hardened of soldiers experience when faced with a beast that wants to maul you to death. At the very least, it'll make you flinch.

People who flinch when they have me in a bind usually don't live very long.

In the split-second Dante's appearance surprised them, I drove my MK-9 deep into the leader's belly just below his sternum once, twice, and on the third stab I angled it up to pierce his heart. By the time my blade slid out of his body he was dead on his feet already.

Dante pounced at the back of the knees of the man with the Hi-Point 9mm. He landed hard on his face, rolled over, and pointed the semi-automatic at Dante. It wasn't the smartest decision he'd made that night. Dante's jaws clamped onto the wrist and blood spurted out as he tore the hand free from the arm with three monstrous tugs. He barked, inches from the man's face, and flung gobs of spittle onto him.

The one I'd stabbed just then finally fell onto his back, dead. It all happened in about three quarters of a second. As calmly as possible, I used the dead man's pant leg to wipe the blood off my knife. Then I sheathed it back by my shoulder, put my belt back on, and retrieved the double-barreled shotgun from the cab of my truck.

"Now then," I said, making a show of looking as casual as possible. I broke open the shotgun to make sure the two loads of buckshot were still loaded before snapping it shut.

"Simons says: if you enjoy having both your hands then I recommend tossing that away."

The one with the .38 looked at the gun like he'd forgotten it. He tossed it aside. Dante left the one-handed man to growl at him.

Dante's eyes are a golden yellow, and at night they practically glow. I'm pretty sure right then he looked about as close to a demon as that man would ever see.

"Put your belt around your buddy's arm. I have a few questions for you gentlemen, and I'd prefer if he doesn't bleed to death first. Oh yeah, pull those stupid masks off, too."

He stared back at me, afraid to move. I pointed at the other guy writing on the floor and clutching his stump as blood continued to spurt out in rhythmic pumps.

"Chop, chop."

Slowly, he slipped his mask off. He avoided my eyes as applied his belt like a tourniquet around his friend's bicep. Once the bleeding slowed, they shared a look. No doubt wondering what play to make. Silently planning how they hell they were going to get out of this alive. Spoiler alert: they weren't going to.

But then I saw it. It had taken me a second in the dark, but there it was. They both had small radios wired to their ears. I kept my gun trained on them and checked the heart-stabbed corpse. He had one as well. I pulled it from his ear and put it to my own.

"What's going on over there?!" someone asked. "We're four minutes out. Keep that asshole busy."

Shit. They had backup.

I turned back to the two cowering from Dante on the ground. "Go ahead and unplug your radios. Good news: your buddies are on the way. Bad news: that's not really enough time for how this usually goes. Four minutes? See, that's going to be something of a record so I'm going to have to get creative."

I put my Boomstick back in the truck, opting instead to draw both my tactical MK-9 and my Apex knife. I approached them with a blade in each hand like some slasher maniac from a horror movie.

"See your buddy over there?" I asked, cocking my head towards the guy I'd stabbed through the heart. "He's the lucky one who got the cleanest death tonight. You two got the short straws. But, the clock's ticking, so I'm going to have to skip the foreplay."

With a flick of either wrist I sliced an ear off each of them. Yeah, I kept my knives that sharp. Blood gushed, hands clamped to their fresh wounds, and they howled in pain.

"First question. How many people?"

"What?" asked the shooter who still had both hands.

I put the tip of one of my knives into his nostril and pulled slightly. "Your backup. How many people?"

The man's lips sputtered like wheels spinning in the mud unable to get traction. I pulled a little harder on my knife, just an ounce more and I'd slit his nostril open.

"Eight!" he bellowed. "Two cars, four shooters each!"

Double shit.

Even if they were as amateur as these three, eight against one Cole West out in the open were not good odds. I still had a chance this guy was bullshitting though.

"Hey," I said, turning to his one-handed friend. "Is he telling the truth or—"

The man with the missing hand stared straight ahead with lifeless eyes. I checked his stump and saw the fresh pool of blood around the asphalt beneath him.

Triple shit.

"Great job on the tourniquet," I said, prodding the loose belt with the flat of one of my knives. The lone survivor of the hit trio squirmed, and I realized I still had my other knife stuck up his nose.

I checked my watch. Time was running out.

"Next question: meeting place. Where. How'd you get the gig?"

"Ruby," he said, panting. Blood began to leak out of his nostril. "We met at Ruby's, I don't know who—"

The screech of tires cut him off. Oncoming headlights lit the two of us up. His eight friends were ahead of schedule. His eyes went wide, no doubt grasping for the last bit of hope that his backup was about to save his life. I dashed that hope away by sticking a knife up through his ribs and piercing his heart. Out of time. I had maybe three seconds before his backup shot me down; I hopped in the truck, clicked my tongue to signal Dante to jump into the bed, hit the ignition and gunned it without a moment to spare.

When I joined up with Black Spear, they were supposed to be

the baddest of the bad. On my first mission I'd had legitimate reason to be afraid of my own teammates more than the enemy we'd faced. Our outfit had been the most fearsome group imaginable. Technological overmatch applied to the shooter level, each individual trained to unparalleled tactical excellence, and an executive charter direct from the President, which granted ruthless rules of engagement. Black Spear was a horror story the enemies of the nation told themselves while huddled in their caves. So why was my heart beating so fast I could feel it in my neck?

It's not supposed to be like this, I thought.

Hit teams canvassing our previous mission sites. Ambushes butchering our teams and desecrating their corpses. My own squad so efficiently dismantled by a lone man, I didn't have the words. We hadn't just lost today: we'd been *beaten*. We operated in the dark, pushing back against the shadows, and now Mr. Black was here on the shadows' behalf to push back.

My hand trembled on the steering wheel as I sped through the industrial area away from the foundry, so I removed it. I stared at it, confused like it was some kind of traitor. It felt like something was coming to a head. My fuck up, the loss of our friends, and now this on top of all the previous skeletons Bernice would kindly remind me I still had crowding my closet. The shake in my hand got worse, and I smacked it against the dash as if that would fix whatever was wrong.

The two cars gained on me. There was no way I'd make it back to the freeway in time. Some invisible vice clamped tighter around my chest with every beat. It wasn't just that the eight Legion shooters were pursuing me. I was being *hunted*.

Fear. It's never far from my mind, I mean you have to be a fool to be fearless in this line of work, but this was different. The scope of what I found myself up against made me feel small in a way that had become unfamiliar. My heart beat even faster at the realization that I was losing control of myself as much as the situation.

You won't make it to the freeway.

Nameless buildings passed by my windows as I accelerated way past seventy. A bad part of my brain wondered which one they'd stash my body in once they caught up to me. Generic warehouse number one, condemned factory number two, or how about that new construction site at the end? The construction zone caught my eye. Six stories of initial structure, mostly just the concrete and rebar support columns and foundations for each floor. Maybe they'd haul me in there, pour concrete over my corpse in one of the foundation fill spots.

No, I thought to myself, practically screaming it in my head, *don't think like that.*

The shadows pushed back against us, and that scared me. That was okay. Thing about fear is, you can use it. A cornered and frightened wolf is far from helpless. I tightened my hand into a fist and forced the tremor to stop. Legion had shaken me, shaken us, but Newton's Third Law said that for every action there was an equal opposite reaction. You blow up an airport, break my team, and kill my friend? Yeah. Standby for one hell of a reaction.

I steered right and burned through the chain-link fence surrounding the construction site. The truck screeched to a halt, I whistled at Dante to hop out, and I headed to the dark inside. Various tools were left behind by the day crew. Hammers. Saws. Nails. Belt sanders. Something Black said to me came to mind. He'd taunted me saying he wanted to see how dark I'd become; he was already convinced that I was just like him. A monster.

Maybe that was it. What I had to do to remind myself that I was a goddamn frightening nightmare in my own right. It occurred to me that I'd left the Boomstick and handgun in the cab of my truck. That had not been an oversight.

They wanted to hunt me?

"Let them come," I said as I stepped into the shadows.

CHAPTER 22

Raven. 12:05 a.m.
Construction Site
Los Angeles, California

"He went inside!" shouted Raven.

Raven wasn't his name. Nor were the others in his car named Bear, Jaguar, or Lion. Their call signs had been assigned when they'd taken the job, and everyone got their own NFL animal for the week. As far as names went, Raven wasn't bad. He'd hate to be the loser in car two that got stuck with Dolphin.

The other car pulled up alongside theirs and four more mercs spilled out. Raven was lead for this gig, and he took half a moment to sketch out a game plan in his head before turning to share it with the other men. They all wore ballistic vests over nondescript clothes and had brought whatever burner weapons they'd had available. Raven himself wasn't even certain who was or wasn't Branded among them, but he was fairly certain he was the only Demon. That was how it worked: compartmentalization. Raven had a handler, and the handler provided gigs, everything else was beyond his purview. A job was a job was a job.

"Car two," he said, indicating Panther, Bronco, Cardinal, and the unfortunate Dolphin, "start at the top, work your way to the ground floor. Flush him down to us. We'll start here and clear towards you."

The second team moved to the trunk of their vehicle and retrieved the long guns stored within. Cardinal and Dolphin grabbed what looked to Raven like Chinese made AKs, while Panther and Bronco opted for a pump-action Mossberg and Remington respectively. Raven popped the trunk of his own vehicle and divvied out the armaments to his team. Two more shotguns for Bear and Jaguar, an M4-style rifle for Lion, and his own Kel-Tec KSG shotgun. For good measure, Raven took out a crate of flashbang stun grenades and handed one to the others, just in case. That his own weapons were far nicer than the other seven's was not lost on Raven, which made him wonder again whether or not they were even Branded. If they weren't, this might be their initiation.

"Pistol and a shotgun in his vic," noted Bear. He raised his chin at the cab and Raven nodded. "Why'd he leave them behind?"

Raven smiled as he twirled a finger in the air to signal them to move in. "Simple . . . he's ready to die. Let's go grant his wish."

Dolphin followed tight behind Panther, who led the way with his shotgun. A flashlight at the end cut through the darkness as they ascended the stairs. This guy, whoever he was, had decided to hide like a rat somewhere in this construction site. He was unarmed, on his own, and didn't have a chance in hell. Sucked to be him.

The guy was, however, kind of a big fuck and the site was dark as shit. Even without a gun, he could probably do some damage. That thought had Dolphin nearly bumping into Panther, who hissed a warning for him to back up. They reached the top floor and fanned out. Six flights of hard concrete stairs had his legs screaming and made it difficult to walk in a combat stance.

"With me," Panther said in a hushed whisper. "Bronco, Cardinal, check the other side."

Dolphin nodded, unsure if Panther could even see him in the

dark but followed his lead. The top floor was empty. A blank space with little more than some worktables, piles of 2x4s near boxes of loose nails, and assorted equipment. Rolls of bright orange extension cords snaked this way and that, and Dolphin wondered if he should call them out as a trip hazard for the others. Dolphin scanned his weapon across the open floor and eyed a shelf with several tools. There was a gap in the middle and Dolphin absentmindedly wondered what manner of tool might've fit there.

A loud machine whine had Dolphin leaping out of his skin. He and Panther exchanged a look with Cardinal and Bronco, who waved them towards the noise while they continued checking their own half of the floor. The ear-splitting screech went on and on. Dolphin found Panther hurrying towards it.

They rounded a corner and found the source: a table saw had been tripped on.

"The fuck . . ." muttered Panther.

He turned about to look behind them but his flashlight illuminated nothing. Panther cocked his head at Dolphin to kill the saw. He immediately looked for the off switch. Two things happened as Dolphin knelt down to search for the plug. First, he heard the wet meaty sound of a solid object impacting flesh. Second, something wet splashed against the back of Dolphin's neck.

Dolphin bolted upright, one hand instinctively wiping at the blood that had rained down on him and gagging at the sight of Panther's head halfway through the table saw's blade. The blade continued chewing through flesh, bone, and gray matter as Panther spasmed unnaturally on the table.

The third thing that happened was Dolphin realized which tool belonged to the gap on the shelf, as a three pound, short-handled sledge crunched between his eyes and sent his own skull fragments into his brain.

"He's here!" Bronco yelled to his teammate.

Seeing Panther's head split down the middle and Dolphin's face cratered gave him a moment of hesitation, but then the Remington boomed in his hands. The bastard moved too damn quick and vanished into the shadows as buckshot pelted nothing at all. Panther and Dolphin were down, down bad. In that one glimpse Bronco got of the target, he saw what almost looked like a rifle in his hand.

"He's got a gun! Think he grabbed one of their pieces!" he said as he racked a fresh shell into his shotgun.

"Where is he?!" shouted Cardinal as he came up beside Bronco. He rattled off a burst from his AK. The bullets hit only the table saw and their own dead teammates. Whether it was an act of panic or if he'd mistaken their bodies for the target, Bronco didn't know.

"He went that way," said Bronco, using the barrel of his shotgun to gesture around the corner.

"Let's get him," growled Cardinal.

"Slow down!" hissed Bronco. "I said he's got a gun now."

Cardinal gave him a strange expression, then eyed the dead bodies of Dolphin and Panther. Both Dolphin's AK and Panther's Mossberg were still held in their fingers. Even the pistol in the back of Dolphin's trousers and the one in Panther's shoulder rig had been left behind.

"They still have both of theirs. You're spooked and seeing things. Let's get this asshole," Cardinal said.

Bronco took one last look at a bloody hammer left atop the table saw before following Cardinal's lead. He could tell Cardinal was antsy. The man was eager for the kill and was rushing to get it before anyone else could. The two of them headed in the direction the target had escaped down. It looked like he was circling back to the stairs.

Bronco felt exposed in all the dark of the construction site. Too much open space where walls *should* have been, and now it felt like their guy could be lurking in any corner. While Cardinal plowed ahead with his weapon pointed to the front, Bronco tried his best to pick up the slack by shining his light to their flanks.

Nothing, he thought.

His eyes went back to the front where Cardinal was about to pass the doorway to the stairwell. An orange extension cord crossed their path. Just as Bronco was about to say something, the cord went taut and cinched around Cardinal's ankle. The man went down hard, his AK letting off a negligent burst before flying from his hands as he landed flat on his stomach. Bronco brought up his own weapon. Looking down his sights, all he could see was Cardinal's wide panicked eyes.

No shot . . .

Then Cardinal's eyes impossibly went wider as someone yanked the other end of the cord and pulled him screaming into the dark.

Bronco thought of screaming 'Cardinal' but knew it wasn't his actual name. All he could manage was a weak and frightened "Hey!"

The beam of his flashlight shook horribly as he took careful steps in the direction Cardinal had been taken. There was a blood curdling scream from further on up. Bronco picked up his pace. There were drag marks in the dust on the floor and Bronco followed it like breadcrumbs. It led around another corner, and Bronco braced himself to round it.

He brought the stock of the shotgun into the pocket of his shoulder before taking a breath to steel his quaking nerves. He'd go on three.

One.

Two.

Something pressed into the space behind his jaw, just below his ear. Bronco went petrified stiff, his eyes going to the side as the object jammed hard against his skin. It felt pointed, almost like a needle. Bronco had been mistaken after all. The target hadn't been armed with a gun. Well, not exactly.

The target pulled the trigger on the Ramset concrete nail gun, setting off a .22 caliber powder load, and sending a two-and-a-half-inch nail straight into Bronco's skull.

Raven's team hadn't even finished clearing the first floor when they heard the gunshots. Sounded to him like one round of 12-gauge, and then a string of 7.62 from one of the AKs. A few moments later there was another AK burst. He sent his three men towards the stairs with a flick of his finger. Lion looked giddy, as if excited at the prospect of the hunt being over so soon. Raven did not mirror the feeling. There was something to the gunshots that did not scream 'mission accomplished' to him.

"Eyes up," Raven ordered. "Don't let this sumbitch spook you."

Lion took the point. The beam of his flashlight cut into the stairwell, he cast it upwards to clear the way above them before heading to the top floor. They got to the third floor when they found Cardinal's dangling body hanging in between the stairs. He was strung around the neck by an orange power cord, two large knives plunged to their hilts just above his collar bones. His dead eyes stared ahead. The corpse swayed slightly back and forth, and the cord creaked and stretched under his weight.

Raven did a quick visual inventory of Cardinal and found that his pistol was still holstered at his side, but his AK and the flashbang were gone.

"Oh, my God," breathed Jaguar.

"No," a voice whispered from a few floors above. "No God here. Only me."

Raven aimed to the top of the stairs and sent a three-round

barrage towards the voice. He swore he saw the silhouette of a man for just a second before it slipped away. The shooters hurried up the stairs.

"Which floor is he on?!" Bear snapped.

"Top," said Jaguar. "I think."

"*Push*," Raven said through grit teeth.

They stepped out of the stairwell onto the sixth floor. Their flashlight beams all went in different directions to try and spot their man. All they found were bodies of their own.

"Keep it tight," ordered Raven.

The others pushed forward, maintaining no more than four feet distance between each other, while Raven brought up the rear. Lion's light picked up something bright and orange, and he focused on it. It was a five-gallon plastic pail, but laid atop it was what had to be Cardinal's AK rifle. Lion's beam sliced through the shadows all around him, and once he was sure the target was nowhere to be found he approached the discarded rifle.

"He just left it?" Lion asked. "Who is this guy?"

"The target, that's all," answered Raven impatiently.

Lion slung his M-4 and reached for the AK before Raven could stop him.

"No! Don't!"

The second Lion lifted the rifle off the pail, a small metal object beneath it sprang into the air. It was the metal safety lever of Cardinal's missing stun grenade. Raven had just enough time to shield his eyes before it went off. Flashbangs are meant to be non-lethal, since there's no fragmenting metal shell around it and minimal blast upon detonation. However, if placed in a large bucket tightly packed with nails and screws, it was more than adequate at dispersing them.

The nails and screws exploded into Lion, shredding the arm that had grabbed the AK and leaving the side of his face a nail-ridden mess. Amidst the fog of disorientation, Raven managed to see a large shadow separate itself from the darkness. It moved forward, scooped up six heavy duty, eight-inch nails, and approached Jaguar, who had his back turned. Raven tried to say something, but everything was ringing. The nails protruded between each of the shadow's knuckles. When Jaguar turned, the shadow began punching up and down his body. Again and again, he punched and stabbed the nails into each of Jaguar's shoulders, at the sides of his ribs, down into the inside of either thigh, and back up again before delivering two spiked jabs into either side of his neck. Then, just as quicky as he'd attacked Jaguar, the shadow melted back into the dark.

It took three seconds.

Jaguar slumped against the wall behind him, tried to say something, but all that came out was blood. Bear finally got back to his feet, saw Jaguar and Lion both practically reduced to hamburger meat, and screamed a panicked wail. He fired his shotgun into the empty blackness. Raven did the same.

Six men dead in the span of minutes. Raven sensed more than saw movement and zeroed in on it.

"There!" he said, his light just catching a glimpse of a boot before it disappeared behind a concrete support pillar. He and Bear split up to catch the target from either side of the column. They approached in rapid steps, but there was nothing there.

"Next one," Bear said and raised his chin at the next column closer to the edge of the floor. Raven nodded. They maneuvered to clear behind the column. Once more, they found nothing.

Raven heard something whirling through the air. It whistled towards him like a frisbee, and on instinct Raven ducked out of its way, but then Bear was clutching at his neck. No screams. No words. There was a ten-inch circular saw blade embedded in his windpipe, preventing anything from escaping his mouth but blood. One of Bear's hands fumbled uselessly at the saw blade, his other squeezed the trigger of his shotgun on reflex. Buckshot impacted the ground and ricocheted upwards, some of the pellets rebounding in Raven's directions and snapping into his thigh and hip.

Raven grimaced and fell to his knee for a moment. Bear's eyes rolled into the back of his head before he tumbled backwards off the edge of the building to plummet to the hard concrete below.

"Where are you?!" Raven yelled into the dark.

He wasted a few rounds shooting at spots in the dark.

His eyes frantically darted around. He saw Lion looking like a pincushion with over a dozen nails embedded in his face. Jaguar sat against a wall, gurgling through holes in his neck as he bled out from too many stab wounds to count. Dolphin lay on the floor in a corner with a hole where his face used to be, while Panther's head was split down the middle and his feet twitched with rhythmic spasms.

"Fuck this," Raven whispered as he hobbled down the stairs. He'd have to reach out to his handler, call for more backup, call in *all* the backup. First thing to do was to get the goddamn fuck out of here. Each step down the hard concrete stairs sent needle pulses of pain up his ricochet wounds.

Raven didn't notice that the two knives were no longer in Cardinal's suspended body.

He reached the bottom floor and forced his leg to move faster as he neared his car. When he stepped out from the inner darkness of the building, he happened to look up and find Bear's body. After falling from the top floor, he hadn't quite made it to the bottom. Instead, he'd gotten caught and impaled by half a dozen rebars from an unfinished external column.

A low growl drew his attention back to the ground in front of him. Yellow eyes glared up at him from the black furred pelt of a living demon. The enormous dog growled again. Low, threatening, and filled to bursting with the promise of sharp fangs and rent flesh.

"Good doggy," Raven said softly.

Slowly, he began to raise his Kel-Tec shotgun to aim it at the hound. He never got the barrel above waist level.

White hot fire laced across the knuckles. Raven heard his weapon hit the ground before he actually felt his severed fingers fall away from his hand. Blood spurt from the grievous injury, and Raven spun around to draw his sidearm. The shadow lashed out with another knife and severed three more of Raven's fingers from his other hand. The mercenary howled in pain and stumbled sideways on his hobbled leg.

The looming shadow stepped closer with a blood-slick knife held in either hand. He tilted his head slightly as he looked at Raven's miserable wounds, then sheathed both blades.

"Who the fuck are you?!" Raven demanded.

Shock was setting in from his ruined hands. The target picked up Raven's shotgun and aimed it one-handed at Raven's chest. The buckshot hit the center of his ballistic vest like a freight train. Two or three ribs cracked as he was knocked on his back.

"Who . . . ?" Raven tried to ask again, but every breath felt like his chest was filled with broken glass.

He tried to prop himself up to a seated position, which only hurt his mangled hand even more. The man shot him in the chest again to put him back to the ground. Raven tried to beg but couldn't get his tongue to work. His eyes fluttered from pain and blood loss. The barrel of the shotgun hovered a mere inch from his face, but then the man shifted the aim to Raven's foot.

He didn't exactly feel the man blow his toes off, but the sight of it brought forth fresh screams from him all the same. The barrel drifted then to Raven's remaining foot. The shadow paused and looked to Raven with eyes so cold he felt his own heart freeze over.

He spoke then. A single word, a question. He barked it with a voice that sounded like a mallet smashing upon an anvil.

"Where?"

CHAPTER 23

The mercenary had talked. He'd spilled what little he knew, which was barely anything, and then had practically begged me to finish him with the gun rather than let Dante have a go at him. I obliged.

I drove at a respectable—yet not suspiciously overcautious—seven miles per hour faster than the posted speed limit. Normally, I drive how I want to drive and trust Rain to hijack certain frequencies should a police car get interested so she can tell them to back the hell off. But, this being not exactly an official business trip, as well as the fact that I had a couple dead bodies haphazardly covered with a tarp in the bed of the truck, I thought it best to be a bit more inconspicuous.

Dante sat on the passenger seat next to me. The big dog was alert, ready to spring should the need arise. I did my best to pat his head and let him know that everything was okay, and that he was a good boy. To say that he and I had gotten off to a rocky start would be hilariously understating just how bad it was. In fact, I still had the scars on my leg from where he'd tried to turn me into a snack. It had taken months of readjustment and training from one of the best military dog trainers in the country before Dante trusted me. More than once during that time, Rourke had all but ordered me to put him down Old Yeller-style.

I'd refused. Maybe it was old fashioned stubbornness, or maybe I had a soft spot for fellow lost causes. But look at us now: two animals, nigh inseparable, born for war yet doing their damnedest to keep the world from it. We were kindred spirits, he and I. A pack of two whose loyalty was not something others should test.

The HUD on the dash showed me that Bernice was calling. It was unusual for this hour, but I figured this was an unusual situation and Rourke had probably told her what was going on. I moved to decline the call when the phone answered it on its own.

"Send me to voicemail again, boy, and we're going to have problems."

"You've got some tricks," I said.

"I had Rain force the call through," she answered. "You need to come in. You're not alright, Captain."

I wondered if I should tell her that I had just offed about a dozen men and strangely felt back in my right mind from it. Dante whined next to me, and I decided to hold onto that little bit for now. I checked the tarp in the rear-view to make sure the bodies were still hidden.

"Nah, gotta disagree. I think I'm doing okay right now."

"Boy, even from here I can smell that bullshit stinking."

Never one to sugarcoat it, that Dr. Bernice Candy.

"Fine," I relented. "I'll be there first thing in the morning, Mom."

"Trying my patience here . . ."

"Love you, too. Pass the phone to Rain, I've got something that needs her attention."

"Excuse me? Aren't you supposed to be recuperating or bedside with your men right now?"

"*Please* pass the phone to Rain?"

There was silence, a few muttered curse words from Bernice, and then Rain was on the line.

"What've you got?"

"I'm sending you some fingerprints. The first set is Black's, the other are a couple low-level Legion members. I've also got some phones I'll need you to crack and backtrace later. Run them through White Shield, I need to know everything."

"Prints? What the hell's going on here, boss?"

"That is exactly what we're about to find out. Sending them now."

"Boss, I really think—"

"Out."

I hung up.

I needed to keep the momentum going. The gravity of the case was still pulling me, and I knew that if I let myself or Rain stop for even a moment, we might lose the trail. You must strike the iron on the anvil when it's hot. This was no different. Bernice would have to wait. Hell, Tag and Billy would have to wait. They weren't going to heal any faster if I visited them, but Black most certainly would get further away if I let him.

I felt the gravity again. Its pull was nearly magnetic in the way that I found my thoughts flowing in a certain direction. It was Black's names. There was more to them, and the fact that not even White Shield was able to locate Mister Dragonab should've been a clear enough sign. The names swam through my mind's eye again and again as I obsessed over what it was that I couldn't see. There had to be a clue hidden right under my nose.

And then I saw it. I nearly slammed on the brakes as my heart felt ready to burst straight from my ribcage. I immediately called Rain back.

"I work fast, boss, but not that—"

"Stop, listen! The names!" I stammered.

My respectable seven miles per hour above the speed limit doubled and continued to climb as I put the pedal to the floor. "Look at the list! Evan Uric, Milo Whail, Stew Cleo, Grant T. Dragonab, and Allen Diekly."

"I've been looking at the list, and we aren't any closer to—"

"The names are all anagrams! Look at them again and rearrange it."

I didn't even need to say so, the quietness on the other end told me that Rain was already working it out.

"Oh . . . oh fuck this is bad."

The list was a partial misdirect. Black Spear's numbers were scattered to the wind trying to protect Uric, Whail, Cleo, Diekly, and Dragonab. The problem was they were the wrong people, and Black had already crossed a name off his list while we were playing into his little goose chase. Because Allen Diekly was really Daniel Kelly. Milo Whail, William 'Billy' Ho. Grant T. Dragonab, Brandon Taggart. And Stew Cleo, yours truly Cole West. The last one, Evan Uric, was Cerberus's old captain Eric Vaun. The fact that we hadn't heard from Vaun in so long had me wondering if Black hadn't already crossed him off the list earlier.

"He came here for us," I said.

"Fuck this, I'm letting Rourke know now. What else can I do?"

"Meet me at the hospital." I hung up. The speedometer needle passed into the triple digits, and I questioned whether or not I would be the last person left on Black's list by the time I reached my friends' room.

CHAPTER 24

Cole West. 1:40 a.m.
Scripps Memorial Hospital La Jolla
San Diego, California

I cut through the lobby with my hand stuck firmly in the pockets of my jacket. My Para Black Ops .45 was sitting there with the hammer lowered, one in the chamber. Every set of eyes that glanced at me as I rushed towards the elevator could be one of Legion's in hiding. The charge at the nurse station. The old custodian mopping the hallway. The man in the baseball cap restocking the vending machines.

For we are many . . .

Just because I'm paranoid doesn't mean they aren't out to get me. I wanted to laugh at myself for thinking something so cliché, but the concern was genuine. Thus, the gun in my pocket. Hell, I would've brought the shotgun if I thought I could hide it inside my jacket. I'd settled on bringing Dante along. San Diego has a massive military community and that meant more than a few with disabilities who needed service animals, so no one even gave the big dog a second stare. He and I both had that look, I guess. He whoofed at a package of beef jerky on the bottom of a vending machine, and I clicked my tongue for him to follow.

Try as I might, I couldn't keep nightmarish images from flooding my mind. Thoughts of opening Billy and Tag's room and finding both of them murdered in the worst of ways. An obsidian blade through each of their hearts, or their heads removed and put atop a spear of their own like Valkyrie's. The worst thought was what if I'd gotten to their room and they weren't there at all? All Black Spear operators were erased from the system entirely, if Legion abducted them there would be no way to even start a search. They would just be gone. Period. It would be as if they hadn't existed at all.

But the door opened, and there they both were. Sleeping, but no more injured than when we'd left the foundry. Rain was also there, peeking her head around a corner and letting out an uneasy breath when she saw it was me.

"Jesus, boss, you just about gave me a heart attack."

"Cardiology is downstairs, you'd be fine."

She closed the door behind me after looking out into the hall then spoke to me in a hushed whisper, "I just got here. The list, boss! How are you not freaking the fuck out right now?"

I pulled my hand from my jacket pocket and the gun with it.

"Do I not look worried?"

Seeing me armed seemed to settle her a bit. She eyed the side of it, the spot where Black had left his fingerprints. I picked up on her train of thought and asked.

"What did you find?"

"You're not going to like it," she said.

"On this day? Try me."

"I'm serious."

"What could you possibly tell me that could make this any worse?"

"Nothing."

"Exactly. So, spill it."

"No, boss," she said, stepping away from the door and further into the safety of the room. "That's what I found: nothing. No matches *anywhere*. I ran it through White Shield's entire database.

No links. I mean zero. Birth certificates, arrest and court records, I tried checking military enlistment physical exams, I even went through Apple's facial screen unlock library. Nothing! The guy is really a fucking ghost."

If there was a cherry on top of this shit sundae of a mission, then this was it.

She shrugged. "I've got another White Shield analyst taking a second look at Black's list at Home Site. The parchment seems fancy; maybe it was special ordered and we can find a lead there."

"What about the other prints I gave you?"

"Those jokers? We pulled plenty," she said. Clearly the intel gatherer was a little elated that she could provide something actionable on the other Legion members. "All had multiple priors. Colorful records for sure, but nothing particularly epic. Not Legion epic, at least."

"They were low-level."

"Clearly. I pulled each of their phones' GPS logs, looked like none of them had crossed paths until earlier this evening when the three of them met up in one location. From there they apparently went straight to the foundry to wait for you."

I thought back to what the last Legion thug had told me before I'd killed him.

"He said they were sleepers, got a call like they'd gotten before and did as instructed. Good little soldiers who never peeked behind the curtain."

"They tell you anything else?" Rain asked. "Are they . . . in any condition to tell us anything more?"

My face betrayed nothing. Part of me wondered what the odds were that a security guard would check under the tarp in the bed of my truck. I had a clean-up crew on speed dial and if they worked as quickly as they usually did, then the bodies would be gone before I got back to the garage.

"Don't worry about that."

I heard the door handle behind me turn and I put my gun behind my back, but it was only the nurse. A memory of Daryl Hannah as an assassin from *Kill Bill* all dolled up undercover in nurse's garb popped into my head, so I kept my gun ready.

"Oh, I'm sorry. I didn't know they still had visitors!" the nurse said in a cheerful whisper. "It was already so late when the last one came by, I didn't think anyone else was coming."

The nurse went about checking Tag's vitals. Something she'd said sat wrong with me.

"What other visitor?" I asked.

She gave me a funny look. "Sharp-dresser, black suit? Nice guy. Handsome. He was here about an hour ago. He left them that. Sweet, huh?"

I looked at the counter she pointed at and found a small card and a single white rose. Inside the card were three simple words. *See you soon.* I showed the card to Rain, who tried and failed not to let her fear show in her eyes.

"He was here."

The fucker was playing with us. Circling his prey and refusing to bite. What was up with that? Too easy to kill two men in hospital beds? No challenge? I pulled out my phone to call Rourke. He'd come in here, into my men's room, and nobody had been able to stop him. Black really was a ghost, just like Rain had said.

I froze in place.

The gravity slammed the puzzle pieces in my head together like a mouse trap snapping into place.

Fuck.

Fuck, no.

I wanted to be wrong about what I'd realized but knew in my heart I wasn't. I put the phone back in my pocket. The conversation I needed to have with Rourke would have to be in person. It would make it that much easier to strangle the old man if I was right.

CHAPTER 25

The drive was a blur.

My hand found itself resting upon my holstered pistol all on its own. I like to consider myself a fairly reasonable guy. Having a stoic outlook on life means I'm not exactly prone to angry outbursts most of the time. This wasn't one of those times.

I shoved into Mr. Rourke's office without so much as a courtesy knock. I'm pretty sure if you could find a rough draft of Moses's stone tablets, you'd find that 'Thou Shalt Not Covet' only beat out 'Thou Shalt Not Upset Mr. Rourke' by a slim margin. Kara Mason was a barely perceivable shape that moved to the doorway and halted me with a firm hand on my shoulder. With a subtle look she encouraged me to move my hand away from my hip holster. She could fold me in half in a single breath if she wanted to, and we both knew it.

Rourke looked away from his computer screen to take a passing glance at me before giving Mason a dismissive nod.

"Kara, I don't think even West is dumb enough to try anything."

Bastard was still refusing to call me Captain. She gave an unamused little snort and stepped out of my way.

I stood before the Director of Black Spear, glowering at him and yet choosing my words very carefully.

"You know more about Damien Black than you're letting on."

"I see your knack for rest and relaxation is as astute as ever," he said.

I looked at Mason out of the corner of my eye, unsure of how much to say in front of her. Maybe she already knew.

"I pulled a complete set of Black's fingerprints, and you know the funny thing? Rain couldn't find a single match," I said. "But there was something about the lack of information about him. Something familiar."

Only now did Rourke look away from his screen to give me his full attention. "Are you going to make a point, West?"

"It was how completely blank his profile is that tipped me off. He's a ghost. It's what we've all been saying, again and again so often I'm getting kind of tired of hearing about it. You can't find anything on him. It's like all his records—birth certificate, social security card, fingerprints, all of it—were just erased from the world."

Rourke stared at me, that champion poker face of his refusing to give anything away. He just sat there waiting for the other shoe to drop.

"And I realized something, I've only seen that level of complete erasure in one other place. Us. That's why we can't find anything on him. Because you got rid of it. Because he was Black Spear. Wasn't he?"

Rourke suddenly looked very tired. That grim mask of his faltered, and for a moment I saw regret in his eyes. I might even be so bold as to say his expression looked painful.

"Yes. He was."

DARK BEGINNINGS 3

"This is three times the distance of my furthest shot," Adrian said.

"All the fundamentals of marksmanship apply, and since your brain is supposedly a sponge, you shouldn't have an issue incorporating the quick lesson I gave you," said Crimson. "That scope will magnify seven times better than your M-16's optic did."

Adrian replayed the information Crimson gave him earlier and adjusted the scope accordingly. The target would be fifteen-hundred yards away, that was just about two-hundred yards shy of a mile. It occurred to Adrian that he should find it troubling that he'd just referred to it as a "target" and not a person. Strangely, he did not. Their hunting trip was what Crimson had called "straight-forward". Jade had told him that meant assassination. Crimson had at first withheld the name of their quarry but had in the end relented.

Leonid Petrenko, an ambitious stateside *Pakhan* for the Russian mafia. His ambition made him sloppy, which had put him right in their crosshairs. This was unfortunate for him, because Spectrum's sole objective was to flatline him. No sifting through belongings for a classified dossier, no interrogation for actionable intel. Straight-forward.

Gold, who Adrian had learned was the team's tech wizard, had hijacked communications between Petrenko and a buyer interested in some of his smuggled AKs. Gold had fashioned a voice modulator that made it sound like he himself was the buyer, at which point they'd given Petrenko's phone a ring to finalize the meeting details and make some last-minute adjustments. The buy was moved to a meatpacking plant that Petrenko's organization owned. Having it on home turf where plenty of his men would be standing guard was a plus for him. For Spectrum, the plus was the quarter mile stretch of road leading to the plant that would give them a clean opportunity to take him out.

Adrian was posted on a rooftop further down that road. His scope was dialed in and there were plenty of markers along the road to gauge distance. A small flag by a gas station, a waving banner on the street corner, and a tattered streamer marking the start of the plant fence-line. All would give him an indication of the wind speed and direction.

As of now, Adrian's job was simple overwatch. Observe Petrenko's car in real-time as it went down the road and update the team on its position as it neared the plant. Cobalt, the team's explosives expert, had emplaced an explosive on the road that when triggered would appear to simply be a tire blowout. He would be sipping coffee at the gas station, waiting for the vehicle to pass. Gold would hack the phones of Petrenko and his entourage to ensure they didn't call for help. Any cameras in the area would also be shut down.

Crimson and Jade were the strike team. They were emplaced on opposite sides of the street and would approach the vehicle. Gold would roll the windows down remotely, using the onboard computer, and they would eliminate the target. Adrian had the utmost faith it would be swift and deadly. Adrian and his sniper rifle were the contingency in case anything went wrong. Which, from the sounds of how planned out this was, was not a high probability.

"It's almost showtime," Crimson said. "All callsigns, this is Mr. Crimson. Radio check."

"This is Mr. Cobalt, read you loud and clear. Cup of joe is hot. Detonator is ready."

"Mr. Gold here. Read you, Lima Charlie. Phones and vehicle's on-board computer are mine."

"Jade," she said simply. Adrian heard the tell-tale sign of a pistol hammer lowering. "I'm ready."

Adrian took a breath, lowered his eye to his rifle scope, and keyed his radio. "This is Mr. Black. I've got eyes on the target."

CHAPTER 26

"Damien Black wasn't just one of our operators," Rourke said. "He was one of the most promising recruits that has ever been brought into this program. So promising that I handled his recruitment personally."

I decided to let go of just enough of my anger so that I could sit in the chair opposite Rourke's desk. Mason sealed the office and then unlocked a filing cabinet.

"But from the moment he became part of the Black Spear Initiative, he was deeply troubled."

"Your psyche evals didn't flag Black for being a self-described prophet of death?"

"Sometimes it's hard to see the cracks until after the dam breaks," Rourke replied. "We tried to get a handle on him. Either process him out or pull him from field work temporarily until we could get him the help he needed, but before we could, Black went rogue. He killed his entire squad and then spent the next seven days assassinating ambassadors from seven *different* nations in seven *different* countries. No one hired him, he was making a statement. Announcing himself to the world."

"I'm here, and open for business," I said, picking up the train of thought. Rourke nodded. "He broke bad and got away from you? That doesn't ring true. Why didn't you have a team try to take him out right after?"

"He did try," Mason cut in.

Rourke held up an open hand to settle her. "Within the hour of him turning on his squad, I personally oversaw a strike team to apprehend him. That was the night he gave me *this*."

He turned his head and pulled his ear down. There was a scar I'd never seen before, the tell-tale mark of a bullet-hole that had long since healed over.

"After they removed what they could of the bullet, I spent the better part of a week in a coma while Black hit ambassadors seemingly at random."

As if the memory caused him pain anew, Rourke winced and pulled one of those white pills out from his pocket. I'd known the Director to have a habit for the pills for some time. Evidently Black's bullet left some lingering pain. Rourke swallowed two pills dry and grimaced.

"As is the standard with all our operators, Black's personal information had already been expunged from every database at his time of recruitment."

"You didn't want the world finding out that he was one of ours."

"Black's actions would have constituted an act of war. Rogue agent or not, he was a former American asset. It would have been our country in the hangman's noose, and it would have changed nothing because he was still in the wind."

"All this time you knew," I said. "You kept us in the dark about him and sent us in anyway. Kelly *died.* I watched my fucking brother bleed out in my arms! The rest of my squad is in the hospital, we're the real ones on his kill list, and you wanted to keep your secrets? And all the while I've been thinking we were safe here at Home, that we could circle the wagons here, but he knows our every move and every base, doesn't he?"

"Don't be dramatic. His time predates Home Site, he's never been here. Doesn't know its location. Almost everyone from Black's time is either dead, retired, or transferred to more administrative positions," Rourke said.

I took note of Mason bristling at that last part.

"And who he was before doesn't change anything. The monster he is now has nothing to do with that. Finding out which hospital he was born in isn't going to give you some clue on how to find him. His fingerprints won't tell us why he's gunning for you."

Mason handed me a file folder. It was sparse but inside were a handful of heavily redacted documents on Damien Black. A few photos of him in civilian clothes looking happy, which struck me as all kinds of wrong.

"I don't believe for a second you're telling me everything," I said and closed the folder. "But just in case you're actually feeling like being inclusive with your bullshit need-to-know basis, what's Morpheus?"

I caught Mason flinch at the mention. Rourke yielded as much as a mountain would to the wind, but I wasn't about to back down. I stood up and leaned over his desk, my face was maybe eight inches from his own.

"Black mentioned it at the foundry. When I asked you, you were extra shady about dismissing it. Which, for you, is kind of saying something. His kill list was all anagrams for my squad, but that's not what he's really here for. Morpheus is his endgame. What is it?"

Rourke considered for nearly a full minute. If he thought the silent treatment was going to get me to back off, he was sorely mistaken. I used the back of my hand to gently close his laptop then pushed it aside so that there was nothing on his desk between us. The staring match ended, and he finally spoke.

"Morpheus was a Cold War project. It was a radioactive device that was intended to incapacitate and disrupt enemy forces. Its development hit one too many walls and suffered one too many disasters. Morpheus was shelved and scrapped a long time ago, West. It's deep in the basement, and no one's ever going to dig it up."

"Sure, except it definitely isn't and you're definitely lying."

Rourke looked unfazed. "If that's what Black is after, then he's going to be gravely disappointed. It's gone."

I gave him my best crocodile smile. "You know how I know you're still lying to me? If it was really scrapped, then you would've given me the files on it. How dangerous could something be if it's been destroyed?"

I'd faced engineered plagues with Rourke. I'd gone up against next-gen nanites and mech suits that looked like they'd crawled out of a sci-fi movie with him. All that crazy shit, yet here and now was the closest I'd seen him to looking scared.

"More dangerous and frightening than you could possibly imagine, West."

"Who's running point on this now?"

"On that front I actually have some good news. Sit down."

I postured in front of his desk for another breath. A small part of me hoped I could provoke him into swinging. Rourke might have thirty or so years on me, but there was still a monster underneath that three-piece suit. I wondered what it was made of.

"Sit down, or I'll have her make you sit down."

I did as requested.

"We are about to drag Legion kicking and screaming into the light," Rourke said. "This latest intel fills some of the more concerning gaps we've had in recent years. Some, but not all. Interpol is going to be spearheading a joint task force with one purpose: compiling all intel on Legion and destroying them."

"Isn't that what White Shield is for? Having access to global intelligence secrets?"

"Normally, yes. When we need to circumvent the norms of international policy and due process then we can simply dig at our leisure. But the implications of Legion being networked across the global playing field, and that they nearly burned the world in the Warmaker case, requires a more public coordination. Dots will be connected, clues uncovered, and they will be rooted out. The power of organizations like Legion's relies upon their anonymity. Not unlike ours, hiding in the shadows and swimming in secrecy is what grants them their power. Dragging them into the public light and branding them as just another terrorist organization will see them cut down to size."

I fought like hell to keep my eyes from rolling. "You're putting a lot of faith in the international community's ability to put their bullshit aside and work together to common cause."

"Common cause is always easier with an actual flesh and blood enemy. White Shield can pull every file from every computer on the planet, but what about detectives who had a hunch that never made it into an official report? What about special investigators, who reached a dead-end, and their file isn't digital at all, but left forgotten on somebody's desk? White Shield's database is far from infallible, and we can only help complete the picture by bringing in outside opinion."

"Hip hip hooray," I said, mock clapping. "So, what about me? Who's hunting Black? I'm just supposed to watch this task force's highlights on NPR?"

"One man or this entire cabal? Eliminating Legion will bring Black with it. As for you," Rourke signaled Mason over, who handed me an airline ticket. "The Interpol task force is meeting in Vancouver in three days, at which point Legion will officially become the global intelligence community's public enemy number one. Hard for the cockroaches to hide when every set of eyes knows about them and is looking. Director Goode will be in attendance. I'm sending you to attend the initial summit meeting to act as Goode's primary security officer."

White Shield's Director, Micheal Goode, and I had initially not gotten off to an amicable start. That was before we stopped the entire west coast from being bombed to ruin. He'd managed to withstand a decent amount of torture before that, too, which sealed it for me that Goode was more than just a little guy with a thirty-pound brain. He'd taken a bullet to the stomach for me that very night. I wouldn't mind an opportunity to return the favor for him if anything hinky happened in Vancouver. It occurred to me that flying me to Canada, which was far outside any semblance of proper jurisdiction, was Rourke's ulterior motive. Though Black Spear usually didn't operate on foreign soil *with* their permission, having me attached at the hip to a VIP at such a high-profile public conference would make it nigh impossible for me to get my trigger on.

I stood up once more and, almost politely, placed Rourke's laptop back in front of him.

"I don't like being on the sidelines, and I don't like waiting for the bad guys to make the first move," I said. "That being said, I owe Goode."

Rourke indicated the door without looking at me. "Have a nice flight, West."

I stopped at the door and gave him a smug grin. "Three days 'til, boss. Plenty of time to get into trouble before then."

Mason cut a look at me that would've cracked marble and slammed the office shut behind me. I stared at the door for a good five seconds, and then my smile stretched wider.

I looked down at my hand, and the thumb drive I'd plugged in and removed from Rourke's laptop when he wasn't looking. I pocketed it and walked in a hurry down the hall as I called Rain. It was time to see just how many secrets the old man had been keeping from me.

CHAPTER 27

The thumb drive felt radioactive in my hand. It wasn't just that its contents intimidated me; it was the fact that I'd crossed the man himself to get it. My time with Black Spear had made breaking rules a habit, but this was Rourke. I figured some tracing program was copied onto the drive and, at this very moment, Rourke had guys coming to nail me to a cross. That was *not* paranoia.

However, if Rourke wanted to send some tough guys my way they were going to have a hell of a time getting the drive back. All I had to do was get it to Rain first. I rounded a corner, checking over my shoulder as I did, and found myself bumping right into Bernice.

"You're keeping odd hours for somebody who's off case, West."

"Speak for yourself. Plus, there's no windows," I said with an exaggerated shrug. "Hard to tell what time it is."

The frown she gave me was so guilt-inducing, I almost confessed to every wrong-doing I'd ever done, up to and including that time in third grade I swiped a juice box from the cafeteria. Bernice had a superpower when it came to making a man feel small. She didn't bother calling me a liar. She didn't even threaten to call Rourke on me. All she did was point a finger at her office door, and I sheepishly walked in.

"You say it's strange I'm up, but what's my shrink doing up at this hour?"

"Looking for you, obviously," she said.

I didn't bother making up a story about how she didn't need to worry about me. Those pleasantries were a faraway memory. I found my favorite spot on her couch and let the plush leather envelop me. Bernice first filled a glass from a pitcher of cucumber water and took a half-full roll of Tums from her desk before finding her own seat across from me.

"Pretty sure dealing with you is bad for my ulcer, boy."

"Isn't it barrier-forming to use language like that? Calling me boy might make me feel small and less receptive to your counseling."

Bernice chewed two Tums and washed it down with the cucumber water while looking over her nose at me. "Really? We're going to pretend you've ever been receptive to it?"

"Point taken."

She set her glass down on the coffee table between us and leaned forward, hands on her knees. Instead of scolding me or getting into her full psych eval mode, she just gave me that look. The Mom look. The one that stripped away all my finery until I was nothing but the inner child.

"Cole, you need to slow down," she said. "You're hurting. You've *been* hurting. Throwing yourself and your team at every mission you can just so you don't have to sit still and feel it all."

"You're saying it's my fault? Kelly. He got killed because I took the mission."

"Boy, you know damn well that's not what I'm saying. Don't you try posturing up them walls between us and don't disrespect me by twisting my words in such an obvious way. You're still having nightmares, aren't you?"

"Can't have nightmares if I don't sleep."

Bernice hit a button on a remote and a small fireplace on the far wall came to life. I flinched back, eyes wide, my pulse jumped to a breakneck pace. She lowered the setting until the fire dulled to a low burn. I forced my breathing to halt altogether just so that I wouldn't start hyperventilating. The moment passed and I slathered a new layer of false composure over myself.

"Oh, sorry. Just trying to set a more mellow mood," she said.

"That's a cheap shot, Doc."

"I imagine someone like you is going to run into some fires now and then. You think I'm being unfair here? What happens if you freeze like that in the field? Kelly wasn't your fault, but *that* would be. The longer you put this off, the harder it will be for you. We wouldn't be here if you devoted some actual deliberate time to this. To grieving."

"Vengeance seems more worthwhile at the moment."

"You have some lead Mr. Rourke doesn't know about?"

"I think it might be the other way around actually."

Her eyes fell to the thumb drive in my hand. I slipped it into my pocket before she asked. Bernice stood and walked to a small safe in the corner. The dial spun in her hand back and forth as she unlocked it, then retrieved one black-leather personnel folder from the stack within.

"One of the hardest battles I've had is convincing Rourke that my sessions would be completely confidential," she said. "I told him this can't work without trust and if the operators knew the boss was privy to all that was discussed in here, they would never step foot inside. No digital reports. No updates that get run up the chain. Just my own notes."

"And you trust him? Who's to say he didn't just bug your room?"

"The fact that he's also sat down on that very couch more than a few times."

I looked at the leather sofa through a new lens. Being on the shrink's couch constituted some of the loneliest moments of my life.

Being made to lay my soul bare and expose all my weaknesses, fears, and insecurities was not exactly a comfortable feeling. But being reminded that I wasn't the only one who'd been here, and that Rourke himself had sat here? It made me feel a tad less alienated from the tribe.

"The reason I tell you that is because I need you to understand just how seriously I take everyone's privacy," she said. "I only ever disclose to Rourke if a Black Spear operator is compromised if and when I believe they are a danger to themselves and their team. And even then, I don't give specifics. Just my recommendation. I don't disclose the more detailed information about who I see to anyone. Ever. It's an agreement Rourke and I came to when I came on. It's a rule that I'm going to break for you now."

Before I could ask, Bernice handed me the black-leather folder. At first I thought she was going to be giving me Rourke's, and then I hoped that maybe Black had been a client of hers, but when I opened the folder the name inside was the last person I expected to see.

"Captain Vaun?"

"Cole, I think we both know that he's probably dead. Nobody's seen head nor tail of him in almost a year. Rumor around the water cooler is he might've gotten too close when looking at Legion after the Warmaker case," she said. "That's half the reason why I'm letting you look in there. Not so important to keep a dead man's secrets."

"And the other reason?"

"Because I don't think Legion killed him," she said. There was something underneath the sadness in her tone. Was that regret? "Look at the file. He sat down with me after his friend Major Wilcox was killed at the onset of the Warmaker case. And you know what? He sounded just like you sound right now. Vengeance. Anger. That *need* to make somebody pay for hurting your brother, no matter how altered your judgment might be. We both know where that path led him."

That path had brought Vaun face to face with Wilcox's killer: an enforcer for Samuel Cain named Phobos Marstelli who had a proclivity for karambits. They'd crossed blades, and while only Phobos and Vaun himself know exactly what happened, it was clear Phobos was the winner. Vaun had gone into the fight angry and Phobos cut him down, bad. For reasons known only to Phobos, he'd let Vaun live. But to say Vaun survived wasn't the full truth. His wounds weren't only physical, but those ones were permanent and debilitating, and he was left with the realization that he was no longer fit to lead Cerberus Squad. He was a broken shell, and he'd retired with the notion that he'd do his own investigation into who'd been pulling Cain's strings. It was something to give him direction, and maybe a way to redeem himself in his own eyes.

"I said I don't think Legion killed him," she said again.

"Then what? He's sipping Mai Thais in Barbados? Vaun never struck me as the 'leisurely retirement' type."

"No. I don't think he ever got close to Legion, Cole. I think when he left, he never had a trail to follow. I think the weight of *that* failure, coupled with losing command of his squad, got to him."

I put together what she was alluding to, and more so what she was warning me about myself.

"You're worried that I'm either going to get myself killed going after Black, or I'm going to kill myself because I can't find him."

She pursed her lips. I was just about done with this session and ready to storm out before stopping short.

"You ever hear of Les Brown?" I asked.

She nodded.

"He's a motivational speaker. He's got this quote about the graveyard. He says it's the richest place on earth, because when you go there you see all the hopes and dreams that never came to pass. Goes on to say that you should close your eyes and picture being on your deathbed, and that all the ghosts of the ideas and dreams you had will be staring at you and asking why you didn't act on them."

She nodded and leaned back a little, wanting me to continue.

"But you know what I see when I close my eyes? It's not the ghosts of my dreams or goals. They're the ghosts of all the people I didn't save. Vaun. Kelly. Valkyrie. All those poor bastards I burned alive stopping Cain. It's the ghosts of the ones yet to die that I *can't* save. My team. Madison. The guy that runs the taco truck down the road. Everyone that dies from here on out is on me. My deathbed is already crowded with ghosts, and I'm not about to sit this out and let more fill up the room."

Bernice's face wrinkled and she scribbled a note.

"Madison, huh? Not 'Doctor Archer'?"

Shit.

"Relax," she said. "It's cute. And while I definitely don't think you're in any condition to be dating anyone, maybe you'll be more receptive to level-headed wisdom if you hear it from her."

I had this feeling that Bernice already had her suspicions about Madison and me, and she had just been waiting to find out for sure. Heavy thumps of boots running down the hall outside made me tense up, and my hand went to the flash-drive on reflex.

"I think that's about all we have time for right now," Bernice said. "Is there anything else you want to talk about?"

I stood up and walked towards the door, taking a peek outside. The coast was clear.

"Yeah, actually. I might've used some construction equipment to kill eight men, stabbed a few others, and fed one to my dog. Feeling really broken up about it, doc."

I rushed out of her office and closed the door behind me before she could ask. Her words of caution, though well intentioned, fell on deaf ears. There was a rage burning in my chest, and it wasn't going away no matter how many conversations with her I had. So, if I couldn't get rid of it, then maybe I could focus it. Point that fury in one direction and let it loose. I wasn't going to let it cloud my thoughts, but that didn't mean I was going to let Black get away unscathed. I was going to find him. And I was going to cut his fucking heart out.

CHAPTER 28

The five Immortals played poker while Simon called his superiors with updates from the other room. It was the first time Black had been left unattended with them. Well, the first time they'd been awake. Late in the night he'd gone throughout the penthouse to get a closer measure of Legion's elites. They were like monks in the way they rested. It was more of a sustained meditation than actual sleep. Black had no doubt that had he gotten within two paces of one, their reflexes would snap them from their trance.

Now they appeared much more like actual human beings instead of conditioned killers. They shared jokes and smiles with one another while the Frenchman, Henri, dealt the latest hand and the others anteed in. If it wasn't for the various weapons upon the tables—and their signature masks within arm's reach—they could easily be mistaken for a group of mates like any other.

Black approached their table and pulled one of the chairs out slowly so its legs dragged and squealed along the floor. He was pleased to see that not one of them flinched despite the jarring sound.

"Deal me in?"

"*Oui, Monsieur Black,*" Henri said.

It was an okay hand. Two of hearts, six and seven of clubs, jack of diamonds and spades. A single pair was better than nothing. He committed his cards to memory then placed them face down on the table. The others finished looking at their own and began placing bets and checking each other for tells. There really weren't any, these men were trained to be in control of their every action. This game would come down to the luck of the deal rather than being able to read the opponent's hand.

The scarred Irishman, Declan, raised.

"Never thought I'd work alongside you," he said. "Let alone play poker."

"Why is that?" Black asked.

He matched Declan's bet.

"Because you're *him*," said Scaglin. "*The* Mister Black, in the flesh. There are so many stories. So many names. 'The Magician with a Knife.'"

Black smiled and flicked his wrist, one of his obsidian blades appeared in his palm. Scaglin looked like a giddy child. With another flourish, Black made it vanish.

"*Le Peintre*," said Henri.

The Painter. Black had acquired that moniker after a client in Paris specifically requested that he make the scene as colorful as possible. Not too many jobs had been attributed to that particular alter-ego.

The round of poker went on with the raven-haired Harrison claiming the pot. Black didn't need to win. He was rather enjoying finding out how much they knew of him. He still possessed just enough of a soul to relish admiration. They'd initially been apprehensive around him, but Black saw the truth now. To them he was a legend. Legion had done extensive homework because Black had gone to great lengths to leave various dead-end trails in his separate identities. He found himself oddly flattered by it.

"What about 'Papa Shadow'? And 'The Ghost'?" asked Hogue.

"Not the Ghost, no. But I am a great admirer of his work. Nor am I the Surgeon; I've heard tell of people trying to credit me with some of his artwork."

Hogue mouthed the name Papa Shadow to himself once more. Black checked his latest hand. It was a winning one. Full house: jacks full of nines. Black didn't need to win, but he did enjoy doing it. He raised boldly and watched the others' confidence wane. Yet, strangely, only Scaglin folded. Black found that interesting.

"I heard of the Columbians sending one man to take out an entire chapter of the La Realeza Cartel," said Harrison. He matched Black's raise and went higher. "They called in the King of Blades."

"*Lord* of Blades," Black corrected. "That's actually my favorite one."

He heard soft footfalls of expensive leather-bottomed shoes behind him. Simon's call to his masters had concluded.

"Having fun?" Simon asked.

"Oh, are we ever. Just getting more acquainted with my fellow servants of death."

The Immortals brightened. With that, Black had elevated them to his own level. Not only were they playing cards with a legend, but they were one with him.

Simon prickled. Clearly, he wasn't enjoying these newfound bonds Black forged.

"Deal me in."

"We've already—"

Simon cast a look at Henri who stopped himself. The blank face of the Immortal took over and once more there was an emotionless killer at the seat, he just happened to be dealing cards.

"No one will argue your skillset," Simon said to Black. "Among assassins you are without peer. The ace killer."

Simon showed Black his newly dealt hand. It was crap. Ace of hearts. Nine of diamonds. Five of spades. Three of spades. Two of clubs. Only way he'd win is with a High-Card, which definitely did not beat Black's Full House.

Simon squared his shoulders, "But I think you mistake skill with actual power."

He set his useless hand onto the table before him and frowned.

"You are the very best player in your game, that much is certain. But the ones in power make the rules."

He raised his chin to Declan, who placed his own cards face-up on the table. Simon looked them over and then exchanged his two of clubs for Declan's four of spades.

"You may wield death freely, but that does not give you power. Because that freedom was given to you by us."

Next he raised his chin at Scaglin, who then exchanged his six of spades for Simon's nine of diamonds.

"Legion oversees all. We are the dealer, we own the pot, and *we* determine the winner."

Lastly, he held up his ace. Simon flung it across the table to Harrison, who politely handed over his seven of spades.

"You see, Black, all the cards already belong to me."

Simon used his thumb to riffle through his new hand, then grinned wide as he set it down. "How about that? A straight flush. I believe that makes me the winner?"

Henri collected the cards and started to shuffle for the next round before Simon held up a hand to stop him.

"That's enough. We have work to do."

All signs that the Immortals and Black had bonded disappeared. Once more they were Simon's fierce and loyal soldiers. Black had to consider the possibility that they had only been acting. Or maybe Simon's leash simply held more sway over them than he'd thought. Very tricky, these clandestine organizations.

Black looked at the pot at the center of the table. Simon's winnings. He would prefer not to lose again. Winning felt better.

CHAPTER 29

It was always amusing when prey thought itself more clever than the predator. He'd chosen the café downtown for their meeting. Holt had to give him credit for the forethought; it was a public venue after all, which would dissuade rash behavior from either party. Putting a bullet between his eyes would prove bloody difficult when there were roughly thirty witnesses eating their overpriced breakfasts.

The driver pulled the car to the curb, and Rinx turned towards her.

"The chair, ma'am?"

"Stuff it, Dorian. I can handle things well enough on my own."

Most of the time she tolerated the wheelchair and relied on others to cart her about. It was, of course, safer that way. Less likely to slip and break herself. It had the added effect of displaying her power. Holt was master of any room she walked into, regardless of her frailty. This meeting, however, required a different presence.

She needed to be seen as her true self: Lady Death. It wasn't enough to be feared for the army of protectors who would kill for her; she needed to be feared for what she herself would do.

"Dorian, be a dear and pass me my cane."

The cane was a beautiful thing, one of a kind. Its shaft was primarily made from a rare type of glass called *fulgurite*. *Fulgurite* was only formed when lightning struck a beach and fused the sand, and usually not in pieces large enough for anything useful. An expert craftsman had carved ivory to complete the rest of the shaft, the resulting effect was white marbled with a crystal sheen. Gold filigree inlayed the ivory and trailed up in a thorned rose pattern to a solid gold crook handle top. It was the perfect sum of elegance, precise reinforcement, and rare parts overcoming brittleness. It was her.

The inside of the café bustled with patrons. Normally, Holt would have at least six Immortals to ensure no one got within two arms' distance from her to prevent accidental bumping and jarring of her person, but the truth of the matter was she always resented that. An entourage of protectors quickly felt like a prison escort when they wouldn't even let her handle her own personal space. Most people were polite enough to part way for her when they saw the cane, the rest cleared her path when they saw her face. Fragile as her bones might be, her expression was hard as bedrock. Holt had no trouble at all getting to her morning meeting.

His eyes looked past his menu and saw hers.

"Oh," he said.

This one was a far cry from a silver-tongue.

She lowered herself into the seat opposite his with calculated grace. It wasn't like a lovely bird descending to earth, but a leopard priming to pounce.

"You can stop pretending to look over the menu and just order the same Denver omelet you get every time, Carl."

Carl Tannhauser let the menu fall to the tabletop and nervously looked around the restaurant. He was looking around for her Immortals, no doubt, but their absence didn't make him any safer. Not that he'd ever seen them without their Kevlar faces, anyhow.

"You're having me watched?" he asked.

"We watch *everyone*, dear. It's your own fault for having such strong habits. I'd think that a Senior Manager for the CIA's Directorate of Analysis would understand how harmful patterns and routine can be."

He visibly withered in his chair. Holt heard his foot tapping incessantly under the table, a staccato rhythm in tune with his anxiety. This one had been under her thumb for quite some time. She'd nurtured him like a sapling, tending to his growth, and seeing to it that his reach grew far and his roots deep. But trees that bore little fruit didn't last long in Holt's orchard.

"I'd think someone in your position would know to dress down," he said in a forced whisper. "White suit, gold cane? Security detail out front? It's like you're trying to draw attention to us."

Holt's grim expression shifted into a tight-lipped knowing smile as she leaned forward and rested her chin on the top of her cane. "That's what you wanted though, isn't it? Attention. Why else would you choose to meet in such a crowded eatery. You're worried that something *terrible* might befall you for your recent failures."

"Failure? I have buried reports for years. If it wasn't for me, Legion would have—"

Her cane slammed upon the floor, freezing both Carl's tongue and his tapping foot.

"Do not *speak* our name," she hissed. "Do not speak of your deeds as if you are owed for them. Look how high you've already been elevated for your efforts. How much has been spoon-fed to you in exchange for your assistance in keeping larger matters hidden."

"It's out of my hands. I've done what I can, but at this point anything I do will be like trying to tap the brakes on a runaway train. It's going to happen. Le —er, the *organization* could never have stayed hidden forever."

Holt rapped her fingertips along the cane's shaft. Excuses annoyed her. One of the best perks of the position she held was that most people were smart enough not to offer them to her. They knew better than to try. They knew what failure reaped. Having to hear Carl's felt like fiberglass in her ears.

"They're talking about a joint task force," said Carl. "An *international* task force, at which point it won't matter how many agents I redirect and files I alter."

The maelstrom of restaurant activity surrounding them played against her nerves. Clattering forks and knives on porcelain plates, waitresses taking a litany of different orders, and Carl's unending list of excuses all swirled into a cacophony that had her ears ringing.

"Can't bloody hear myself think," she whispered.

"What?"

"I said . . ." Holt tapped her cane to the floor thrice. ". . . I wish we could have a more private conversation."

The other customers, all sixty of them, as well as the waiters, waitresses, busboys, and hostesses, froze as one. The immediate quiet hit Carl like a brick to the chest. Every single person in the café looked to their table. Then, as one, they stood and filed out of the building.

"Now then, where were we?" she asked.

"How did . . . ? What . . . ?"

"You're not as clever as you think, my boy. We own this restaurant you've been frequenting. This is our world. All the pieces, the players, even the board upon which it's played. All of it."

This bit of theatricality had been Rinx's idea. He might play the role of muscle-bound protector, but the boy had a devilishly wicked mind. Holt was convinced that it was *too* trite. Like something out of a Hollywood film, and yet the utter dread on Carl's face said that all the effort put in to prepping this fun made it all worth it.

"Jesus, oh Jesus . . . You really are going to kill me."

Carl's forehead beaded with sweat, and he shrank away from Holt's gaze. Instead, he looked to her hands, maybe expecting to see a gun. There was none to be found. As a matter of fact, Holt had never actually fired a gun. Anything larger than a .22 was sure to shatter every bone in her hand. No, Lady Death's methods had always been more sophisticated than a ball of lead.

"My boy, I have already killed you."

His confusion was the sprinkles on her tart. With one bony finger she prodded Carl's empty coffee cup.

"Headaches lately, yes? Probably just work stress, you told yourself. An extra cup of coffee or two to dull the sting. It makes it hard to sleep, which of course compounds the problem, but it's nothing to worry about. The job keeps you far too busy to take an afternoon off to see the doctor, at least not for something like a bloody migraine. It wouldn't have mattered if you had scheduled one, mind you. The damage was done."

Holt was suddenly tired of seeing his open-mouthed breathing and decided to break it to him straight.

"Polonium, my dear Mister Tannhauser. We placed it within your cellphone not too long after your string of disappointments began. You're a dead man already."

His hand whipped out from under the table, a compact .38 aimed at Holt's chest. This reaction from him was surprising, though not entirely unexpected. She didn't even flinch back or dignify him by looking at it.

"You still have some time to get your affairs in order," she said. "Time to spend with your family and perhaps tend to some last matters on our behalf before you expire."

"You kill me and expect me to—"

"Take your finger off the trigger and toss the gun away." There was such authority in the way she ordered him that he hesitated, and the revolver started to shake in his hand. "Right now, you have the happy ending. Perhaps sooner than you intended, but happy nonetheless. Do anything other than exactly what we say, and you get the alternative ending."

"The alternative?"

The butt of the gun lowered to rest upon the table.

"Your family," she said. "They die with you, just as painfully and slowly. You should live just long enough to see your infant daughter suffer and die from radiation sickness; your wife may outlive you if she doesn't kill herself. Your daughter's death will bring the FBI to your doorstep, at which point you will be arrested and found guilty of helping terrorists smuggle a dirty bomb into your nation's capital. Not wise to keep Polonium within the walls of your own home, dear boy. You will spend your few remaining days as a pariah, despised as a traitor—and a stupid one at that—with the knowledge that your wife will wither away on her deathbed hating you."

The gun became a faraway thought.

Carl slumped down in his chair, brought lower than any man should be. Rinx appeared behind him with his breakfast omelet prepared. He placed it in front of Carl and then offered his arm to Holt to help her stand.

"You'll probably consider putting that revolver through the roof of your mouth quite often in the coming days. You have my permission to do so as soon as your work is done, and not one second sooner. Now, eat your bloody omelet. We'll be in touch, Carl."

Carl Tannhauser looked around the café. Before today it had been one of his favorite places. A familiar place that he'd always felt safe in. He used the side of his fork to cut a small morsel from the omelet, forced it into his mouth, and tears ran down his face as he sat all alone.

DARK BEGINNINGS 4

"Target is on approach to you, Cobalt."

"I see him," Cobalt said.

Adrian spotted him through his scope, leaning against the outside of the gas station, detonator in hand. The explosive charge was out front, Petrenko's vehicle would drive right over it in the next-

"Shit."

"What is it, Cobalt?" Crimson asked.

Adrian had already seen it happening, "Apparently Petrenko is low on fuel."

The vehicle pulled into the gas station, completely bypassing the emplaced charge, and stopped next to one of the pumps.

"Gold, can you get into the computer and make him pull over?" Crimson asked.

"Give me just a minute. Windows and phones are one thing, killing an engine is separate but shouldn't be too hard."

Adrian adjusted slightly and found his reticle hovering over the back windshield where Petrenko's head was. The sniper rifle was the contingency plan, but Crimson had yet to give him the green light. One of the vehicle's occupants stepped out, except instead of removing the nozzle from the pump he headed on inside.

"Don't think you have that long," said Adrian. "Looks like he's just here to grab a Snickers for Petrenko."

"Cigarettes," Cobalt corrected. "Menthols. Blegh."

Less than thirty seconds later Petrenko's goon was walking out.

"Time's up, Mr. Gold. Car's leaving," Adrian said.

"Call the play, boss," Jade said. "If he gets inside the fence-line this is about to get damned sloppy. Quick and quiet goes out the window the second he gets off this road."

Crimson considered the options.

"We'll do an Abbey Road. You cross and take the driver and the body-man in the passenger seat. I've got the side, Petrenko and the second bodyguard. Gold, you have the windows still?"

"Oh yeah."

"That's a Plan B I can work with," said Jade.

"Thought the new kid was Plan B?" asked Cobalt.

"That's a hell of a shot, but if Black has it then he can feel free."

The thump of the XM500's gunshot, even suppressed, reverberated off the rooftop the second Crimson was done speaking. The half-inch thick round crashed through the back window, completely obliterated Petrenko's head, then penetrated through the driver's head in front of him before exiting out the windshield. The car swerved hard into a brick-faced building. Its rumpled hood sparked, and Adrian saw fuel dripping out the bottom of the car. Adrian figured a stray spark would find the puddling gasoline any moment, and if the two unconscious bodyguards didn't wake themselves, they'd be given their own premortem funeral pyre.

The comm line was silent. Nobody had expected Adrian to actually take the shot, much less prove his accuracy wasn't mere fables.

He took a good look through the hole in the back windshield and the mess of collected brain matter inside. The interior resembled a Jackson Pollock painting in red and gray. It was an image that, like everything else, would be forever etched to memory.

CHAPTER 30

Cole West. 5:30 a.m.
The Platform
Pacific Ocean

The button, and all the hell it contained, was just below my fingertip. One little press and I could end it all. With the twitch of my index finger, I could activate the Firestorm nanites and torch everyone—guilty and innocent—to stop this war from happening.

"Just do it," Black said.

His hand went over my own and guided it towards the button. I didn't want to push it, not again. Madison was next to me, her face an anguished mask. This mess was partly her own, yet here she was urging me *not* to push it. But somebody had to.

"Come on, burn them already."

Black's hand was gone and now it was only my own on the detonator. Too many lives in my hands, countless souls hanging by a thread. Except that wasn't entirely true. I already knew precisely how many souls there were. Two-thousand four-hundred twenty-eight. The tips of my fingers brushed the keyboard's surface. Smoke filled the room the second I touched it. That familiar odor stung my nostrils. Burned hair and cooked meat.

"There it is," Black said, drawing out the s like a snake. "Burn them. Show the world that black heart of yours."

I hit the button, only this time it was me who burned. The fires first lit at the edges of my fingers and toes, but the flames hungrily crawled towards my chest and scorched my face. Skin sizzled and bubbled, flesh charred black, and I screamed as I burned and burned.

I turned to Black, but he was gone. Instead, I found myself staring into my own eyes. A dark twin stood in his place. He gave me an unrecognizable smile, so much crueler than any I'd ever given, and laughed as the fires consumed me to nothing but ash.

My own choked scream woke me with a jolt.

This wasn't the Platform, and the button was months in the past. I was in the safehouse we'd moved Tag and Billy to. Cold beads of sweat covered my forehead and scalp. I forced myself to take a few breaths and slow down my heart rate, then looked to the beds where my comrades slept to make sure I hadn't woken them. They were out cold.

"You want to holster that, boss?" Rain asked from behind her computer.

My pistol was in hand. I hadn't realized it.

"Bad dreams?"

"No." Not my best lie, not by a mile. "You get anything from that drive yet?"

"Plenty."

"Morpheus?"

"Eh, that's where it gets hinky."

"Hinky?"

Rain looked at me with the purest expression of contempt possible. "Did you really think that *Mister* Rourke, Grand Poobah of Black-Ops, wasn't going to have security measures? This is the guy who instead of carrying a suicide pill with him, he carries that Plan C suicide bomb. The same guy who'd rather vaporize himself and everything in a city block rather than let his secrets get loose. So, yeah. There's some roadblocks."

She turned the screen around so I could see it. Several large, encrypted files were password protected.

"I didn't think a little thing like that would stop you."

"I appreciate the faith, boss, but this isn't the type of encryption I'd plan on dicking with," she said. "I put in the wrong thing, and it's likely to wipe the drive, burn my computer, and shoot up a digital GPS flare that'll have a kill-squad on our ass in five minutes flat."

"Those kill-squads are coworkers. I think we'd be okay. What did you get?"

"You see, that's the interesting thing."

Rain pulled up a list of locations, they were spread out across southern California, western Arizona, and northern Mexico.

"What am I looking at?" I asked.

"Spots White Shield determined to be of potential interest. Known hangouts and havens that Black or his friends might use."

"I'm waiting for it to get interesting."

"When you had me do a background dig on the goons that jumped you at the foundry, I told you they'd never crossed paths before. Yeah? Well, that's true. Except they had all visited this place at different *times* last week."

Rain highlighted one of the locations and expanded an image of a bar: the Ruby Lounge in Tijuana. The name belied that it was a total dive. The perfect spot for someone to broker a job to low-tier thugs without anyone batting an eye.

"You're going after them?" a voice behind me asked.

I turned and found Billy sitting up in his bed. His fractured jaw was still wired shut and he spoke through tight lips.

"He's not getting away that easy," I said. "You should tag along if you're up for it. Might end up in a bar fight, just try not to take any more hits to the face."

Billy had always been the funniest guy on the team. I expected him to laugh or maybe throw a quip back. He did neither. Billy scowled and stared at me, and his expression was so hard I paused.

"My friend is dead. My other friend was cut to ribbons by a man half his size. All on your watch. Your call. Why the hell would I follow your lead now?"

It was all coming to a head. For weeks he'd been challenging me out of some misplaced resentment. Maybe he was pissed that command was given to me and not him, or maybe he didn't think I measured up to Vaun's legacy. I wanted to believe he was just hurting since no one had ever beaten him as bad as Black had, but I knew that wasn't the entire truth.

"Because Vaun chose *me*."

There was a look in Billy's eyes I'd never seen before. No humor. No warmth. For the first time ever, I looked at the killer who'd always been hiding behind the smiles and the laughs.

"He chose wrong," said Billy.

It crushed me hearing those words. To hear the utter hatred my teammate had for me in that moment. He rolled back onto his bed and pawed at the side of his broken face. I could only bear the silence for a moment before it chased me out to the quaint kitchen.

Rain had already moved her computer here when she'd seen the tension between Billy and me getting tight. Rather than give me a pep talk, she just offered me an Oreo from the sleeve she'd dug into.

"I take it you're going solo for this little bar recon mission?" she asked.

"I guess on a positive side, if it's a dead end I can just stay there and get plastered."

"Not fair," she said through a mouthful of Oreo crumbs. "Whoever's in charge of stocking safehouse pantries should be fired."

She opened one of the cupboards to show me how barren our supplies were. Evidently the Oreos were the only edible thing she'd found. Black's little bouquet tease at the hospital had forced us to move Billy and Tag with zero prep. I'd picked this safehouse because it was the least used. I guess that should've clued me in that its stocks of food and water would be low.

"You started your field training blocks, right?" I asked.

Rain set the Oreos down and gave me a nervous look. "Um, which parts?"

"Low profile. Blending in. Counter-surveillance and how to lose a tail on foot."

"Oh Jesus, you want me to go with you to the bar? I haven't passed the weapons handling portion yet."

"No, I have something else in mind," I said, and gave her a large stack of bundled hundred-dollar bills. "Go shopping and try not to lead them back here."

"What?"

"Black knows our names and faces, but not yours. We can't count on Rourke sending any help our way. We're on our own on this. And we kind of need to eat. I'll leave Dante with you. He'll keep you safe."

Rain riffled a thumb through the cash, counting it. "You just had ten grand in burn money sitting around in case you had to bug out?"

"Not exactly."

I set my backpack on the counter next to her, unzipped it, and proceeded to pull out five more bundles. My pack still held plenty more.

"Hard earned spoils of war, Miss Harper."

On the tail end of the Warmaker case, and at the height of Samuel Cain's conniving bullshit, he aimed to discredit everyone on Cerberus Squad and brand us traitors by making it look like we'd received enormous bribes from foreign nationals. The bribes were fake, but the wire transfers to our accounts had been real. I guess he'd counted on us getting killed before we would spend any of it. Didn't really work out for him in the end.

It was time to check the Ruby Lounge. I topped off two extra magazines from the lone box of .45 ACP I had left and slid them onto my belt. I was really missing the extensive armory at Home Site right now. I considered taking a short detour on my way to the bar, but didn't want to chance Rourke snatching me up. This was just a little recon, though. Check the bar, ask a few questions, and maybe have a drink before taking off. Didn't need a full arsenal for that.

"Why do you do this?" Rain asked as she peeked into the backpack. "This money . . . you could walk away and go buy your own freaking island. You could happily retire anywhere and be whoever you wanted to be."

My favorite hooded leather jacket—which had lost both sleeves in the field and was technically my favorite vest now—was hung on a hook. I grabbed it en route to the door. I took a long time putting it on as I thought about her question.

"I wanted that, once. But I don't think guys like me get the happy ending."

Rain started stacking a sizable pyramid on the counter out of money bundles.

"Okay, and do you really want to be the type of guy who has to say shit like that?"

"Want has got nothing to do with it."

"Then what?"

"You know I had a very similar conversation with Kelly. Before he . . ." The words caught in my throat.

I froze and just sort of tapped my hand on the counter until I could find my tongue again. Rain was polite enough to wait.

"At first, back when I was the squad FNG, I would've done anything just to prove to the others I was hard enough to survive this. Face a bioengineered plague, take on an army, walk through fire. Then one day you catch a look in the mirror and realize none of it washes off. The blood. It stays no matter what. So, if there's no getting clean, what's the harm in adding a few new layers on top?"

"Boss, I don't want to take Rourke's side but maybe you should sit this one out, get your head clear."

"My head's clear, Rain. If I'm stuck in this life, then I might as well keep swinging." I stopped at the door and pointed at her pyramid of greenbacks. "Don't go spending all that in one place."

"Ha freaking ha."

Dante whined. I knelt and pressed my forehead against his face, giving him a few pats, too. I signaled him to protect Rain and he gave me an affirmative *whuff* as the door closed behind me.

I was truly on my own now. Not even my loyal canine for backup. I smirked as I pulled my vest's hood up and climbed into the truck. Good. It just meant I wouldn't have to share any of the revenge.

CHAPTER 31

Devin despised owing favors to his friends. The only thing he disliked more than owing favors to his friends, was owing a favor to Rain Harper. She'd been White Shield support for less than half the time he had, yet she had one hell of a chip on her shoulder. Devin credited that to the team she was assigned. Cerberus was nothing less than infamous.

Still, he wasn't entirely opposed to double-checking her work. It presented an opportunity to find something she'd missed. *That* would feel good. Devin wasn't such a bitter prick that he was blind to the factors at play here. Her team had taken casualties after all, and she'd been providing mission support when an entire squad got slaughtered. Not to mention a literal terrorist attack at LAX. As much as Devin would want to shove it in her face, if and when he found her mistake, he wasn't that petty.

The parchment Rain's team had retrieved from Mr. Black was an interesting piece of evidence. It felt like something out of a fantasy novel. To call it mere parchment was a bit misleading, when Devin saw it he'd remarked that it was more like a scroll. What type of people had her team been up against if they issued hit orders on scrolls?!

Rain's latest update from Captain West claimed the names were misleads. Go figure. *He* probably could've figured that out for her. With the names being a dead end, she'd asked Devin to analyze the parchment itself. The ink Mr. Black's employers used was a beautiful metallic gold. Unique. Devin loved unique things. It made it easier to narrow down.

Just as Devin prepared to scrape a sample of the ink, his hand froze. There was something in the scroll. Something woven within the fine fabric. He grabbed a set of precision tweezers and prodded at it, exposed it, and finally removed it. The object in question was a long metallic fiber.

Devin squinted at it under a microscope.

I've seen this before, haven't I? he thought.

He had.

The second his mind made the connection he flew into a panic. He knew exactly where he'd seen the metallic fiber before. It was quite similar in design to a covert tracking device.

CHAPTER 32

He felt a stirring in his soul, like his great need was finally close to fulfillment. A new opponent to play with, a new great kill, a new soul for the thirteenth blade. It was enough to make even his pulse quicken with anticipation.

You won't win.

The voice came to his mind so suddenly and clearly, it actually gave him pause. Over the years the memory of Adrian Rasp, his last greatest kill, had fluttered into his mind here or there. Most of the time it was little more than a sensation. He could sense how Rasp would have reacted, but this was the first time that he could hear his voice.

The ghost of Rasp living in his memory had annoyingly begun to show itself in Black's thoughts more and more as of late. It was partially why he had agreed to this job. Kill the memory for good, replace him with someone even more worthy of Black's attention.

The more Black consciously tried to ignore Rasp's words in his head, the more they took form. It was like running an eraser over the same spot on a piece of paper until it ironically became the point of all focus. He closed his eyes and instead brought to mind what Rasp had looked like when Black had buried him. How helpless. Weak. The thought cleared his head, and he found himself thinking once more about the matters at hand.

"Soon," he said.

Simon turned to him from the other seat in the back of the vehicle and arched an eyebrow. "Come again? You alright in there?"

"I said we're almost there."

"How far out?" asked Hogue from the driver's seat.

Black looked at the screen on his handheld device. An infrequent blip pulsed on it, and Black observed the surroundings outside his window to gauge the blip's location.

"Pull over here. It's just down the block."

Black stepped out of the vehicle, Simon and the others following suit. The five Immortals were garbed in their black body armor and each fit their masks over their faces before exiting. Black looked down the road towards their destination. Towards Home Site, Black Spear's main hub on the west coast.

"So good to be home . . ."

DARK BEGINNINGS 5

Adrian had once read an article that proposed the average human brain had an equivalent storage capacity of 2.5 petabytes. That was equal to the memory required to play .mp3 music nonstop for two-thousand years. Which is to say that, unfortunately for him, he had a long time to go before he'd reach that alleged cap and be able to forget something.

Killing someone was no small thing. Those that have done it manage to move on in their own ways. Some compartmentalize by saying that aspect of them was different than who they were when they went to bed. Some justified it by saying it was necessary violence or that they were in the right. None of these were options for Adrian, and they didn't help him stomach it all any easier. There was no compartmentalization possible because all his experiences were firing all at once like some maddening simultaneous painting. He'd tried to explain it to one of Black Spear's counselors in passing, and he realized the poor man was drastically underqualified to even understand what Adrian was dealing with.

Crimson began to take notice of something off about him. But, like a coach unwilling to bench a star player after so much success, his concern had never gone further than simply asking if Adrian was okay. Of course, he was. Feeling some type of way inside his head with all the dark things he'd been doing didn't mean he'd forgotten what normal was. And so he'd conducted himself how he knew he was expected to. Crimson didn't ask again.

Which brought Adrian to this moment, sitting alone in his quarters. With no one else there. No one to distract him. The great canvas that was his memory washed over him. He would sit there as wave after wave of sensory memory crashed through his mind.

The touch of the three little pearls of blood on his wrist, from when he'd eliminated the KGB assassin named Konstantin Semyon on the streets of Moscow. He'd used a deftly placed stiletto and even now could feel the tacky grip of the knife's handle in his palm. Then there was the smell of Lucca Santini, a hitman for the Veleno Crime Family, voiding his bowels into his own pants when Adrian shot him from behind the driver's seat. The stench of shit and harsh gunpowder in the air, all mixed with rich leather upholstery was horrible. The sound of La Realeza cartel accountant Mayra Lopez's shriek, which turned into a gurgle when Adrian had stabbed her through her neck. The sight of Leonid Petrenko's brains disintegrating, and the trapped bodies of his guards burning when the crashed vehicle caught fire.

Lastly, there was taste. In Adrian's opinion, it was the worst. In his mouth he could taste earthy tobacco intermingled with the coppery flavor of aerosolized blood. That memory came from when he'd slit the throat of an executive for Alpha Wolf Security, who'd been selling security vulnerabilities of American bases they held contracts for to enemies overseas. The man had been smoking a cigar when Adrian killed him, and the puff of smoke spilled forth from the clean cut in his neck only to cloud Adrian's face and fill his mouth.

Those were only five snapshot memories. Adrian had already built four months' worth of snapshots with Spectrum. Every action he was required to take had been etched into his brain as solidly as a chisel into concrete. They didn't understand. No one could. By Mr. Rourke's own estimate, there had never been anyone quite like Adrian.

The slight chime on the electronic clock next to him let Adrian know that he'd been sitting alone in his quarters for five hours now.

No. Not alone. And he wasn't in his quarters. His body was, but he was elsewhere adrift in the vast library that was his mindscape. A library with every book and every page visible all at once. Each glance was another bloody streak upon the canvas. An endless feedback loop that never stopped.

Worse still, there was a part of him that didn't care if it did. It was a quiet, dark little spot in his mind. A blank patch that didn't flinch at the pain. Like a black hole, it could take it all in and not change in the slightest. With every dark deed he added to his accomplishments, Adrian felt like black oil was covering up who he used to be. Not for the first time Adrian wondered who he would be once the final brushstroke had been painted.

CHAPTER 33

Cole West. 8: 30 a.m.
The Ruby Lounge
Tijuana, Mexico

The bar wasn't hard to find. My little incursion with Legion's cronies at the construction site did a solid job of renewing my confidence after Black effectively ruined it, but hopping south of the border was a horse of a different color. Running solo presented certain tactical disadvantages. Operating on foreign turf, however close it may be to home station, complicated that further. It pretty much cemented the fact that I did not have any backup coming, and if I ran afoul of authorities Rain would have her work cut out for her in springing me loose.

The Ruby Lounge looked surprisingly busy for the early hour. After checking my watch, I realized it was Saturday which made a little more sense. A few shots of liquor in the morning with a side of some greasy bar tacos was still the best way to kill the hangover from Friday night. I was losing track of the days, though, which wasn't a good sign. I lied to myself and said that I'd get plenty of sleep once I put Black in a coffin. And see Bernice every day for a month. First thing's first, though . . .

Thirty minutes into scoping out the Ruby Lounge from my truck across the street and I decided I'd seen enough of the outside. I didn't know what or who I was looking for, but I trusted the feeling in my gut that was pulling me forward. I left my Boomstick in the cab of the truck but kept my .45 ready just inside my jacket. No reason to go full buckshot on people just yet. All I was doing was asking some questions.

I was so focused on the bar's front door as I crossed the street that I walked right into a bum and nearly knocked over his shopping cart. A couple of crushed empty cans fell to the sidewalk, and he slurred some insult at my mother in Spanish. I was going to offer to help but he had that crazy look. Old hooded jacket hiding his face, shoulders hunched and a bent crooked posture, a long scraggly beard poking out from behind his hood, scratching at himself and muttering nonsense. The dirt on his face was so thick, it was hard to believe there may be skin under there. The little twitching mannerisms could be a sign of either meth use or a serious mental condition. Neither of which I wanted any business with. Basically, the last person you want to bump into. That is unless you have a pistol with seven rounds and one in the pipe ready.

The bum picked up his stray cans, tossed them back in his cart, and then draped a soiled blanket atop his collection to keep anything else from falling out. He carried on his way, pushing his cart with an awkward limp and calling my mom a whore. I made a mental note to get some coffee ASAP so that I could sharpen up. Walking into a crazy homeless person is about as red flag as you can get when it comes to realizing you're losing situational awareness.

"Don't mind Crazy Ken," someone said behind me. He spoke English, which threw me for a loop. I turned to see a tall red-bearded man with broad shoulders and a full belly hauling a bag of trash to the Ruby Lounge's dumpster.

"You on a first-name basis with many hobos?" I asked.

"Hell, nah," he said. "It's just what we all started calling him. Ken might be whacked out worse than a space monkey, but he hasn't bothered anyone. Just comes by to sort through our trash."

I followed the bearded man back inside the Ruby Lounge and realized he was the bartender. A majority of the patrons inside looked to be Americans. There were ten or so other people; four played pool, two tossed darts, and a couple others in the back casually drank beers while watching morning tv. George Thorogood was belting out his drink order of a bourbon, scotch, and beer from a jukebox in the corner. But no dark figure in the back-corner booth. No sinister meeting of a villain hiring tough-guys for Legion.

"You've got the look bad," the bartender said as he wiped a glass clean.

"Come again?"

"You're checking for entry and exit points, haven't put your back to a wall, and are looking over everyone else here. Not to mention you're in a bar on your own at eight a.m. What branch were you in?"

I raised a confused eyebrow at him, and he cocked his head at a framed photo behind the bar of a soldier in Afghanistan. It took me a second to recognize the bartender without his beard.

"Nine years, forty pounds, and one knee replacement ago that was me. Corporal Eli McAvoy, Third Rangers Company A."

"Marines. Sergeant Cole West," I said, extending my hand. I used my previous rank, it felt wrong to say I was a captain considering I hadn't become one until after the Corps.

We shook, and he filled two shot glasses. As he did so I noticed for the first time the various military flags pinned to the walls. Evidently the Ruby Lounge was American veteran friendly. With the rising housing costs in the San Diego area, it was becoming more and more common for vets to go full ex-pat and move to Tijuana.

"Call me Mack. First shot's on the house for any vet," he said.

He downed his drink and went back to manning the bar. As a force of habit, I dabbed a small test strip into my liquor before I raised it. The test came back negative for any poison or drugs, which made me question whether I had the right feeling about this place after all.

I threw the shot back and shook my head, angry at myself for possibly following another false trail. Whoever hired the three goons from before was probably long gone.

"How long have you been out?" Mack asked as he cut lime wedges.

I found the question strange.

"What makes you think I'm out?"

He shrugged. "Can't remember the last time I caught an active Jarhead without a fresh shave. The bald and bearded look seems like a go-to for most when they get out."

I itched the beard that I'd grown out for the Siberian assignment. There was a mirror behind Mack and after checking myself out in it I realized I'd lost the clean-cut squared-away Marine look a long time ago.

"It gets easier," Mack said. "That feeling like you don't have a place back in the world. Just give it time."

"You're giving my shrink a run for her money right now."

"I don't know about her, but I've been there, brother. I've lived it, I've seen it. It does get better. We're the lucky ones, not everyone gets to come back."

His words snagged me like barbed wire. Mack noticed immediately. He thought to himself for a second, nodded, then reached to pour me another shot.

"Who was he?"

I wasn't looking for charity so I pulled a ten from my wallet and he reluctantly took it.

"He was . . . my guy. The one who despite all the shit we'd been through never stopped smiling, you know? *That* guy. Good soldier, better friend."

Mack pursed his lips and nodded. There was sadness in his eyes that told me he knew all too well what I was feeling. I took the second shot and felt that pleasant burn bite the back of my throat. I knew full well that drinking on the case wasn't the smartest move, but it already looked like I'd struck out on finding Mr. Black or Legion's trail.

"I'm usually not one to turn people *away* from my bar," Mack said, "but this right here is only ever going to be a temporary salve. Speaking from experience, mind you. If you want a more permanent fix, you need an outlet. A hobby, or a group."

"I've already got a hobby at the moment."

"Yeah? What's that?"

"Hunting," I said.

As an afterthought I reached into my pocket for a photocopy of Legion's demon brand and put it on the bar table.

"Speaking of which, don't suppose you've seen anyone with this come through here recently?"

Mack brought the picture up close to his face and squinted at it. He stroked his beard with one hand deep in thought.

"You know, come to think of it, I have seen a few guys with this mark around here."

A glimmer of hope sparked in my chest, but then just as quickly it faded. Mack smiled and it was like all the warmth and friendliness in him had disappeared. I felt movement behind me, a quick glance in the mirror behind Mack showed me that all the patrons had dropped what they were doing. Their attention was square on me. Mack let the picture fall to the ground and leaned over the bar towards me. He turned one of his arms over and there it was: an identical demon brand seared into the inside of his forearm.

"Matter of fact, I've seen quite a few people with it around these parts."

I should've trusted my gut. On a plus side, I was in the right place after all.

CHAPTER 34

I pulled my .45 and brought it up to eye-level. "Sorry, Mack."

His head kicked back and gave the wall behind him newfound accuracy in the bar's namesake. As his body fell, I saw a sawn-off shotgun in his dead hands that he must've pulled from under the counter.

The jukebox in the corner finished the George Thorogood song and followed up with Black Betty by Ram Jam. Fitting.

I rolled over the bar and fired my mag dry behind me. Two more of them dropped, eight left. Each of them had pulled pieces and had me pinned down. Bullets zinged overhead and destroyed the lines of glass and bottles above me. A cocktail shower of various liquors drenched me. My nostrils burned at the sharp vapors. The shooters blasted the mirror on the back wall, stealing away any line of sight I could use it for.

I pulled one of the two back-up magazines I had and slapped it into my gun. They were getting ready to push on me, so I poked my pistol over the counter and fired three shots just to keep them back. Ammo count was not looking good right now. When they returned fire, I crab-walked along the bar and spotted the back door that led out to the alleyway where I'd first bumped into Mack. My one chance was to make for the alley and get to my truck.

One of the shooters got brave and ran right up to the bar, thinking he could put a bullet through the top of my skull if he surprised me. It almost worked. Almost. Instead, when I heard him jump onto the bar top, I put one through the bottom of his head right as he leaned over. The ceiling was spray painted with fragmented bone and bright red chunks.

Amidst the chaos I had just a second to think about how being in this particular bad spot was entirely my fault. That whole 'squad being undermanned' problem, and the overdue recruitment I kept putting off, was really biting me in the ass here.

I emptied the rest of my magazine blindly over the bar, being rewarded with a sharp cry of pain. Dead people don't scream, so at best I winged another of them. I inched towards the doorway. There was a mere four feet between the edge of the countertop and the door, but that's a whole lot of distance to cover with a whole lot of people shooting at you.

Their bullets punched through the hard wood of my cover. I reached for my last magazine when one of their rounds coming through got lucky. It was truly a one in a million shot that drilled through the wood and blew the magazine right out of my hand. The bullet destroyed it and .45 ACP bullets catapulted around me as the spring within the busted magazine uncoiled.

"Not my fucking day." I picked up one of the bullets.

I slipped it into the open chamber of my gun and sent the slide forward. One in the chamber. It would have to do. I waited for the briefest of pauses in their onslaught and then I rolled at the door. I timed it perfectly so that my shoulder slammed into it with all my mass and momentum. The heavy door opened just enough for me to squeeze through before closing behind me.

I got up to run and felt a hand on my wrist trying to pull me back inside. One of the shooters had been quick on my heels, but he'd gotten careless in his haste. He must've thought I was empty because he genuinely looked surprised when I turned back, pressed the barrel of my gun to his nose, and blew his brains out the back of his head.

Now I was empty.

There was about three seconds before the rest came through behind him, so I took the time to muscle the dumpster in front of the door. I hit the wheel locks into place, then turned and ran down the alley as fast as I could. The alleyway stretched like I was in a nightmare. Bright daylight at the end of it seemed to get further away the harder I ran.

A man walked into view and blocked some of the light. I thought for a second that one of the shooters might've decided to flank me, or maybe some local *policia* were responding to the gunshots. The idea of spending some time in a Mexican jail cell was preferable to being dead, but then I saw the familiar shopping cart and realized it was the hobo Mack had called Crazy Ken. The hunched vagrant's cart stopped with a squeal, and his head swiveled towards me. I heard the Ruby Lounge's backdoor explode open and the screech of wheels on pavement as they shoved the dumpster out of the way.

"There he is!"

I ran faster.

Crazy Ken's entire posture transformed as he turned in my direction. His back straightened. He stopped his worrisome twitching. And though he still walked with a slight limp, his gait looked purposeful rather than the aimless wandering of the mentally unwell. The man reached into his shopping cart to pull out a bedroll, then shoved the cart aside.

"I've been waiting for you," he said.

His hoarse voice was strangely familiar. The bedroll fell away and in his hands was an automatic shotgun with a full drum mag. He walked down the alleyway with his half-limp and the shotgun aimed from the hip. There was nowhere to go. This was the end of the road.

"Get down," he said.

I dropped flat to the pavement and rolled like a log out of the way as he fired. He held the trigger down and filled the alleyway with buckshot. Though his face was still hidden under his dirtied hood, I could see his mouth twisted into a snarl that bared all his teeth. A full-throated war cry ripped forth from his lips and wrestled with the deafening shotgun for who would be the loudest.

The gang of Legion soldiers were torn apart by the storm of lead coming their way. I saw limbs blown from their bodies. One man took a full load to the chest and had his entrails explode out the back. My savior dropped the empty drum magazine, slapped a fresh one in, and continued to fire.

BOOM BOOM BOOM BOOM BOOM BOOM BOOM.

Spent shells rained down as he finished mopping up the rest. Every inch of the alley from the walls to the grimy cement ground was drenched in blood. There was only one Legion member still breathing, but just barely. His thigh was shredded to hamburger and red soaked through his shirt at the shoulder.

"Wait . . ." he said.

The vagrant lowered the barrel towards the man's face and finished him. Ken stood there, wreathed in a thick gray cloud of gun smoke, and he let the empty shotgun fall to his feet. The air was thick with vaporized blood and the cloying smell of burnt powder. He looked around the alley at all the dead before making his way over to me.

"We need to move," he said, extending a hand to help me to my feet while pushing back his hood to reveal his face. He used the back of one of his dirtied sleeves to wipe away some of the grime caked on his nose and forehead.

Despite the dire situation, I found myself frozen to the spot. This man was no stranger to me.

"Vaun?!"

DARK BEGINNINGS 6

"Have I done something wrong?" Adrian asked.

Rourke shifted in his chair and looked over the report Crimson had provided him. It was a list of his growing concerns regarding Adrian's state of mind. Adrian was no fool, he'd never set foot in this facility before and besides Crimson, who had brought him, no one from Spectrum was here. This was not a mere routine meeting.

"Of course, not. There are just certain considerations we need to take into account. You've been with Spectrum for what, six months now?"

"And eleven days," Adrian added.

"In that time you've completed nearly thirty high-risk missions, each one has gone flawlessly in no small part due to your participation."

In the span of a second, six months and eleven days' worth of memories flashed through Adrian's eyes. He had pulled the trigger eighty-six times, but there were also the other methods he'd mastered since. Garotte wire, knives, explosives. Each life he'd taken was imprinted in him as if he'd claimed a very piece of their souls and joined it to his own.

Crimson had been using Adrian to assist in profiling. He would watch their targets, learn their habits, and use it to plan their ops. Within a day of watching someone, Adrian knew everything from which shoe they tied first to how many times they would chew their food before swallowing. Whether they licked their lips after taking a drink of water or not, whether they walked up steps two at a time or took them singly. All that encyclopedic knowledge on targets was in his head, and it didn't go away just because he'd killed them.

"I'm having trouble sleeping."

Rourke took a long time looking over Adrian. The boy looked troubled, his shoulders sank and there were bags under his eyes.

"I know, Adrian," Rourke said. "That's why we're here. Crimson is worried about you. We want to help."

"Help?" he said with a sheepish laugh. "I can see all their faces so perfectly that I could draw a portrait of each one. If you want, I could write in explicit detail exactly what each person did second-by-second on the days leading up to their deaths. I know the exact foot-pounds of pressure it took for the knife to pierce the chest of four of them. Or just how many breaths they took before their hearts stopped."

"Do you want out?" Rourke asked bluntly.

"No, no, I don't."

The answer surprised Rourke, but only a little.

"It doesn't matter if I walk away or stay on, I'll remember it all regardless. Which is exactly my point, sir. How do you plan on helping me? There's no fixing it."

Rourke steepled his fingertips. "No, there's no fixing it. But perhaps we might ... *chip* it in precisely the right way."

The allure of relief piqued Adrian's interest and Rourke could tell right away.

"It's a radical therapy, Adrian. Bleeding edge technology. You would be the first candidate, and if this works we can save so many more."

An elevator door opened, and Rourke rose from his chair, Adrian did the same and followed him inside.

"What do you know of the MK-Ultra Projects from the sixties and seventies?" Rourke asked as the elevator descended.

"The old Cold War programs?" asked Adrian. "Hypnosis and psychopharmacology for enhanced interrogations and mind control. If I'm not mistaken, their experiments were aimed at creating sleeper agents and to develop methods of breaking hard targets. Most of which was deemed illegal, and the Company did everything they could to dispose of their files."

"MK-Ultra was a disastrous fool's errand," Rourke said. "Developed during a time of heightened paranoia. This, however, is the quantum leap forward."

Rourke brought Adrian into a brightly lit room. An apparatus that looked like a cross between a dentist's x-ray machine and a laser cannon straight out of a science-fiction movie was attached to the ceiling. Technicians in white lab coats adjusted it and took calibrations. A woman watched them and tapped her foot impatiently, her arms crossed.

"Adrian, this is Doctor Erin Childs," Rourke said.

The woman turned around and gave him a vigorous handshake. "Adrian, pleasure to meet you. Welcome to the Darkheart Project."

Adrian walked into the center of the room and found a table with strong leather straps across it. It was shaped like a T so that when someone laid on it their arms would be outstretched to either side.

"This certainly isn't what I thought of when you said therapy, sir. What is it?"

"This, Adrian, is what awaits when we get to Phase Two," said Childs. "But we're getting ahead of ourselves."

Childs signaled her team to carry on without her as she walked in step with Rourke and Adrian out of the room to her own office. She gestured to a chair and Adrian sat. Rather than take a seat behind her desk, she sat atop the desktop and spoke with the tone of voice more akin to a friendly teacher than a covert military scientist.

"Total transparency: we're moving towards uncharted territory here, Adrian," she said. "Phase Two will involve a unique form of radiotherapy. The laser device you saw in the other room will focus this energy at your prefrontal cortex. Are you familiar with what—"

"It's the personality center of the brain," Adrian said. "You're looking to lobotomize me?"

Childs held up a hand. "Nothing so imprecise. We don't want to eliminate aspects of your skill set and personality. We want to separate them. By introducing a sort of schism, we can divide the man you are from the soldier we very much still need you to be."

Adrian found himself rubbing his temple. To say this sounded drastic would be a gross understatement, but at this point he would do anything just to be able to sleep again.

"Phase One will mostly consist of behavioral modification therapy," she said. "Basically, we have to knead the clay before we take a crack at molding it. A very intense program of hypnosis sessions and a cycle of psychotropic medications will prepare you for the Phase Two procedures. Think of that as a primer. We begin building a door frame and a room before we move aspects of you into it."

In his head Adrian pictured that blackness that had been spreading in him. Could it really be so simple as to cordon it off within his mind? Section it away? He thought of his vast mindscape library, each piece like an individual filing cabinet, and wondered if maybe the blackness could be filed away as easily.

Rourke placed an uncharacteristically reassuring hand on Adrian's shoulder, "I'll be handling those sessions personally. I'll be there with you every step of the way."

Adrian nodded. "Okay. Let's do it."

Childs smiled and hurried out of her office to begin getting things in order. Once the door latched behind her, Rourke let out a long sigh and dropped himself into her chair. The silence smothering, Adrian couldn't help but break it.

"I'm not entirely convinced this is a good idea," Adrian said.

He looked Rourke in the eye. He found not an ounce of uncertainty in his steady gaze.

"What's your concern?" he asked plainly.

"Phineas Gage."

"I'm sorry?"

"Phineas Gage. Have you heard of him? No? Railroad worker who was injured in an explosion in 1848. A one-point-one meter long metal spike pierced through his head, and it passed through and damaged his prefrontal cortex. Stories conflict, but they say he was a completely different person after his injury. Less refined, more violent."

"You're worried that by separating Adrian Rasp from Mr. Black, we're going to lose some of your humanity?"

"Sir, I'm worried that you're going to get exactly what you've always wanted: the perfect killer."

Rourke forced a smile. It was an ugly expression and did not belong on the big man's face.

"If Mr. Black is the perfect weapon, Adrian Rasp will still be the perfect holster to hold it. Everything will be okay."

A flicker passed in the man's eyes, and Adrian realized with disappointment that it had been the first lie Rourke had ever told him.

CHAPTER 35

Predators at the top of the food chain don't worry about others hunting them. Perhaps that was why Black Spear's facility had been so easy to infiltrate. Who in their right mind would have the audacity to break into a place where America's top assassins worked? As it turned out, Legion did. And they were quickly proving that the top of the food chain belonged to Legion and Legion alone.

The two security sentries at the road checkpoint could have potentially been a problem. Scaglin had removed said threats via a high-powered rifle on a rooftop down the road. The two roving guards around the perimeter of the building might have been able to alert everyone that something was amiss, had Harrison's double-edged daggers and Declan's axe not found their necks. Then there were four men posted just within the front door, and they would be the last line of defense. Without them, no one else would sound the alarm. Black himself had walked right in, flicked a hand in their direction, and then pushed a button on a small detonator. It wasn't until he pressed it that the four men realized that what Black had flung were miniature sticky-bombs.

The explosions were relatively small, but enough to blow the guards to pieces and destroy most of the security station. Anyone else in the building would be smart enough to know they were under attack now, but it didn't matter. It was already too late. The nightmares were already inside.

Simon and the Immortals, minus Scaglin, who remained on the other rooftop, joined Black in the front lobby. Black found one of the intact computers behind the security desk and started typing away. There was a series of clicks as all the electronic locks on the floor opened, and the bulletproof metal shutters lowered over all the exits and windows.

Black had a presence to him that Simon was not at all comfortable with. The assassin was supposed to be his weapon, and this mission was supposed to be Simon's alone. Yet more and more, Black wrested bits of control from Simon and ingrained himself with the Immortals. Simon wasn't naïve. It was clear they admired him. They were of the same ilk: killers, and nothing more regardless of their prowess. If anything, Black was more than aware of his role and seemed to relish it.

"Now come nightmares," Black said. "Now comes darkness."

He pressed one last button and the lights went out. Booted footfalls from down the hallway grew closer, their pace slowed as the building drowned in shadow.

Black gestured in their direction down the hallway. "Gentlemen, happy hunting."

Simon hung back with Black in the lobby for a moment while he donned his night-vision. He did a brass check on his pistol to confirm he had one in the chamber. Next to him Black smirked.

"I heard that. Plan on getting your hands dirty this time?"

Simon gave the killer his full attention. Black stared back at him as if he could see perfectly in the complete darkness despite not having a pair of night-vision of his own.

"You've been quite amusing, Black. I'll give you that. It's fun to watch your work and your tricks. Not unlike a juggling clown."

The comment only made Black's dark smile widen.

"I aim to impress and entertain," he said, taking a bow with arms outstretched and a knife held in each hand. "Shall we cue the next performance?"

The four Immortals set forth blanketed in shadow. And the bloodbath began.

CHAPTER 36

"Do you have a car?" he asked as we ran from the Ruby Lounge's alleyway. Well, I ran, and he hobbled as quickly as he could.

He. Captain Eric Vaun. My predecessor, the guy who recruited me, the guy who for all intents and purposes I thought was dead five minutes ago.

"Truck. Across the street. Where have you been?!"

Instead of answering, he reached up to his face and pulled the beard away. It was a fake, held on by very convincing latex and makeup. Next he pulled off the scraggly wig, revealing clean hair beneath. In an instant the vagrant vanished, to be replaced by the professional I knew.

"Seriously, Vaun, what the fuck?" I unlocked the truck and climbed in.

He jumped and slid across the hood, then hopped into the passenger seat. He'd shed the dirty trench coat at some point, as well.

"No time, we need to get out of here."

I hit the ignition and spared just a moment to give my passenger an appraising look. "You know we thought you were dead, right?"

He stared straight ahead.

"This is big, Cole."

"Yeah?"

Vaun grabbed my Boomstick from the floor, pointed it in my direction, and fired out my window. The Legion soldier who had been running towards us with a revolver in hand took the buckshot to the chest and fell dead in the street.

"*Very* big. Drive."

CHAPTER 37

He hummed a tune to himself as he walked down the pitch-dark hallway with a knife in each hand. *Paint it Black* by the Rolling Stones. Dim red emergency lights had popped on over doorways along the corridor, but they did little in terms of brightening visibility. Not that Black had any issue with that.

Two soldiers faced him with weapons ready. They didn't know Black was there until he was on top of them. The blade in his left hand plunged into the first one's throat, the other stabbed low in the second's gut below his ballistic vest. Black spun, eviscerating the second man while all but decapitating the first. Their blood splashed against the walls and door behind them, appearing more black than red in the darkness. He flicked his hands to whip the excess blood from his blades, then waved them to the beat of the song in his head as a conductor would.

Black continued humming his song as he journeyed deeper into the building. The Immortals were hunting elsewhere, occasionally the staccato of automatic gunfire signaled that one had come across more easy prey. The way it echoed across the porcelain tiles and vacant halls sounded like lively drumbeats to Black's song. It brought a smile to his face. This had been a long time coming.

Around the corner he heard the telltale shift of weapons and gear adjusting. From the sounds of it, at least six waited for him. There was a high-pitched whine at the edge of Black's ears that could only come from night-vision goggles. Unluckily for them Black had an answer for that as well.

He reached behind his belt and pulled two grenades, removed the pins, then lobbed them around the corner. The first was a flashbang. Black was too busy bobbing his head to the tune running through his mind to hear it go off, too busy humming to hear them screaming in surprise.

The second grenade went off; a black smoke bomb. Whoever wasn't completely disoriented from the flashbang would see only a black cloud filling the hallway towards them. The one closest to the smoke didn't have time to scream when it enveloped him, and he found Black waiting within. The next three managed a quick panicked yelp as he put a knife through sides, chests and necks. Number five screamed the loudest. Black let the scream go on, choosing to slowly stab the obsidian through his eye and give it a twist rather than finish him quickly. Number five howled, and Black slid the razor-sharp knife along the inside of the man's thigh to open his femoral. The scream rose an octave.

Black wanted the sixth man to hear it.

The smoke crawled towards the last guard and washed over him. As he disappeared into the smothering cloud, he fired wildly in a wide arc in front of him. The magazine ran dry. He reloaded and emptied the next one while backstepping to the door behind him. He didn't hit anything. Black already stood behind him. He turned the man into a pincushion. Stabbing, slicing, cutting at all the places he knew the Kevlar vest had weak spots. The back of the shoulder, the seam between the ballistic plates, high above the collar at the base of his neck. The first wound alone would've been fatal. Black delivered nearly twenty in the span of five seconds.

The final death blow he inflicted was to the base of the man's neck. His aim was perfectly delivered so that the blade avoided the vertebrae. The point of his knife pierced all the way through and out of his Adam's Apple, Black then wrenched it sideways and severed through the vertebral arteries. He held him upright as the blood sprayed out the back of his neck to the door behind him. When the initial spurt slowed, he let the shaking body fall to the floor with the rest of the dead.

Black whispered to himself about painting a red door black as the sixth man's blood drenched the final door. The dull red emergency light above the doorway pulsed weakly. Black gripped the doorknob and took his time opening it. How long had he waited for this moment? How many times had he *dreamed* of being at this very precipice?

"Hello, Father," he said as he entered Rourke's office. "The prodigal son has returned."

DARK BEGINNINGS 7

"How many more times do we have to do this?" asked Jade. The way she squirmed in her chair you'd think it was made of fiberglass rather than rich leather.

Crimson didn't bother looking up from his newspaper. "The boss says one or two more sessions."

"Are they even working?" asked Cobalt. He sat across the room and craned his neck, trying to listen behind the door to hear how Adrian's session was going.

"The kid doesn't sleep, Crim. All he does is train and read."

Gold looked up from a book he was reading. "What's wrong with reading? Just because you've blown too much demo to have a working brain anymore doesn't mean the rest of us have to pretend to be troglodytes."

Cobalt fixed his baby blues on his friend and frowned. "You're reading Tolkien. Adrian reads nothing but technical manuals, tactical handbooks, and encyclopedias. I walked into his room the other night and found him poring through Gray's Anatomy."

"Love that show," joked Jade.

"The sessions *are* working," Crimson insisted, refusing to hear any objections. "Unless any of you magically got a PhD or two while I wasn't paying attention, I advise you all to shut the hell up. Mr. Black is one of us, and we're going to continue getting him whatever help he needs."

"Adrian," murmured Jade. She pulled her hood up over her head, something she was wont to do when unhappy at a situation. "Not Black."

Crimson nodded, then made an exaggerated show of reopening his newspaper. "One or two more sessions, then they're ready for D-Day."

D-Day, as in Darkheart Day. The day when they would take Adrian to Phase Two and progress from hypnotic suggestion and mental reconfiguration to the first session of outright applied radiotherapy. 'Unique radiation' is how Rourke had described it to Crimson, but there was no amount of radiation he was comfortable with shooting into one of his soldier's brains.

At the end of the day, Adrian was a kid. So young he couldn't legally buy alcohol yet, and yet he'd accomplished more alongside Spectrum than many operators do across their entire careers. That impact wasn't lost on anyone. Not him, not Rourke, not on any of Spectrum. It had been an elephant in the room since day one. Elephants can be damn big dangerous animals, though.

Crimson had no family, no kids, no spouse. He was quintessentially married to the job, and each and every member of his squad was as close as blood to him. He felt a fatherly need to protect Adrian, an unfamiliar situation for him and yet that loyalty was undeniable. The problem was, how do you protect someone from their own mind? How do you protect them when their very purpose, the reason they were gifted the skills they were born with, was becoming a danger to them? Rourke had convinced him to see the truth: the only way to truly protect Adrian was to reach Phase Two.

The back door opened. Dr. Childs walked out with Adrian in

tow. The young man looked peaceful. Behind him, the doctor was practically beaming. All evidence to things going well.

"Adrian," Crimson said and stood. "How'd it go? How are you feeling?"

Adrian looked at his squad leader and blinked a few times. His eyes came into focus, and he gave Crimson a puzzled look.

"I . . ." He hesitated, eyebrows scrunched into momentary confusion, and then his face lit up in a smile. "I don't know?"

Crimson was equally confused and looked to Childs for an answer. She was similarly smiling and watched with rapt attention as Adrian looked about the waiting room with a strange sense of wonder.

"We've been building the doorway and opening a room for him," she explained. "Today, we saw if we could put anything in there. Major, phase one is a *success*!"

Crimson did a double take between the doctor and Adrian. "Really? What'd she tell you in there, son?"

Adrian excitedly waved his arms, and then just as quickly bit down on a knuckle as emotion came over him. "I don't know! I can't remember the last time I *didn't* remember something."

His other squad mates came over to speak with him and Crimson took the moment to speak aside with Childs.

"So, the schism that you were talking about, you've done it?"

"Yes," she said. "It's merely an outline right now. Think of it as a faint line in the sand, but with Phase Two we can make real progress. It's one thing to suppress and compartmentalize ten minutes, it's another to transfer whole personality aspects. We're on the forefront here, Major. Every step is uncharted territory."

"That's what I'm afraid of."

"Don't worry," the doctor said, and fastened on a smile that Crimson had seen before on Rourke. "Everything's going to be just fine.

CHAPTER 38

Darren Rourke. 9:10 a.m.
Home Site
San Diego, California

"You're no son of mine."

"No?" Black walked into the office, giving the room appraising looks, with his wrists clasped behind his back. His fingers touched the handles of obsidian blades hidden up either sleeve. "How can you say that? After all, you made me."

Kara shot Black twice in the chest. He went down and disappeared into a puff of smoke from a grenade he'd pulled from his belt. The cloud billowed out and the assassin vanished.

"Ah . . . Miss Mason," Black hissed. "Don't think I'd forgotten you."

"Slippery shit," she cursed, fanning her pistol from left to right.

Rourke stood like a resolute statue behind his desk, refusing to show the smallest sign of fear. This was *his* office. No one was going to scare him here.

"Of course, I don't think you'd ever forget me either. Not after that beauty mark I left you with last time," said Black, his voice impossible to track.

Kara shot into the smoke but was rewarded with nothing but the hollow sound of a bullet striking the wall. She kept herself between the cloud and Rourke, finger curled and ready along the trigger.

"Come on, come on . . ."

"Are you getting jumpy, Mason?" he whispered. "I wonder how much you miss field work. How many lies you've told yourself about how *great* you were. It's only fitting that death sent me to remind you."

A knife whistled through the air and sank deep into Kara's shoulder. Her dominant arm went limp and her handgun clattered to the ground. She stumbled backwards, her back to the pane-glass along the wall. As she stooped to pick up the pistol, Black stepped forth from the shadows. Tag's revolver was in his hands. The barrel pointed steadily at her face.

Black seemed to consider for a moment, then adjusted his aim and shot her square in the chest. The .44 magnum round practically took her off her feet and sent her back against the window behind her. Black's head tilted curiously, either surprised that the glass had held up or impressed by Kara's vest.

"Body armor and shatterproof glass, asshole," she said through grit teeth as she pulled Black's knife from her shoulder and readied to return it to its sender.

"Bob?" Black said, a finger on his ear.

There was a series of distant booms and then several bullets hit the glass. Mason spared a glance over her shoulder to see that the bullets hadn't penetrated, but left huge running cracks. When she faced front again, Black ran at her with a spinning kick that crashed into her chest with the force of a freight train.

Mason hurtled through the window, supposedly unbreakable shards of glass raked against her skin. Her arms flailed wildly about her in what she would've called a shameful moment of panic. Then, she plummeted to the ground below.

Wind swirled into the darkened office and swept the smoke

from the room. Kara Mason, Rourke's right hand and most loyal of all his soldiers, was gone. Just like that.

"Now then, finally some privacy."

"Where's Adrian?" Rourke asked.

Black adjusted the cuffs of his jacket sleeves and shrugged, "Don't ask stupid questions, Father. I buried him a long time ago. I've buried so many over the years, I do appreciate the kill teams you've sent my way. They were always fun exercise."

Rourke thought about going for the pump-action shotgun under his desk but knew there was no way he could get to it in time.

"What are you after, Damien?"

Black leaned across Rourke's desk, positively beaming that the old man had relented in calling him by his true first name.

"Morpheus."

He plugged a small device into Rourke's computer and a green light began to blink as it mirrored the hard drive. Rourke figured that was the goal, but there had to be more to it. Black was a self-described servant of Death. Whatever his endgame, there would undoubtedly be a massive body count along with it.

Rourke's eyes caught something on his computer screen, and he couldn't help but smile. A subroutine logged anytime a file was copied from his hard-drive, and apparently Black wasn't the first person to do so.

West . . .

"Someone's a few steps ahead of you," Rourke said.

A tight-lipped scowl fell across Black's face as he saw the same thing Rourke had. It was an interesting tell, because as long as Rourke had known him Black had never been one to get upset by another person. He was on another tier from people. Which made his reaction all the more curious.

"Why are you fixated on him?"

"Some people are meant to be broken. Then all the little pieces can come together in such interesting ways."

He removed the device from Rourke's computer and stowed it inside his jacket pocket.

"You would know better than most, Damien."

"That's what you still don't understand. You didn't break me, you *perfected* me." Black's nostrils flared, and there was a wicked look in his eyes. "You brought me up from the lowest abyss. Took all the potential I ever had and made it flesh and blood."

"Then tell me, why is the perfect killer afraid of West?"

Again, the same tell. The slightest of twitches at the edge of his smile. The smallest flicker in those shadowy irises.

"He challenged me. Took all those souls with a push of a button. I thought it only fair that I challenge him back. I'll hurt him. Hurt his friends. Do whatever I have to so that when I kill him, he's at his very best. His most deadly. I want him to see that, though we may be brothers in death, and his heart is as black as mine, he is beneath me."

The blowing wind gusted around the two men, neither so much as flinching. For the briefest of moments Rourke understood Black's twisted logic. His rules. It really was all a game to him.

"That blackness inside you? It's not a heart," Rourke said. "It never was. It's a damned hole. An empty pit. You'll never kill enough, never *be* enough to ever fill it. What you really can't stand is that, in this entire world, there's no bastard as empty as you."

Black smirked. "That may be so, but I'm still better than any of the men you tried to replace me with. Certainly more than Sergeant West is."

"*Captain* West," Rourke sharply corrected, "is ten times the man you ever were."

Rourke couldn't hide the bit of pride that snuck its way into his tone. There was a warmth that came with it. A fondness. He even smiled.

Black rounded the desk and shoved Rourke against the wall, his hands gripping tight around Rourke's jacket. There was a beat where Rourke wondered when he would feel a sharp stab into his chest, but then Black released him and helped him straighten his jacket.

"I'll need you to send West a message for me," Black said as he turned to walk away. "Call it a parting gift."

"What is it?" Rourke finished adjusting his jacket buttons and looked up, but Black had vanished.

"Some messages don't need to be told." Black's voice whispered like a ghost from the open doorway. "They need to be witnessed."

Rourke stood puzzled for a second as the wind howled in his office. Something felt off in his jacket pocket and he reached in. It was his Plan C device, a next-gen explosive failsafe he always kept on his person. A bit more dramatic than a suicide pill, but more often than not Rourke traveled with classified material that couldn't be allowed to fall into enemy hands. Plan C was designed to vaporize nearly a city block to prevent that.

Except the device had already been armed, and the timer was nearing zero.

"Well played," Rourke said as the detonation sequence finalized.

CHAPTER 39

She'd never understood when people said 'butterflies in their stomach'. That always had such a gentle implication in her mind; a more accurate saying would be 'rattlesnakes repeatedly biting her gut'. It was exactly what she felt walking down the aisles of the grocery store. Venom, stabbing her insides, and coursing through her veins. There was nothing remotely pleasant or tender about the way her stomach roiled.

West's giant dog seemed to pick up on her unease and gave a deep "*Whuff*" that sounded a lot like "Be cool, you're embarrassing me."

Rain gave Dante a pat on the shoulder and threw an assortment of canned meat in the shopping cart. Thankfully, it seemed like her paranoia was mostly unfounded. Though most of the other customers in the supermarket did look in her direction, their eyes were always fixed with admiration on the jet-black, yellow-eyed monster that accompanied her. So far, the only one to give Rain herself any attention was a curious old man who no doubt thought a little girl like her had no business owning a dog so big, or maybe he just thought her vibrant blue hairstyle was odd. Dante had chased him away with a mere look, which had brought such a smile to Rain's face, she promised to buy her furry bodyguard some treats. Brontosaurus bones or whatever it was West fed this thing.

Shopping for others was weird. Shopping for others that were basically on the run from both their own people and a secret society was even weirder. It didn't help that normally Rain's shopping list consisted of a pallet of instant noodles and sugar-free Red Bulls. Trying to figure out the nutritional needs and eating habits of three very physically active men who she could only assume were on ridiculously high-protein diets was more than out of her wheelhouse. They'd have to do with Spam and corned beef because Rain was about as skilled at cooking as she was Olympic gymnastics.

She kept forcing herself out of her thoughts and into the world. She needed to keep her attention on her surroundings no matter how unassuming they were. This time she wouldn't be watching the situation unfold from behind the safety of her computer. The training wheels were off.

Satisfied that no stalker was waiting to ambush her by the produce section, she wheeled her cart to checkout and started loading her items onto the belt. She did her best to blend. It wasn't an easy thing to do when you have electric blue hair with a Mastiff in tow.

The cashier scanned and bagged her items with nary a glance up from the conveyer.

"What you feed 'im?" the cashier asked, not bothering to even look at Rain.

"Whatever he wants."

Dante gave her a whine and put on an Oscar-worthy performance looking hurt. Shit. She forgot the doggie treats. Rain turned around to make a quick dash to the pet aisle when her eyes caught a tv in the corner of the deli area. The local news was on, covering a story on an accident at some building. Some sort of gas leak had caused an explosion, first responders were on scene, but it didn't look like anyone had made it out.

Rain stopped dead in her tracks when the reporter gave the address. Home Site. It was gone.

CHAPTER 40

"Where have you been?"

Our drive had been silent until now. I'd been waiting for Vaun to let loose with the intimate details of the vast conspiracy he'd uncovered, but after nearly two hours on the road I'd gotten fed up with waiting. Vaun shifted in his seat. His eyes kept darting around from the side-view mirrors to the cars we passed.

"Around," he finally said.

He was skittish, and that fact was terrifying enough on its own. I hoped it meant that Vaun had just been on his own for too long and wasn't used to such scintillating interaction, and not that he was broken in some way I didn't know how to fix. His mental state hadn't been the strongest *before* he'd disappeared on us.

"Don't suppose you can tell me what or where Morpheus is?"

"No," said Vaun. "Why?"

"It's what Legion hired Black to get. Some Cold War relic, a radioactive weapon. Rourke is being exceedingly vague, which is nothing new. He swears it was scrapped, and the garbage buried a long time ago."

"Hmm. We'll just have to ask him a little less politely."

I checked the rear-view mirror, but this section of the interstate was fairly empty. I'd expected an ambush before the border back into the states, but no dice. Maybe we'd offed their entire cell in Tijuana. I sort of doubted our luck was that strong, though. It was that kind of week after all.

I wanted to be patient with Vaun. I really did. He was a mentor, more than that he was a friend. I didn't have any way of knowing what the hell he'd been through since he fell off the grid. All the same, playing coy wasn't ever my go-to method when I needed to know something, and I'd been white-knuckling it with my own shit as it was.

"Damien Black," I said, the name like poison in the air. "You never told me about him."

"You're Cerberus Squad's captain now. You could've read our previous mission reports at any time. If you didn't know he was the one who killed John Crow, it's because *you* didn't want to."

He had a point.

"You could've warned me."

The leather on the steering wheel crinkled in my grip.

"You're right. I should have, but Rourke blacklisted him on our target list. Number zero. No attempts to find, capture, or kill. I . . . I thought maybe that would be enough to keep you, and the team, safe. That John Crow would be the last of us to—"

"Kelly," I said.

Vaun went still. *Very* still. You could've heard his heart stop for that second if you'd been listening for it. There hadn't been a good moment to tell him until now.

"Vaun, he got Kelly."

It wasn't fair of me to throw it in his face like that, and I felt dirty for having to do it, but I also needed him to know that the mission had gone personal.

"I swear to God, we'll get him, Cole."

"Me," I said, and took my eyes off the road to look at Vaun and make sure he heard me. "It has to be me."

The rest of our trip back to Home Site was void of further conversation. As much as I wanted to know everything he'd uncovered, neither of our heads were in the right spot. I settled instead for some mileage therapy. I reached into the center console and thumbed the top off my pills, then popped two and gulped them down. With each mile that passed in the rearview, I felt myself regaining a little bit of control. Vaun very obviously saw but turned to look out his window instead. If he had thoughts on my own generous medication mandates, he was polite enough to keep them to himself.

By the time we neared Home Site, I was running on pure ice. All my bullshit was balled up nice and tight and locked away in that pit deep in my head. No skeletons in the closet clawing for attention. No wandering thoughts to where Madison was or how my loose cannon act might affect her, or us. I was okay with my mountain of personal crap staying down in the dark for the foreseeable future. I was operating clean and clear rather than running off emotion. That's why I noticed something was wrong before Vaun.

I saw the flashing red and blue lights and assumed the worst. I could think of a dozen different reasons for why first responders would be at a Black Spear site, but none of them were close to what waited for us as we rounded the block for the Home Site fence-line.

Nothing. Absolutely nothing.

Our base of operations, my home, the place of refuge for myself and all my allies, was completely gone. A few fire trucks were packing up their hoses as I pulled to a stop. There was barely any rubble. It was as if someone had simply plucked the building off the ground and left a smoldering foundation behind. I couldn't help but do a run-down of how many men and women must've been inside at the time.

"We can't stay here," Vaun breathed. "They're probably watching for anyone to come home."

Fuck. I wanted to scream at him and ask what was wrong with him that he could be so cold. As it turned out, he'd taught me well because I was just as callous. I reluctantly shifted the truck to reverse.

A bloody hand smacked my window, leaving a red print on the glass.

Her face was hidden behind a layer of soot and it took me a second to recognize her. Kara Mason. One hand was clamped firmly against a bandaged wound on her shoulder that had already soaked through red. The arm hung by her side and her clothes were nearly shredded across the back and sleeves. Bits of shattered glass still clung to her. There was a fury in her eyes I'd never seen before. She looked like a wounded animal. Not scared. *Dangerous.*

Her lips pulled back into a feral snarl.

"Where. Is. He?!"

CHAPTER 41

Vaun tended to Mason's wounds while I drove us to the safehouse. To say she'd taken a nasty fall was putting it lightly, but thankfully her body armor beneath her modest blazer saved her spine from shattering on the pavement. She was lucky. That said nothing about the two or three ribs she'd cracked on the landing, and that was already glossing over the stab wound to her shoulder. All across her arms and back were shallow slices where skin met glass when she'd gone through the window. Vaun had applied a field expedient stitch job to the worst of it as I'd done my damnedest to avoid every bump and pothole on the highway.

We needed to regroup and figure out our next move. Mr. Black used to be one of us; he'd already proven that everything from our comm frequencies to the locations of our black sites were compromised.

Rourke was gone. It was something I hadn't thought possible. The man represented more than just the unyielding statue of Black Spear command. He was our very connection to Washington. No Rourke? No line to that shiny red phone in the Oval Office. It also raised questions as to whether or not the executive order granting us autonomy remained in effect. The one and only physical copy may be ashes around Home Site's foundation right now.

The aftermath of a titan like Rourke's passing would be a veritable shitstorm that I couldn't fathom. It wasn't out of the realm of reason to think that Black Spear itself would crumble without him manning the helm. Bottom line? We were pretty much operating without any official authority, which meant there was a big old proverbial clock ticking down before any surviving Black Spear teams were ordered to stand down.

Mason shrugged off Vaun's attempt to help her inside upon our arrival. I did the secret knock I'd previously told Rain about so she wouldn't shoot one of us in a panic. Mason was already shoving past me and going inside before I turned the knob. She found one of the bathrooms and locked herself inside.

"Give her a moment," Vaun said. "She's . . . well, protecting Rourke was her job."

Vaun went to check on Tag and Billy but stopped short when Billy was already standing in the doorway. One look at his purpled face and swollen eye was enough to break even Vaun's stone resolve. These had been his people—his responsibility—long before they were mine.

"You're back?" Billy managed despite his wired jaw.

"Sorry it took me so long."

"Save your apologies for the dead," Billy closed the door to his room in Vaun's face.

Rather than sulk, Vaun asked Rain to show him to the second floor, which housed a modest operations center. He unzipped a backpack and went about unloading the fruits of his investigation. At first he moved at a manic pace, but little by little, as the larger picture began to be pinned to the corkboard, he grew more composed. By the time he finished tacking up the last picture to the wall, he looked like his old self again.

His display was far more organized and far less irrational

conspiracy theory than I expected. In fact, he didn't even use any string to draw connections between photos. There were plenty of surveillance photos, some photocopies of accounting forms, a few weapons acquisitions invoices, and then what looked to be a diagram for some sort of rank structure. He gave me a look as if to ask whether or not anyone else would be attending his brief besides myself and Rain. I shook my head, and he just nodded.

"I don't know about you," I said, "but I feel like the walls are closing in on us. Why don't we assume they are, and you give us the short and sweet of it all since we're pretty pressed for time here."

Vaun considered for a moment. Clearly the depth of what he'd uncovered took up a large amount of real estate in his head and asking him to distill it down to the CliffsNotes version was giving him pause.

"Okay then," he said, his eyes scanning along the wall as he decided on where to begin. "I guess we can start here. Where we all crossed paths for the first time."

The picture he pointed at was a man I recognized. Abraham Jackson, the leader of a defunct militia called Terminal that had tried to assassinate the President back when I was still the Cerberus Squad's FNG. The last time I'd seen his face, I'd used two loads of buckshot erasing it.

"We know that when Jax started Terminal, most of the financial support came from his second-in-command, Robert Batson. But that only explained roughly two-thirds of their accounts. They had a sponsor. Someone who helped them with connections to purchase their weapons, secure the land for their base, et cetera."

"Legion."

"Precisely. That's their game. They live in the shadows and step to the edge of it only to pull others' strings to further whatever their larger motives are."

"Larger than Terminal offing the President?" Rain asked.

"That's a troubling thought."

"With chaos comes opportunity, with opportunity profit. The more discord and death they sow, the more control they wrest for themselves. Their power grows, all without stepping onto the stage themselves. They're content to spread their fear and manipulation from their position of total anonymity through their agents and proxies."

"They must have made an exception," I said.

I signaled Rain, who brought a case folder to Vaun. Within it were the photos of the Valkyrie Squad massacre, their spiked heads and the Latin message carved into their tongues. "Because they don't seem to have any qualms about hiding who they are from us. Any theories on that?"

"Yeah. We seriously pissed them off."

CHAPTER 42

Kara Mason. 1:00 p.m.
Black Spear Safehouse
La Jolla, California

The sink became tinged a pale red as she washed the dried blood from her body. She refused to look in the mirror until she was certain that the reflection would no longer be an embarrassment. When she finally did, the broken thing that stared back at her was no less shameful.

She shook her head and gingerly slipped one arm out of her tattered jacket, then awkwardly pulled her injured wing out of the other. For a beat she held the garment. About to hang it neatly on the hook, she gave a disgusted snarl and threw it into the wastebasket in the corner. Once more she looked into the mirror, barely recognizing herself.

She was *Mason,* damn it. The Sledgehammer. The one who terms like "glass ceiling" had never held any meaning for. It was such a laughable concept to her, because she'd done nothing but surpass her competition and destroy their small expectations her entire life. Yet here she was, broken. Beaten. A loser.

Her red-stained white blouse came off next. She was glad to be rid of it. The professional attire required of her position as Rourke's body woman had always felt foreign to her. For years now she'd worn the clothes and played the part, all the while eagerly wishing to lace her combat boots back up and return to the field. Except today she'd shown that she'd committed the worst sin imaginable among soldiers: she'd gotten sloppy.

Rourke was gone now. Along with dozens of her brothers and sisters in arms. Losing Major Cruz—losing *Maggie*—at the onset had been hard enough. Now she couldn't help but feel like she was growing cold to all the loss. She welcomed it, let that emptiness wash over her like an ice bath. Felt it sap all the warmth and joy from her. In that moment, she opened her eyes again. The sight before her filled her with disgust. Long raven hair matted against her skull from both blood and sweat. The remnants of conservative makeup she still hadn't managed to wash away. Even the well-maintained fingernails belonged to someone who cared more for their appearance than their purpose.

Kara leaned forward and rested her elbows on the sink.

"Just who the fuck are you trying to be, girl?"

DARK BEGINNINGS 8

"Are you ready?" Crimson asked as he walked Adrian towards the table.

Adrian looked at the leather straps that would hold him in place, and the intimidating Morpheus apparatus above.

"Yes."

He reached into his pocket and retrieved two prescription pill bottles, then took his dosage of both. If everything went well, it would be the last time he'd have to swallow those foul tasting psychotropics.

"The whole squad is in the next room over, we'll be here waiting when you're done."

Adrian nodded. One last step before the point of no return, but he'd passed that point months ago when he'd pulled the trigger on Leonid Petrenko. He fought back the oncoming storm of memories that smothered his vision as he climbed atop the table. Childs entered the room alongside two technicians and set to work ratcheting the restraints into place. Crimson gave Adrian one last comforting pat on the shoulder.

"See you on the other side, son. We've still got a lot of work to do."

Adrian nodded with a smile and watched the major walk out the room.

He drew in a deep breath. With every passing second, he was more and more eager to get on with the procedure. He slowed his breathing, channeling a Buddhist meditation exercise he'd read five years prior to center himself. The physiological and mental shift happened naturally after. Adrian could actually feel himself slipping into the state that Childs and Rourke's conditioning had prepared him for. It was like slipping into a set of worn leather boots.

The procedure table lowered into place and the large laser mechanism swiveled down overhead. A technician placed a plastic marker over Adrian's forehead and then used a felt pen to draw an outline almost like a crosshair for where the radiation would be applied.

Not a lobotomy, he reminded himself. *Laser-precise mental surgery.*

Dr. Childs and the technicians exited the room; behind a pane of observation glass, he could see a crew monitoring instruments. All wore heavy full-body suits for their own protection. There was a deep hum from somewhere in the facility, and the Darkheart Project came to life. Lights and indicators alongside the laser blinked on to indicate it powering up. The hum grew in intensity until Adrian could practically feel the vibration in his lips.

He closed his eyes, ready for it to begin. Ready for this to end.

Childs spoke to him through a speaker in the corner of the room, but Adrian was elsewhere in his mindscape. He looked about at the darker parts and wondered if he would even notice or miss them once they were cordoned off into the other room Rourke and Childs had been preparing.

There was a barely audible pop, and he felt a slight tickling on his forehead. He realized the laser was firing, but still he kept his eyes closed. It would work. He knew it would.

But, too late, Adrian realized their folly. They'd been right about everything up to this point. The only mistake was in preparing and making the doorway: because doors could open both ways. As the Morpheus Engine reached its full power and the laser fired its precision spike of energy, Adrian screamed.

The dark spots in his mindscape exploded with blackness, filling everything until Adrian was drowning in the pitch oil. That infinite library of thoughts and memories flooded with the black, covering every page. Within his own head he was falling into a pit, a pit that laughed and swallowed him whole. He fell and fell into the dark until he was merely a pinprick within the black and fell further until even that disappeared. Down, down, down.

The door had been opened, and Mr. Black locked it shut behind him.

CHAPTER 43

His sponsors often arranged for him to fly via small private planes. It was an extravagant show of wealth that Black had grown numb to. Legion's plane, however, was at the very top of the list when it came to impressiveness. The plush leather seat wrapped around him so well, it threatened to make him relax. Black had already taken notice of the sophisticated instruments that kept the aircraft cloaked to their enemies. There surely was a sizable ordinance hidden beneath the unassuming civilian façade, although Black had yet to confirm his suspicions.

Another thought had taken root in his head. His veins should be filled to bursting with exhilaration. Black had done what no one else could have; he had felled a titan. Rourke, dead by his hand. Yet it had given him no gratification. That hungry darkness within him just smiled and opened wide for more. Black would throw further souls into the pit soon enough.

"*It'll never be enough . . .*" a ghost of a memory whispered to him. It was the ghost of Adrian Rasp.

"Only one way to find out," Black said with a wicked smile.

The nagging whispers had only grown louder. Now, he didn't

bother to ignore them. Rasp's ghost could scream bloody murder at him for all he cared; his time taking up space in Black's head would be up before long.

Black closed his eyes and focused inward for a moment. He imagined his heart, not the physical one, but the darker *truer* one. The shadowy hole.

"Back to the bottom," he said to himself as he cast Rasp's memory back into it. Silence once more. *That* was satisfying.

When Black opened his eyes, he found Simon had moved to the seat across from him. There was a soured expression on his face almost like he had a bout of constipation.

"You were talking to yourself."

"Yes."

"You know the weirdest thing about you being a sociopath?" he asked. "You care so little that you don't even think to lie."

Black shrugged. "I'm many things, Mister Ellis. Murderer. Assassin. Finder of artifacts and killer of titans. But I'm not a liar. Lying is . . . beneath me. A man should be honest above all else."

"That best be the truth, for your sake," said Simon. "Because if you *don't* know where Morpheus is, and this trip turns out to be for nothing, I don't know how much longer we can retain your services."

His less than subtle threat hung in the air between them. Black looked past Simon's shoulder to where the Immortals sat. There was only Harrison, Scaglin, and Hogue. The other two were up in the cockpit. Black's fingers pulsed with anticipation, but then he decided against it. He could stay the course. For now.

"How far out are we?" Black asked.

Simon craned his head around to ask Declan from the front of the plane. For one delicious moment Black wondered what Simon's exposed neckline would look like with a knife in it.

"About twenty minutes from the facility."

Black opened a laptop and used the data he'd mirrored from

Rourke's hard drive to drill through several security firewalls.

"Black, what are we walking into here?"

Rourke's stolen access codes tore into the digital systems. With a few keystrokes Black began to disable the safety measures in the nearing facility.

"Chaos, Mister Ellis. You wanted Morpheus? I thought a demonstration of its effect would be in order first."

An almost imperceptible flutter went across the muscles of Simon's jaw. The man had fought back a nervous gulp, but that effort alone was as damning as the act itself. Black chose not to milk it. He was too busy thinking about how close to Morpheus he was. Soon enough, it would be his, and soon enough, he would finally shut Adrian's ghost up for good.

CHAPTER 44

"Jesus," I said, taking another look at the intricate web Vaun had drawn on the whiteboard.

"The Terminal case, the Warmaker business, and nearly a dozen other missions Black Spear has been involved in," said Vaun. "Legion has either indirectly been associated with or outright orchestrated it from the shadows."

"You were right about us pissing them off. But their goals in this instance are two-fold: taking us out *and* retrieving Morpheus."

"Which is still a huge question mark," said Rain. "We're shooting in the dark here, because we won't have a starting point until we can decrypt Rourke's files."

"How's that decryption going?" Vaun asked.

She rolled her eyes, annoyed at the insinuation that she would withhold Morpheus's location if she'd already unlocked the files. "Your reputation precedes you, Vaun. If you ask West, he'll more than vouch for mine. So, believe me when I say that we're working with the Mount Everest of data encryptions. It's just going to take a little bit more time."

Vaun nodded, clearly rubbing her the wrong way had not been

his intention.

"You sure Rourke didn't drop any clues about it when you pressed him?" Vaun asked me.

"We talking about the same Rourke here? Not the guy to let anything slip. All he said was that it was shelved, scrapped, and buried deep in his basement or something like that."

"Wait…" he said in a hushed whisper. His whole posture changed, it was as if I'd just walked across his grave. "You're certain he used those *exact* words?"

I jogged my memory, then gave him a nod.

"Shit," Vaun breathed. "You didn't use those words before, you said it was 'buried garbage'. It's not his basement. It's *the* Basement."

I gave him a queer look as his eyes widened with understanding. "Okay, you want to fill me in?"

"Even operators trade ghost stories, except our scariest are the ones that are real. Once upon a time, there was a black site research installation that suffered one too many accidents. It was decommissioned and retrofitted into a deep storage facility for tech deemed too dangerous to ever see the light of day," said Vaun. "*That's* the Basement."

"Rourke's very own Raiders of the Lost Ark Warehouse. Great. So, say Legion gets to the Basement. Even if they don't get their hands on Morpheus, they'll still have access to weapons Rourke wanted forgotten. Any idea what we're looking at? Biological? Chemical?"

"Asking the wrong guy," said Vaun. "I've only heard of it, never been."

"I have," Mason said behind us.

She leaned against the door frame. She'd hacked off her shoulder-length raven with clippers, practically shaved at the sides, and she'd switched from her tattered business attire to an athletic tank and a pair of cargo pants. When she crossed her arms the stitched wound at her shoulder didn't seem to give her any trouble.

In a word? She looked lethal. Sledgehammer was ready for some payback.

"It's in Washington state. Being by the director's side for so long meant I occasionally snuck a peak over his shoulder at his computer. I can take a crack at the password encryption, too, if Ms. Harper can't get it."

Rain bristled.

"Wait, if we know where Black and his Immortal entourage are headed, why don't we just call in the cavalry and have a battalion of Rangers there waiting for them?" she asked.

"The director was killed," Vaun said.

"And?"

"And without Rourke our line to the President is cut," Mason chimed in. "We have no Executive Authority. The CIA has already been circling like vultures for months now, trying to convince the President to dismantle Black Spear. I wouldn't be surprised if all our assets were being absorbed into the CIA's Directorate of Operations."

"Which means our only option is to head them off ourselves," I said. "Good. Black's mine. No one else's."

Vaun gave me a wary look. Just saying Black's name was like drops of battery acid on my tongue.

"We can take Rourke's plane," Mason said. "I can get us into the hangar, and it's the only thing fast enough to get us to the Basement before them."

"Billy and Tag are in no condition to fight," I said.

"Just you and me, and Rain for on-site intel support." Vaun nodded. "As long as Kara doesn't mind keeping an eye on things here?"

Mason tapped the brace along Vaun's bad leg. "You're in no condition to fight either, Vaun. I've done guard duty long enough. Don't worry, I won't let your protégé get hurt."

It was a hard truth to speak, but a truth nonetheless. If we were going up against Immortals and Black, then Vaun's leg would be a problem. Rather than say anything else, Mason just gave each of us a hard look and threw her hands out to either side.

"We going to waste any more time?"

A half smile etched itself across Vaun's face. One of his signature looks and something I hadn't seen since his return. "Okay, people, you heard the lady. Load up and punch out."

"Rourke's plane has a pretty sizable on-board armory," said Mason.

"And if Legion hits us enroute to the airfield?" I asked as I set weapons cases onto the table in the center of the room.

"Good point," she admitted. "See, I knew there was a reason you made Captain."

I buckled a gun belt around my waist and holstered my .45 on my left hip. As I thumbed rounds into spare magazines, Vaun came closer and leaned against the table next to me.

"Is your thinking clear, West?" he asked.

I tapped a fully loaded magazine on the table, then slid it onto my belt. "Clear as crystal on what I'm going to do."

He hesitated before speaking again. In that short span I filled a second magazine, tapped it, and belted it.

"Revenge is unprofessional, West."

"Yeah? That didn't stop you from going after Phobos Marstelli for what he did."

"Exactly my point. Look what it got me. Cole, look at me."

I set the half-loaded magazine on the table and looked at Vaun. I took notice of the newer age lines across his face. How much weight he'd lost since last we'd met. The scars that were grisly trophies of his last failed hurrah. He'd been brought to death's door by another man's blade, and that encounter came about on a path of revenge.

"You don't look like you're ready, and you're acting like you want to go at this ill-prepared. I went off half-cocked and look what it got me. You see this?" Vaun asked. He held a double-edged karambit in his hand. "He let me keep my life and this, both as reminders that I'm only alive because he let me go. You know what they say about revenge; if you go on a journey for revenge, you better dig two graves."

"Good idea." I attached my MK-9 knife to my vest. "That way, when I cut Black in half, I can bury the pieces separately."

Vaun spoke very carefully, his voice full of caution and restraint. "West, the mission is Morpheus. Black is secondary."

"Kelly," I said, gritting my teeth together to keep from screaming. "He killed Kelly. He used Tag's gun and blew a hole in his throat. I had to watch him drown in his own blood. And then there's Rourke. And more than twenty of our friends. You really trying to talk me out of this?"

Vaun looked hurt. "Damn it, no. I want him dead, too. I'm saying you need to go into this with a level head. You're carrying enough baggage upstairs as it is. You want to go for vengeance recklessly, as I did? I promise you, Black won't be as merciful as Phobos. That animal will rip you apart in ways you cannot imagine."

As hard as it was to do, I took a deep breath. Held it, felt it, then let it out slowly.

On that long exhale I felt the fire in my belly die down and all the bad thoughts and memories in my head grow quiet. That monster I'd been battling with inside was willing to play by the rules if there was something on which I could focus all of my regret, guilt, pain, and rage. Black provided that in spades.

Vaun took notice of the change.

"Yeah," he said with an encouraging nod, "*now* you look ready."

We left the second-floor briefing room and found Rain and Mason had already finished their prep. When she saw that I was ready to go, Mason gave me a lift of her chin and went to start the car. Dante, who'd been dutifully guarding the front door, sprang up with tail wagging when he saw me. I scratched behind his ear and gave his muscled shoulder a pat.

"Don't worry, you're coming with this time." Dante *whuffed* enthusiastically. "I still need someone watching over Rain, buddy." His *whuff* dulled to a disappointed grumble. I winked at Rain and then clicked my tongue for Dante to follow me to the car.

Vaun stood in the doorway to the recovery room where Billy and Tag still rested.

"You going to be okay sitting this part out?" I asked him.

He shrugged. "It'll give me some time to catch up with the boys."

A car horn blared outside. Evidently Mason was growing impatient.

"West . . ." Vaun said.

I stopped at the front doorway.

"Black tore through Cerberus like it was nothing. He broke Billy as if he was some amateur. What are you going to do if you cross paths down there? How are you going to beat him?"

The question hung heavy in the air. I thought back to how Black had picked us apart, and how, in his own way, he'd taken a piece of each of us when he killed our brother. Until the day I died, I knew I'd never be rid of that image of Kelly helplessly dying in the rain. My hand went to my pocket on its own, finding the .45 ACP bullet I'd recovered when I returned to the foundry. The one I'd promised was for Black. That bullet answered it all for me.

"I don't know how I'm going to win," I admitted. "I just know that I'm not going to fucking lose."

CHAPTER 45

There was no way to hear the screams from here. Fifteen-hundred feet of dirt and then twenty feet of concrete separated the highest level of the subterranean facility from the surface. The wailing cries of the damned and the crazed would never make it up here. When Black disabled the Morpheus safeguards, the security feed showed him how quickly the Basement's occupants had been affected. But he didn't need to watch the cameras or hear their screams to feel what was happening down there. It felt like death.

Black basked in that feeling as he leaned comfortably against an old fifty-five gallon barrel. The elevator that led down to the Basement was in front of him, hidden within a small concrete entrance.

"Good Christ," Simon breathed. Unlike Black, he had felt the need to bear witness to Morpheus' capability through the laptop.

"I would not think you a religious man, Mister Ellis," Black said. He took notice of Simon's pale complexion. "Or squeamish, for that matter."

A symphony of pain came to Black's ears from the laptop's speakers before Simon could close the screen. It was a beautiful composition.

"You didn't need to kill *everyone*."

"I enjoy exceeding your expectations," Black answered. "Besides, not everyone died. There are some that respond differently."

"Yes, the so-called 'Kruegers' you previously mentioned."

Black smiled. "Chaos made flesh. I trust this will suffice for confirmation?"

Simon slid a cell phone from his pocket. "Indeed. Lady Holt will be most pleased."

While Simon called his master, Black reached into his jacket and drew out Brandon Taggart's .44 revolver. He twirled it around upon his finger, recreating a set of tricks he'd watched from a western movie. Black spun it slow, spun it fast; he rotated his wrist and flipped it around backwards. He took a new appreciation for the bluntness of the gun while his hand seemingly moved on its own. Six shots was all it held, but each bullet was a wrecking ball.

Packing that much punch in such a limited capacity meant a man would know each pull of the trigger would need to be special. Intimate. Already Black had used three bullets, and he knew both had been truly memorable. It dawned on him that perhaps he should have used one of the three remaining magnum rounds to kill Rourke, but then he decided it wouldn't have mattered because West wasn't there to see it.

Black opened the chamber, gave the revolver a tap to pop one of the bullets into his palm, and then used his thumb to push it onto his knuckle. He rolled the bullet back and forth along his knuckles as he'd seen some people do with a coin. Funny how such a small piece of metal was strong enough to take a man's head off. Black found himself wondering whose bullet this was. Everyone had one, but whose would this become? Who could he hurt West the most through?

The magnum round caught the light beautifully as he paused and pinched it between thumb and forefinger. It was no wonder Taggart had such a fondness for the weapon. People tended to find favorites in this line of work.

That thought made Black reload the bullet and holster the revolver after one final spin. Loath as he was to admit, he knew all too well about having favorites. He reached down to his ankle to retrieve the thirteenth blade that was hidden there. Nearly all of his most remarkable kills had been done with this very blade. Black was rarely sentimental, but this was the exception. When he held the knife, he could feel all the souls it had taken trapped within the Portoro marble handles. All their pain had been drawn into the obsidian like a sponge. Black ran his thumb along one of the white marbling swirls. Ghosts, locked in stone.

Cole West would be next. He sheathed it back to his ankle and fixed his pant leg. Only West was worthy of it, no one else would be honored by its edge. Some prey deserved more than a bullet.

Simon returned with his Immortals in tow.

"Lady Holt is quite pleased. Now just the small matter of retrieving it."

As if on cue, the Basement elevator dinged. A man, panicked and bloodied, hobbled out. He clutched at his hand which was missing several fingers. There was a moment when he looked at all of them with a glimmer of hope, no doubt mistaking them for his rescue. That hope was dashed away when Black sent a throwing knife whistling through the air and into his Adam's apple. It pierced through to his spine. Death was instant.

"My dear Mister Ellis," he said, going down to a knee to pull the knife from the corpse. "Retrieving it is the fun part. Tell your entourage to don their party masks, and don't forget to take their vitamins. We won't want anyone ending up like, well, whoever snacked on a little finger food."

Black used the toe of his shoe to prod the stumps of the dead man's missing digits.

The six men stepped into the elevator, descending into hell. Only one of them smiled.

CHAPTER 46

"Flight time," I said to Mason, "how long?"

I raised an eyebrow at Rourke's private plane. It looked like luxury, that was for sure, but we needed speed more than anything else right now.

"Ninety minutes," she answered, grabbing a gear bag from the trunk. "Give or take."

"That's pretty damn fast."

"We took the pleasure of upgrading Rourke's jet," said a voice from behind the plane. "Consider it the lovechild between a Gulfstream G-5 and Lockheed's F-35."

The voice was too familiar to me. No. Not her. Not now, damn it. Madison Archer walked into view with a rolling pelican case in tow.

"Captain West, good to see you again."

We both put on our best poker faces and gave the obligatory totally professional handshake. When I felt her palm in mine, it was like static arcing between us. There was so much I wanted to say to her. I needed to let her know I was sorry for keeping her at arm's distance but beg her to get as far away from me as possible. I wanted so badly to tell her that she needed to go deep underground, that I would promise to find her after. Instead, all I could do was ask what was in the pelican case.

"Rad suits with integrated detectors," she said. She didn't skip a beat in keeping up appearances. "Kara didn't give me much to work with as far as what we're up against with Morpheus, only that it's a Cold War weapon with possible nuclear or radioactive hazards, so I pulled some of the prototypes we've been developing for dirty bombs. The suits have an outer layer of dense polymer to stop beta particles, a liner layer of synthetic composite powder comparable to iron-rich volcanic ash to attenuate harmful radiation, and strategic shielding at the good bits—torso, groin, neck, armpits—made of a fine wire tungsten mesh which will block gamma and X-ray while remaining relatively flexible."

"Strategic shielding?" I said, arching an eyebrow.

"You know anyone else who can work with fine tungsten wire woven fabrics faster? I did what I could with the time provided, and this way it saves on weight."

"Lighter than lead, at least." I took the case from her, then cracked half a smile. "What are you calling them?"

"I said they were prototypes. I know Samuel Cain was all about his cute little nicknames, drawing on Norse, and Roman, and any other mythology he thought sounded cool, but I think coining a clever acronym is a little premature."

My smile held. I knew she got a kick out of being able to name new equipment, for her it was like discovering new land. She sighed at length and pinched the bridge of her nose.

"AEGIS," she admitted. "I like AEGIS. Advanced Emergency Gamma Irradiance Suit. Because it's a shield?"

Mason and I exchanged a look, then spoke at the same time.

"AEGIS is good."

Madison snapped immediately back into brilliant scientist mode, "The suits have an estimated protection threshold of five to seven

Sieverts. Estimated. I really want to stress that part. It's like a bullet-proof vest: you shoot enough bullets at it then it's going to break, and every second you're down there will be like you're taking rounds. If there's been a radiation release, you will be okay from the residual irradiation, but I wouldn't use these to go walking into any nuclear reactors any time soon."

"Noted," Mason said. She brushed past me, snatched the handle of the case, and walked right up to the plane. "Burning daylight, West."

Rain followed her up the steps to the cabin, which gave Madison and I precious seconds for a goodbye.

"I wanted to—"

"Don't," she said. "Whatever you want to say to me, you tell me when this is over."

"It's not safe. They have eyes and ears everywhere. You need to disappear."

She laughed. "Cole, whatever they're using to listen in and peek at us, I guarantee I make something better. Don't you go worrying about me, tough guy."

"Damn it, I'm serious," I said in a sharp whisper. "When Black . . . when he . . . "

"Cole," she said firmly. "I'm a big girl, and you said it yourself that he's headed to the same place you are. So, get a move on, and put that piece of shit in the ground."

I didn't know how I should say goodbye, or if Mason and Rain were watching, so all I could do was hold out my hand and wish her luck. It was a damn insult to her. It was a damn insult to whatever this thing budding between us could turn into. There was a very real chance we wouldn't see each other again. Maybe Black would get the best of me down in the Basement, or maybe Morpheus was more dangerous than we thought. But if Legion was watching us now, I couldn't endanger Madison further by letting them know how much she meant to me. So, a handshake was all I got. As if we were only coworkers. Nothing more.

Of all the suffering I'd endured the past two days, that hurt was a completely new one.

I turned and boarded the plane before I could accidentally hold onto Madison's hand just a second too long. Rain was already seated with her laptop open, working on decrypting Rourke's Basement files using the codes Mason had given her. Mason herself was in the cockpit, finishing the pre-flight checks.

"Here, I know you're geared up and loaded already, but I figured you were partial to that double-barrel of yours and these might come in handy," she said. She handed me two boxes of shotgun shells she'd pulled from the onboard armory. "White shells are the newest Hades loads. Armor-piercing incendiary shells; I've seen one burn through two car doors and still torch the guy on the other side."

"Haven't worked with these in a while. Last time, I cooked Samuel Cain's helicopter with some."

"Yeah, well I don't know why you stopped carrying them, but these are even better."

There wasn't exactly an easy way to say that firing off a load of flaming buckshot could trigger a PTSD flashback, so I avoided her fishing comment entirely. I could've made a smartass comment then, but this was really the closest Mason would ever be to doing something nice and I saw it for what it was. She hit a switch, and the plane's engines roared to life—much more powerful than I expected—and we taxied towards the runway.

"It's good to have you in the field," I said to her.

The sincerity seemed to throw her for a loop, as if she didn't know how to act when someone wasn't wearing that hard warrior mask. After a moment, her expression softened. She gave me the smallest of nods. Then something I would've thought impossible happened. She smiled. Despite needing to repay the blood debt written with Rourke's death, she was in her element. For the first time in a long time, Kara Mason was exactly where she was meant to be.

Fury or not, that had to feel good.

She hit the throttle, and Rourke's plane shot down the runway like a bullet. Madison hadn't been boasting about its speed. The landscape on the peripherals of the windshield blurred as Mason pushed it faster.

"They're a distraction," she said quietly once we were well in the air.

"What are?"

She scoffed. "Relationships, West."

"Don't know what you mean."

"You two aren't as good at acting as you think. I've pegged you two as an item for a while now, pretty sure Rourke knew for months."

I stirred uncomfortably in my seat. "Why wouldn't he say anything?"

Mason tapped a few buttons to set the autopilot, then turned to face me. "Either he didn't feel a need to bring it up until it served a purpose for him," she said, "or maybe you should consider the possibility that he actually saw you as an asset. Cracks and damages and all. And maybe having her kept you together enough for fieldwork. Regardless of what you might believe, Rourke thought you were good. That you could end up being one of the best."

It was hard to picture Rourke thinking that highly of me. Harder still was the gut punch realization that, if Mason was right, I would never be able to hear it from him directly.

"Also, you're an idiot," she said.

"No argument there."

"You should've kissed her goodbye. Let's just hope that Dr. Archer's smarter when it comes to her tech than she is in her taste in men," she said and prodded the pelican case with her boot heel.

"Still no argument here."

A screen near the controls showed our flight path to the Basement. Every second it got shorter, I couldn't help but see it as a fuse burning down.

DARK BEGINNINGS 9

Red was always his color, but now he was drowning in it. Crimson's blood spilled forth from half a dozen cuts across his torso, and all he could do was lay on his back as it filled his lungs.

It had all happened so fast. The procedure only took two minutes, and then Crimson and Childs entered to release Adrian from the table. The boy had smiled at them both. And then he took a pen from Childs' clipboard and stabbed it through her eye socket. Before either of them could so much as shout in surprise, he'd removed the pen and blinded her other eye, then pushed the maimed woman's flailing body into Crimson. They'd toppled over, her own blood splashing in his face and momentarily blinding him, as well.

She'd fallen to the ground, and then Adrian was there with a knife in hand. Where had he gotten it from?

"You always kept it at your hip," the young man said and, in the blink of an eye, he slipped it into Crimson's chest six times as easily as if he were made of butter.

The stabs were so quick, so precise, it wasn't until Crimson had fallen to the ground that they even began to bleed. But bleed they did, and now he would bleed to death.

"Adrian . . . ?" Crimson rasped, each breath a struggle as his body cavities filled with blood.

"It's a good knife but you can have it back." He straddled Crimson's chest, only to stick the blade up to the hilt in Crimson's sternum.

Crimson croaked. He could *taste* the steel in the bottom of his esophagus. His killer held the handle of the knife and used it to pull Crimson up to a half-seated position so they could see each other face to face. There was nothing in the young man's eyes. No remorse. No mercy. No light.

"Black . . ." Crimson realized with horror.

"In the flesh," Mr. Black said with a wicked smile. He gave the handle a twist and felt the crack of bone and fresh arterial spurt of Crimson's heart.

"Thanks to you. Now then, let's go see how the rest of our squad is doing, shall we?"

Rourke pushed into the hallway with no regard for clearing any corners. The three remaining members of Spectrum Squad—Cobalt, Jade, and Gold—flanked him with weapons up and at the ready. Rourke took one look around the room and there was a slow deliberate exhale from his nostrils.

"Holy fuck!" breathed Cobalt. "What the hell did this?"

Rourke didn't bother answering. The walls were splashed with red from the dozen slaughtered Darkheart technicians. Cut to ribbons seemed grossly understated to the condition they were left in. A bloody trail led from the procedure room at the end of the hall and, despite knowing the culprit was long gone, Rourke stormed ahead anyway.

"Oh, *damn*," cursed Jade as she stepped in behind Rourke and found her squad leader's body lying on the floor. His eyes stared lifelessly at the ceiling; his own knife plunged deep into his chest.

Forcing himself to see the scene analytically, Rourke took quick flicking glances around the room. Doctor Erin Childs' body was the only other one in the room. Her eyes were nothing but gouged out cavities, a final moment of anguish etched upon her face. The murder weapon in question, a blood-soaked pen, was discarded on the floor next to her.

A PA system blared on. Both Rourke and Spectrum flinched.

"Admiring my handiwork?" mocked Black through the speaker. "I admit, it was a bit rushed. Which is a shame since these two were the first kills that were truly all my own. Those others in the hallway outside were more fun. But really, I've been warming up for you, Father."

The lights went dark and there was an electronic whine as the room locked down. A moment later red emergency lights flipped on.

"Adrian," said Rourke. His booming voice was as unshaking as ever. "Stand down. There's no way out of this."

"*Not* Adrian," Black corrected. "Not anymore. Thanks to you, your good dead doctor on the floor there, all your wonderful therapy sessions, and the lovely jolt of Morpheus straight to Adrian's brain."

"Whatever went wrong in your procedure we can fix. You're *still* Adrian, no matter what you've convinced yourself. We plotted into uncertain waters, but we can still walk you back from them."

"Boring, boring, *boring,* Father," sighed Black. "I'd rather play a more interesting game. I've been prepping for a while now actually. All those times you were blanking bits and pieces of poor, traumatized, Adrian's memory, I was taking the time to set the groundwork. And now it's finally gametime for all five of us. I hope you have more fun than Crimson did."

"You son of a bitch," hissed Jade.

"Who wants to play next?"

The electronic lock on the door beeped as it disengaged. Rourke signaled the three operators, and they pushed back out into the hallway outside. The red emergency lights overhead painted the grisly bloodshed they'd already seen in a new otherworldly color.

"Pick a door," mused Black. Three doors in the hallway unlocked. "What've you got to lose? Just remember: nobody lives forever. I'm here to remind you of that."

Gold adjusted his glasses. "Are we actually going to let him split us up?"

"Fuck that," Cobalt scoffed.

"Come now," Black chimed in. "There's only one elevator out of this facility, and it'll stay disabled until we narrow you contestants down to one. You can play by the rules, or you can starve to death in this hallway. The problem with Mr. Rourke maintaining such secrecy in these facilities is no one will *ever* come looking for you here."

"He killed the major," said Jade with a barely restrained snarl. "I don't give a fuck if he is a kid. He's dead."

Without another word she chose a door and pushed through, weapon up and at the ready, with no hesitation at all. The electronic lock engaged red and latched behind her.

"Jade!" Gold shouted.

Rourke took one glance at Spectrum's tech expert and could tell he was cracking apart. And, like a dog smelling fear, it would only draw Black to him sooner.

Cobalt sighed and reluctantly walked through the middle door. "I've got a demo-charge with your name on it, Mr. Black."

Gold, with far less confidence, defaulted to the last door available. At a loss for any final defiant threat, the man gave one last uncertain look to Rourke before stepping through the threshold.

Once all three doors were sealed behind their respective operators, Rourke looked up to where he knew the security camera was watching him.

"What?" he asked. "No door for me? I don't get to play your little game?"

There was no answer at first. Rourke fixed his unblinking attention at the expressionless camera, waiting for Black to speak again. Then, another door unlocked and automatically opened. Rourke peered inside. It was one of the security substations complete with a row of monitors. From the looks of it, everything was locked out except for the screens.

"You don't get to play yet," he said. "First you get to watch."

"Watch what?"

"A demonstration of the weapon you've created."

CHAPTER 47

Our wheels touched down on a short private airstrip adjacent to the Basement. A thermal scan as we descended showed no one on the ground. Nobody alive, at least. Rain had finally gotten into the security systems, but everything was already unlocked. I knew it for what it was: an invitation. Black wanted us to come down there, down into the dark. I was more than willing to accept the offer.

The camera feeds showed that nothing had left the facility since Black and his Legion friends had gone down, which meant we weren't too late. Yet.

"Watch our backs," I said to Rain. Mason and I approached the elevator. "I want to know where Morpheus is, and I don't want Black sneaking up on us."

Rain's voice came through the comm channel. "The Basement has seven levels. The top two are leftover from when it was a research facility and are unused, third should be living space and administrative areas, four through six are all the deep-storage for dark tech, and the seventh looks like the engineering floor where the generators are."

We walked by a dead scientist; he was covered in strange wounds I had trouble identifying but I knew the knife-puncture in his throat the second I saw it. Black's handiwork for sure. I did a quick pat down of him and found a badge that ID'd him as a Doctor David Bertrand. Among his pockets were a few prescription bottles.

"Anything?" Mason asked.

"Maybe," I said as I looked over the bottles. "Prazosin, Clonidine, and some KI pills. Potassium Iodide. Both are nearly empty, which is interesting since it looks like the prescriptions were filled just two weeks ago."

"Potassium Iodide prevents your thyroid from absorbing radiation, probably a prophylactic for whatever weapons are down there. What are the other two?"

I found myself picturing my very own bottles of the same medication I'd left back on the plane. "Various uses, not the least of which is PTSD. Helps with nightmares and other sleep disturbances. Or so I hear."

Talking about it threatened to breathe new life into the fires that haunted me, but I managed to wrestle those memories down deep back to the bottom of my mind.

"Yellow Pages, you find which floor Morpheus is stored on?"

"Morpheus will be on six," Mason answered for her. "The levels are based upon hazard. The deeper we go the more dangerous. Six."

"Those generators must be something real scary," I joked as the elevator doors closed behind us. It fell on deaf ears. Tough crowd. The elevator hummed as we began our descent. I felt the pressure in my ears as we went deeper and deeper.

"Abandon all hope, ye who enter here," said Mason. I think it was her own form of a joke. There was a blip on my wrist-mounted computer screen. A quick glance showed me that we were already picking up rising radiation levels, which was a little unnerving considering we hadn't reached the first basement level yet.

"Yellow Pages, picking rising rad levels. Dose rate of point one milli-Seiverts."

Quick lesson on irradiation: dose rate was roughly the amount of radiation you were exposed to per hour, and total dose was how much you'd already taken. Think of a speedometer and an odometer. A tenth of a milli-Seiverts per hour wasn't bad, it was equivalent to getting a chest x-ray every hour. Elevated, sure, but not exactly Chernobyl territory just yet. I was still glad we'd both preemptively taken doses of KI tablets.

The readout bar on my wrist-computer went higher.

"We're up to point five milli-Seivert," I said. Mason had the stock of a 5.7mm P90 submachine gun pulled tight to her shoulder, but her eyes were glued to her own detector.

"One milli-Seivert" she breathed. "What can the AEGIS stand?"

"Six Seiverts," Rain answered. "But I feel I should remind you that you are both wearing *prototypes* and maybe we shouldn't push them unnecessarily."

I tried to give Mason a reassuring shrug, "Metric system at work. We could stay here for six thousand hours. This is like getting a CT scan every month."

The elevator dinged as it reached the first floor.

"Or drinking water from the Fukushima evacuation zone," Rain added. "Toxin: get out, now."

I tapped Mason to indicate I was moving and stepped out into the hallway outside. Everyone on Cerberus Squad had learned that when Rain was running our overwatch, we jumped when she said jump. There wasn't time to ask why she was advising things, and our lives quite literally depended on us trusting her.

Red emergency lights flashed slowly along the walls. The hallway Mason and I found ourselves in was thankfully empty.

"Okay, Yellow Pages, want to tell us what we're looking for if Morpheus is five levels below us?"

"Security station," she said. "Someone disabled the safety protocols in the entire Basement. That's why the radiation is leaking from the Morpheus device. I'm locked out, I need you to get to the station and link me in so I can turn it all back on. Left out of the elevator, then follow the blue line on the floor. It'll take you right there."

"Got it. You got eyes on Black?"

"Negative. Cameras are down on floors five through seven. Too much interference. Process of elimination? They're holed up there."

We pushed forward. It was the emptiness of the Basement that was getting to me. I expected to come down into a bloodbath, but so far we were greeted only with a suffocating stillness. I descended into this darkness eager for answers and instead it was like the universe was laughing at me with more blank spaces.

"Body," Mason said. I'd spotted it right as she said it. Another lab-coat wearing scientist was facedown just outside the security station. I covered her as she took a knee to give the corpse a once over. "Funny, there's no wounds. Radiation isn't high enough to have killed him?"

She rolled the scientist onto his back. The man's dead eyes were wide open, frozen in whatever their last moments of terror had been.

"Heart attack maybe?" I said, only half-kidding. "Put yourself in his shoes. Knowing what's held downstairs and then alarms start going off that there's a containment failure?"

"Maybe," she said and started to frisk his pockets. "Curious. Check these out."

She pulled three prescription bottles out of his lab-coat pocket. Prazosin, Clonidine, and KI.

"He kept it on him," I noted.

"Come again?"

"The Prazosin and Clonidine were right there at his hip. Why would he need it on his person? It's a daily dose, he could've just as easily kept it in his medicine cabinet or at his bedside."

Mason held the bottles up to her eye before stashing them in a pouch on her vest. Something wasn't right here. Shit, nothing had felt right all week but this here was like we were about to go fully off the rails. That gravity I'd been getting pulled by seemed to be drawing me closer towards the edge of some endless pit. And, God help me, I was willing to leap into it if it would mean getting my retribution.

"That's not the only weird thing," she said.

I arced an eyebrow in her direction.

"This makes two big brain types in research get-ups. Why would you need lab coats or active scientists for a defunct storage facility?"

I mulled it over. "The old man had secrets from everyone, Sledgehammer. You included."

"West, you taste metal?" Mason asked.

"Callsigns only, Sledgehammer," I said.

But I did. There was no other way to describe it, just a strange metallic taste like ozone in the air after a lightning strike. We shouldn't feel anything through our suits, though. I checked my wrist and was reassured to find that readings were holding steady at five milli-Seivert. The levels weren't deadly, but considering how much concrete separated each level of the Basement, and there were five floors between us and Morpheus, it just promised that it would get worse the deeper we got.

"Toxin, I need you to plug me in," Rain said. "I have no eyes on the bottom floors, which means we have no way of knowing how hot it is down there. Unless you want to melt into a puddle, get me an uplink so I can get these systems online!"

"Yeah, yeah, I hear you."

Mason was already in the security station, which was little more than a large booth surrounded on three sides with bulletproof glass and security monitors. Weapon lockers lined the back wall. I took notice of the fact that nobody had even bothered to unlock them when they'd come under attack. Too many questions, too few answers down here.

"Computer's dead," said Mason. She tapped the keyboard and moved a mouse around but the monitor stayed black. "Yellow Pages, we've got emergency lights flashing. Looks like something tripped a breaker. Please tell me there's a quick fix that doesn't involve going all the way down to the generators on seven."

"Affirm, Sledgehammer," she answered. "Just around the corner should be a utility room with a switch box."

"I got it," I said to Mason. "Watch the hallway. Keep the comm traffic active. Back in two."

She gave me a simple nod and took a position watching the corridor that led to the elevator.

I followed Rain's directions further down the hallway, took a left, and kicked my way through a locked door to the utility room. The panel for the breaker was at the back, I slung my rifle and made my way for it. Just as I opened it and started to flip the appropriate switches, a rapid beeping came from my wrist computer. I looked at the display.

The rate had spiked to 100 milli-Seivert. Firmly in Chernobyl territory now, and not just at the powerplant but dead center *inside* the reactor.

I tapped it a few times, certain that an increase that sudden had to be an error, but before I could clear it up a faint scent found its way to my nostrils.

It was an all too memorable smell, and it wasn't the metallic taste from before. No, this was the stench of burnt hair. Scorched flesh. Melted skin and singed clothing. It was the reek of what haunted me the most: the smell of a human body burning alive.

The door opened with a creak behind me, and I could hear the licking flames crackle as I turned to face it. But what stood waiting for me in the doorway defied reason. A man, muscular in build, burned alive before me. The flesh peeled away from his face until it was nothing but a scorched skull wreathed in flame. A red, raw, charred arm reached in my direction, and the burning man stepped into the room. It filled with his choking smoke.

The burning man screamed and ran right for me.

CHAPTER 48

I thought he was coming to me for help. But then as I tried to wrap my mind around what I was seeing, and how that scream was so full of agony and anger, I realized too quickly that the burning man meant to share his pain with me. His footsteps left small bits of flame upon the floor as he closed the distance. Flecks of charred flesh and ash dusted from him in his wake like blackened snow.

The moment of hesitation passed, and I lifted my rifle. At least, I tried to. It became impossibly heavy, as if stuck to my side. Thinking it somehow had gotten snagged up on some of my gear, I shook the sling off my shoulder, let the weapon fall to the floor, and drew my sidearm. I lined up a shot at center-mass, more than eager to put him out of his misery, and squeezed the trigger.

Except the trigger wouldn't budge.

The trigger weight on my .45 was only about four pounds, and I was easily pressing with three times that, yet it was practically cemented in place. My hands trembled from the effort, my sight-alignment on the pistol's front post was lost, and in that span of a breath the burning man was upon me. I was smothered by the heat and stench of scorched hair and flesh coming off him. One of his hands, burned away to nothing but blackened bony digits, reached for my neck as I found my back to the wall.

My heart hammered in my chest. I swung a heavy right hook, but it was like I was punching underwater. There was no power behind the punch. No speed. By the time my knuckles connected with his charred jaw, it carried no force at all. He batted my hands away, the flames licking at my skin through my suit's sleeves. The burning man's hand wrapped around my throat. My airway closed in his grasp, and he threw me to the ground behind him.

The entire time he screamed, a bellow that sounded to my ears like a roaring fire. Uncontrollable. Unfathomable in its fury. On and on it went. The louder he screamed, the hotter and higher the flames upon him seemed to grow. They ate at his flesh yet he did not falter. He did not flinch. He did not stop.

The fire spread from him to the floor and walls. In seconds they climbed until the room became a furnace. I tasted smoke through my mask and choked on it. I scrambled backwards on hands and feet, trying to put as much distance between myself and this monster as I could. My hands felt cool metal behind me. My rifle.

I grabbed it up and took aim. This time it didn't get snagged on my side. I pulled the trigger and held it down until the magazine went dry. I didn't know I was screaming until the gunfire ceased. But the burning man was unfazed. It was as if the bullets had just passed right through him. I reloaded and fired again. Nothing.

The burning man's anguished roar started to sound like laughter.

My own scream turned into a panicked whimper. I don't know if I've ever felt so powerless before. And, God help me, I was scared. Something was wrong with me. I shook like a child. Fortitude built from years of facing fear evaporated as that scream tore into my ears, sounding like razor blades slicing across my eardrums. None of it made any sense, but that didn't matter. All that mattered was that I knew this thing was going to kill me.

"Cole . . ."

The thing spoke. Its lips were gone, its throat too impossibly burned to give it a voice, yet it called my name. Its voice like dried leaves scraping together.

"Cole!"

"Fuck away from me!" I shouted, yet the shout came forth as barely a whisper.

"Cole!" This time, it sounded more human. Almost as if the vocal cords belonged to someone else.

Somehow, I stood. The burning man was a mere arm's length away, and I'd risen to die on my feet. I'd been witness to the unnatural in Black Spear. Men reduced to rabid animals that spewed blood to spread their madness, future tech that seemed pulled from science fiction movies made into reality, and cultists whose zealous beliefs in their rituals made me question the very rules of science. As the burning man neared me, I accepted that he was some demon cast forth from hell. And he walked the Earth to take me from it.

"Cole!" the thing said.

My ears bled just from listening. The fire crept across the floor from its feet like some living thing, and there was nowhere for me to go. It came upon me, climbing up my legs and covering me to my face.

A scream escaped up my throat unrestrained, but it dribbled from my lips barely a whimper. A pathetic moan. I writhed on the ground as the fire burned right through my AEGIS. It blackened my skin next and melted the mask from my face. I threw my arms out to either side as I burned, submitting to the pain and welcoming it to finish me.

"Cole!" said the burning man, now standing right in front of me.

Its voice sounded . . . feminine?

"Please!"

I huddled to the ground and felt very cold. Blackness enveloped me. The darkness was so suffocating, and I thought that this is what death must be like. An endless nothing that awaited me, me and all the friends I'd failed.

"Cole, please . . ." the woman's voice pleaded.

No.

This couldn't be.

Jesus, what was happening? Thinking was hard. Like my brain was clogged in the muck. And then I heard a different voice. Not the woman's, but a familiar friend.

"Wake up, bud," Kelly said.

My eyes snapped open.

The fire was gone. The burning man was gone. My suit was intact. My whole body quaked violently. I finally clenched my hands into fists just to get them under control. Cold sweat trickled down my back. I couldn't stand. Instead, I pulled myself onto one knee.

"What the fuck is happening?"

DARK BEGINNINGS 10

Gold trembled as he descended into darkness. His door led to a stairwell down to a lower maintenance area, which unfortunately for him had far less emergency lighting than the hallway above. He was no coward by any measure, but the circumstances on hand had him quite literally shaking in his boots. He'd seen what Adrian Rasp was capable of when he went dark. The killer within Adrian was dangerous enough, but now Gold was playing Mr. Black's game and all on his own.

With the darkness giving him no other option, Gold fished his phone from his pants pocket and thumbed on the flashlight. The beam cut through the shadows, and Gold sliced it away back and forth. The device gave him a bit of comfort. Crimson had his authority, Cobalt had his detonator and explosives, Jade had her knife, but tech was always Gold's tool of choice.

Keeping his eye on the front-sight of his weapon, Gold flicked with his peripherals on his phone's screen as he attempted to access the facility's systems. Mr. Black was an unrepentant monster, but how savvy could he be with computer systems? There was a reason Crimson had kept him behind sniper scopes and out of Gold's mission support lane.

"Come on, come on," he said with grit teeth.

If Gold could get into the network, then they could circumvent Black's entire stupid game. If he hadn't been distracted by his nerves, he would've thought of that immediately. It did not go unnoticed that Crimson would've immediately caught their mistake.

Suddenly the emergency lights went dead, and he was blinded for a moment when the brilliant white lights switched back on. The only problem was it hadn't been Gold to trigger them.

"Tsk, tsk," Black said with disappointment. "No cheating, Mr. Gold."

The image on Gold's screen was replaced with a frowning emoji face. Before Gold could think of anything else, his phone grew hot. It took only a moment. And in that moment, he mistakenly thought it was simply heating up from the flashlight, but then sparks flew from the device as a boobytrapped thermite charge ignited. There was a white-hot flash that he was too busy squinting at to realize his entire hand had burned away. Charred flesh sloughed from his bones as the fragments of the molten phone dripped to the floor.

The pain came then. Overwhelming. Excruciating. It sent rivers of lightning up the mangled stump at his wrist and sent Gold hobbling to a knee. He was forced to drop his pistol as his one good hand reached up to the handrail to keep from falling down the stairs. The handgun clattered along the concrete steps to the bottom. One second, he felt agonizing heat, and in the next Gold practically shivered.

I'm going into shock.

"Always so reliant on your gear. Always so comfortable staying apart from the *real* bloodshed," Black said.

Except this time his voice did not come disembodied from any speaker but above Gold at the top of the stairs.

"I placed that thermite in your phone last night."

His former ally stood silhouetted in front of the bright white lights, soaked to the elbow in blood. The edges of Gold's eyesight blurred. He risked a look behind him where his lost pistol lay hopelessly out of reach. With a desperate grunt, he pushed off the handrail and bounded toward the bottom to retrieve it. Gold didn't make it down two steps before Black's foot cracked across the side of his neck like an axe into a tree. Everything below Gold's throat instantly went numb and his body rag-dolled, hitting each and every hard-edged concrete step along the way.

The broken mess of Gold's body came to a flopping end at the bottom where he let out one final, strained, exhale while blood oozed forth from his broken skull.

Cobalt came prepared. He *always* came prepared. He laughed at people who said, 'don't bring a knife to a gunfight' because he had no qualms bringing explosive charges on every mission. Today was no different. He had no intention of playing into Adrian's psychotic gauntlet. Sure, he'd made a big display of reluctantly choosing his door, but that was show for the camera. He'd stuck his wad of chewing gum into the door latch, which kept it from fully sealing behind him and had just as quickly slipped back into the previous hallway.

Unsurprisingly, neither Gold nor Jade had been clever enough to make it back. Jade was too stubborn and currently too angry to do anything but bull straight into the fight. Whereas Gold would likely need a moment to get his wits about him before he remembered he could hack the locking mechanism.

"Damned stupid genius," mused Cobalt.

He approached the locked down elevator. Sure, there may be a more subtle way out of this, but Cobalt hardly had a reputation for subtlety. He'd set a charge, blow the elevator doors, and haul ass up the shaft. Once above the surface, he'd call in the cavalry. Sometimes the only way to beat a game was by not playing. All Gold and Jade needed to do was not get themselves killed while Cobalt went and saved everyone's asses.

It occurred to him that Mr. Rourke was nowhere to be found. The big spooky bastard had always given Cobalt the creeps, and he wasted no more time wondering just where Rourke had gotten off to. Holed up in a supply closet, maybe? Already escaped through a secret private elevator only he knew about?

Cobalt smirked with amusement. The truth was he couldn't get out of this hole fast enough. He reached into the pouch on his belt to retrieve the explosives, more than ready to make his own door and get the hell out of here.

He prepped the explosive but just as he readied to place the charges against the elevator door, motion at the end of the hallway caught his attention. Cobalt whirled around, dropping the plastique at his feet and whipping his pistol up in a two-handed grip all in one fluid motion.

Black stood across the corridor from him, leaning against the wall as casually as possible.

"You're too predictable. It's boring, really. No artistry. No beauty. Just a hammer born to swing and smash at things."

Cobalt stood his ground, quickly eying Black up and down and seeing he held no weapons. "Well, you know what they say about everything looking like a nail."

If Cobalt aiming a gun at his face worried him in the slightest, it didn't show. Instead, he examined a fingernail without a care in the world.

"You really should change them more often."

"Change what?"

Black slowly smiled. There was such malice in that grin, it gave Cobalt pause. He hesitated.

"Your detonator frequencies," said Black.

Too late he saw the identical remote detonator held in Black's hand. Cobalt's blue eyes went wide as he looked at the prepped explosive charge on the ground at his feet. Black hit one button, eyes aglitter as the charge detonated. The blast was directed upward, turning the man into nothing more than a geyser of meat that splattered across the ceiling.

Black finished inspecting his fingernail and patted the detonator with genuine appreciation before stowing it in his pocket. There was something intimate about getting up close, but he had to admit that he'd grown to share Cobalt's appreciation for bombs. Black tipped an imaginary hat at the gory chunks splattered across the hallway and ceiling. Cobalt's lessons on bombs would continue to prove useful.

He hummed to himself as he turned to the door Jade had gone through.

"Two down, one to go."

She was in her element. At the end of the day, Jade was a fighter. Take away the tech, take away the overwatch, take away the whole squad, and she would still be a fighter. It didn't matter when there were only the red emergency lights overhead, and when the normal lights came back on it didn't change a damn thing. She would kill this monster.

The loud boom she heard a moment ago came too close to be anywhere but from within the facility. It sounded like Cobalt was getting up to his usual fun, and a part of Jade hoped there was enough of Black leftover for her to still cut to pieces.

Jade stalked forward on the balls of her feet. Out of sheer habit she'd pulled her green hood tight over her head. It always helped her focus. Every muscle was ready to strike in whichever direction the danger came from. She gripped her sidearm at the high ready position, but she wanted to use the knife. A bullet would be too quick for what he deserved. Skewering Crimson like that? On his own blade, no less? Yeah. She owed Black a whole lot of pain.

Jade's door had led her to what appeared to be mostly living areas for the facility's staff. Modest sleeping quarters, a quaint little fitness room with treadmills and a few free weights, and a small cafeteria style room lined with tables. She stepped into the cafeteria and nodded to herself.

Fuck this cat and mouse shit.

She looked around the room and spotted a security camera in the corner. Shooting a hate-filled stare at it, she held up her handgun in plain view, removed the magazine, and then cycled the slide back to eject the round from the chamber. Then, she placed the empty weapon on the table and slowly drew her knife from her belt. Her shoulders heaved with every breath that filled her lungs like fire.

"You going to keep me waiting all night?" she asked. "You and me: let's go."

A form peeled itself away from the shadows outside the doorway, and he appeared. There was something unrecognizable about him. Sure, the looks and features were the same as the young kid she'd worked with for months now, but everything else appeared different. The way he moved. The expression on his face. The emptiness of his eyes. A night and day difference.

"No tricks," she said, flipping her combat knife back and forth between a forward and reverse grip. "No bullshit. Just a private bloodbath."

The smile that stretched across Black's face was nothing less than jubilant. "That's the spirit."

He approached her unarmed, but that didn't mean shit to her. Jade snarled and slashed with her knife in a lightning quick back and forth motion. The edge of her blade whistled through the air, and Black nimbly side-stepped out of the way. She continued to press her attack. A thrust that would've pierced his throat, a wide sweeping crescent cut that would open him up from neck to navel, and a quick double stab that would take either eye out.

If only any of the strikes had landed.

Black slipped each of her attacks as easily as if she was moving in slow motion. When he deftly checked her backhanded slash with the point of his elbow, she realized the truth. He wasn't just moving faster than her. He was anticipating what her next move was before she'd even done it. Taking backsteps to position himself outside her attack before her arm could swing, dropping his level and ducking the cut even as she was making it.

Don't get sloppy now, she scolded herself.

But all the same she felt her frustration getting the best of her. Desperate to lay just a single blow on her opponent, Jade leapt at him like a feral animal and drove the point of her knife for his chest. Black dodged, shifting to the side and fully outstretching his arm to clothesline her. He chopped the side of his pointer finger's knuckle straight into her neck.

Jade felt her windpipe close up. She skidded to a stop. Her knife remained in her hand, and she lashed out even as she choked. Still, her blade touched nothing but empty air. Every second that passed felt like an eternity as she tried to force breath through her swollen throat, to no avail. Though she kept trying to keep up her flurry of attacks, each swing grew more and more sluggish.

Her vision rimmed with black. She gagged and choked, furious at herself for failing at this task. Furious even more that she'd been lain so low by a *single* fucking hit. One final time she swung at Black's neck, but his hand snapped up and effortlessly caught her wrist. He squeezed. Hard. Her knife fell from her hand.

Lack of oxygen finally took its toll, and she fell to her knees. Black lowered himself down with her, one of his hands clutched around her throat. His grip was concrete, but at the same time there was almost a tenderness in the way he held her neck. Too late she saw the truth. It wasn't her that he was so infatuated with, it was her *death*.

Black stared at her with rapt attention, watching as she choked miserably.

"Disappointing," he breathed. "You're not even worth killing, are you?"

Somehow she mustered the will to spit in his face. That only seemed to amuse him more.

"Maybe next time you'll put up more of a fight," he said, wiping away the spittle that stained his cheek. "A little . . . *incentive* may be needed. Something to remind you of me. Something to fuel that fire."

Jade's eyes bulged as blackness reached out its arms to take her. Any second now she'd pass out, but she would stare this son of a bitch down as long as she could.

"I made this just for you," said Black. From seemingly out of nowhere he produced a long stiletto. The blade looked strange, as if it were chipped from black glass. "Obsidian. Easy to get past metal detectors. Now, try to hold still."

Despite her injured throat, and still being on the verge of unconsciousness, Jade managed to scream as he carved into her face.

The woman fell to the ground, and Black smiled proudly at his handiwork. Yes, this one was touched by death now. Should she come back, she would be all the better for it. Right as Black was wondering if perhaps he had shown too much restraint with the mark he'd graced her with, a gunshot ripped through the air.

Black spun around, his obsidian dagger in hand, and found himself looking at Rourke. Gray smoke trailed from the end of his gun barrel and the fist that held it was steady as stone.

"You going to bring me in, Father?" Black asked. "Get a peek under the hood and see if you can figure out what went wrong here?

Or, maybe, everything *did* go right?"

Rourke squeezed the trigger, and a bullet tore through the fabric of Black's shirt right at the shoulder. He'd missed by millimeters. Missed on purpose.

Black arched an eyebrow playfully, "Struck a nerve?"

"Why did you do it?" Rourke asked him. "These were your teammates."

Black looked from Rourke down to Jade's broken form on the floor. "Why? Why not. Life and death is just a matter of time, and death always wins. My eyes are open to that now. I'm just speeding up the process for everyone."

"Drop the knife, Adrian."

"*You* opened my eyes."

"I won't say it again."

"*You* gifted me this. And in return, I'll share this gift with the world."

"Final warning."

Black's knife whistled through the air, straight as an arrow, and Rourke shifted to take the knife to the shoulder rather than his face. It sank an inch deep, and in the time it took him to reassess his aim Black was already on top of him. He didn't so much as hit Rourke as he dismantled him. A dizzying combination of quick thumping punches that broke down his shooting stance, a kick to the inside of Rourke's thigh that hobbled him, and a chop with the edge of his hand that ripped the pistol from Rourke's fingers. Black scooped it up and pressed the barrel up behind Rourke's ear against his jaw.

They looked each other in the eyes then. Maybe not seeing anything recognizable in each other, or perhaps Rourke saw something of a mirror in Black's eyes that scared him. Nietzsche warned about staring into the abyss, and in that moment Rourke thought that for the first time he fully understood what the philosopher meant. There was an abyss staring back at him, and it was an abyss of his own making.

Black pulled the trigger.

CHAPTER 49

"Cole!" Rain screamed.

A tremor ran through my hand as I tapped my earbud. "Call—callsigns only, Yellow Pages."

I went to retrieve my rifle, then left it where it lay when I saw that I'd completely expended my ammo for it. I couldn't remember the last time my hands shook this badly. I told myself it was just adrenaline running its course, but that lie got caught in my throat and nearly choked me. I was scared shitless, plain and simple.

"I kind of threw that to the wind when you didn't respond the first ten times!"

"Yeah, well about that—"

"Never mind, Toxin, get back to Sledgehammer, *now*!"

I snatched my sidearm from the ground and bashed through the door of the utility room, leaving the mystery of what I'd just experienced in my taillights. I found Mason on the floor. She held a double-edged stiletto in a death-grip but floundered about on the ground. While she slashed wildly at the air with her knife, her other hand reached up and tore her mask off her face. She made choking gasps and clutched at her own throat.

"Yellow Pages, what the fuck is happening?" I asked.

I took a knee next to Mason, pinning her arm to the ground to keep her from cutting me. Her eyes darted around the room, focusing on strange unseen things.

"There was a radiation spike a minute ago at the same time you went dark on me," she said. "You both started acting weird. Next thing I know, you snap out of it but she just stopped breathing."

I twisted the stiletto out of Mason's hand. She fought back with the wiry strength of a cornered animal, making a damned challenge out of it. Her mouth moved like a fish out of water. I checked her airway but it was clear. Mason thrashed on the ground as I tried to make sense of what I was witnessing. It was like she was drowning on dry land.

Precious seconds ticked away as her face grew purple.

"She's choking, Toxin," said Rain. "I think you're gonna have to give her a tracheotomy, and do it fast!"

I took just another moment to look at the strangeness in front of me. I opened the med kit at my side. I wasn't even sure what I was going to reach for. Bandages, antiseptic? I considered using Mason's stiletto to open an airway in her throat, before I made up my mind.

"No," I said, taking a different item form the med-pouch on Mason's hip, "I need to wake her up."

I stuck the adrenaline needle in her thigh and hit the plunger. Mason's eyes shot wide, her pupils gone to pinpricks, and she sucked in a desperate lungful of air. A second later, she shoved away from me, rolled towards her knife, and came to her feet with it ready in hand.

"West?" she asked.

Her eyes darted around the room, and she reversed the stiletto in her grip. She backed her way into a corner as if she wasn't sure whether I was a friend or a threat.

"I'm really starting to feel like a broken record about the callsigns here."

I backed off to give Mason some space; both to collect my thoughts and so she could bring herself back down to earth. The security station's computer had been smashed. I could only assume in Mason's episode she'd knocked it over. So much for Rain enabling the safety protocols.

I pulled Dr. Bertrand's pill bottles out and passed them to Mason. "Take two of each."

Mason eyed them warily, and while she must've thought it a weird instruction it was no weirder than what we'd both just experienced. She popped the caps off both and swallowed the pills dry. While she did, I reexamined my wrist display.

Dose rate was holding at 20 milli-Seivert. Severe, anyone not rocking a AEGIS would be facing acute radiation sickness.

"I think I know what's going on here."

"I'm all ears," she said. She found her P90 submachine gun and checked to make sure it was loaded.

"Morpheus. What if its radiation was, I don't know, different? Everyone that works here having PTSD medication can't be a coincidence. What if it was a preventative dosage just like the iodide tablets?"

"What are you saying? That the radiation is, what? Causing hallucinations instead of tumors?"

"I'm saying you and I were just sleeping with our eyes open. Some sort of waking nightmare."

"That would explain why the adrenaline snapped you out of it," said Rain. "And why Toxin came through."

"Why is that?" Mason asked, clearly bitter that I'd been affected differently.

"Because I've been taking those for months," I offered, raising my chin at the pill bottles.

Mason squared her shoulders and nodded. I was surprised how quickly she had come around to this new theory, but then again, I imagine she'd seen more than her fair share of the unbelievable after working alongside Rourke for so long.

Back in the hallway I found all the other doors had electronic locks marked red. When I tried to open one, the handle wouldn't even turn. It looked like whatever mayhem Legion had worked on the security systems had thrown the Basement into some partial lockdown. I came to a door with a greenlit lock, inside was what looked like a research area. Lab equipment and plenty of computers lined the wall.

"Didn't you say this place was decommissioned a long time ago?" I asked.

"That's what the report says," Rain answered. "Why?"

I ran a thumb along the top of the computer monitor. Not a speck of dust collected on my glove tip. "Because this computer has been used recently."

I pulled what looked like a thumb drive from my pocket and plugged it into the computer. It was a mobile uplink that would let Rain work her magic and get into whatever secrets the hard drive held.

"I don't think this is connected to the security systems, but pull what you can. Sledgehammer and I are pushing on."

"Gotcha, Boss."

I eyed Mason's submachine gun with unrestrained jealousy as we worked through the floor.

"I'm glad one of us isn't down to their pistol," I said.

A strange expression fell across her face.

"I threw it away," she said. "It was too heavy to swim with. I was sinking."

I filed that bit away for later, and didn't press her further.

We made our way to the stairwell, ready to delve deeper but fully aware what awaited us. Locked, just like the rest of the hallway.

"Yellow Pages, gonna need a different route. Stairs are locked off."

"Only other way is the elevator, Toxin."

Mason hissed, "Just pop one of those Hades shells on the lock and let's fucking go."

"Not that door," said Rain. "You want to get through that, you'll need a weapon that's measured in megatons rather than barrel gauge."

I rapped a knuckle on the steel door and frowned. It felt as solid as a bank vault.

"We're wasting time we don't have, damn it. The AEGIS suits won't hold up forever, and the deeper we go the quicker this candle burns."

As if to reemphasize my point, our wrist displays beeped to warn us that both our AEGISs had just crossed the one Seivert total absorbed threshold. Given the dose rates up until this point, that math wasn't mathing. Not for the first time I thought the Morpheus radiation was playing by some funky rules.

Just as I turned to move back to use the elevator, I heard a *ping* further down the hall. One of the doors had turned green.

"Trap," Mason said bluntly.

"No shit."

We stacked up outside the door, then I shouldered through and she covered left. But there was no one inside. No one living at least. It was a break room of some sort. Three bodies were inside, two wearing lab-coats and one in security fatigues. The security guard's pistol was in hand, its slide locked back on an empty chamber, with brass casings littering the ground around him. I squatted down and looked from his perspective, finding a collection of bullet holes on the far wall. He'd been shooting at nothing. It looked like he'd used the last round on himself.

The two science types were worse off. One had pulled a fire-axe from the wall and taken it to the other. Both his legs had been lopped off at the knee, and the axe itself had split his head so deeply, the blade came to rest between his collar bones. The axe-wielder himself was laying on his back with eyes staring dead at the ceiling. All the fingers on one hand were chopped off; judging by the axe nearby he'd done the deed himself. He looked like a vegetable, and a check of his pulse showed he'd gone some time ago.

There was a cheesy motivational poster hung on the break room wall. It showed a man scaling a mountain with a triumphant smile on his face and sported two simple words: No Fear. Except, the axe-wielder had used one of his severed fingers like a marker to add some color to it. Blood dripped down the poster's surface. More of it had drawn a chilling frown over the man on the poster's smile, and two new letters were scrawled in large grisly marks.

The additional letters changed the message of the poster entirely: Know Fear.

This wasn't a trap after all. It was more show and tell.

I considered how lucky Mason and I had been that we were in separate rooms when the rad spike hit us. I could have easily shot her dead by accident, or she could have gutted me with that stiletto of hers. Seeing the break room murder scene started to put into perspective what use Legion would have of Morpheus.

We returned to the elevator, wary of any more doors unlocking that contain crazies who were still alive this time. While Mason covered our rear, I hit the button to call the elevator.

"Toxin, you have a second?" Rain asked.

"Go."

"Okay, something hinky is definitely going on. I'm working on breaking through this hard drive—give me about two more minutes on that—but the date stamps on some of these files? They're new. Like, as of last week new."

"I'm thinking this shelved Morpheus project was a little less shelved than we've been told," I said.

"Looks that way. Okay. Whoa. There's a lot of info here. Looks like everything Morpheus related diverges under two umbrellas of research, a Morpheus Engine and something labeled ... Project: Darkheart? That mean anything to anyone?"

Mason stiffened. She tried to mask it by sweeping her P90 back towards the stairwell, but I still caught it.

"Sledge, if you—"

The elevator door dinged and hands grabbed me from behind. The elevator occupant pulled me off balance and into the car. I landed on the crumpled body of a second person, a quick glance at his bloody face looked like he'd been beaten to death and there were a few stab wounds at his neck.

"Get away from me!" the man yelled and kicked at me on the floor.

His eyes frantic, his face feverish, he held a blood-stained ball-point pen. A curious murder weapon. I'd be downright insulted if that's how I died. Mason whipped her P90 at him and fired, but he got a lucky slap at it and bullets riddled the wall just above my head. I drew my Boomstick, stood, and pressed both barrels up under his chin. I was hoping that it would snap him out of his craze. That the threat of buckshot to the skull would somehow scare him back to reality.

Instead, he tried to bury his pen through the eye lens of my mask. I had no choice. I pulled the trigger. The Hades shell turned his head into fireworks. Fumes of incendiary chemicals mixed with vaporized brain and skull matter exploded up to the ceiling in an inverted shower of cinders.

Mason stepped into the elevator car, glancing at the mess painted above us. "Glad you didn't use that method to wake me up."

I looked at the decapitated body and felt a pang of remorse. It wasn't the guy's fault. I had enough innocent blood on my hands as it was, I didn't need Legion forcing me to add more.

"Wait, you hear that?" she asked. It sounded like bacon cooking. "It's like ... oh *shit!*"

The Hades round finished burning through the ceiling, and the cables above, and the elevator fell to the bottom of the shaft.

CHAPTER 50

She lost them. West and Mason's signals had dropped several layers deeper into the Basement before disappearing altogether. Their comm feed was nothing but static. Rain told herself all that was just indicative of closer proximity to Morpheus and higher rad levels, and not a sign of anything more disastrous.

Dante whoofed in the aisle, cocking his head in the direction of the stairway. He was apparently pretty annoyed to be stuck on guard duty yet again.

For a second, she considered calling back to Vaun and letting him know that West had gone dark. Instead, she resolved to give them more time. That would let her delve deeper into the hard drive, and when they came back up on comms, she'd be able to give them a better read on what they were dealing with.

The encryption wasn't hard to break. She chalked that up to the fact that someone would have to both know where the Basement was—one of the darkest and best kept secrets among America's black sites—as well as gain access, so at that point bothering with next-gen uncrackable encryption wasn't viewed as necessary. Everything was saved and kept onsite, no network connections at all. Until West plugged her in, that is.

What she found was nothing less than daunting. There were entire volumes of files. Records, testing reports, progress notes, and technical information that, on the surface, was hard to understand. Warehousing inventories with ambiguous labels. All of it dated back decades. Realizing she was looking at a smorgasbord of DoD's forbidden and forgotten relics, she narrowed her search down to only the files that mentioned Morpheus.

Even that didn't narrow the pool of files significantly enough.

Rain's eyes swam from the sheer depth of information before her. It was like trying to find a single street name on a map of an entire major city. She tried to narrow it down further, using the keyword 'testing'. If there were testing reports. hopefully there would be more conclusive details on Morpheus's capabilities.

Instead, the results showed her how many testing subjects had been forced to undergo Morpheus exposure, and the numbers filled her screen. She swallowed back bile at the thought of how murky these waters she'd been wading into were. Subject after subject had died; the notes on the report only listed the level and length of exposure and then time of expiration. Report after report was the same. *Subject expired after two minutes of exposure to Morpheus; level five. Subject expired after ten minutes of exposure to Morpheus; level three. Subject expired after thirty seconds of exposure to Morpheus; level seven.* And on and on and on.

Until she came across the first that was different. *Subject triggered Krueger Effect after one minute exposure to Morpheus, level eight; transferred to seventh floor.*

"Krueger Effect . . ." she whispered to herself.

She ran a quick search of the files, this time to see if there were any matches for 'Krueger Effect'. There were plenty. More than fifty of the testing reports listed similar results, as well as what looked to be a lab memorandum on it. More worrisome was that the memo was dated from nearly twenty years ago.

"Effects of exposure to ambient energy released from the Morpheus Engine vary depending on several factors: the level of exposure, the length of exposure, as well as the individual subject's biometrics all determine how quickly and severely they are affected. The unique qualities of the Morpheus Engine's radiation affect the synaptic centers of the brain that deal with fear and the body's natural sleep state.

Acute minor effects include anxiety, tachycardia, perspiration, and shortness of breath. Severe effects include auditory/visual/tactile hallucinations, psychosomatic pain, seizures, and loss of motor control. These may culminate in death both through brain stroke or through accidental cause, or the subject reduced to a vegetative state.

"However, for reasons yet to be determined, certain subjects undergo what has been called the Krueger Effect. Exposure to high levels of Morpheus radiation may trigger an inverse reaction in certain individuals. The fight-or-flight response is accelerated, the adrenal glands are overloaded, the Amygdala enlarges, and all mental faculties are reduced to nothing but violent instinct.

"Higher-brain functions all but cease, and there has been no demonstrable recovery in these individuals long after the Krueger Effect is triggered. These Krueger subjects will need to be researched further for the Darkheart Project. All Krueger subjects will be transferred and contained on the seventh floor."

Rain finished reading and looked back at the digital 3-d schematic of the Basement, and both West and Mason's last known locations. Either they were dead from falling down the elevator shaft, or they were alive and at the very bottom. On the seventh floor. The Seventh Circle of Hell. Being dead might be a slight shade better circumstance.

CHAPTER 51

I awoke to a taste of metal in the air. It dawned on me that I'd noticed it upstairs as well, but down here it was much stronger. Where was down here, though? It was too dark to see anything. When I felt around with my arms outstretched like a blind man, I found all four walls of the elevator car. I flicked a flashlight on to get a better look at the state of things.

That metallic tinge on my breath was making my head feel funny. Afraid that I was about to have another nightmare hallucination episode, I pulled the adrenaline needle from my own med-kit and gave myself a dose. Its effect was immediate, and I had to fight just to stand still. But everything was clear, and no nightmares came clawing out of my mind, so it was a fair trade for a risky heart rate.

"Sledgehammer, you still with me?"

Mason shook herself once and got to her feet. "I'm here. What's the rad level?"

I checked my detector and had newfound doubts whether I was seeing things clearly or not. The levels kept switching between a blaring red indicator for two hundred milli-Seivert, a dull yellow for ten micro-Seivert, and then registering a green zero.

"I think my gear took a hit during that fall," I said.

She checked her own and shook her head, it was registering the same.

"Or Morpheus doesn't play by the same rules of the science we know."

I pointed at the doors, and she helped me force them open. I jammed my MK-9 knife under the door to keep it from shutting on us. She exited first and aimed into the shadows while I pulled myself out behind her. I retrieved my knife and the elevator doors closed on damaged rollers.

What awaited was most assuredly *not* an engineering floor for the facility's generators. There was a long concrete corridor leading from the elevator with several cell doors on either side. I knew just from looking that this wasn't more office space. It was some sort of prison, or worse yet maybe an asylum.

"You seeing this?" I asked, not sure if I should trust my eyes.

The beam of my flashlight found what looked like scratch marks on one of the walls, dug with human fingers.

"Creepy sanitarium aesthetic? Yeah, we're on the same page there."

"Good. Just checking."

When we reached the first cell I peeked through the small window on the door. It was pitch black inside, but for a second I thought I saw a pair of eyes looking out at me. Then it was gone, the cell's occupant vanishing. I shined my flashlight into the cell and caught a glimpse of pale skin, so pale that I knew it hadn't seen the light of day in too long, and the person inside scuttled away from the light. He kept just to the edge of the beam's cone, watching me through the window.

An arm shot through the window and nearly grabbed me by the neck before I stepped back. The cell held *two* occupants. They both howled and threw themselves at the door. The one forced both his arms through the small space and flailed about in some insane effort to reach me. The banging and screams woke those in other cells and the corridor suddenly became a cacophony of madness.

"Let's get the fuck out of here."

I moved down the hall at a much brisker pace. Mason gave no argument. Right as we neared the end of the line of cells, I heard a loud buzz. Like an electronic lock being disengaged. One by one the cell doors slid open with a deafening *clang*. Mason and I ran from the open cells as their occupants spilled forth. I counted maybe thirty, slavering and vacant of all reason, clawing their way for us. They were fighting each other to get at us, like a pack of rabid dogs tossed a single steak.

The hall turned a corner and led to a much more open area. This one looked more like a morgue, or possibly a medical examination room. The only exit was on the far side, a set of double-doors with an electronic lock glowing red.

Mason scoffed and turned back towards our pursuers. The buttstock of her P90 was pulled to her shoulder. For some reason my thoughts went to the scientist I'd blown away upstairs. The one who had attacked us on instinct rather than any malicious intent.

"Wait," I said, pulling her barrel down. "They aren't themselves."

"You must be joking?"

"We could've killed each other but managed to snap out of it. We got lucky."

"I could just shoot them in the legs . . ."

"Come on. You take the fifteen on the left, I'll take the fifteen on the right."

My challenge seemed to change her mood. "Okay then, try to keep up."

The horde of emaciated prisoners entered the room, and we moved to meet them. On my very first day in Black Spear, my very first hour really, I'd made the mistake of thinking Mason was

Rourke's secretary. I'd quickly been corrected, and Kelly himself had warned me that Mason was the very last person I'd want to fight. For quite some time now, I'd been keen on seeing her in action with my own eyes. And for once, reputation and reality were one and the same.

Kara Mason was no meathead commando. She was not gifted with the genetic handicap of higher bone density and an inclination towards greater muscle mass. Which meant when she fought, she fought in ways that a guy like me most certainly would not. It was like seeing your first two in a binary world of ones and zeroes. She pivoted on nimble ankles and attacked with short snapping kicks to the side of their knees, she boxed their ears with cupped hands to pop eardrums, she stepped with lithe agility to maneuver between them in ways I never could. Where she was lacking in strength, she made up for by seeing vulnerability. Where others saw a limb, she saw load-bearing structures, then applied appropriate force to knock them down. She fought like an architect.

Me? I was a wrecking ball. Strength was something I had in ample supply, along with the knowledge of how to use it. While Mason shattered knees and attacked from the unfamiliar angles, I had no reason to go any way but head-on. The thing about fighting amped up nutjobs is that they're focused solely on killing you with no regard at all to their own defense. The first two I encountered swiped at me with curled claw-like fingers. I smashed one's face with a left straight, knocked the second to the floor with a hook to the jaw, and stomped his chest to finish taking him out of the fight as I moved to the next.

There was a break in the combat flow just long enough for me to see how Mason faired. I watched her strike nerves and twist joints. She used the mass and momentum of her larger attackers to redirect them into others. When they fell, she leapt upon the three of them like a wild animal and knocked each of them out in turn with an elbow, a fist, and a dropped axe-kick. And then she sprang to her feet for more.

There was no strategy to their attack. No direction. They lacked unity, some violently tearing pieces off of one another before they reached us. I came upon two of the crazed prisoners strangling each other to the floor. Before one could kill the other, I cracked their heads against one another like two coconuts. Both went limp onto the floor.

One maniac fell down dead before me with a deep gash through the middle of his back. The culprit was behind him: a larger madman who'd gotten clever enough to pull a fire-axe from a wall. He swung it in a wide arc, not even going after me or Mason but desiring to kill everyone he could. The axe blade came down for my face and I caught the shaft with one-hand. My free hand delivered an uppercut so damn hard that he was out cold before he hit the ground.

I tossed the axe far away, and then had to duck to avoid the body of another Mason used Judo to throw across the room. She gave me the smallest of apologetic shrugs before having to slip a wild punch aimed for her face. Moving as if made of oil rather than flesh and blood, she twisted to the side of her attacker and chopped his throat with the blade of her hand. He went down hard.

We cut through them like twin scythes through a field of wheat. Her, graceful as the wind, but carrying the force of a hurricane. And me, as straightforward and unyielding as a boulder hurtling downhill. Earlier I'd estimated that there were thirty or so of them. It turned out my count was short by nearly ten.

It didn't matter.

CHAPTER 52

He sat safely in the Central Security room, observing West and Mason take on the facility's Kruegers. The Basement's numerous cameras fed him a live feed of the show on the wall of monitors before him. It was from here that he'd baited the two along, unlocking the doors necessary to bring them closer to him. Knowing Mason most likely had the very set of Rourke's access codes Black was using, he'd taken the liberty of creating his own and erasing the others. Now he, and he alone, was master of the Basement and all its locks and secrets.

He was only slightly surprised that Mason survived her fall from Rourke's office. Perhaps he hadn't actually wanted to kill her before? He'd impaled her through the shoulder but could've just as easily put his knife through her eye. What if it was her, and not Cole, who could become his next greatest kill? So far, she'd endured the Morpheus effects as well as West had. The possibility was tantalizing. She did have history with him, after all.

Black rose from his chair as the Kruegers continued to drop like flies before the two skilled fighters. He'd been firsthand witness to Mason's prowess before, one glance at her and he knew there was little new to her skillset. It was all familiar. The same rhythm to her movements, the same tendencies and choice of combinations, the same old song and dance.

No, she would not be his prize.

It was West who interested him. There was a certain ferocity to the way he fought. Black could see the beast underneath the skin, itching to get out. With every blow West landed, Black saw that dark heart within him trying to take hold. Black began to mimic West's movements. Feeling the script of West's strikes and letting his mind key them all to memory. They became twin images of each other, though only one was aware of it.

There was a beautiful combination of disciplines in West's style. Black recreated West's hook—pure American boxing—and lashed out at the air with a Muay Thai *teep* push kick in synch with him. When West delivered an upward diagonal elbow strike into a Krueger's collar bone, Black had trouble identifying the style. It looked to be from a Filipino style, perhaps Silat? Black imitated the strike, smiling as he saw the potential follow-ups in his mind's eye, smiling even wider when West used one Black had predicted.

Even an expert in hand-to-hand like West had weak spots. And just like that Black had learned them by heart. This is why Black was unequaled: he already knew what his opponents were going to do, and how to counter it. An employer of his had once mused that watching him fight was like watching someone play rock-paper-scissors, except Black could use both hands in the game. There was a tempo to fighting, a beat that each punch or kick flowed to, and Black knew how to cut in between the notes.

The final Krueger fell on screen, and as West's shoulders and fists dropped, so did Black's.

"How much longer?" Simon asked from behind him.

He'd stood at a distance the entire time, and only now must have felt safe enough to approach. Black tapped a few keys to bring up a reading of the radiation levels on the sixth floor.

"Not much longer," he said. "Morpheus has been building up that stored energy for years, electromagnetic interference is just one of the residual effects. If we didn't purge the excess energy from the core, we likely wouldn't be able to transport it safely, let alone allow your Immortals to remove it from here without it driving them mad. Speaking of which, I believe it's time?"

Simon reached to his pocket and took another dose of the pills they'd brought along. If he wondered why he hadn't seen Black take any since their descent into the Basement, he didn't ask. The radio clipped to Simon's vest squawked before he could address it.

"Sir?"

It was Declan.

"Speak."

"We've almost finished rounding up the remaining research staff. The last of the security team has been neutralized."

"Excellent. Re-up your doses, all of you."

The radio went quiet. Simon stepped closer to the wall of screens. His attention was on the one that Black had previously told him showed the Morpheus storage cell. When Black had first removed the safeguards to purge the accumulated Morpheus energy, all the cameras on the bottom three floors had instantly gone to static. Now only one camera remained affected.

Simon's finger brushed the screen, the static had dissipated somewhat. He could almost see its picture at this point. They were so close to their goal now. Simon's pointed finger curled into a fist when he saw West and Mason on another monitor.

"No more games, no toying with your food," said Simon. "Those two can't be allowed to interfere. Kill them. We are paying you a fortune, if you expect to see a penny of it you will do as you're ordered."

Simon turned to leave the room, no doubt desiring to have the last word in the conversation. Black scoffed, and unable to restrain himself snickered. The sound stopped Simon dead in his tracks.

"Money? What a disgusting thing," Black said. "They are but slips of paper and cotton, covered in other people's bacteria and grime. Passed around, changing hands a hundred times over, then collected by the millions and joined in such a small space. All that accumulated filth festering together? The very thought sickens me."

The way Simon looked at him then was so satisfying. It was the precise moment he realized how little he had to hold over Black.

"I never needed, or wanted, your money."

This time Black dismissed Simon with a wave of his finger and turned his back on him. Soon enough Simon would see that his leash never had a hold over Black. He'd been respectful enough to let the illusion of control remain until now. Simon still didn't understand *what* Black was. As if money would be what drives him.

When he looked at the Morpheus cell's camera, the static had all but cleared. It was time.

CHAPTER 53

Cole West. 4:30 p.m.
Seventh Floor
The Basement

There was a dull fire that throbbed all the way from my knuckles, through my elbows, and up to my burning shoulders. Unlike the ones that had haunted my dreams so often as of late, I welcomed this one. This one fueled the anger building inside. It was like throwing morsels to a hungry dog, knowing that the meal it truly wanted was nearing. Black had threatened to unleash some darker true self within me. He might not be too happy with the results.

"Not bad," said Mason.

She knelt down and zip-tied one of the unconscious prisoner's wrists together. There had been a basket full of plastic bands on one of the medical examination tables in the center of the room, and she'd wasted no time in ensuring the ones we'd put down were restrained.

"We really have time for that?"

"You wanted to keep them alive," she scoffed. "You saw how amped up they were. I don't want to find out that, among other things, Morpheus lets them bounce back twice as fast as a normal person."

"Point taken."

We made quick work of binding the rest up once I pitched in to help. I surveyed the crowd of broken bodies around us. They weren't dead, but some would need a long recovery, and others could probably use a cast or two. I'd tried to keep the brain damage to a minimum. Killing was something nearly unavoidable in this life, but I had to admit that I found myself oddly proud that we'd managed to knock this crowd down without having to pull a trigger. There were enough notches on my belt as things were. And yet there was still enough space left for that one mark I came here for.

"You want to drag them back to their cells, chief?" she asked.

I checked my watch to see how long it had been since we'd dosed ourselves to stay awake. "No time. All we can do for them is get Morpheus as far away as possible and hope this wears off. And we can't keep injecting ourselves with adrenaline, or our hearts will freaking explode."

"Oh, definitely," she said, prodding the sunken eye sockets of a particularly withered looking prisoner. "I'm certain this charming bunch will spring back into model citizens any moment now."

I ignored her sarcasm and found myself by the double doors at the back of the room. At some point in our throwdown, the electronic lock had been lifted. It was pissing me off that Black wanted to play this cat and mouse shit with me, but if it got me another step closer to him then I wasn't going to turn down the open invitation.

Instead of finding Black on the other side, I found something more disturbing. Which, considering the week I'd had so far, was really saying something.

At first glance, it looked like an autopsy room. The three corpses on examination tables in the middle of the space confirmed my theory. The first body's skull had been sawed open, the brain removed and set on a separate table in the corner. The second had its chest cavity sliced and held open with surgical clamps and forceps, several organs pinned with markers. The third was facedown, its entire spine exposed. A series of needles were wired into spots along the vertebrae, placed directly into the spinal cord. The problem was that all three had IV and blood bags hooked up to them, which meant that they'd been alive at the start of whatever sick examination had taken place here.

I wanted out of this room. Immediately. The walls made my skin crawl, and the thought of how many people had lain on these tables before these three made my stomach do a somersault.

"Kruegers," said Mason. She'd picked up a clipboard full of notes from the middle table and did a quick read. "That's what the crazies are called. Looks like they were doing research on everything from brain activity, to neural conduction, to organ function."

"Why?"

"To try and prevent it from happening further," Rain's voice said in our ears. "Whatever electromagnetic voodoo interference was going on seems to be diminishing. The GPS in your suits ghosted me for a minute there, and I've been talking to myself trying to reach you until just now. Anyway, these three here weren't always prisoners, it looks like they were researchers working here who at some point snapped. Records show that this Krueger Effect has been spiking, the cases of staff succumbing to it accelerating over the course of the past two years. Used to be maybe one a year, more recently they were rotating staff regularly because one or two would pop a month. These three were all in the span of a week."

"All the more reason we should get the hell out of here as soon as possible," Mason said.

"No argument here," I said. "Yellow Pages, find us an exit, please."

"Way ahead of you," she said proudly.

Rain guided us deeper into the Basement, turning down more dark corridors and through further doors she'd unlocked for us until we finally came to a large cargo elevator.

"Presto. You can ride that up to the sixth floor, get to the

Morpheus Engine before them, then bring it back and I'll take you all the way up to the surface."

She'd called it a Morpheus Engine, which was a new term. Clearly, she'd been busy delving through the Basement's files while we'd been disconnected.

"Sounds like a perfect plan," I said as I pulled the heavy cargo sliding door aside and stepped aboard. "Now I've only got one more question, but you're going to read my mind and not make me ask it."

"No, boss, I don't see Black. But those cronies with the creepy masks are on the third floor. They—well, they just finished killing everyone."

"Were they crazy? Kruegers?" asked Mason.

"Neither were. The Basement staff was definitely affected, but most of them just screamed at nothing or whimpered on the floor. I think a couple had heart attacks. Whatever preventative dosage of antipsychotics they have everyone here on is nowhere near enough to counteract the higher Morpheus levels once the safeguards were disabled. Which, by the way, I'm still locked out of. Oh, and the Legion look like they're just fine."

Mason and I locked eyes through our masks and understood what Rain's update meant. It meant if Legion was thinking as sharp and clear as we were at the moment, we'd have a hell of a fight on our hands if we crossed paths. It also meant that they'd known more about how the Morpheus Engine worked and how to mitigate its effects.

I hit the button for the sixth floor, the panel blinked a few times but the cargo elevator didn't budge.

"Hang on," said Rain. "Aaaand . . . bingo."

The panel light turned green and the car began to ascend slowly.

Mason jumped back abruptly and looked to the ceiling, "Jesus. Considering the black budget these facilities are built off you'd think they wouldn't have leaks in the ceiling."

Her eyes went to the floor where she stepped away from the growing puddle on the floor. There was only one problem: there was no leak in the ceiling, and I didn't actually see a puddle.

"Sledgehammer," I said, forcing as much calm into my voice as possible. "There's nothing there."

She did a double take from the floor to ceiling, then pressed the heel of her palm against her temple. "This place is messing with me. I'm good."

"I'm not so sure."

Her gaze kept going from mine to the top of the elevator, I imagined she was seeing more and more water raining down.

"You can't do this alone. And I don't need you sidelining me or babysitting me, West. I'm fine, damn it."

I reluctantly nodded. Mason squared her shoulders and faced the cargo doors with her weapon at the ready. I used that moment of mutual trust to come behind her and wrap my arm around her neck. It doesn't matter how legendary a soldier you are, or how capable a fighter you are: once a choke is sunk in good, and with an arm as big as mine, there's not shit you can do but pass out. Cutting off the blood supply to the brain will have someone my size out cold in under ten seconds. To her credit, she fought it for thirteen.

It was for her own good. I used the last zip-tie on my pocket to bind Mason to the handrail then scooped her submachine gun off the ground. For whatever reason, I could still fight off the Morpheus energy more easily. I didn't know how much longer that would be the case, which meant I needed to make every second count.

"Yellow Pages, Sledgehammer is compromised. Take her up to the surface."

"Can you do this on your own, boss?"

"I have to. Just give me the shortest path."

The elevator reached the sixth floor and I stepped out, closed the door behind me, and watched as Rain sent Mason up to the top.

That taste of metal in the air was stronger here. Unsurprising. I took that to mean I was getting closer.

Just for shits and giggles I checked my malfunctioning wrist display. Dose rate of 250 milli-Seivert, and my absorbed dose was allegedly up to three Seivert now. In this business, we'd call that a turnback dose. As in, it's time to turn back around and get the hell out of dodge.

Fuck it. In for a penny, in for a pound.

"Down the hall," said Rain. "You're looking for cell two fourteen."

Solid steel doors lined each side of the hallway. With every step I took, I found myself wondering what other secrets I was simply walking past. What other forgotten weapons did Rourke have buried here? The further I got from the elevator shaft, the more that taste of metal disappeared. Instead, I smelled burnt hair and charred meat. I told myself it wasn't real and to keep going.

"Rain, do I even want to know what's behind these other doors?"

"Seems like a story for another time," she said. "Rad levels rising, and I'm getting some strong interference. We might lose comms the closer you get to it."

A flicker of light to my side like a small dancing flame tried to draw my attention. I put it out of my head and walked a little faster. My earbud squelched, and Rain's voice disappeared.

"Two fourteen," I said to myself, eager to hear any sound that would keep me grounded.

I shouldered Mason's P90 and took off in a trotting run. Rather than feeling that rising fear in my belly, I felt eager. I was almost out of here. The last cell on my left before the hall ended in a corner was two zero eight. I turned the corner, and there it was.

Two fourteen. The cell was already open. And someone was waiting for me in it.

"Took you long enough," said Black.

I was already squeezing the trigger as he tapped a button in the doorway, but my bullets rattled off of a steel emergency door that instantly slammed into place. He tilted his head a little as he looked out at me through the Plexiglas window.

Here I was at the finish line, and I'd just watched Black cross it before me.

He should've died. The amount of blood loss, not to mention the severity of the gunshot wound to his head, should've been a death sentence. Somehow, Rourke had clung to life. He'd hovered on the edge of death for three days in a coma, and on the fourth awoke screaming in agony. The damage was done. Irremovable bullet fragments meant he'd have chronic nerve pain for the rest of his life, and it dawned on him then that Black hadn't botched his kill attempt. His gift was pain, and he'd *meant* for Rourke to survive. To live, and to live in pain, knowing that every day he breathed was only because Black had allowed it.

The doctor had prescribed him some pills that would supposedly numb the pain without dulling his mind. Rourke popped two of the small white pills and swallowed them dry, eager for a relief from what was already creeping on. He sat in the hospital room of the only other survivor from the massacre in the facility, and he didn't want to be distracted by the hurt when it came time to talk.

"Where is he?" the operative known as Jade finally asked. Her face, stitched and bandaged, made her voice sound muffled. She'd tried to discharge herself on the second day, but had been forced to remain in place until her and Rourke could have this conversation out.

Rourke's own jaw was wired shut, but the pills would hopefully see him through this conversation.

"Gone."

"We have to go after him."

"No."

Jade propped herself up on her elbows to shoot Rourke a withering stare. "No? Look at my fucking face, *sir*. Where's my team? In the morgue. He doesn't get to just walk away from that."

"The situation is complicated," Rourke managed to say. The aching flare across his jaw was putting up a hell of a fight. "Black Spear operators are ghosts. We erase their records, Mr. Black knows this and is using that to his advantage."

"The facility," asked Jade, "can we bring him back there? Undo it? Bring Adrian back?"

Rourke exhaled slowly. "Project Darkheart has been shut down. Total erasure. All equipment is being moved off-site, digital records wiped. This time tomorrow, the entire facility will be filled with concrete. I won't risk this happening again. Not ever."

"Is the equipment being destroyed?" she demanded.

His silence was enough of an answer, Rourke was many things but for some reason couldn't bring himself to be an outright liar in this moment.

"No, of course not. Because how else could we try again and learn from our mistakes?"

"I promise you, Ms. Mason, this project is dead."

She traced the line of cut in her face over the bandages, deep in thought. "If we find him, *when* we find him, I want in."

Rourke nodded, then moved on to the next order of business.

"Ms. Mason, Spectrum is dead. But you're not. As it happens, I have need for a new squad. And a new squad leader. What do you say, Jade?"

Mason looked out the hospital window. In her mind, all she could think of was finding Black. And smashing in his skull with a damn hammer.

"If Spectrum is dead, then I'm going to need a new callsign."

CHAPTER 54

We stared each other down through the doorway. I gripped my weapon so tight, I thought the metal would crumple in my hands like tin foil. He never blinked the entire time, just stared out at me. The bastard was still clothed in that perfectly pressed black three-piece suit of his, and not one strand of his slicked-back oily hair was out of place. He didn't even wear a protective mask. That mocking grin of his was on display before me. The tension in both our eyes was nearly enough to rend the metal barrier between us. Then, as if a switch was flipped, he raised his chin up at me in appraisal.

"Did he go easy?" he asked. "The marksman."

I thought back to the foundry, and Kelly dying in my arms.

My friend.

My mission.

My fault.

"Easier and faster than yours is going to be."

Black puffed out his cheeks.

"Whew, dying like that? What a horrible way to go. Choking on your own blood? I believe the bullet pierced his spine so he wouldn't have been able to cough, let alone fight it. That's no way to go for people like us. No. People like us go down swinging."

"Like us? I'm *nothing* like you."

"No? Keep telling yourself that. Your accomplishments number in the thousands. I wonder, how many more did you cut through just to get to this point, to get to me? I see you, West."

I wanted to crush his skull beneath my boot and tell him he was wrong, but I was helpless to do anything except beat my hand against the door.

"Ba-*bum*. Ba-*bum*," Black clapped his hands together to the rhythm of a heartbeat. "Can you hear that black heart of yours beating yet? It's growing so strong."

"You want a beating? Open this door, I'll give you a beating."

I unclipped Mason's SMG, let it fall to the floor, and drew my knife.

"No, this is more your style, right? Let's go a round or two, Black. Come on. Let's carve each other up a little. You and me."

I slammed the pommel of my knife onto the door.

"Come on! That's what you want!"

A knife was in his hand and he rhythmically tapped it on his hip, tempted by the offer. This knife was different than all the others I'd seen him use. Longer. His other hand danced around the button that would release the door. I know he wanted to do it. But at the last moment his fingertip pulled away. He lazily dragged the tip of his black dagger across the window and it scraped against the glass leaving a fine line at my eye-level. Then he turned the dagger lengthwise so I could see its black marble handle veined with white swirling whisps.

"You see the ghosts in there?" he asked, his eyes fanatic wide. "The souls locked in the stone? They're lonely, West. I can't wait to add you to the collection."

Then he turned his back on me and walked further into the cell.

"But no, not just yet."

At that he stepped to the side, and I found myself at a loss for further threats for him. Because I finally saw it. The Morpheus Engine.

My first thought was that its appearance was underwhelming compared to its effects I'd already experienced. The device was about the size of a fifty-five gallon barrel, with a large hexagonal shaped base and top. A small keypad was at its top, along with some control dials. Its gunmetal surface didn't glow with any sinister light, but there was a strange distortion in the air around it that resembled waves coming off asphalt on a hot day. Black rolled his fingertips along the top of the device, deep in his own thoughts.

"That's it, then?" I asked. "I thought it would be scarier."

Black frowned, then spoke to me politely as if we were colleagues. "It's the safest thing in the world when it's powered down. The outer shell is constructed of lead alloys that completely shield the core's energy. Some of the residual electromagnetic interference can still occur, but none of the harsher effects."

"Everyone losing their minds down here may beg to differ."

He gave me a wicked look.

"That's because it wasn't powered down. I had to buy time for you to get here." He gave me a casual shrug and the corners of his mouth pulled down in an exaggerated frown. "I told the good Mr. Simon Ellis that the engine needed to purge its built up energy, but the truth is I just wanted to have a bit of fun. Cranked it up a few notches and disabled the safety measures to see how everyone fared. Tell me, how did you enjoy the Kruegers downstairs?"

I kept my eyes on him but tried to form a plan by using my peripherals. Seeing if there was another way into the room, or if there was some way to get Rain to unlock it for me.

"They're still breathing."

His disappointment was palpable.

"Right. All that rage and no willingness to let it loose in full. I practically gift-wrapped them for you," he said, wagging a disapproving finger at me. "And, I might add, they came practically free of any moral fretting you might've had about killing them. They are empty shells ripe for reaping. Nothing but rage and violence inside. You had no reason to hold back. They *can't* be saved."

"I can try," I said. "And don't worry. I won't be holding back with you. How many people do you think I'll save by killing you? That death god you preach about will be awfully torn up about all that life preserved."

His eyes narrowed. There had always been a predatory glint in them, but now there was something else. Curiosity.

"What are you after, West? Vengeance? Redemption? Saving these people will not bring you peace, because the lengths you'll have to go to if you want to stop *me* will only make your soul darker."

I thought of what he had asked. Strangely, it didn't come across as another jab. The truth is, I hadn't stopped long enough to really ask that question myself. I wanted him dead, yes. But for who? For Kelly? For me? Killing him wouldn't make things right with everything I'd done, and I doubt putting one demon into the ground would quiet all the other ones in my head.

But it was a good place to start.

I don't know if it was a trick of the light, but that blur in the air surrounding the Morpheus Engine seemed to increase. The taste of metal filled my mouth. My head went foggy. I ignored the warning from my wrist that the AEGIS was reaching its failure point. Six Seiverts? Six hundred? What difference did it make at this point.

"What are you?" I asked. "No mask. No gear. But you're right next to it, and it isn't doing anything to you."

Black's hands embraced either side of the device like it was some divine artifact.

"Because this birthed me. The Darkheart Project. Experiments with the Morpheus energy, working alongside hypnotherapists and psychotropic medications to crack a man's mind *precisely* rather than shatter it like the Kruegers below. Its unique radiation is what split Adrian's psyche and drew me up from the shadows; it is what switched our places. Made Black flesh, and Adrian nothing but a whisper in the back of my head."

With every second Black stood near the Morpheus Engine, he seemed to stand straighter. His presence radiated through the room more and more. It was as if he grew stronger from its presence rather than going mad from it.

"He's still there, isn't he?" I asked. "Deep down, Adrian's fighting you. Trying to get back control."

"Indeed." Black sighed. "His whispers have grown more bothersome of late. But no more. Now, I bury him for good."

At that Black entered a pin code into the keypad atop the Morpheus Engine. A top panel slid open. Four cylindrical fuel rods rose from the core of the shell. Colored a slate gray shade, a sickly green sheen glimmered off each rod like motor oil on water. The emerald shimmer was not unlike the inner whorls of an abalone shell, impossibly catching light that wasn't present in this dark cell. I squinted and held up a hand just to keep looking in Black's direction. But it wasn't brightness in my eyes, rather it was like the brightness was in my head. A harsh light going directly into my mind, scraping across my skull like a scalpel.

It was overwhelming. I squeezed shut my eyes shut to block out the sight of the Morpheus rods, but it only made the effect worse. When I opened them again, Black was reaching for the core without hesitation. Defying all reason and logic I understood, he eagerly grasped the fuel rod with his naked hands. I felt the entire room crackle with energy. Black grit his teeth as the green energy arced from the rod and up his arms.

Or was I seeing things again?

I realized he was screaming, an angry roar held back by a

clenched jaw. I howled with him as an ocean of pain crashed through my mind.

And then, as if he were packing up a suitcase for a business trip, Black reinserted the fuel rod and closed the core access panel. The effects dissipated somewhat, but that burning smell snuck its way towards my nostrils. Telling myself it wasn't real didn't make it go away.

Black adjusted a cuff link. He fixed his tie.

"That's better." He tilted his head as if listening for something, then smiled with satisfaction at the silence. "Now then, still with us, West?"

This was a thousandfold worse than when I'd faced the burning man. Every ounce of me—body, mind, and spirit—had been torn asunder. It was as if a million shards of glass had been funneled into my brain. Thick sludge pumped through my veins and slowed every heartbeat. If there was a well deep within which I drew willpower from, then I now found myself scraping nothing but sand from the bottom of it.

All I managed to say was an unemphatic, "Fuck."

I rose up from the knee I'd fallen to. I picked my knife up from the ground and slammed its butt against the window again.

"What are you afraid of, Black? Face me, damn it."

"My own fears," he said, showing me his back once more and approaching the Morpheus Engine controls, "aren't the ones which you need to be concerned with."

I heard him flip a switch and crank a dial. Tunnel-vision set in at once, and I knew I had moments before the nightmares clawed my consciousness away once again. I needed to get through the door. Fast.

I pulled my Boomstick from the scabbard upon my back and aimed for the locking mechanism. On the other side, Black turned the dial higher. An invisible knife corkscrewed behind my eyes, entangling itself around my retinas, and I fought just to keep my eyelids open. To stay awake.

And still the dial turned.

I aimed for the lock and fired, and a belch of flames burst forth onto the door.

"No," I whispered.

It should've been loaded with slugs, not Hades rounds. The incendiary load spread across the entire threshold, and I had to step back lest I be consumed by them. Metal sizzled against the burning thermite, but the barrier held.

"What do you say, West?" Black now stood as a silhouette through the small window. "Why don't we take this all the way to ten?"

"Black, no!"

The outline of his profile became wreathed in flames. They consumed his visage, burning it away to a cackling skull. Where moments before Black had stood, now I looked once more upon the burning man of my nightmares.

"No, no, no! Wait!"

I didn't see him turn the dial to the final setting, because the fires waiting in the darkness had already taken me. Body, and soul.

CHAPTER 55

Mr. Black. 4:55 p.m.
Level Six
The Basement

He was complete. The cracks that Adrian had slipped through were thoroughly sealed. Forever. Black had at last finished the perfection that Project Darkheart had started. Adrian Rasp was gone for good. There was no sleeper agent, no alternate personas. There was only the darkness. Only Black.

Having basked in the nourishing power of a maximum Morpheus pulse, Black deactivated the engine and called Simon on his radio.

"It's done," he said. "Have your Immortals fetch the trucks, and I'll bring your weapon to you."

Simon's voice came back, slightly staticky from how close Black was to the Morpheus Engine. "Well done, Mister Black. Well done, indeed. We're headed up to the surface now. I trust that other matter is concluded?"

Black disengaged the security door. "Which matter would that be?"

"Your so-called 'greatest kill'? Was it everything you'd hoped for?"

Captain West was gone. The man convulsed on the floor while his eyes shifted between staring catatonia and rolling into the back of his head. He was lost in whatever nightmares Black had sent him to. The mind could only take so much. Black walked past his twisted body, utterly disappointed that there would be no waking for him. Black's thirteenth blade would go unused, no more soul claimed and interred within its marble handle. Perhaps he had overestimated his prey?

"Cole West is no longer among us," Black said absently. "I'll be with you in just a moment."

There would be no satisfaction if he simply cut the man's throat here and now. Nobody was home upstairs, which meant it wouldn't count as a kill. The soul was elsewhere in some faraway hell. Black gave pause in that hallway before going to find a handcart to move the Morpheus Engine. He was curious about something. What if West *did* climb back up from the abyss?

No. No one came back from that. No one. Morpheus cleaved through peoples' minds and either left them braindead or turned into mindless savage Kruegers. The power of Morpheus was absolute. Not even Adrian Rasp managed to return from the depths, though that pitiful maggot had tried. The only reason Damien Black wasn't alongside West down in that nightmare abyss was because Black *was* the pit.

Cole West was just another man, but Black was death.

CHAPTER 56

Cole West. 

I shouldn't be here.

Wherever this was, it was wrong. My skin felt like it was covered in fiberglass. Fiberglass that *moved*. It itched and burned as if the very air around me was harmful. The taste on my tongue was nothing but ash. It coated my mouth like I'd been spoon fed charcoal.

At first, all I heard was my own ragged breath, but a crack of thunder silenced even that. A flash of lightning illuminated the horror before me for a second. Bodies of men and women, stripped of clothing, and strung up on hooked chains. Blood dripped down them to the floor below. There was a ringing in my ears, slowly rising in intensity.

For whatever reason I felt drawn back to my feet. More lightning flashed, but rather than a boom of thunder it came instead with a sharp screech that sent my fingertips into my ears. The darkness receded more, showing just how much death surrounded me.

"I'm in hell."

They dangled from the chains like grim marionettes. Some freshly dead, some older. Spikes and hooks pinned them to the chains through their mouths, or suspended them by their ankles, while still others hung by pierced wrists with their bellies cut and entrails freed. The metal links rattled against each other in the vast open room.

When the lightning screeched again, I saw that I was in a grand hall, like some throne room pulled from an ancient castle. The ceiling was too high to see, the chains ascending into the impenetrable dark above, and the walls on either side of me too far away in the shadows. There was a long blood red carpet before me, drawing me down the hall.

Great pillars of stone flanked the pathway every twenty paces or so. They rose up high as towers with crude metal spikes adorning their sides. I saw a man, starving and sunken down to nothing but skin and bones, stuck through the back upon one of the spikes. He tried to pull himself off amid horrid moans, then went limp and his slack body was impaled further.

The hooked corpses were too many to count, and they filled the wings on either side of the carpeted path and seemed to go on forever. Something compelled me to walk down the carpet. I kept my eyes on the path ahead, refusing to look at the numberless dead around me. Still, I could feel their empty gray eyes upon me as I passed.

I heard a sizzle. Behind me, wherever I had stepped, I left a patch of burning carpet. A smoldering footprint with every step. Yet, strangely, the carpet waited until I took another step before the previous spot lit up.

"This isn't real," I said to myself.

I didn't recognize my voice, or that my thought had turned to speech until it was already said. My own mind was barely audible within my head.

"Not. Real."

Saying it out loud didn't change anything. I slapped myself, hard. But that somehow only made what I saw with my open eyes more real. It was as if this place was fueled by pain.

"None of this is happening . . ." I said, just shy of screaming the words.

This time saying it brought a tiny sliver of understanding. I held it close, held it tight, like a wanderer holding the last torch in the darkness.

"It isn't happening," I said with more force, willing that torch in my mind to burn just a little brighter.

The thought became an anchor. It grounded my mind in this hellscape.

I couldn't help myself and glanced at one of the dead on my left. The wrongness I saw was so strong, it was like looking at razorblades. I winced, covered my eyes, and continued down the hall. That ringing was rising in volume until I couldn't even hear the screech of another lightning bolt. When its flash illuminated the room, I saw Black standing before me for just an instant, and then he was gone.

The dead began to move. Little twitches, just enough to make me look at them. But looking at them hurt. Then the little twitches turned into violent shakes. Tremors ran through every one of the bodies, the inhuman spasms went faster and faster until they blurred before me. With every step further it felt like knives drilled deeper into my ears. Every sound I heard sent another twist into the invisible daggers. And every second the dead caught my attention was like pouring hot glass into my eyes.

My eyes began to bleed. I screamed, a pitiful wail that echoed off the stone walls of the grand hall. Just as the shrieking thunder came to deafen me, it was all snuffed out. All became silent, and all the dead became still.

I felt something behind me. When I turned, I found myself before a throne. Unfathomably tall and carved of dark stone, it rose higher in the air than a skyscraper. The seat was hundreds of feet above me, but what sat upon it dwarfed all other horrors I'd witnessed so far.

It was nothing less than a titan, towering above me. This being, because that was the only word I could think of to describe it, was clothed in hellish black armor. It was as if every piece had been forged from thousands of swords, *millions*, and somehow, I knew that each of those blades had a cruel and wicked history. Merely looking upon this great darkness sent more blood running down my eyes.

This was hell. Though it looked nothing like what Sunday School had described, I knew it in my bones. And if I was in hell, then this monster was its ruler. Looking upon it, despite the blood coursing down my face, I could see the malice emanating from it. It was cruelty given form. Pain forged into metal. Something about it felt older than imaginable, older than the devil I knew.

And then it spoke. Just a single word.

"YOU..."

Its voice was like an ocean of blood crashing upon a rocky beach. Deafening. Powerful. Hearing the hurricane force of its breath put me to my knees.

"BELONG... HERE..."

The hooked corpses around me shook once more, flung into blurry unnatural convulsions by this dark god's words. When I tried to look away from the devil on the throne, I found myself transfixed. The more I stared, the more I bled. From eyes, ears, and now mouth. I had to tear my mask from my face just to keep from suffocating. I choked and dug my fingers into my face from the pain. A thick coppery taste filled my throat. Then, the bodies began to burn. All at once the mass of mutilated bodies became a funeral pyre that filled the hall.

My nostrils were too drowned with blood to smell the stench of the inflamed dead. The seated tyrant turned its wrists over, and I saw he held lengths of chains within each hand. Hundreds of links in its palms like they were bracelets. When it gathered the chains up in its hands, countless dead came with them. Countless burning bodies drawn up into the air.

I screamed. Long, hopelessly. My throat ran raw as the blood-slicked scream turned into nothing more than a feral cry. Beyond fear. Beyond pain. Taken to a point past what it even meant to be human anymore. There was a tug around my feet and looking down I saw a thick coil of iron links around my ankles. It went taut and dragged me across the stone floor towards the dark throne.

The devil in metal loomed over me. Its throne became an inferno as the chained bodies burned down to nothing but skeletons. Lightning struck next to me, so close I could feel it in my chest, and the flash showed me some of the bodies yet to be consumed by the fire.

I recognized their faces. Kelly. Tag. Billy. Rain. Vaun. Mason. And then there was Madison. One by one they joined the blaze, but Madison was the last. I couldn't bear to watch her burn. I instead wished the fire to take me first. I wanted death to claim my soul, to end this madness and set me free. If this was hell, then dying was an easy way out.

But the flames never came near me. And it was only then that I understood. The devil didn't want me dead; he wanted me to serve with him. He held me in his hand, and my cries went silent as I simply had none left. My eyes filled with blood, and I went blind in the dark.

Though I could see no more, still I heard it speak to me.

"YOU… BELONG… HERE…"

Another bolt of lightning flashed, and this time it struck me full in the chest.

PART 3

UNBREAKABLE

*"Maybe you need to know the darkness
before you can appreciate the light."*

—Madeline L'engle

CHAPTER 57

The lightning arced through my heart. I sat up, screaming. That tormented throne room, and its seated terrible king, disappeared. I was back on Rourke's plane, both Rain and Mason standing over me. They looked at me with wide frantic eyes. Mason had a set of defibrillator paddles in her hands. It only took a second to do the math.

"Fucking hell, Boss," said Rain. "We lost you there for a minute."

"Two minutes," Mason corrected.

She set the paddles down and walked away. I took a long while to sit up fully and clear my head of all the fog.

"Okay, what the hell happened? How'd I get back here?"

"You tell us," said Mason. "I came to topside—fuck you, by the way—and comms were dark. Elevator controls were locked out, whatever happened down there caused too much interference. Rain tried unlocking a back way in for me, but there was nothing. I doubled back to the cargo elevator and found you there. Somehow clawed your way back to the surface before doing your best vegetable impersonation and having what looked like a heart-attack."

A big wet tongue slapped the back of my neck, and then Dante was nuzzling me. I didn't realize I was shaking until I held him close. The shakes died down a little. If the ladies noticed, they weren't saying anything.

"Morpheus?" I asked, bracing for what I already knew.

"Bugged out," said Rain. "Everything electromagnetic went to shit for a few minutes. I got pushed out of every system. By the time I got back inside the Basement's network, Legion was gone. Nothing in the air the satellites caught, so they must've switched to a car. By now they're on the highway, heading who knows where."

Too much forested tree coverage for satellites to track vehicles. You don't become an international cabal like Legion without learning how to lose a tail.

"You stole the boss's plane?" Kelly laughed.

That laugh used to bring life to a room. Now it made me wince. He was spread out on the seat across from me, sinking into the plush of the char and letting out a loud sigh.

"Bud, let me tell you. This is *so* much comfortable than the metal slab in the morgue where I've been hanging out. It's way too cold in there, by the way."

I averted my eyes, not wanting anyone to catch me looking at a ghost. More so, I didn't want to see Kelly's pale dead skin or the ragged hole in the center of his throat. The massive entry and exit wounds didn't seem to be giving his ghost any problems speaking.

"We've gotta keep moving," I said, rubbing my temples.

"Technically you were dead a moment ago," said Mason. "Vaun and the others are clearing out of the safehouse, we'll regroup and figure out our next play. But you won't be doing us any good if you keel over again or go Krueger, so just cool it for a minute. Try to get some rest."

She went to the cockpit. Rain followed suit.

"Alone at last," grinned Kelly. "You know honesty is the best policy—I mean, so I'm told. Not exactly true in our line of work—

but yeah, good call on not saying anything to them about little old me."

I waited for the cockpit door to latch closed before speaking. "You're not real."

"First of all, that's cold," he said, propping his feet up on the table in front of him. "Second, I'm only here because of you."

"Yeah, I got you killed. I got Billy's face broken. I let Black kill Rourke and every other friend back Home. I already know it, Kelly. So, if you're planning on haunting me about some shit I already hate myself for, you can save it."

Kelly's ghost whistled.

"It's just the Morpheus exposure," I said, rubbing my temples. "It'll fade. And so will you."

Kelly enthusiastically swiveled his chair back and forth. "Maybe. But you did take a massive dose, maybe it cracked you just a little? You're not a Krueger, but let's face it, you've been walking a razor line of sanity for a while now. It wouldn't take much to push you over the edge to Crazytown. Or maybe the Morpheus Engine really *is* magic?!"

It better fucking not be. If Kelly wasn't just a figment of my strangely irradiated brain, then that meant the painful place I'd seen was real too.

"It'll fade," I said.

I closed my eyes. The plane went silent, then the only sound was the engines firing up and us taxiing down the runway. I forced deep breaths, trying to re-center myself, but it felt like stacking pieces of a Jenga tower that kept collapsing. Calm escaped me. When I opened my eyes, Kelly still sat there, reclining comfortably in the chair.

He raised an inquisitive eyebrow in my direction, "Get some sleep, bud. I'll wake you when we get there."

CHAPTER 58

Handing out tickets was one of his least favorite parts of the job. But, given the current downpour, Tack would rather write the guy the ticket and get him to slow down than see his car wrapped around the guardrail a couple miles down the road. The highway was slick. The last thing he wanted was to close out his shift was another wreck.

Tack rapped a knuckle on the window and the driver rolled his window down, "Alright, Mister Fawcett, there's your license back. Just slow it down for me, alright? Rain, brakes, and high speed don't mix well."

Yeah, maybe he was getting soft for letting the kid off with a warning. Most teenagers got the pucker effect when they saw red and blue lights flashing behind them, after that they tended to drive ten-and-two as if they were taking their first driving test. Tack patted the roof of the car to send him on his way.

"You have a good night n—"

He stopped short when he saw something in the tree line beyond the car. A snap of twigs that made the hairs on the back of Tack's neck stand straight up. The passing headlights from the highway lit it up in quick flashes. It was hard to see clearly, but Tack could tell it was big. Real damn big.

"Officer, is everything—"

"Stay right here for me."

Even from here, Tack could smell it. The filthy fur of a wild animal. The odor always got worse from being wet, but underneath that something even worse. Something rotting.

When he was a boy, his grandpa had shot a bear on their property. It had limped away and disappeared before gramps could finish it off. A week or so later, it came back. The bullet-wound had festered, and the animal had gone mad from infection and pain. It came upon Tack, only five years old then, and even at that young age he thought he was going to die. He'd ran, and his dad had scared it off with a rifle. They'd never seen it again, and though it'd likely died of infection they never found its corpse.

Here it was. Tack knew it. It had finally come to get him. He thumbed the leather catch on his holster and brought his revolver up in both hands. The bear burst forth from the tree line and charged at him.

That terrible smell hit him before the bear neared. It was enough to make his eyes water. The kid in the car, Fawcett, was screaming at Tack but he couldn't be bothered with it. He emptied all six chambers in the bear's direction. His hands were trembling so badly that the last shot went wide. The driver's side window cracked and Fawcett clutched at his neck. His screams turned to wet gurgles.

Tack reloaded, but when he looked back up the bear was gone. Yet that rotting fur stench grew stronger. He was practically drowning in it. For some reason it started to feel like a screwdriver was twisting into his temples. A scream came forth from Tack's lips, he wasn't sure why. Impossibly, Fawcett answered them with an inhuman roar. Above his neck was the head of a bear. It looked at Tack, and when it roared a second time maggots spewed forth from its mouth.

He shot the bear-man again and again. Wriggling maggots spilled forth from the bullet wounds and onto the asphalt near Tack's boots. Something monstrous screamed from Tack's side, but it didn't come from a man's throat. This one was the scream of a semi-trailer engine as Tack stepped right into its path.

The dash-cam on Sheriff Aaron Tack's cruiser caught everything. What started as a routine traffic stop ended in an unprovoked shooting. The sheriff had been turned to hamburger by the oncoming truck, so much so that no autopsy would be able to determine what had caused his apparent psychotic break.

A second camera had also recorded the events, but this one had watched with satisfaction. Simon finished the video and signaled Black to kill the Morpheus Engine, then made the call.

"Well?" Holt asked.

"I'm sending the footage now, ma'am," Simon said. "Let me know if any other test-runs will be needed."

CHAPTER 59

We circled our wagons at the closest Black Spear site to the Basement. To say that we were given less than a warm welcome would be a horrible understatement. The head of Pike Site, Commander Burt Galleon, greeted us at the fence line with lips so harshly pursed, you'd think they were superglued together. Burt Galleon was a ten-year Black Spear vet, and if his reputation was accurate, then he ran the tightest ship imaginable. Which is probably why he didn't care much for us showing up at his doorstep.

Galleon headed Storm Squad, one of Black Spear's finest. Funny thing was, they'd all kept their distance when we arrived. Turns out there were whispers going around the Black Spear teams that Cerberus Squad had acquired a more deserving moniker: Cursed Squad. Seemed like every time another squad teamed up with us, they tended to get ghosted. Achilles Squad was the first, choking on teargas and shot dead in their sleep back when I was an FNG. After that came Hydra, who had been ambushed by the Marstelli twins when we worked the Warmaker business. And, of course, most recently there was Valkyrie. I wondered just how much Galleon knew. It was one thing to know a sister squad was killed, another thing entirely to learn that their heads had been spiked and a message etched into their tongues.

Vaun brought the others up north from the safehouse on the second day. *He* was given a reception akin to a long-lost family member. Obligatory jokes were made between him and Galleon. He said Galleon's mustache was looking grayer these days, Galleon countered by making a less than sincere compliment on Vaun's new cane and the collection of scars Phobos Marstelli had left him.

"Your face has seen more knifework than a Real Housewife of Beverly Hills."

"Yeah, well you look like a 70's porn star who refuses to retire," said Vaun.

"Speaking of retirement, how's that working out for yourself?"

"You got me there."

"Shit. Damn good to see you, brother."

They shook on that, and after the two spoke privately everyone else warmed up to us a little. Perhaps the curse was stronger in me than it was Vaun. Cerberus, broken as its extant members were, was at least all in one place now. The only problem was Legion had vanished. It felt like we were all just waiting for the other shoe to drop.

That's what was fucking with me the most. We were being forced to play reactive rather than proactive, waiting for Mr. Black to make his next move known and try our best not to play right into it. They had already claimed Morpheus, but for what purpose eluded us. The worst part about having no leads was the down time it gave me. My mind was still playing tricks on me days after Black had unleashed the Morpheus Engine's pulse. The one time I tried to sleep, the dreams had been so terrifyingly vivid that I bolted upright and woke the entire floor with my scream. I've since refused to lie down or close my eyes longer than a blink.

Commander Galleon found me in Pike Site's modest dining

hall, nursing a large mug of coffee that had gone cold some time ago. The hour was late, and we were the only ones there, but he decided to take the seat right across from me. He'd brought the pot of coffee over and offered to top me off.

"Let me guess," I said, holding out my mug, "you're here to tell me that I should be sleeping? That sitting around isn't a good use of my time?"

"Maybe I just think it's sort of sad seeing you drink coffee by yourself," he said, filling a cup of his own. From the corner of my eye, for just a second, Kelly sat next to me. When I blinked the chair was empty. The absence only felt colder.

"I'm not alone, man."

He gave me a queer look but thought better than to ask.

"Yeah, down time can really send those skeletons in the closet sprinting for daylight. Better get used to it, though," Galleon said. "All teams are grounded. Word coming down the pipe is that Sloan is looking to shut us down."

"Sloan?"

"Walter Sloan."

He drew the name out with palpable distaste, grimacing like he needed to clean food stuck from between his teeth. Galleon took a long sip of coffee before continuing.

"Deputy Director of Operations with the CIA, he's been vocal for quite some time about how the Black Spear initiative needs to be absorbed into the company. Feels it's dangerous to grant us so much autonomy. Up until recently, he's had some very vocal opposition on that topic."

"As in Rourke."

"As in Rourke," Galleon confirmed. "Problem with being as secret as we are is that when the top guy goes belly-up, us shooters are more or less kept in the dark as far as what happens next."

Rourke. Another death at my feet. The man was an absolute

juggernaut in our world, and the vacuum he left behind would only continue to send out ripples.

"Thanks for letting us crash here," I said.

I clinked my mug against his in a toast, doing so before he could pull it away lest my curse touch him.

He gave me a modest shrug. "Professional courtesy, Squad Leader to Squad Leader. That, and a favor was owed."

"Glad Vaun didn't mind calling it in."

Galleon gave me a hard stare. "It wasn't Vaun I owed. If it wasn't for Dan Kelly, a couple boxes of .50 BMG, and a high-powered rifle, my entire squad would be in graves right now."

He let that hang in the air, and I chose not to cheapen the moment with more moping.

"Think you can get the rest of your people to play nice, too? The second we get a trail we could use some back-up. These Immortals are some heavy hitters."

"Don't worry about my guys. You're a captain now, West. What's up with yours?"

The question hit like a hook to the jaw. I'd avoided Tag and Billy since they made it up north. I'd first used their recovery as an excuse, but after Vaun told me Tag was stubbornly up and helping Rain with the Basement's files, and Billy was self-medicating with Pike Site's wet bar, I'd continued to make myself scarce. There was just so much shit between us all. It's hard enough to look at your shortcomings, harder still when those failures are marked in the flesh and blood of your own men.

"It's a good question," the returned ghost of Kelly said.

He flickered, like a light going out, and was gone again. Hopefully that meant my brain was knitting itself back together. I could still taste metal in my mouth every now and then. Little by little that was going away too, though.

"My White Shield liaison and my computer guru are both

ripping through the data files we retrieved," I said. "They'll find some weakness. Some way for us to track the Morpheus Engine. Then we can get all in synch before we finish this. 'Til then, I can wait just a little longer and take my time with *that*."

"Speaking of White Shield, the Director himself has been calling me to get through to you. It's a little annoying, considering I haven't told anyone you're here."

"Director Goode? Pretty sure he knows everything. I was supposed to help him with some dog and pony show joint task force conference, that was before everything went to hell."

"You're ignoring the White Shield Director's calls? There's reckless and then there's, well, all the words I have sound too similar to 'stupid.'"

"Jotting it down on my To-Do List," I said and wrote 'Call Goode' on my forearm with a felt pen.

Galleon itched his mustache with his thumb. "Looks like you're about to cross one thing off that list."

I raised an eyebrow, but then saw he was looking past me. I turned and saw Rain in the doorway. She held a stack of papers and was giving me a thumbs-up.

"We got something!"

Galleon and I looked at each other again, and his face went all tight-lipped again.

"Time's up, Captain."

CHAPTER 60

If there was a more apt name for Lady Holt's superyacht, Black surely could not think of one. He'd at first been taken aback by the sheer size of the vessel. It dwarfed all others in the water, larger by an order of magnitude. It, like everything else about her, was a demonstration. That constant was something Black admired about the woman: her power. She simply exuded it.

Black's power was death, something he wielded better than anyone. Those that feared his name did so out of an understanding of what he was capable of. Lady Holt, however, held something else entirely in her hand. Hers was the power of influence, of control, and of position. With a snap of her fingers, she could end a hundred men's lives a hundred different ways in every corner of the globe. The fact that literally snapping her fingers could break her own fingertips was an irony Black did not overlook. If anything, it further spoke to her authority.

An unusually high wave lazily rolled against the side of the ship, not hard enough jostle her but enough to bring Black back to the present. Simon and his entourage were summoned to Lady Holt's court to present their prize personally. As Black was the only one with intimate knowledge on the Morpheus Engine and its effects, he was brought in tow. His payment, and their business, was to be concluded upon delivery.

Simon and the brittle woman discussed the recent trial runs they'd enacted prior to arriving. Her towering body man, Rinx, escorted Black to a balcony deck outside and told him to wait until he beckoned him back.

But Black was not some loyal dog that could be summoned at a master's whim. It was growing old playing this part for them. He slid open the door and stepped through. Rinx stood in his way, placing a hand firm as iron on Black's chest, and looked to Holt for approval to break him. Instead, she used a delicate finger—little more than a bone wrapped in paper-thin skin—to beckon Black closer. Black shouldered past Rinx's hand and stalked into the room. The armed sentries around the room, each adorned in identical tailored black and white suits, held their weapons tighter as he approached.

"I can't recall the last time someone dared to be so bold around me," she said.

She gestured next to Simon, much to his chagrin. Black eased himself in, finding greater pleasure in Simon's discomfort than the cushioned seat itself. Simon sat as rigid as a man attending his first important job interview. Tight-lipped, back straight, left hand upon left knee and right hand upon right knee. Up until now he had always adopted the position of the man in charge, yet now Holt had his balls so tightly clamped in a vice that he'd diminished like a whipped pup. That Black was next to him for it made it all the better.

Meanwhile, Black was stretched out and perfectly at ease. Simon looked at him from the corner of his eye, so Black stared back and draped his arm along the backrest. This game between them of who was at the top of the food chain had grown stale. Now, with the addition of a better opponent, Black was done pretending to be under Simon's thumb.

"The wire transfer has been initiated, ma'am," said Simon. "The trials we've run have shown us everything we need to know about the next phase of—"

"This man knows nothing," Black interrupted.

Simon bristled. Holt cut a glance to Simon, perhaps expecting him to refute Black's claim. Just as he prepared to speak, she instead gestured to Black to continue. Simon physically choked on his words. The assassin offered Simon a handkerchief when his chokes turned to stifled coughs.

"Those scientists were playing with the Morpheus Engine for decades, and even then, they'd barely tapped the surface of its science. Mister Ellis here toyed around with it for barely a few days, do you think he's mastered its use?"

Simon's hands balled into fists. "My Immortals copied their entire database, ma'am. Everything they learned over the years is at our fingertips. We know what they knew."

"Firstly," said Holt, "they are *my* Immortals, my boy. You don't sit at the table yet."

Simon's eyes fell to the ground and his cheeks burned red. He began to twist the Praetorian ring on his finger. A ring that should have been a mark of prestige, and instead was merely an unearned family heirloom. This job was supposed to fast-track Simon to a loftier position. Instead, Black would steal the moment from him just when it was within his grasp. This was death by a thousand cuts for his soul, and it was such an intoxicatingly rare pain for Black to savor.

"Secondly, your childish competition between each other is utterly beneath me. Our endeavor's second phase is above all else."

"Of course, ma'am," he stammered. "I just thought it prudent to remove outsiders before discussing—"

"Leave us," she commanded. Much to Simon's dismay, she meant him and not Black. Simon hesitated, for only a second, before rising graciously and walking away with tail tucked securely between legs.

"All of you . . . *out*."

The suited security guards promptly followed behind him, leaving only Lady Holt, Black, and Rinx, who still stood behind him.

"Pity that," she said almost sadly. "Young Simon's grandfather was once my Praetorian. Dear Dorian there was hand-picked to replace him when a sniper's bullet meant for me took the use of his legs. You've seen that silver ring Simon wears? That little bauble belonged to his grandfather before him and now the poor sod carries it like a damned security blanket. It's a shame the Ellis bloodline has led to one with such lofty ambition and such little, well, I'm not sure what it is he's missing."

"He's too human," mused Black. "Not a monster. Not like us."

Holt gave him an evaluating glance, weighing what he'd said. Then, very slowly, she nodded. It was the sincerest of acknowledgments.

"To many, knowledge is a certain power," Black said. "To presume to learn from someone is to take a piece of that power for yourself in some small way. That's why the others won't ask you. They're afraid of dying for that piece. I'm not, so I'll ask: who are you, really?"

She pursed her lips, then gave Rinx a little flick of her finger. He bowed his head slightly then went to a nearby wet bar to fix two drinks for them.

"Knowledge is power. Violence is power. Money is power," she said at length. "So many kinds just there for the taking. Names, though. They hold one so very different from the others. You yourself have quite a colorful assortment of them. Lord of Blades. *Le Peintre*. Papa Shadow. Such mystique, such legend. Some call me the 'Glass Queen' behind my back. They don't think I've heard, but I hear it all. 'Lady Death', now that one I prefer. Tell me, do you think they deemed me Lady Holt out of mere respect?"

Rinx returned with two highball glasses. Holt took hers and

waited for Black to drink first. There was a challenge in her eyes, two-fold. The first was to take a drink unafraid of poison. The second was to see if he dared further his line of questioning, dared to nibble further on that fruit of knowledge.

Black drank deep.

"Who are you?"

"I am Lady Margot Holt, firstborn daughter of Prince George, Duke of Kent. Born to a nameless whore and forgotten by the crown, thirty-seventh in line for the throne."

And there it was. The secret that explained the power. The respect. The birthright and familial esteem, which would lead someone to climb so high in the shadowed world.

"What do you think that was like?" she asked.

She set the highball aside and her grip tightened along her gold and crystalline cane. That platinum ring of hers caught the light differently and seemed to glow as she craned her head to look at Black. The words she spoke burned her tongue like flitting embers.

"Being born of such privilege, such high birthright, yet the very bottom of the bloodline? You couldn't even find my end of the family tree on Wikipedia. I'm sure some dusty tome in a forgotten library makes mention of my father's affair, but certainly nothing of me. History tends not to focus on powerful men's mistresses or the offspring they bear them. King George the VI was an embarrassing risk for the empire because of a stutter, what do you think they'd say of me? Adorned in casts and scars, already walking with a limp before my sixth birthday. The crown would never be mine."

Black wondered how long these truths had lived like snakes within her, fighting to slither to the surface. He knew that there were no illusions between the two of them. The only reason she allowed him to know this was because in the end, unlike the others, he didn't care. The thought of taking advantage of this information would never even cross his mind. The grave takes all, royalty and paupers alike. *That* was Black's truth, and it mattered more to him than hers.

"Imagine knowing your whole life that no matter how far you rose above your station, the highest point would forever be out of your reach," she said.

Black didn't need to imagine, though. He felt that in his soul. It's what West had stolen when he'd reaped those thousands of lives. He'd stolen away the mantle of being death's favorite.

"And so, my dear boy, I found my own. I discovered my own throne wreathed in shadows."

"Is that what this has all been about?" he asked. "Hurting your family?"

"I'm beyond such trivial matters now."

"I don't know if everyone would consider the crown of England anything trivial."

She scoffed, "You know the funny thing about power I've discovered since taking it? The crown is so far below me, I cannot even see the bloody thing."

Black emptied his glass. Holt twisted her platinum ring carefully around her finger, perhaps wondering what was on Black's mind, perhaps wondering if she should give the order to have Rinx break his spine.

"Now then, what do we do with you?" she asked. "Our business is concluded, but perhaps you were interested in a more long-term service?"

She abruptly stopped turning her ring around. Black took a closer look and saw that there was a skull signet on it. Its empty eyes stared at him invitingly. Once more he thought of the power this woman wielded. This queen who sat perched atop her shadowed throne. This was something he hadn't realized he was after. Something more than what he'd been: death, wielded on an entirely higher tier.

Black rose from his seat and knelt before Lady Holt.

"Will you serve Legion?" she asked.

Black kissed the cold metal of her ring. "Yes, to the death."

CHAPTER 61

Rain's hand was so jittery, it threatened to spill her sugar-free Red Bull onto the tile. I tried not to be a little worried about what she and Tag had turned the room into. Reports covered every square inch of wallpaper. There were dozens of photos—from old grainy black and white ones to newer HD ones that could've been taken yesterday—and they spoke of a story that went back decades. It reminded me of Vaun's own conspiracy web he'd pinned to the walls of the safehouse. More and more, I saw that it wasn't a sign of crazy, but rather how twisted and interwoven the truth was. Not just that, but the scale of it. I was starting to miss straightforward cases that dealt with superviruses, a Siberian tundra, and a single sniper shot.

"Alright then, Miss Harper, take a deep breath and tell the class what you learned," I said.

She picked up a laser pointer and her eyes darted around the room as she tried to figure out where to begin.

"Okay, okay, okay, so first off . . . alright, *here*! The Morpheus Engine. During the first test runs, they were experimenting with the effect it had on the EM spectrum. Radio waves, basic power and utilities, electronic digital systems, stuff like that. Which it did, *but* that's when they figured out that the radiation it gives off is unique."

"Unique how?" asked Vaun.

"Unique in the sense that it seemingly plays by its own rules. It can be measured similarly to gamma waves and beta particles, but it doesn't affect organic matter the same way. Some of its effects can be suppressed through doses of Potassium Iodide to limit absorption in the thyroid, but even then, the Basement staff had to supplement that with antipsychotics. That's why everyone had those bottles on them down there. Subjects who underwent multiple exposures never developed any cancers, but they did go batshit crazy. Cap, you took a full-blast in close proximity, but have no radiation burns. No measurable acute radiation syndrome. The Morpheus waves, for whatever reason, affect the mind more than the body. Low levels can cause anxiety, paranoia. Mid-level doses will trigger full tactile and audio-visual hallucinations."

"We got a very intimate experience of that, yes," said Mason.

"Yes," Rain nodded.

Her laser pointer found several screen-captured images from testing footage. Each of the subjects looked terrified as they fought back or succumbed to some invisible horror.

"The mind makes it real. One person sees a pack of dogs chewing his legs off, and his mind tells him he has no legs and can't walk. The pain receptors fire off to his brain until he has a heart attack. Another guy sees armed insurgents charging his position, so he empties a machine gun into a squad of friendlies. A third person thinks they're being strangled, so their brain tells their lungs and throat that no air is getting in. They stop breathing and suffocate."

"Or drown," Mason whispered, her brow furrowing in remembrance.

"It's a chaos weapon," said Vaun. "It doesn't matter if it doesn't kinetically destroy a city. You turn it on, and everyone inside will tear the place down themselves."

Somehow that possibility seemed too small for Legion. They decapitated an entire squad to send a message. They murdered the head of America's blackest of black ops organizations in his own office just to drive that message home. No, simply destroying a city wasn't enough.

"What fuels it?" I asked. "I mean, it's called an engine so can it, I don't know? Run out of gas?"

Tag gave me a signature grunt from the far side of the room. He pointed at a schematic printout, which caused him to momentarily wince at the still fresh knife wound in his shoulder, and broke it down for us.

"'Reactor' would be a better word. Four rods make up the core, and the weapon was designed to accumulate its radiation and discharge pulses at various levels to the surrounding area. Exposing the rods, of course, would expose anyone in close proximity to a high dose."

"What are these rods made of?" I asked. "If those are the heart of this thing I'd like to know where they come from and, more importantly, if there's any more Morpheus rods waiting to be made."

The blank look on Tag's face was less than reassuring. He reluctantly pointed to Rain, who took over and brought our attention to a picture of a large crater.

"Either of you familiar with the Willamette Meteorite?" she asked.

"Nope," I said.

"Yes," said Vaun. He shrugged at me. "Nat Geo, you should watch it sometime. The Willamette was the largest meteorite discovered in America. Thousands of years old."

"Kudos to you," said Rain. "It's comprised of mostly iron and nickel, but the other materials in its makeup were at concentration levels thousands of times higher than any naturally occurring on Earth. Stuff like Iridium, Platinum, Palladium, and the Morpheus metal. The Willamette Meteorite held most of the Morpheus ore ever discovered. The material for the four rods were extracted and smelted from it."

Something she'd just said snagged me like a thorn. "Hold up. You just said 'naturally occurring', so there *is* more of this stuff?"

"According to the Basement's reports, yes. Trace elements have been found in the earth all over the world, just at concentration levels so much lower that they're practically nonexistent. We're talking point-zero-zero-one parts per million at the most. Gold is four-hundred times as abundant. Some areas are anomalies and, for some unknown reason, have higher concentrations. People would experience heightened levels of fear or outright hallucinations in some of these spots."

Vaun pondered that and nudged my shoulder. "Makes you wonder, huh? How many ghost stories and haunted houses were caused by this stuff being in the soil? How many nutjobs went psycho just because their house was built on the wrong ground?"

"Exactly!" said Rain.

She finished her sugar-free Red Bull and crunched the can in her fist.

"Fucking *exactly* what I was thinking. After they extracted all the Morpheus metal from the meteor, they took ground surveys across the country trying to get more. Couple places had soil samples with elevated levels that stand out. The suburb of Amityville in Long Island. Roanoke Island in Delaware."

I took a long breath through the nostrils. I wanted to absorb everything they'd dropped on me, but it was just too much to grasp. I needed a handle. Just a way for me to squeeze this all down to a manageable size. Make it small enough for me to swallow without my brain exploding. I guess Rain noticed I was about to scream from sheer frustration, because she shook her hands as if brushing away the topic.

"Cool history lesson," I admitted. "Do we have any good news on how to keep ourselves from going full *Nightmare on Elm Street*?"

As if on cue the door to the conference room opened and Madison Archer bustled in with her arms full of black cases. "Sorry I'm late. Did you start without me?"

Rain gave her an enthusiastic thumbs up. Mason's face scrunched in amusement, and she cast a brief glance in my direction.

"Dr. Archer has something that just might help," Rain explained.

Madison handed one of the black cases my way, I set it down between Tag and myself. We both flipped the latches and popped the lid. Inside were several earbud radios, which looked nearly identical to the standard ones we carried on every mission.

Mason snuck a peek over my shoulder at the case's contents. "Pretty sure we already have these, Dr. Archer. Though you have been working around the clock and this *is* the third gear drop-off you've done this week, so maybe we should cut you some slack."

Madison chose not to rise to the bait and instead gestured for Mason to insert the earbud to see for herself.

"Wow!" Mason said with mock surprise. "How utterly underwhelming. You're not getting sloppy on us are you, Doctor?"

Instead of answering, Madison hit a single button. Mason winced in pain as a quick sharp screech pierced her ears. She clawed at the earbud and threw it back into the case before balling her fists at her sides and staring death at Madison.

"That was *unpleasant*," said Mason.

"Good," Madison replied, her face betraying nothing. "That's kind of the point. These modified earbuds are your first line of defense. Your Cicadas. I re-tooled one of Samuel Cain's Screech prototypes for this. A constant high-pitch whine will stave off and disrupt the body's natural sleep cycle to keep the bad thoughts away. It'll be low enough that you'll barely register them, but your mind will. We can spike that volume to give you a quick jumpstart should you be exposed to Morpheus. Think of them as a mildly annoying dream repellant."

"You said 'first line,'" Galleon commented. "What's the backup plan?"

Madison swiveled a second case around and popped the lid. Inside were a series of auto-injector needles.

"Call these your Kick needles. Cocktail of adrenaline and antipsychotics. Everyone will be prescribed some lower dose pills, because the Kicks pack a hell of a punch. Emergency use only. You overdo these and you're likely to have your heart burst before the enemy can do anything to you. Especially you, Captain."

She looked at me, and I realized with shame that she knew about my little episode of briefly dying at the Basement. I wondered who from my team had spilled the beans and decided it had to have been Rain.

"Any questions?" she asked.

When there were none, she gave me one final professional nod before taking her place at the back of the room.

There were too many things I wanted to say to her, and too many bigger things at work in this moment to spare the time it would take.

"Enough of that, let's get to the *other* good news. We have a lead on where they are," said Rain. "We set a White Shield satellite to monitor any radiation spikes and, sure enough, we got a hit. The past two nights at exactly twenty-eight minutes past midnight there was a high ping that matched the Morpheus Engine's energy signature."

"It's Black, he wants me to know where he is," I said.

"Why do you say that?"

"Because two-thousand four-hundred and twenty-eight was the final body count from the *Firestorm* nanites. That's how many people I killed to stop Samuel Cain's war. Black worships death like some great god, and he thinks I've taken his place as its favorite by giving it a more worthy offering."

I looked at Rain's map and spotted the two dots where Black had purposely released Morpheus energy. There was a third dot marking the Basement's location. Combined, the three breadcrumbs showed a steady trail headed northwest.

"So, the million-dollar question: what's northwest?" asked Mason.

"Fly out of Seattle International and disappear," suggested Vaun. "Or hop the border and cut to the wind. Vancouver's port isn't just the biggest in Canada, it's the largest on the entire west coast."

Something about Vaun's idea was sticking in my ear a little. For some reason I definitely agreed that Vancouver was Legion's destination, I just wasn't entirely sure why. I folded my arms across my chest to think and looked down to the ground, hoping to pull an answer out of thin air. Instead, I caught the answer already written across my own arm in Sharpie. It was the reminder I'd written myself after talking to Galleon: Call Goode.

CHAPTER 62

Cole West. 10:00 p.m.
Pike Site. Seattle, Washington

The pieces didn't so much as slide together as they slammed into place so fast, my stomach flipped over itself. Intelligence chiefs from every major nation were meeting to pool their resources. They were going to stitch all their incomplete intel together into a net to drag Legion into the light, but Legion was less than obliged to leave the shadows.

A cabal like them, with their power rooted in being unknown, would do anything to maintain control. Bringing them into the spotlight, giving the enemy faces and identities, would loosen the stranglehold on everyone stuck under their thumb. We could find and freeze their money, identify and take down their command structure, or disrupt their means of communication for their entire sordid ranks. That, of course, was dependent on making Legion a public threat rather than the boogeyman behind the curtain that only black-ops folks like us knew about.

"We're going to need all hands on deck," I said. "Injured or not."

"Good," said Tag. He was far from healed, but it didn't bother him in the slightest.

"Count me and my boys in," said Galleon from behind us. He

gave me a shrug. "Cursed or not, you're family."

"Appreciate it, Commander."

Just as I headed out the door to gear up, Vaun caught me by the wrist. He waited until everyone else had cleared out of the room before he spoke.

"All hands means *all* hands, Cole. You going to talk to Billy or what?"

Instead of answering him, I just pushed past. I'd been avoiding this conversation; Vaun knew and was straightforward enough to call me out on it. But the last words we'd shared were less than cordial. I wasn't Kelly. I didn't have the years upon years of friendship and trust he'd built with Billy. I had a couple of good ones, and those might not be enough for us to bounce back on.

I found myself outside Billy's temporary quarters before I knew it. I thought about knocking, then for some reason thought I'd better just open the damn door and get this over with. Like ripping off a band-aid, except this was bound to be more painful.

He was inside, sitting in a chair with tired eyes to the ground. The room reeked of booze and I had to fight against the empty bottles on the ground to push the door open. An unopened bottle of whiskey rested in Billy's lap. Bottom shelf plastic bottle with a generic label, which didn't bode well. Stranger still was what looked like a bible held lazily in one hand.

"Gonna stare, or you gonna speak?" he managed to ask.

His jaw was still wired shut, muffling his words and making them sound somehow angrier.

"Not that you and I have had many heart to heart conversations lately, but I never took you for a believer," I said, raising my chin towards the bible in his hands.

Billy scoffed, or rather did his best despite his injury. The bible was old and faded. There were dog-eared pages to serve as book-marks for important passages, and when Billy riffled a thumb through it, I caught a blur of notes taken in the margins.

"Not mine," Billy said, then he held the weathered book in front of his eyes as if trying to decipher its messages through the cover. "You know they cleaned out Kelly's locker before Home Site was taken out? Besides some uniforms, and a few photos, all he had in it was this and a necklace."

Billy set aside the bible, and I noticed a small silver cross chain on the table next to it. I couldn't recall ever seeing Kelly wear it before. I wasn't sure what to make of either of them. It looked like Billy was having a similarly hard time trying to understand how an accomplished killer like Daniel Kelly could simultaneously believe in an almighty God above and the promise of salvation.

Billy apparently chose not to dwell on that conundrum any further and instead turned his attention back to the unopened cheap whiskey.

"Planning on adding that to the collection?" I asked, using my foot to send one of the empty bottles rattling across the floor.

"Maybe. Haven't had a sip today, figured I'll make up for lost time. Easier to break over someone's head when it's empty anyway."

He looked up from the ground then. One part joke, one part threat. This band-aid wasn't coming off easy.

"Awfully hard to break a plastic bottle. How'd you manage to tank all this down the past few days with your mouth wired shut?"

Instead of saying anything, he just held up a simple bendy straw. Billy rolled the bottle back and forth in his palms. I could see the debate in his eyes. He wanted to crack it open and drown out the noise again. I was tempted to let him. Hell, I was tempted to join him. But there were some truths we both had to face first.

Kelly's lifeless form lurked at the back of the room, shaking its head in disappointment at me.

Tear the band-aid off, Cole.

Before I could speak, Billy grumbled another barb.

"You remember that bullet he took for you?"

The memory flashed before my eyes. Kelly tackling me from the path of a bullet, and the bullet punching through his shoulder instead.

"Of course. Saved my life on my first day."

Billy slowly turned to face me. "You know it still hurt him? It just, well it didn't heal right. His shoulder. He never bothered bringing it up to you, did he?"

I tried like hell not to let Billy's reveal cut me too deep. He barreled on when he saw his words were drawing blood.

"Of course, he didn't. Why would he?" Billy spoke softly, no need for menace in his tone. He hurled every word at me like a murder weapon. "That was him, wasn't it? Classic Kelly. But it hurt him. Every time he hugged a rifle stock into the pocket of his shoulder, every pull of the trigger and every kick of recoil. Every. Damn. Time. It hurt."

Then, he had to go and add one final cherry on top.

"You know, I just realized that the bullet that killed him was actually the *second* one he took for you."

He let me simmer in it. Feeling the heat of his anger, and the cold of our friend's absence. Kelly left a hole in our world and, like it or not, it felt like Billy and I were marooned on opposite sides of that hole.

"I miss him, too," I said.

As soon as the words passed my lips, I felt like it was the wrong thing to say. Despite his ruined jaw, Billy managed to scoff.

"You miss him? Yeah? Why's that?"

"He was . . . he was the best," I managed. "He was a hero. How many times has he averted disaster, how many lives has he saved?"

"You think that matters one measly fuck?" asked Billy with a mirthless laugh. "He died scared, helpless, on a back-alley rooftop and nobody will blink or notice. You think he'll even be granted military honors at his funeral? Think any of the officers he served under before Black Spear will show up? You think a *single* goddamn politician, or anyone in Washington who sent him forward to do what he did best, gives a shit?"

The venom in his words stung to hear. Worse still, they echoed the same painful concerns I'd thrown at Rourke in his office before.

"Nobody cares when a ghost dies, nobody but us," said Billy. "The only ones who will bat an eye that he's gone are those of us left behind to carry his coffin. I guess we should count our blessings that his body was already at a funeral home and not in the morgue at Home Site, buried in the rubble."

That fact was one I hadn't managed to think of yet. How much worse would this be if we were unable to even bury our friend? I read the writing on the wall and saw that Billy was seconds away from retreating into himself once more. Just another moment and he'd likely start guzzling that booze, and then he'd be truly lost to me.

"He's dead," I said.

Billy looked at me again. There was such anger in his eyes. Beneath it, fighting to the surface and him fighting even harder to keep it down, was the pain. I kept my stare on Billy, refusing to look at Kelly's ghost behind him. When I took a deep breath, Kelly flickered and vanished.

"He's dead, Billy. And that's on me. My call, my team, my—my soldier who died. My fuck up. So yeah, feel free to hate me about it. I already do."

There was so much loathing in his expression. But then I understood. That look was one I'd been seeing more and more elsewhere. I'd been seeing it in my own reflection. His anger wasn't for me, not entirely at least. He hated himself. Billy was the best fighter we had, and Black had folded him like origami. It wasn't that I'd gotten Kelly killed: it was that he'd failed to stop it.

"What do you want from me, 'Captain'?"

"We're in for a fight, and I need you in it with me. You're the *best* and you know it. We've got another shot at stopping them; I figured you might want a piece of the payback."

Billy held up the bottle and took one last look at it before setting it on the table next to him, unopened. "Correction: I *was* the best."

He pointed to his jaw. Time was short, and now that the band-aid was coming off, I wasn't in the mood to cater to his wounded pride any further.

"Alright then, how about this? You take that bendy straw of yours, and you suck it the fuck up. Boo-hoo your face got broken. We still have work to do."

Billy rose to his feet, and though I stood several inches taller he still looked up at me with one last vestige of challenge in his eyes. "That an order, sir?"

"There are bigger things happening right now than what's going on between you and me," I said carefully, then I put as hard an edge into my voice as I dared. "And you're goddamn right it's an order."

He nodded, and there was a change in the air. It was like the strings between us that had coiled tighter and tighter had suddenly been cut. For now, at least. This was the way it was, commander and subordinate, and we were both finally accepting it. My team, my call. I just hoped I was making the right one by bringing him back into the fold.

CHAPTER 63

It was almost time. Tomorrow morning the curtain would rise, and he would usher in a grand audience to the dark. He'd spent the night knapping several fresh obsidian blades in preparation. If all went according to Lady Holt's instructions, Black wouldn't even need to draw one. Still, he'd gotten them shaving sharp in case she was wrong.

Speaking of which . . .

Black made his way downstairs, headed to the foyer where the Morpheus Engine waited. The estate they'd taken occupancy in was yet another Legion asset that spoke to their limitless wealth and influence. The architecture was a mix of neoclassical and modern aesthetic. Marble columns lined the foyer walls while the carpet was stitched with an intricate geometric pattern. Traditional gold balustrades along the stairs accented the dark-grey wooden steps. It was all a mix of old and new. It was something Black was trying to open his mind to accepting. New ways of thinking. New methods of inflicting pain.

The Morpheus Engine, placed center-stage, seemed almost like an art piece in a museum. He checked his watch as he stepped towards it; he was right on time for his recent nightly routine. Lady

Holt's plan was an interesting one, but its subtlety would not provide Black the closure he needed. Which is why for the past few nights after Simon and the Immortals went to sleep, Black triggered a short pulse. It was a minor thing, not large enough to induce a Krueger Effect to anyone in the building, nor was it powerful enough to affect anyone outside the immediate area. But to anyone looking hard enough, it would get them looking in the right direction.

West lived. Black knew it in his bones. Somehow, the big man had climbed out of the hell within his own mind. It was meant to be the two of them in the end, after all. Serendipitous. Fated. It would all lead to Black giving West the most *beautiful* end imaginable.

"Come to me, West," Black whispered as he tapped the button twice to activate then immediately disable the engine. "Come to your death."

Perhaps he was insane, but he swore he could taste that bit of Morpheus energy in the air. He licked his lips in appreciation and smiled. Yes, it was almost time.

The light in the corner flipped on and there was Simon. He sat in a leather leisure chair with a large pistol on his lap. The scowl stretched across his face made Black's smile vanish. Two Immortals stepped out from behind the tall marble columns where they'd hidden. Declan and Henri. Two more, Harrison and Hogue, appeared from the shadows at Black's left and right. The last, his favorite, Scaglin, descended the stairs from behind him.

"You've proved valuable, I'm not too proud to admit," Simon said. He stood and pointed the gun at Black's chest as he approached him. "For that, I'll allow you two minutes to explain why you've left them a trail. Then, you die. It'll be quick. Clean. Simple. All the ways you hate."

"Two minutes?" Black said slowly, then sucked a contemplative hiss through his teeth. "You know, we all only have two minutes to live, you ever think about that? I do. All the time. Two minutes is all any of us have, but each time we take a breath we reset the timer."

Black took a long inhale through the nostrils to make his point.

"I tire of your ramblings. What are you even-?"

"Borrowed. Time," Black said angrily. "Everyone is living on it, fighting off what always comes anyway. Desperately bartering for just another year, another day, another two minutes. One more breath. One more chance. I exist to *end* the negotiations. Everyone's time is borrowed, but the bill comes due. I'm here to tell everyone: time's up."

Black's knife went through Simon's mouth and out the back of his head. Before his finger could so much as twitch along the trigger, Black pushed him backwards and punched the blade into the column behind him. The tip audibly cracked off against the marble, and the room went utterly silent.

"I'm here to collect death's dues."

Simon's gun clattered upon the tile floor. His fingers fumbled at the hilt stuck between his teeth, his tongue lolled against the paracord wrapped handle. His final moments were just as desperate as Black had said. He fought so pathetically against what was inevitable. Black watched as blood filled Simon's mouth and drained out the back of his neck. It trickled down the grooves in the column. Black hoped that the man appreciated the beauty in his death, the artistry of the crimson splashed upon the white stone. When Simon's eyes rolled into their sockets, Black took another long breath through the nostrils, savoring this moment. *Tasting* such an insufferable, insignificant man's death.

The Immortals around him were still. They were sworn to live and die for Lady Holt, not Simon. Black reached down to Simon's hand and removed the silver ring of his grandfather from his finger, then put it on his own. He flexed his hand into a fist twice and admired how perfectly the ring fit him. It was like it was meant to be his.

"So, I guess you're calling the shots now?" asked Scaglin after a short moment.

"We can discuss it further, if anyone else would like," said Black and he pulled the knife from Simon's head.

The body fell and spilled more blood upon the tile. Black gripped the handle tight and let them all remember who he was and what he could do. There were no protests.

"Good," he said, disappearing the knife up his sleeve. "Now then, Bob, there's going to be a few changes to tomorrow's scheduled events that I think we should go over."

CHAPTER 64

You give up pieces of yourself the longer you stay in this fight, but those missing spots don't get to just stay vacant. The gaps are always filled by something new. Sometimes it's scar tissue, sometimes it's mental trauma. You clear out old memories and make space for other fresher things. One day you can't remember your best friend from third grade's name, but now you know which nerve in the spine registers the most pain to a dagger. Little by little you give those pieces away, it's like you're installing new software. Eventually the whole thing's been overwritten. Good or bad, that's what you have to work with.

Until something new comes. And then you get to do it all over again.

We'd been working hurt from the start of this, and that fear had dogged us every step of the way. We lost a piece of our team and the fear of losing more seeped into our every crack and crevice. More fragments chipped away from our broken spots the further down this rabbit hole we'd gone. Even now I could feel the nightmare energy the Morpheus Engine had hit me with clawing away inside my head, fighting to show me the horrors once more. So far, I have been doing a damn good job of keeping those monsters in the closet. Because we were close. So close now.

Our helicopter bucked and shook me back to the present. Vaun, who refused to stay back at Pike Site despite my objections, noticed and raised his chin at me.

"Your head on straight?"

I gave him a confident nod.

"Cole, what I said before about revenge being unprofessional? I was wrong."

I set my rifle on the bench next to me and leaned forward. "What're you on about, sir?"

"What I *meant* is, we have to be more. We can't just go around killing people that hurt us first so we can feel better about ourselves. Otherwise, well, wouldn't Black be right? That we're all nothing but darkness inside? We have to be more. *This* has to be more."

"How can it? I've got my eyes on one thing and one thing only."

"Honor," he said. "There's honor in avenging our fallen comrades. There's honor in completing the task at hand. And there's honor in stopping Legion's plan. That's the mission: we stop them because it's the right thing to do, not for revenge."

It felt wrong for him to tell me this, considering he'd gone and gotten himself crippled trying to get his own revenge. I guess that just meant he was more of an expert on the subject. What did it matter *why* I was going to run a knife across Black's throat? If the end result was the same, wasn't any driving motive irrelevant?

I pushed the thoughts aside as our helicopter touched down on the rooftop. Dante's shoulders tensed and I gave him a quick pat to let him know it was go-time. The big furball went quiet as that predator instinct within started to wake up. It was good to have him back, though he'd whined like a puppy when I took him away from Rain. I'm pretty sure she'd been overindulging in the treats department.

Two men approached us from the far side of the helipad. The first was a familiar short man in a dapper light-gray suit, White Shield's director Michael Goode; the other was dressed in such an indistinguishable three-piece suit it practically screamed "federal agency". His reddish-brown hair was combed and parted in a conservative fashion, and he bore a remarkable resemblance to the actor Bryan Cranston. I hoped we would be getting more of a 'Malcolm in the Middle' personality and less of a 'Heisenberg'.

"Shit," Galleon muttered under his breath when he saw the second man nearing us. "Not good."

"Who's that?"

"That's Deputy Director Sloan."

Walter Sloan held up a hand to help keep the slowing helicopter rotors from buffeting his hair, and when he saw all of us off-loaded and fully armed his face tightened into a grim scowl.

"Just the band of spooks I was hoping *not* to run into," he said. Definitely not 'Malcolm in the Middle'. "This little function is invite only, as in for people who actually exist. The last thing I need is to sully our already tenuous standing in the intelligence community by waltzing in a dozen assassins and spies."

"Oh, give it a rest, Walter. This one here is practically a magnet for trouble," Goode said, pointing at me. "If he's here, then it surely can't be far behind. So, tell me, how bad is it, Captain?"

"How many men do you have here?" I asked.

Goode's eyebrows scrunched up. "Standard seven-man security attaché, why?"

"Legion isn't just the topic of discussion at this intelligence summit," I said. "They're planning on hitting it."

"I take it they're going to use the Morpheus Engine I saw in Ms. Harper's reports?"

"Possibly. With Mr. Black's involvement, I wouldn't take anything off the table for certain until—"

"Whoa! *Damien* Black?" Sloan cut in. He purposely positioned himself between Goode and myself. "You're telling me that slippery shit is mixed in with all this?"

"Yes, my team will post as security throughout the building. One of mine is already tapped into local CCTV and watching for any sign. As soon as—"

"Jesus, do you have a hearing problem or something?" he asked. "Son, we're *not* on American soil but you're standing here with enough firepower to level the building. Not good optics, especially in broad daylight. And you said you already have someone tampering with Canadian systems? Do the words plausible deniability mean anything to you, or were you recruited for reasons other than your critical thinking? We were invited here—well, correction, *I* was and Goode is hard for me to say no to—but you? Oh, I don't have a problem saying no to you."

The men behind me, Vaun and Galleon included, stood fast. This was still my lead. I lowered my voice and made sure Sloan felt the promise behind it. "I could make it *real* hard for you to say no to me if you want."

Rather than pull back, Sloan smirked.

"Exactly who is it you think you're talking to, son? You think I'm going to flinch just because you're the oh-so-scary Black Spear? Please, the word's out: you guys aren't the baddest in the bunch anymore" he said, waving his hands around in the air mockingly, and then he jammed his finger into my chest. "I'd already been getting my hands dirty for years before you set foot in Boot Camp. You know the advantage I have over you? I exist. I'm a real fucking boy. I can release a memorandum to the world decrying the Black Spear Initiative as a rogue entity, and no matter how much you screamed it wouldn't matter, because *my* agency and *my* position in it are what's real. That old man Rourke is gone, God rest his over-inflated and entitled soul, and now we can bring you and all your little black-ops buddies into the fold. This time tomorrow your whole program is getting absorbed into mine, so show a little respect."

I wondered what the repercussions would be if I took the finger he was pushing on my flak and broke it. Probably not good, so I switched stances and tried to play to his position.

"Look, sir, we can figure all that out tomorrow if we make it. Right now, I'm telling you there is a very credible threat against you and everyone else in this building. We don't really exist and we don't matter, whatever, I could care less, but the things I've seen aren't *supposed* to be real either. Yet they are. How badly damaged would our reputation with our allies be if they found out we knew there was a threat and did nothing? Like you said, we're just ghosts. But somebody's head will have to be on the chopping block, and you're the only one here who's real."

Sloan chewed his lip. He turned to Goode, who only returned a blank unamused expression.

"Like you said, Walter, it's your call."

His expression brightened, and he clapped his hands like a man ready to negotiate.

"Alright, let's do it," he conceded. "On one condition, though. We need someone alive. I want Mister Black."

It took everything in me not to pick that bastard up by his neck and chuck him off the roof right then and there, but Vaun was at my side and put a hand at my elbow to calm me down.

"This whole thing is a shadow war that we're trying to shine a spotlight on, and Black is the damn cherry on top. He's the motherlode of most wanted, and more importantly he can provide actionable intel on Legion. He's a gun for hire, not one of their dedicated zealots, which means he'll talk. Black. Alive. Yeah?"

He extended his palm towards me almost like a car salesman on their final offer. Time was wasting.

"Yes, sir. We can do that."

Sloan clapped his hands together once more and smiled cheerfully. Instantly, the hard-ass CIA suit looked more like a friendly father-slash-businessman.

"Okay then, let's go remind everyone why they invite America to the table."

He turned on his heels and headed to the elevator with us shortly behind. We let Goode and Sloan ride down it first, alone, so that they could grease whatever wheels they needed to before a group of commandos crashed their little party. While we waited, Vaun gave me a measuring stare, no doubt wondering if I'd been bluffing.

"Sloan's got a point," he said. "Legion is more akin to a cult than any sort of international syndicate. Black isn't a true believer."

"Oh, he's a believer alright, though in exactly what I'm not convinced anyone knows for sure."

Both Cerberus and Storm looked to me for some confirmation on how this would play out. I made eye contact with them all, one by one. They all knew what was on the line here, and what we'd lost so far. But they also knew we had a job to do. Reluctantly, I slipped my hand in my pocket. I found a bullet there. *The* bullet. The one I'd been saving for Black. I dropped it into Vaun's palm. He looked at it, puzzled.

"It's got his name on it," I said. "We'll try to bring him in, but I have a feeling he's going to force our hand. When that happens, I'm gonna need that back."

Vaun squeezed the bullet tight then placed it in his pants pocket. I made a mental note of where, in case I needed to take it back without his permission.

Behind me the elevator door dinged, and we stepped inside.

"You know, there *is* still a chance we're wrong and nobody shows?" said Vaun.

"Please. When are we ever that lucky?"

CHAPTER 65

The elevator doors opened and let us out on a balcony level overlooking a sort of amphitheater-styled conference room below. Tables and chairs filled the floor, which meant that the level below us could only be the home of the impending meeting.

A quick survey confirmed that this level would provide us the tactical high-ground and a 360-degree view below. The only way to this floor was from the service elevator we'd just taken, as well as an open stairwell on the other side of the amphitheater. The stairs also led to an unseen third floor.

I set a reminder in my head to have Galleon's men clear it. Having an entire floor as an unknown above me wasn't giving me a warm and fuzzy.

Sloan stood in front of us with his back turned. He and Goode spoke heatedly with two others I couldn't see. Sloan was animated, arms swinging, and then more reassuring hand gestures.

I could make out the conversation in my head. He was explaining how insane things might be, but then just as quickly trying to convey that everything was going to be alright.

Sloan must've felt eyes on the back of his head, because he

turned around and beckoned me and Vaun over. Strangely, he had a confident smile on his face as if he and I were old friends.

"Yeah, come on over, Captain," he said.

Before walking to Sloan, I shoulder-tapped Galleon and pointed to the third-floor stairwell. "Make sure it's clear."

He nodded and signaled three of his men to join him on his recon.

"Captain, I'd like to introduce you to some people," said Sloan, gesturing to the two suited men and one older woman with him.

He indicated the first man with a short reddish-brown beard, he was rather muscularly built for being a high-up intelligence officer. If you swapped his suit for a flannel, he'd be the spitting image of the mascot for Bounty towels.

"Alain Virieux here is the one we can thank for hosting this little gathering. CSIS, mind you."

The Canadian Security Intelligence Service was our northern neighbor's equivalent of the CIA.

"I have great respect for Mr. Rourke," Virieux said.

That caught me off guard. Black Spear was a secret from even most of our own officials, but I guess you don't build something like that without having a tight circle of allies overseas.

"I must admit that I sincerely hope you gentlemen made this trip for nothing, but I am grateful that you are here. Hope isn't too valuable a commodity in our line of work. You will have the full support from my staff for whatever you need."

The well-dressed lumberjack shook my hand and smiled. If seeing a fully-armed American in blacked-out uniform was strange to him, it didn't show.

"This is Deputy Chief Connor Brawnley, from our friends across the pond at MI-6," continued Sloan.

Brawnley looked as lean as a beanstalk, but he possessed the discerning eyes of a viper. All the same, he politely extended his hand.

"Not the subtlest of statements, hmm?" he said with a sly grin and raised his eyes at the team behind me. "Well, you lads on the ground always do the dirty work while we get to sign our reports and pass them up."

"Isn't there a saying about the pen and the sword?" I asked.

Brawnley's smile spread. "Too true, but I do miss my sword some days. Alas, it is a young man's game. I'll tell you what, though. If you lot are right, then these stiffs might be reminded of just how mad the world really is outside the safety of our desktops."

His grip was deceptively strong. He gave my hand one last squeeze before letting go. That, along with the hints he'd dropped, told me that there were plenty of chapters in Brawnley's book that were closer to mine than I would've thought.

I wondered for a moment if that was the fate of all operators; you either die in the field or live long enough to be promoted to some administrative position. Fighters like Kara Mason resented it, while titans like Rourke seemed to go cold inside once accepting it. A young man's game Brawnley called it, and the good die young in this life. The deadliest survive, but the goodness in them dies.

"I don't believe Mr. Sloan has had the pleasure of meeting the lady here before now," said Brawnley, indicating the older woman next to him. "While I've been in my position for a meager handful of years now, she herself served for decades before retiring. She graced us long ago by agreeing to stay on as an *exceptionally* qualified consultant."

"The Deputy Chief flatters," the woman said. "Margot Holt, charmed to make your acquaintance."

CHAPTER 66

He didn't have much time. The end of the line was coming no matter what. Lady Holt had seen to that. He'd shaken hands with the devil long ago and was too far down that road to turn back now. He had no illusions of what kind of man he was. By all accounts he was a traitor. A coward. An overly ambitious and selfish sap. But, even acknowledging that, there were two things he remained underneath all the bad choices: a father and a husband.

Lady Holt wrote him a death sentence, but writing one for his family was something not even he could accept. Carl knew he deserved to die for what he'd done, and for what he'd turned a blind eye to for years now, but his family deserved better. If his days were truly numbered, then he'd be damned if he wasn't going to spend the precious few he had left trying to right his wrongs.

Carl was never stupid enough to wear a wire or bring an audio recorder with him anytime he'd met with Holt or any of her ilk. They would've known. They would've found it. But there were things they wouldn't have thought to look for. Like the CCTV camera at the small shop across the street from the café they'd last met at, which caught a blurry but clearly recognizable image of Holt as she stepped from her vehicle. Or the set of her fingerprints he'd lifted from the table where she'd told him he was already a dead man. Security footage screen captures from the private dock where she'd anchored well in advance of today's intelligence summit. Carl's entire career had been fast-tracked so that Legion could groom him for a position they could then take advantage of, but he'd been skilled at collections long before he sold his soul.

The digital dossier he'd put together was but breadcrumbs, but he prayed it would be enough to at least get the right people looking in the right direction. Legion had been watching him all this time, which meant he'd had equal opportunity to do the same back. Holt had killed him, the least he could do was ruin her fucking anonymity for it.

All that mattered now was making sure he lived long enough to seal her fate as she'd done to him. He had no way of knowing who was and wasn't under Legion's thrall, so his only option was to go straight to Sloan. His security attaché couldn't be trusted. Carl couldn't go through email. He would have to get the SD card directly into the Deputy Director's hands.

Today, before the hearing, might just be his last chance. Holt was going to twist that meeting into her own purpose, but her attendance would mean it might be the one time she'd be in the open. It would be the one opportunity for Carl to make her pay for what she'd done.

Carl had just three blocks to go before he'd reach the venue. He took the back alleys where no cameras could catch him, none of Legion's eyes would spot him until it was too late. He would simply tell Sloan that there was an update on the brief he'd already prepared for him, and then slip him the card. Sloan would know, and could apprehend Holt right then and there. This was going to work.

Recently his head had been nothing but a hornet's nest as the radiation poisoning ran its course, but here and now it was lessened by something he hadn't felt in so long. Hope. That, and the knowledge that he was finally doing something worthwhile once again.

That feeling, so tempting in its warmth, drew him in. And just as quickly was dashed away when Holt's giant body-man stepped into the alley before him.

Dorian Rinx said nothing. He simply shook his head disapprovingly as two more men came from behind to encircle Carl.

"One might think it suspicious to find you acting this way," Rinx said. He removed his bowler cap and handed it to one of the nameless Legion suits.

"Fuck you," Carl spat. "I'm not doing it anymore."

"You are finished when the Lady says you are. *No one* decides that but her. Not you, not even the coroner or the undertaker."

Carl knew the end was here. Still, better to go out on his own terms. So, he did something so monumentally stupid he knew it would force Rinx's hands. He swung a punch at Rinx's chin. He nearly broke his own hand doing so.

Rinx responded by punching him in the stomach so hard, he felt something burst. Carl doubled over and vomited onto the alley floor. There was blood in it. This is what he wanted. He had to make Rinx angry, otherwise they'd just shoot him and be done with it. If that happened, he'd be just another alley mugging gone wrong.

"Tell the hag I'm done!"

"I would caution you against disrespecting my lady further," Rinx said. He pulled the sleeves of his blue trench coat up slightly to better free his arms to pummel Carl further.

"I told you. I'm out," said Carl. "I'm not going to listen to that *whore* you follow anymore! I hope that brittle bitch falls down the fucking stairs, but only after she chokes on a dozen hobo cocks."

That did it. Rinx was a mountain, but one of exceptional self-control. Very few had ever gotten so much as a rise out of him, but descending upon Carl there was now an avalanche of pain.

"I'm going to use your body as a reminder for others," Rinx said, lifting Carl to his feet with a single hand. "May your broken bones be a warning for them."

"Do your worst," said Carl.

"As you wish."

The punch landed square on his cheek and cracked three teeth. His skull and jaw fractured, Carl sprawled upon the floor. One hit, and two broken bones already. That left Rinx with over two-hundred intact bones to play with.

CHAPTER 67

They called it the calm before the storm. I couldn't think of a more fitting concept. All the VIPs were gathered and set to kick off the summit, the media had arrived outside waiting to interview whoever they could, and here I was waiting for the enemy to make the first move. Despite Sloan's doubts, I knew in my gut all hell was about to break free. The nightmarish floodgates were set to let loose, and this time I wasn't sure if I'd be able to claw my way back to the world of the sane. That is, if I'd ever made my way back in the first place.

Cerberus was posted on the second floor overlooking everyone. Storm had a few on the first as well with a couple others standing watch at the limited entrances and exits. I walked the perimeter of the balcony on the second floor, admittedly wandering a bit to steady my restlessness. Kelly's ghost came into view, grinning happily, and he cocked his head towards a doorway. Reluctantly, I followed his direction and found myself in what looked like a sort of chapel. It was a lot like the ones you see in some hospitals. Little more than a cramped room with a few benches long gone unused, a podium with a dusty old bible, and a stained-glass window behind it that had gone years without a solid cleaning. Nothing but a private space for prayer, or maybe just a bit of solitude.

I sat down. I don't know why I did it, I don't even know why I stepped into the room in the first place. It's not like time was particularly on my side at the moment. My thoughts drifted to the bible and cross recovered from Kelly's locker. I still didn't get it. How can you do the things we do, face the horrors we've faced, and still think the big guy in the clouds has your back? What sense did that make?

All the same, I set my rifle down next to me. It felt so heavy, and I was suddenly very tired. I couldn't remember the last time I prayed. All in all? I figured there wasn't any harm in trying.

"You and I haven't seen eye to eye much as of late," I said, looking up to the large cross at the back of the room. "I'm . . . I'm not proud of what I've had to do."

My next words hitched in my throat. I didn't know why it became so difficult, or why I was even talking. I found myself unable to cry any tears, though. They only would've made me angrier.

"I feel like you stopped listening a long time ago, so I stopped talking. I've got no time for your silence. But I'm taking the time now. I've done enough to know that, well, I won't be welcome in your house when this is all said and done. That's fine. I'm not asking to be welcomed, I'm not looking for forgiveness. But . . . I could use a little help."

My eyes shifted from the large cross to the stained glass window behind it. It had depictions of Christ and saints and others I recognized but didn't know, and all their eyes stared unblinking back at my own. Staring through me in a way that made me feel very seen in an uncomfortable way.

"It doesn't matter that I haven't been able to walk your line, or that I'm too far gone to be saved. What matters is that good men are ready to lay down their lives to stop the bad. That the enemy is many, and we are few, and I don't know if we can stop it this time. So, please, show me. *Show* me that you're listening. I've never asked for anything.

I have no right to. But just this once, grant me this one thing. Vengeance."

Silence

The chapel was so very quiet.

I waited for a sign. Waited for the sun to shine a little brighter through that window, or for some feeling of reassurance to wash over me. But it didn't. I think I'd known from the beginning how this was going to end. One way or another it would come down to the two of us. Just Black, and just me.

The stillness of the room became too much.

"And, if you're not gonna help," I said, grabbing my rifle. My brief sorrow soured into anger. "Then just stay the hell out of my way."

I stormed out, partially relieved that none of my team had snuck in and witnessed my desperate call for help. Once again, all we had was ourselves. Nothing but our own grit, our own will. It would be enough. It would be.

Down below, the summit had begun. Alain Virieux was warming up for his opening presentation and everyone gave their rapt attention.

"Hey, boss, something just came across the wire you might be interested in," Rain said through the radio. "Sending to your wrist now."

The hairs on the back of my neck stood up as grisly crime scene photos popped up on my wrist computer. "Yellow Pages, just what in the hell am I looking at?"

It might have once been a person, if that person had nearly every bone in their body was twisted and crushed as easily as an empty soda can.

"Dead stiff, call just came in. They found him less than two blocks from here. Get this, that's one of Sloan's men. He was supposed to be in the meeting."

"If Legion's planning on attacking here anyway, why the need to kill him before he got here?"

"Good question."

"Pull some magic. Whatever you gotta fake, just make sure we get the body and not the locals. Anything else?"

"No, all quiet outside still. Everything is—"

She trailed off.

"Yellow Pages, not filling me with a lot of confidence up here. What is it?"

"I'm running all the plates for the media vans outside to make sure it's all kosher," she answered. "And unless Channel 4 sent two teams to cover the same story, we've got a phony out there."

I eyed Galleon, and he used a hand signal to alert two of his men. They moved towards the entrance to the amphitheater, going slowly and calmly as to not cause a panic. My heartbeat drummed in my ears. Not faster, but harder. Black had taunted me about a growing darkness again and again, and even to me my heartbeat felt like that darkness was waking up again. Something in me knew it was almost killing time.

"I hijacked the local PD's channel. I've got two officers going to check out both vans now," said Rain.

"Alright, boys, this might be Go-Time. Dose up."

Everyone rogered up and popped their meds. I prayed that along with Madison's Cicada, it would be enough to stave off any Morpheus effects, barring anything but a full blast like I'd taken before, that is.

My attention drifted to Virieux's presentation below.

"There is a threat we all face that is nothing short of a monster," he stated. "Unbeknownst to us, this monster has thrived and grown under all our noses."

I looked across the balcony to where my brothers stood. Tag gave me a knowing nod. Billy's face was set in a tight-lipped scowl, yet he shook a Shaka at me. Kelly's ghost popped some finger guns at me before I shook my head and sent the mirage away. My brothers, trusting in me again for the moment and standing by me to the bitter end.

"None of us die today," I said into the radio.

I don't know if anyone believed me, but they all gave an oorah back. It was a promise to each other that we all agreed on. Have each other's back. Hold the line. Fight back and don't let our fears get the better of us.

"At best, we have all at least caught a glimpse of this monster," Virieux continued. "Mere hints and clues reaching out from the shadows. And that is why we are here: to drag this threat into the light. To give identity to those who would commit acts of terror on a global scale under a veil of anonymity. Ladies and gentlemen, we must lift that veil."

Something was nagging at me. Black was frustratingly clever, I didn't believe that his plan would involve such an easily spotted vehicle.

"Sleight of hand . . ." I whispered to myself.

"What's that?" Galleon asked.

"Something Black's done before. If he's making us look out on the street, it's because he's nowhere near there. If our eyes are low then he's going to be . . ."

My mind finished the thought. My eyes shot to the ceiling and looked, with dawning horror, at the skylights that peeked through the roof. There the news choppers circled above, but there was one helicopter larger than the others. It was a twin-rotor military-style Chinook and hovered much lower than the other news helicopters. Something trailed below it by a cable.

"They call themselves Legion," said Virieux.

Before I could warn anyone, the helicopter's cargo crashed through the glass above. I saw it fall, passing by my level, and coming to a rest ten feet above the meeting below. The Morpheus Engine was rigged like a wrecking ball below the Chinook. Razor-sharp shards showered onto the people below as Virieux's speech was overtaken by panicked shrieks.

I couldn't give them the attention I wanted. My eyes were fixed on the engine humming before me and that metallic taste quickly filling the air. That familiar pull that started behind the eyes as you slipped into the welcoming confusion of a dream state came on, but I shook it away. Had to stay awake. Had to fight against the dreaming.

In my head, I said it again and again. Stay awake. Remember what's real. I was still saying that to myself when the engine finished powering up and released its pulse.

CHAPTER 68

This was *not* the plan. They were to discreetly use the Morpheus weapon on a low level; the intent was to reduce the conference to a panicked wreck. Undermine their investigation in the public's eye by showing how incompetent and unreliable this entire ordeal was. But this? This was madness. Madness for which she was only marginally prepared.

The inoculation she and Rinx had taken saved them both from the insanity that claimed the others, but her own weaker thoughts were fighting to make themselves seen and real in her eyes. Even without the sensory hallucinations, the reality around her was brutal enough. One of Deputy Chief Brawnley's aides was on her knees, clawing her own eyes out with perfectly manicured nails.

Lady Holt watched with mixed fascination and disgust as Walther Sloan's security attaché fought amongst themselves in an attempt to get Sloan out. Two of them, their sidearms seemingly forgotten, tore each other apart like feral beasts. Their fight lasted until one slammed the other's skull to mush upon the tiled floor. A third had crawled into a corner and curled into a quivering ball as he sobbed like a child. All around her were individual moments of bloodshed, of panic, of submission, and it was all woven together into a tapestry of death.

One of the conference attendants-turned-Krueger reached out for Holt. Rinx stepped from behind and nearly took its head off twisting its neck 180-degrees around.

"Ma'am, it's time for us to leave."

"Have them clear a path for us, my dear," she said.

Dorian spoke into a wire in his sleeve and then gunshots rang out from above. Her Immortals up above shot into the crowd as Rinx took her by the hand and led her away. The crazed horde was too busy killing itself and each other to bother with the two of them, and the bullets that rained down into them were ignored.

Holt knew the Black Spear rabble were mixed amongst the room. Some of them tried to return fire and stem the chaos, but the chaos contained a will of its own. It was a free-for-all between the Kruegers killing everything they saw, the unseen Immortals who shot those in Holt's way, Black Spear's soldiers pretending they could still take control, and the terrified husks who hadn't yet been reduced to drooling messes on the ground.

She took it all in and happened to notice one of the cameras from the media team still filming. It was feeding all of this to the world outside. Perhaps this situation could still work to their advantage.

"Black is a bolder insect than I expected. I want you to hurt that boy very badly when we get out of here, Dorian."

"It would be my sincere pleasure." He slammed another Krueger to the ground before delivering a precise stomp to the back of their neck.

"Let's leave Black to his game. Have the Immortals meet us below."

Dorian gave her a curt nod and spoke to his wrist again. As he led her from the chaos, she looked up to the balcony above and happened to match the gaze of the soldier standing there. That thug. Darren Rourke's little blunt instrument. Cole West. Lady Holt was many things. In her life she had deceived royalty and commoners alike. There was one thing, however, that she could never hide. Lady Holt was not weak. She was no victim. Countless followers had voiced how tangible it was to be in the presence of her power. And, in that one moment when West looked at her, he saw it. Her strength. He saw the truth of what she was.

There was no hiding it anymore. Instead, she draped the truth about her like a cloak, stared back at West, and allowed a slight smile to stretch across her lips as Rinx led her from the fray.

CHAPTER 69

"Toxin to all points," I said. "We have a new high-value target: Margot Holt is Legion."

"Got our hands full as it is!" Galleon radioed over his own gunfire. "This is—this is *insane*!"

"She'll just do this again if she gets away. Kage, go with him and don't let her get away." They gave a less than enthusiastic affirmative, and I pushed on. I looked at the skylight where the helicopter drew the Morpheus Engine back up and out like a lure being reeled in on a fishing rod.

"I'm going to the roof."

The abattoir of howls and bloodshed below was drowned out by a heavy engine, and a second later a semi-trailer smashed into the room in reverse. A buzzer rang and the truck's back gate lifted. Kruegers, thirty or forty at least, spilled forth and entered the fray. I had enough time to spot the driver slipping away. He wore the black armored facemask of an Immortal. Just as I was readying to relay new orders to Storm and Cerberus two more trucks barreled through the walls in reverse and released their mad cargo. Two more drivers, two more Immortals. And fifty more Kruegers scrambling from the trucks.

Legion had been generous enough to provide the three trucks' worth of Kruegers with hand tools like hammers, crowbars, or axes. Some had machetes or crude cleavers. The pandemonium reached new lows as the crowd joined the bloodshed and confusion.

"Boss, you awake?" Rain asked. "I'm upping the Cicadas for everyone, time now."

The hiss in my ear kept me straight, but I could still see the nightmarish flashes between every blink. The wallpaper peeled away to reveal raw flesh beneath, the carpeted floor turned to bones and discarded limbs that crunched underfoot as I sprinted to the stairs, and a heavy downpour of blood rained through the shattered windows above. Whispers from the ghosts of my life—both good and bad—tickled at my ears. Some whispered threats, others pleaded for help. I feigned deafness to it all. My own shadow rose from the floor to strangle me. I bit my tongue to keep the scream back. This wasn't real. It was just Morpheus and Black fucking with my head again.

"Friendly, on your six!" Tag said behind me as I reached the top floor. Dozens of skeletal hands with long claws burst out from the fleshy wall on my left. I had a moment of hesitation as their talons raked the air inches from my face, but then I felt Tag pushing me from behind.

Not real, keep going!

I passed through them, and they faded like a mirage.

"Boss, I've got all kinds of insane chatter coming across the wire," Rain said over the radio. "What is going on in there?"

"Whatever bad you're hearing is watered down," I answered. "A Morpheus pulse just sent this place to hell, but Black's taking his horror show on the road."

"Toxin," another voice chimed in. Madison's. "The Cicada and medication will only help so much, if you two get too close to the source there's no guarantee that—"

"I know."

"Just, just be careful."

There wasn't time for anything else.

Tag and I reached the final steps to the roof. The taste of metal grew stronger the closer we got. I could feel that strange ache behind my eyes as reality melted away more and more. But then we reached the top, with weapons at the ready, only to see Black's Chinook already pulling away to the edge of the helipad. There, waiting in the helicopter's open back ramp, was Black.

I leapt onto the ramp without thinking, firing my rifle as I did so. The sparks that came from Black's suit-jacket when my bullets hit their mark told me that his stylish attire was more armored than it appeared. So I adjusted my aim and pointed the barrel right at his forehead.

He chopped a hand up, a knife flicked from his sleeve into his palm, and he slashed through my shoulder sling. In one fluid turn he grabbed the handguard, wrenched the weapon away from my grasp, tossed it out the open ramp, then delivered a swift kick to my side. I turned into it, letting my vest's plate take the brunt, and drew my sidearm. I managed to squeeze a single shot off before the helicopter bucked in the air and threw my aim askew.

The round hit him in the shoulder, and despite his Kevlar-laced suit jacket the .45 caliber round still hit hard enough to knock the knife from his hand. He growled and pawed at the spot on his jacket.

"How have you come back?" he demanded. "How?!"

I heard yelling towards the cockpit and realized Tag had come aboard via the side-hatch rather than the back ramp. He was currently threatening to shoot the pilot if he didn't put the helicopter down. The pilot was unconvinced and put the helicopter's nose down hard.

The shift in weight sent me rolling like a log. I came to a stop on my belly inches from the open void beyond the loading ramp. From there I could see the Morpheus Engine trailing beneath us from a cable.

"Do you see?" Black said as he straddled me from behind, one hand holding another knife to my neck while the other manhandled my head. "All those people down there ... all so fucking weak. So much fear, and all of it just waiting to be let out."

With the edge of his knife still pressed against my throat, he reached into his jacket and pulled out a remote. Black turned up a dial and even this high above it I could feel the Morpheus Engine hum with increased power.

"Look!" he spat.

Each one of his fingertips was a bolt pressing into my skull, forcing me to see the city below. I couldn't tell what was real and what wasn't. I saw civilians running in terror, cars crashing and filling the streets with fire, nightmarish creatures dancing in celebration in the flames, and the civilians that weren't fleeing in fear go mad and attack anyone in sight.

We flew north from the city across the harbor with death trailing in our wake.

"I thought you were like me," he said. "I was wrong. You're as afraid as all the others."

I told him how I felt by sinking my teeth into his thumb until blood ran across my tongue. The knife at my neck fell out the window. He rolled me onto my back as he raised a hand to punch out my lights.

"Fuck off him!" Tag yelled and his giant boot kicked at the back of Black's head. Black ducked it then rolled backwards as the big man helped me to my feet.

Black sprang up, pulling another knife from his vest, and pointed it at Tag, "I thought I killed this one already?"

The dagger whistled through the air. I jerked my head to the side. The knife stuck into a cargo net by my face. I went to close the distance between us. Black sidestepped towards the cockpit, spinning as he did so to pull two more of his knives from his belt, and let them fly through the air as he finished his turn.

Tag and I juked and ducked as they came at us. Tag dodged one aimed for his feet as I had to slap one from the air that would've hit me in the eye. Black did another spin, and drew two more throwing knives.

How many of those does he have?!

Once more, we avoided them, and Black found himself with his back pressed against the cockpit. Nowhere else to run.

Black smiled and I saw too late that this time instead of holding one knife in each hand, this time he secreted a third knife between the fingers of one. He yelled like an animal and threw all three at Tag. Tag smacked one out of the air with a backhanded parry, a second pinned to the webbing his vest with a *THUK,* but the third sank low in his unprotected hip. Tag skidded to a knee with a gasp, but I was close enough to charge into Black with all my momentum. I threw Black into the control panel next to the pilot who screamed in surprise.

I reached into Black's jacket while he was dazed. If I could find the Morpheus remote, I could at least stop any more people in the city below from dying.

"Put this thing down!" I yelled as I tried to keep Black from flailing free from my hold.

"We are many!" the pilot screamed and pointed a pistol.

I pushed the gun away before he could fire and slammed his head into the window. Black took that instant to chop his hand across my throat.

Black patted his jacket to make sure I hadn't taken the Morpheus remote, but it wasn't what I'd gotten my hands on.

"Sleight of hand, asshole," I said and held up the detonator for his own sticky-bombs.

Too late he realized that when I'd slammed the pilot's head, I'd slapped one of the stickies to the back of his helmet, and the rest of the explosive booby-traps were still inside Black's jacket pocket. I flipped him the middle finger and used it to hit the detonator. He had just enough time to slip his coat off.

"Sorry, Bob," Black said, throwing the jacket onto the pilot.

Black's boobytraps were small by design; intended to maim rather than kill. That changes when one goes off against your skull and a dozen or so more pop inside the jacket your boss threw over you. The Kevlar-laced jacket directed the brunt of the blast out the side window; the front windshield splattered red with brain matter and skull fragments. Smoke and aerosolized bits of Bob filled the cabin. Black tried to wrestle what was left of the pilot's corpse away from the sparking controls. He used a sleeve to wipe some of the blood off the glass so he could see.

"Oh. Damn," he said softly.

We were headed right for a head-on collision with a hydro-electric dam. Black fought the joystick to pull up the Chinook, which sent me sliding towards the rear and the still-open ramp. An alarm warned that we were too low.

"Tag!" I shouted and grabbed the big man as the belly of the helicopter crashed into the dam. Metal sheared and the entire helicopter broke in half. The Morpheus engine pulled behind our section like a wrecking ball smashing everything. I was flung from the wreckage like a ragdoll. I put my arms up to protect my head as the ground came up to meet me. It was not a soft landing.

CHAPTER 70

He'd seen some shit in his time. Blood, guts, the whole nine yards of bodily fluids and entrails. You sort of get numb to it all. Chaos, however, was a certain flavor of disorienting that one never got used to. Even the bio-threats they'd faced had a sense of design or pattern, but watching someone cave another person's skull in with a hammer betrayed all sense of reason.

Billy took aim and dropped the Krueger with a single shot. Rain's assessment that Krueger's minds were beyond saving didn't make pulling the trigger any easier. Still, he told himself nothing could be done for them and gave chase after Margot Holt. Galleon, with two of Storm in tow, was right there with him.

"She's headed for the garage," said Billy.

Galleon winced as his Cicada increased its screech, then looked to Billy to make sure they were all still sane. "You look like you're having a regular walk in the park."

"Micro-dose to *Tool* enough times, and you get used to that line between fantasy and reality blurring. I'm just ahead of the curve," Billy said with a shrug. "Kidding. Maybe. Not really."

They found a roomful of catatonic civilians drooling on the

floor. Billy knew these people were as doomed as the Kruegers, but he took grim comfort in knowing that at least it wouldn't be him who would have to put them down. One person in the room was still on his feet—though visibly terrified from hallucinations—and swung a long-handled push broom at some invisible creature. Billy ran to his blind-spot and chopped a knife-hand strike to the back of his neck. The man flopped to the floor like folded laundry. He hoped that knocking the guy unconscious would be enough to stop his neurons from firing themselves to insanity.

"Garage is this way," Billy said as he spotted the sign by a set of basement stairs. "Let's go."

He turned to make sure Galleon was still ready, but found instead that the Commander's attention was fixed on one of his men. The shooter in question, an experienced crack-shot who went by the name of Ogre, had let his rifle fall by his feet. Galleon's soldier clawed at his ears so bad, he had started to draw blood.

"Christ, Ogre, where the hell is your Cicada?!" Galleon said, then signaled his second man. "Buzzsaw, talk him down."

"You won't get me, you won't get me!"

Buzzsaw made a move to restrain him. "It's okay, man, just focus on my voice. Let's stay cool."

"You won't get *me*!" he said and swung his knife wildly.

The problem with working alongside the most capable operators in the world is they're just as fast and deadly when they can't tell friend from foe. Ogre's knife sliced across Buzzsaw's cheek and split his mouth open. Buzzsaw's hand tensed on reflex and sent a flurry of rounds rattling across the tiles along the floor. They zipped in a line up the room until one bullet found itself in Galleon's boot.

"Sonuvabitch!" he howled, falling to the floor and gingerly propping his foot up.

"You won't get me!" roared Ogre.

He said it again and again as he readied to finish off Buzzsaw.

But Billy was already there and cracked him across the back of the head with his buttstock, then delivered three nerve strikes to knock Buzzsaw out cold, before returning to where Galleon lay.

He didn't have the time to waste and couldn't trust anyone but himself. They just didn't possess the mindset for it.

"Nothing personal, Commander."

"For crying out loud, Kage, I'm not going to—"

He didn't finish his sentence before Billy's hands had rendered him unconscious. Billy checked to make sure the gunshot wound to Galleon's foot wasn't bleeding too badly, found comfort that Galleon would only lose a toe or two, and then muscled his way through the door to the parking garage.

Did he just make a mistake? Who fucking knew. Billy had seen the signs and knew that, at the very least, Galleon and Buzzsaw were spooked, which meant they were that much closer to becoming a danger to themselves. Also, selfishly, him.

Holt wasn't going to get away from him, and her giant bodyguard wasn't going to stop him either. No time. No games. Billy kept his rifle up as he ran down the hall. The garage was in view, and he could just see the woman he chased climbing into an upper model sedan.

"Freeze!" he ordered as he ran into the lower-level garage. "I said freeze!"

Two shots would do just fine. One to the back of her bodyguard's head, the other to her calf to stop her.

It was dark. Not so dark that Billy wouldn't make his shot, but dark enough that he hadn't seen the figure step from the support pillar until it was too late. The Immortal's knuckles cracked into his chin so hard, it whited out his vision. Billy felt his already broken jaw cant unnaturally to the side. Ligaments screamed against the bone. All his senses went haywire as his nerves were overloaded with pain.

And then it all came to a point as someone stuck a knife in his belly. Billy looked down, saw the blade and handle protruding from his body, and fell to his knees. Warm blood spilled down the front of his pants.

Three more Immortals stepped from the shadows as the first one looked down at Billy. Despite the mask hiding his features, Billy sensed their disappointment.

"We thought you'd be harder to kill than this."

CHAPTER 71

I awoke to heavy raindrops pelting my face. Miraculously, I was alive and unbroken. The tail end of the Chinook was just behind me. It leaked fuel and oil from its underbelly like some dying animal on its last breath. I got to my feet, feeling practically every injury I'd ever experienced in my life with each step. I called out to Tag in the wreckage.

"I'm here . . ." he said.

One blood-soaked hand was pressed to his hip to staunch the bleeding where he'd taken one of Black's knives, the other he used to pull himself from the Chinook. I helped the big man out and draped his free arm across my shoulders to help him walk.

A stray spark fell to the pooling oil and the helicopter became alight with flames. I flinched back from it as visions stabbed at the back of my head. The rain, which moments ago had sent such a chill through my body as it soaked me, transformed into a hellish rain of fire. Though it was still the early hours of the day, all the blue of the sky was swallowed up by darkness.

I reached up to my ear, knowing already that I would find nothing there. My Cicada was gone. Lost amidst the crash landing.

Hellish images already flashed in my vision, and without a second thought I pulled one of my Kick needles from my pouch to give myself a dose.

"We have to go," I said.

I spotted the cable that carried the Morpheus Engine and the two of us followed it like a trail of breadcrumbs. Fiery raindrops fell to my skin, and I forced myself to feel the reality of the cold rain. My clothes unburnt, I shivered. The fire existed only in my head.

The cable led around the wreckage and there, near the nose-end half of the helicopter, in the midst of everything atop this dam, was the Morpheus Engine. There was a bolt of lightning that flashed and then Mr. Black appeared: the only thing standing between us and the engine. He breathed heavily, which was probably the first inclination I'd ever gotten that the bastard was actually human.

"Here we are at last." He smiled. Then, smug as ever, he turned his back on us and approached the Morpheus Engine. "All you have to do is get through me."

He reached into his vest pocket to retrieve the Morpheus remote, then placed it upon the engine.

"Come on, West. Show me that dark heart within you. This is what we've been building up to!"

In a flash he drew a revolver—*Tag's* revolver—and shot my friend twice with his own gun. I caught him as he fell back and lowered him to the ground. His chest was bloody, and I couldn't see between the flashes of reality and nightmare what was real and what was my imagination. One second the injuries were mortal, the next barely flesh wounds. One breath he was a long dead skeleton, the next a wounded soldier.

"Hey, no no no you're okay, brother," I said as his breath grew sharp and shallow. "Stay with me, Tag."

Tag reached up and grabbed the back of my head to pull my ear close. "Go kick his ass, Cap."

I set him at rest against the side of the helicopter's front half and nodded.

"Finish it," Tag said.

Black discarded Tag's .44 magnum to the side, tossing it to the rain-soaked asphalt like it was garbage. He undid his cufflinks and let them fall to the ground, then rolled the sleeves of his jet-black dress shirt up to his elbows. His hair, which until now had always been perfectly slicked back, not a strand out of place, now had locks falling towards his face from the rain. There was a fierce and feral energy radiating about him now.

A bolt of lightning tore through the sky. The fire falling from above flashed back to water, then back again. Black's hand went to the back of his belt, and he retrieved another of his obsidian knives. His other hand went low to his ankle and unsheathed a second knife. This dagger was different. Its blade longer, its handle made of marble. This was the special one. The one he'd taunted me with down in the basement.

"Down to my last two. But, this one?" he said and held the longer blade out for me to see. "I've been saving this one for you. Now, don't be scared. Show me that animal inside."

I used my pant legs to wipe my red-stained palms clean. Yet again my friend's blood was literally on my hands. No more. It would be the last. I stepped through the burning rain towards him. The lit helicopter fuel encircled us like some primordial arena. Watching just behind the fire, barely hidden in the shadows, was an army of the damned. Skeletons, burnt black, all of which I gave no attention.

He was right about one thing: it had all been leading to this. Showdown.

"I'm many things, Black," I said. "I'm the killer. I'm the darkness. I'm fucked up in ways I *know* there isn't any coming back from. But you know the one thing I'm not? Afraid. Of *you*."

I drew my large MK-9 knife in hand and approached him.

"Let's go, motherfucker."

We ran at each other. Lightning struck the nearby ground as we met, so close I could smell the atomized ozone scent burst into the air. Black stabbed with both knives, high and low at the same time, and I cut at him with my own. Our attacks missed by millimeters. I saw the shift in Black's body language as I swung again. That perfect muscle memory of his kicking into gear. I saw him analyzing, remembering my patterns, recalling what he'd witnessed in the Basement, registering how to counter.

And he did so flawlessly.

I slashed sideways but he saw it coming and side-stepped out of its way, delivered a snapping double kick to the outside of my shin and thigh, then followed through with another one-two stab. The only thing keeping me alive was that I saw him coming, too.

Black was fast, but I was strong. I caught one of his wrists in my free hand and squeezed, telling myself I wouldn't stop until the bones snapped in my grip. My knife-hand overwrapped his other arm and pinned it to my side at his elbow to lock it in place. That left the tip of my MK-9 right below his chin. Just one inch. That's all I needed to pop the steel through his head and into the soft palate of his skull.

"Krav Maga, Filipino Kali, don't you have anything I haven't seen before?" he laughed, muscling back against me with impossible strength.

I took an inward look at the book of techniques I had at my disposal and knew that he had a way to reverse all of them. He knew all of them.

So, instead, I took a number from the unofficial book of dirty fighting and smashed my forehead into his eyebrow before pushing him away. Black backpedaled and looked at me with that same wild-eyed smile. Except I could see it faltering. His brow was split, a slow leak of red dripped down his temple to his cheekbone. His smile was a mask, and now that I'd managed to hit him, it was cracking to show the anger underneath.

"Amusing," he said, "but it's not good enough."

I held up my knife, and then turned the flat of the blade towards him so he could see the thin line of blood along its edge. I'd slipped a quick reverse slash at his side when I'd broken our grapple off. He looked down at the cut in his vest along his floating ribs in disbelief. When he glared back at me, the illusion of that smile disappeared. There was his rage. There was his fury. He'd been in my head for so long, it was good to turn the tables and be in his for once.

"You've got perfect memory, Black," I said. "Which means even if you beat me, you'll be able to remember that little wound forever. In every move you make, every swing of your knife, you'll remember when I *hurt* you."

He came at me in a flurry. Left arm, right arm, a pirouette slick on his heels, those obsidian knives came from seemingly every angle. High and low, forward and reverse slashes. The backdrop vanished for an instant as thunder cracked again. There were only our two silhouettes and the flash of our knives, and the burnt damned watching for who would join their ranks first.

Blow for blow, strike for strike, I matched his speed. I wasn't thinking of the next attack or counter; I wasn't anticipating. It was all instinct. If I didn't know my next move, then how could he predict it? Our movements fell into a sort of flow. There was a pure symmetry to our combat as the knives whistled through the air. The footwork was in tandem as we circled one another. At first, I thought he was copying my stance and style, but then realized it was a two-way road. *I* was shadowing him just as much as he did me.

From the beginning he'd been telling me how similar we were. Blood brothers matched by the darkness in our hearts. Right now, fighting him as closely matched as we were, I wasn't so sure he was wrong anymore.

"You see it?" Black asked in between the exchange of blows. "You see this knife? This one's special."

Another feint and reverse cut that came millimeters away from opening up my carotid.

"I killed your friend Crow with this knife. I carved Kara Mason's pretty face with this knife. And as soon I'm done killing *you,* I'm going to introduce each and every one of your friends to it."

Black had wanted me to let that darkness out. He'd taunted and prodded me into letting the animal loose by hurting my friends, all just so he'd have some kindred spirit worthy of facing. So, I let him have it. Everything.

I screamed as I attacked faster and faster. The edge of the dam was behind him and I pushed us both towards it. I saw Black's confidence wane. He'd wanted the animal, and here it was.

I just needed the moment. *One* moment, one opening where I could sink the length of my blade into his chest.

Instead, I overstepped my attack and thrust too far. Black slipped under my arm, cut back and forth with both blades like closing scissors at the underside of my triceps, and went to work like a butcher at my exposed side. He was in close and made quick stabs at all the spots my vest didn't protect. Low by my hip, the outside of my thigh, a slash near my armpit.

In the span of half a second, he'd punctured me like a pincushion. The MK-9 knife fell from my hand, practically in slow-motion. Black kicked at it with the outside of his shoe, sending it sailing off the dam to the thundering water far below.

Twice more his obsidian daggers cut at my chest but didn't draw blood. It wasn't until I felt weight sagging from my torso that I saw what he'd done: sliced away the shoulder straps of my vest.

My armor fell away as he slammed me into the burning helicopter wreckage. The hot metal scorched at my back, and I howled into the fiery rain. I fought through the pain and clamped my hands on both his wrists to keep his knives away. I ignored the blood I felt slicking down my flank. Ignored the hallucinations.

Ignored the voice telling me I was definitely going to die.

The tips of both his knives came at me like twin pincers. The smaller one high, the longer special one he coveted low at my side. I wrestled against that wiry strength. His high dagger scraped along the metal hull of the helicopter towards my face. That horrible screech was worse than nails on a chalkboard, and it drew my eyes. Right in that half second of distraction, Black kicked his knee up and struck the bottom of his other hand. It was all the extra umph he needed to outmuscle me and plunge the marble-handled stiletto deep into my side right above the hip.

"Never bring just one knife, West," sneered Black.

"Good advice," I said and kneed him hard in the ribs at the same spot I'd cut him before. In that split second where he was recoiling, I reached to the top of my boot and pulled my back-up Marfione Apex. I slashed up and buried the broad spear-point deep into his shoulder.

It was his turn to scream now, and his wail reached a crescendo when I gave the Apex's handle a violent twist to further tear at the tendons in the joint. Black's arm went limp and dropped his goddamn precious special dagger into the burning pool of helicopter fuel near our feet.

I wrenched the Apex out and plunged it back down, aiming for his throat, but he pushed away from me. Black eyed the fiery pool and almost plunged his hand into the fire to retrieve the blade, but pulled back with a hiss when the coils of flame licked at his fingertips.

My leg grew soaked from my own blood spilling down my side and drenching my pants. The wound was deeper than I'd thought. I told myself I was okay as I clamped a hand down to stymie the flow. Instead, I felt the jelly of my own intestine pushing out into my palm.

Fuck.

We were both down to one arm. Him, because one was hanging dead from my last wound; me, because one of my hands was keeping me from being disemboweled. Eager to finish the son of a bitch before I bled to death, I charged. Black rolled his last knife between his fingers—a trick I'd seen others do with a coin along their knuckles—until the tip was clasped between his thumb and pointer, and he threw it with a deft side-arm.

I'd seen it coming and sidestepped out of the way as it whirled through the empty air.

No knives left, you piece of shit!

I finished closing the distance between us. He was defenseless. No more blades; his good hand clutched tight to his wounded shoulder. My eyes locked on his. I plunged the Apex for his eye socket. At the last possible second, his good hand left his shoulder and flung a handful of his own blood into my eyes.

Everything went red.

"I lied, by the way . . ." he hissed.

I wiped his blood from my eyes.

He knelt to grab something from his ankle and then leapt up, slashing diagonally.

"I had one more left."

I looked down at my chest, my shirt parted away. It took another second for the flesh to separate where he'd cut me. The grisly laceration went diagonally from my hip to shoulder, and the blood that spilled forth a breath later drenched to my knees. I went from feeling the singe of the fire that dripped down from the sky, to feeling nothing but the goosebump chill of the grave.

I fell to a single knee, and my head dropped down. All I'd needed was the one moment, one opening. Looks like I'd asked too much.

CHAPTER 72

Eric Vaun. 8:47 a.m.
Vancouver, British Columbia

His cane clicked along the marbled floor as he limped along as quickly as he could manage. Connor Brawnley stumbled in front of him. Brawnley's cheek was lined with deep scratches and blood ran down to his neck and shoulder. He held a pistol taken from one of his body-men, and there was a fearful look in his eye. For a moment Vaun thought the man meant to hurt him, but then realized Brawnley had just been spooked by the sight of Dante at his heels.

"Bollocks," Brawnley murmured as he looked around helplessly.

"Apt description," Vaun said.

Death. There was no other word for the ongoing massacre below. Vaun looked past it and saw one saving grace in this catastrophe. When the semi-trailers crashed into the building, the rubble had wedged them in. Which meant nobody inside could get out through the three new holes in the walls. At this moment, the Kruegers were trapped.

"We have to lock this place down. If these—"

Brawnley was cut short when a bullet fired from the melee below snapped him in the eye. The Brit stiffened as if frozen before falling backwards over the railway to the lower-level floor. Vaun spared just a second to try to find Brawnley amidst the swirling chaos before he was forced to turn away.

"Come on, boy," he said to West's oversized dog.

Dante gave him a worried *whuff* and trailed close behind him. The jet-black mastiff was more bear than canine, and Vaun felt thankful he had him by his side to keep the Kruegers back. A worrisome thought came to mind. What if dogs could be similarly affected by the Morpheus Engine? Dante put his worries at ease by powering on ahead and dutifully clearing the way for Vaun like a snowplow made of fur.

"Blackbars, what are you up to?" a voice asked over the radio.

The voice was feminine, but sharp as a knife's blade and spoken as unyielding as concrete.

Kara . . .

"I already tried activating them, but the security shutters aren't going down," Vaun said. "The Morpheus pulse tripped the breakers. I need to flip them."

"The Engine's gone and took a trip across the city, BB."

"This is ground zero, and we've got a few hundred Kruegers in the room below. We have to keep them from spilling outside and spreading."

The comm went quiet for a second. Vaun could practically see Kara talking to Rain about what she was thinking.

"Roger, I'm coming to you."

A Krueger armed with a crowbar soaked red to his elbow bounded at Vaun, but Dante intercepted him and hit him like a battering ram. His teeth sank into the Krueger's wrist and bit deep until the bone cracked. The Krueger was undeterred until Dante applied a similarly precise bite into his throat. Dante's jaws squeezed exactly. There was no worrying at the limb like some savage wolf, Dante looked like a black dog from hell, but he was as trained and disciplined as his human counterparts. It was that same discipline that, for now, kept the dog from succumbing to its own fearful illusions.

"Belay that, Sledgehammer. I've got all the backup I need. Get to Kage, he's on point with Storm going after the HVT."

Vaun could feel her scowling through the radio. He knew she took it personally. She most likely misconstrued his objections as some evaluation of her abilities. Quite the contrary. He knew all too well how much it hurt a soldier's soul to be seen as incapable, but he was being practical when sending her to Billy's aid. The menial task of flipping the breakers was something that even a cripple such as himself could do without assistance.

As if reading his mind, Dante *whuffed* at him. Okay, maybe a *little* assistance.

If his memory of the blueprints he'd looked over was sharp, which it always was, then the utility room holding the first-floor breakers was just around the corner. All he had to do was round this corner and, God willing, there'd only be one or two Kruegers in the lobby between him and the breakers he needed to flip.

As it turned out, God was not willing. Not one damned bit.

There were nearly a dozen people in the lobby in various stages of insanity, the three extremes of fight, flight, or freeze on display in the most horrible of ways. Some cried or sat on the floor, rocking slowly, others broke their fingernails off clawing at the walls as if trying to break through some unseen doorways, one or two might have already been brain dead judging by the drool leaking from the corners of their mouths. Then there were the four raving and murdering each other with pens from the front desk.

Vaun's hand shook at the top of his cane. A moment of hesitation bred from his own self-awareness of his immobility. The best option would be to weave around them, let Dante get involved if any decided the two of them looked more interesting than their current bloodshed. But that would require him to quickstep over the other fear-induced victims that crowded the floor. Not an easy feat to accomplish in a hurry with someone who wasn't that surefooted.

The moment passed, and Vaun trudged on. His cane continued to click with every step. The muscles along Dante's back and shoulders bunched as his reflexes coiled in preparation. It was like stepping through a minefield made of people. And, much as is the case with an actual minefield, getting across unscathed proved far from guaranteed. A young woman with self-induced scratch marks all across her forearms shot out her hand and grabbed Vaun's ankle. The abrupt shift in his own weight sent him toppling over as if he'd stepped into a beartrap.

"It won't come *off!*" she screamed at him. Her other hand raked her fingernails across the very arm that had grabbed him. She scratched deeper until blood and skin filled her nail beds. And she just kept at it. What she was hallucinating Vaun didn't know. Perhaps bugs of a sort, or maybe she had a preexisting compulsive disorder against dirt that was magnified tenfold by the Morpheus pulse. It didn't matter. The madness rooted deep and strong, and he couldn't help her out of it. All he could do was try to keep the more violent ones from hurting others.

"I'm sorry," he said softly as he twisted around to apply the length of his walking cane across her neck like a garotte. She went limp in under five seven seconds.

He was disabled, not incapable.

Vaun forced himself back up to his feet and half-limped, half-hopped on his good leg to the utility room door. There was a howl behind him that defied all reason. It wasn't any language. It could hardly be categorized into any one emotion either. It was a scream of anger, confusion, and pain all wrapped in one. But mostly anger. Three Kruegers turned their attention to Vaun just as he clutched the doorknob.

The reason for their screams were indecipherable, but the

meaning Dante's bark back was unmistakable: back the hell away.

His deep *whuffs* echoed off the porcelain floor and sent the victims who'd gone scared reeling away in deeper fear. But the Kruegers were created by their opposite reaction. Vaun pulled the utility door open and shouted to Dante to follow. Before the big dog could comply one of the Kruegers lunged at Vaun through the doorway. Dante hit him full-on, knocking the man to the ground and biting deep into his shoulder and neck.

Many a dog owner would make the case that their furry friends are smarter than anyone else would admit. That they could understand English and the only problem was their inability to speak it. So, when those big yellow eyes looked up at Vaun, and he gave a quiet little bark before wheeling around to keep the other Kruegers back, Vaun got the message loud and clear. 'Go, I'll keep you safe.'

Vaun let the door close then hobbled around the room in a frantic search. His eyes came across large internet servers, commercial-sized water heaters, and various pipes of anonymous purpose. Then he spotted the circuit breakers on the back wall. Huge light-switch looking panels which, hopefully, were just as easy to flip as their resemblance. Someone had been helpful enough to previously label one panel "First Floor" and Vaun used the flat of his hand to flip all of them off and then on again.

He wondered if the shutters were closing. He wondered if the madness inside this hotel was being contained. All that wonder vanished when a maintenance worker brandishing a screwdriver stepped into view, gnashing his teeth like an animal upon seeing Vaun, and pounced.

The Krueger knocked both of them to the ground and pushed all the air from Vaun's lungs. The tip of the screwdriver stabbed down at his Adam's apple but he kept it back by blocking the Krueger's forearm with his cane. They wrestled with each other. Neither weight nor leverage favored Vaun.

There was a loud crack as the Krueger pushed with all his body weight through his arm and onto Vaun's cane. Vaun could see the wooden shaft bending, and the first sign of fracture right there at the middle of it. If it bent anymore it would break, if it broke, he would lose his defense, and if he had no defense then that screwdriver was going to become very good friends with his throat.

The cane broke.

CHAPTER 73

"Shall we wait for your Immortals, ma'am?" Rinx asked as he pressed the push-to-start ignition.

Holt stole a glance at her four devoted Immortals at the back of the parking garage, "And mess the upholstery with the blood they're covered in? Please, Dorian, let's get on with it. I'd prefer to be in another hemisphere by the evening news."

His dark-rimmed eyes betrayed nothing as he looked at her through the rear-view mirror. The sedan rolled along towards the exit ramp, and Rinx gently eased it to a halt.

"Dorian, dear, you really are my favorite, but I don't repeat myself even for you."

"No, ma'am," he said and stepped out of the vehicle. The suspension lifted nearly two inches without his weight. "Security gate just lowered. Stay here."

He closed the door and went to the control panel. Holt was not one prone to fear, but the twinge at her jaw was sign enough that she wasn't exactly at her calmest. Her hands clasped atop her glass cane in a failed attempt to look at ease. One tapped gently upon the cane's head as she waited for Rinx. The empty car became a prison cell with every passing second. She couldn't even see where her Praetorian was anymore.

Was she scared? That was irregular. Perhaps the Morpheus Engine's effects had pushed past her prophylactics after all.

Something rushed past her window. When she looked for it, there was nothing but the shadows of the garage. It had to be one of her Immortals, or a figment of her imagination. That was the only plausible explanation. They were at the back of the garage, and the Immortals wouldn't have let anyone near her car. They'd throw themselves upon their own blades first.

The security shutter at the top of the ramp began to rise and Holt let out a gasp she hadn't realized she'd held. Rinx returned and she lowered her window.

"Sorry for the delay."

"Bollocks the courtesies and let's get this carriage going, dear."

"Of course. I only—"

A pale-skinned ghoul pounced from behind and wrapped itself upon Rinx's back. Despite all her restraint, Holt couldn't stop herself from shouting. Two more figures came down the ramp now that the security barrier no longer barred them. They both wore policeman's uniforms but were in no condition to maintain the peace.

One crashed into Rinx as he wrestled with the first Krueger, and the other went for Holt's open window. Rinx whirled around to swing the creature off his back, caught it by the leg and neck, and then broke it in half against one of the garage's concrete columns. By then one of the mad policemen had thrown himself into the vehicle. The halfway-closed window broke under his weight and the shattered glass raked across his waistline. He didn't notice.

Holt pulled the latch of the door behind her and spilled out onto the hard ground behind. She felt a sharp pain lightning up from her hip to her back and it rooted her to the spot. She'd likely just broken her hip. Her priceless cane, one of a kind, slipped from her fingers at the same time as the realization hit her. The *fulgurite* and gold shaft shattered. A million fragments scattered upon the cement ground like drops of crystallized rain.

The monster crawling through the window clawed the air before her face. Just as it was readying to leap out at her, Rinx grabbed it about the ankle and wrenched it back out through the window. The jagged glass rent rivers of blood out its back. Rinx lifted it into the air and thrashed it down against the vehicle, brutalizing it as if it were nothing more than overripe fruit being bashed to pulp. The broken thing lay upon Holt's car, twitching horribly.

The sound of rapid footfalls descended the exit ramp. She saw two more figures run down to them and saw Rinx once more move to meet them. He held them back, Holt's great gladiator who would proudly give his life for his patron.

A wretched gnashing sounded behind her. She turned and saw the Krueger that had its spine broken against the column. It was paralyzed from the waist down but still crawled towards her slowly with murderous intent.

"Dorian . . ." she called as she scooted back. The effort wrenched a gasp of pain through her as her midsection shifted slightly along her hips. Chunks of glass from her cane dug into her palms. The cement beneath her seemed to fill every one of her joints with aches as she inched her way back towards the vehicle.

"Dorian!"

But her bodyguard was too busy keeping the ones who'd come down the ramp away from the car. The crippled Krueger dragged itself after her, stripping its fingertips of its skin and screaming its madness. The policeman's corpse was within arm's reach of her, and Holt spotted the pistol snugly tucked on its belt. She'd never so much as held a gun let alone fired one before, yet she was more than familiar with how they worked. Which meant she also knew the destruction its recoil would inflict upon her.

"Dorian!"

Her cries for help went unanswered, and the dreadful thing continued to close the distance. The sounds of Rinx's scuffle reached her ears, and she couldn't tell if he would claim victory in his own battle. With the Krueger's bloody fingers within reach of her immobile legs, Holt drew the policeman's weapon.

She pleaded for her guardian one last time as she pointed the impossibly heavy weapon. But Rinx wasn't there. The Krueger reared upon her with savage jaws open wide, and the shot rang out. Its head kicked back, and it dropped. Her hand folded against the recoiling pistol as if it were made of liquid rather than flesh and bone. The forearm collapsed backwards on an unnaturally made second joint midway up the limb. The pistol flew away to the shadows, unseen as pain beyond words filled her arm to the shoulder.

Holt clutched her broken wing to her chest and tried to keep herself from shaking. She rested her head as easily as she could upon the car cushion next to her, and then Rinx's powerful hands were gently lifting her into the carriage. The last thing she felt before blacking out was something wet upon her face.

A tear.

Her Praetorian wept for her, for his failure.

CHAPTER 74

His hand twitched on reflex when he heard a single gunshot echo through the garage. That involuntary shake stirred him up from wherever his soul had fallen to, while the squeal of tires peeling away finished rousing him back to an ebbing consciousness.

Returning to reality also meant he returned to all the pain of having a knife stabbed in your belly. Billy had heard all the descriptions before about what being stabbed felt like. 'It feels like fire being pushed inside you and radiated lightning', 'it feels like taking a punch to the gut, you can't feel the sharp pain until after that blow fades'. You know what being stabbed really felt like? It felt like having a fucking knife inside you, because there weren't any words that truly did that pain justice.

His hands found the hilt of the large hunting knife protruding from his body, his own blood gushed into his hands. There was a *lot* of goddamned blood.

"Looks like he isn't going to give it up that easy after all," the Immortal who'd stabbed him said.

Billy picked up an Australian accent.

"Not as easy as your mom gave it up," Billy said with a cough. It flecked his lips with blood. He laughed a little, which sent fresh waves of pain through him with every shake. "Heh . . . oh, fuck."

One of the Immortals knelt in front of him, pushing up his Kevlar mask to look at Billy face-to-face. The man was handsome for a brutal enforcer. He held twin double-edged daggers in hand and used one to tap Billy lightly on the shoulder.

"So, do you want us to finish this on your knees or can you get up?"

"Asked your mom the same thing."

This time two of the Immortals broke their silence with snickers of their own. The Australian, who'd since lifted his own mask up, had a deep belly chuckle while the one with the daggers in front of him had a nasally giggle.

"I'd expect nothing less from one of your acclaim," the handsome one said. "I mean the *balls* on this guy!"

"That's what your mom said."

The Immortals were losing it until one with an axe clanged the handle onto the concrete ground.

"Alright, that's enough fun. Finish him, Harrison."

The raven-haired killer in front of Billy sighed and reached up to pull his mask down. "Such a shame to put down a *formerly* acclaimed assassin, *Mamushi*. A lackluster end to an otherwise remarkable career."

Before Harrison finished pulling the Kevlar face shield down, Billy flung his hands up at Harrison's face. The blood, which had pooled into his hands like a bowl, splashed up between the Immortal's face and mask and blinded the man. As the Immortal cried out, Billy exploded to his feet, pulling the knife from his own belly as he did so. He screamed in both pain and fury as he sank it down to the hilt between Harrison's shoulder and neck. The pain from the grinding bones of his broken jaw sent Billy's war cry into a bloodthirsty roar.

Billy remembered how these bastards had slaughtered Valkyrie Squad. He remembered how Valkyrie's bullets had bounced off their armor like nothing. He remembered exactly where the armor would *not* protect.

Billy caught Harrison's twin daggers and threw them at both thighs of the Immortal with the axe. They sank deep and sent the Immortal down onto his knees, unable to move. His axe fell from his hands and the back-spike chinked into the concrete in front of him.

The other two Immortals—the Australian and the Black Frenchman—donned their masks. The masks transformed them. There was a change in them that was so sudden it was like they'd been replaced by two completely different people. The Frenchman kicked out Billy's leg, sending him back down to one knee. The Australian landed a mean hook into his floating ribs before following with a heavy roundhouse punch that sent blood squirting out both of Billy's nostrils. It hurt, real fucking bad, but he was secretly grateful that he'd taken the punch to the nose and not the jaw.

"Not even you stand a chance alone," the Australian said.

The Frenchman moved behind where Billy knelt. He pulled his hip back to load his leg, ready to snap Billy's neck with another kick. Instead, a hand shot out like a knife and chopped the Frenchman right across the throat.

"Who said he's alone?" Mason asked.

The Frenchman's throat collapsed on itself. His own momentum sent him spinning around. He grabbed at his neck, trying to fix what was already too badly broken. Mason slapped his hands down and snapped three quick jabs into his Adam's Apple to further cave in his windpipe. His eyes bulged and fingernails tore gouges in his neck.

The Australian saw this and leapt at Billy. Billy was quicker and ripped the Australian's own hunting knife out of Harrison's neck, then swung it up with both hands. The steel blade went deep into the

Australian's belly. Billy pulled it out and yelled a mighty battle cry as he brought it down like a spike into the top of the man's skull.

"I thought you'd be harder to kill than this," Billy spat.

The Australian's eyes rolled into the back of his head. Billy let him fall back. It had taken all of his own strength for that last burst, and once more Billy found himself falling to the floor. He kept pressure on his wounds and reached to Mason for help, but she had other priorities.

"I saw the footage," she said, approaching the last Immortal, who remained doubled over on his hands and knees, both of Harrison's daggers sticking from his legs. "This axe looks really familiar. You're the one who killed Maggie, huh?"

Mason picked the axe up, then hooked the spike under Declan's mask to slip it off his face. That Kevlar face fell upon the ground and stared up at her. Empty eyes. When she looked back at the Irishman, she saw the same emptiness. Soulless.

"Who?" the scarred Irishman panted.

"Maggie Cruz," said Mason. She held the honed edge of the axe against the Immortal's cheekbone. "My friend. She was the one you killed on the rooftop."

"They're all the same once the masks are on. Nothing but meat ready to be carved. You expect me to remember her?"

Mason stepped back and dragged the axe blade along the ground.

"Don't worry. When you get to hell, that bitch will be waiting for you."

Mason pulled the axe back, then swung it with both hands like a croquet mallet. She put every bit of rage into that swing. The axe cleaved through chin, lips, teeth, nose, and forehead, splitting his skull down the middle with a sickening crunch.

CHAPTER 75

Cole West.
Nowhere.

There was nothing around me. I thought there would be a soft white light, maybe a tunnel beckoning ominously, or even good old fire and brimstone welcoming me to what came next. Instead, it was gray. Just gray. It was like a vast nowhere place. All color, all sensation, all sound was washed out. Smudges swam in my eyes as if the slight gusts I felt at the back of my hands were brushstrokes of some limbo landscape painter.

My every thought was clouded over, not unlike when a dream escapes your memory upon waking. I wondered if this is what dying felt like, simply fading and forgetting. All your life slipping away as easily as a dream. I found myself walking. At least I think I was walking. I took uncertain steps through the colorless void. The ground beneath my feet felt soft, like walking along a beach. I came into a sort of clearing. The gray seemed to part away. There, with his back to me, stood someone very familiar.

"Hey, bud. Cue the *Unchained Melody,* am I right?" Kelly's friendly voice said before he turned to face me. "This is the part where you're supposed to ask whether you're dead or not. You're not, by the way. Trust me. I've got a bit of experience on the subject."

"Kelly . . . ?"

My friend smiled at me. Unlike the other times I'd seen his ghost where he'd been bloodied and pale, and that ragged hole in his throat would stare at me like a reminder of my failure, now he looked as alive as he would have on his best day. He patted me on the shoulder.

"Good to see you, bud."

He motioned for me to follow him as he walked away. For some reason I hesitated. I just couldn't seem to get my feet to move after him. You ever accidentally step on your dog's foot, and then can't bring yourself to look it in the eye and see the pain you caused them? Yeah. This was that, but a couple orders of magnitude worse.

"Don't be afraid, Cap. I don't bite. I think those are zombies, not ghosts."

I awkwardly fell into step alongside him.

"That's the word of the day, isn't it?" I said. "Afraid."

"Oh boy, is it. That Morpheus shit has been beating on your head something fierce, huh?"

I drew in a long breath of the strange gray ether that billowed around us.

"Come on," I said, "my head hasn't been right since the Warmaker mission. All the Morpheus Engine did is finish cracking it apart."

Kelly arched an eyebrow. "Is that what you think?"

"To be fair I am having a conversation with the ghost of one of my best friends. Not exactly selling a picture of mental health there."

"Point taken," Kelly admitted. "But we don't have much time, so I'm going to have to stop playing nice and get through that unbelievably stubborn skull of yours. What are you afraid of, Cole?"

His question punched through my heart like a bullet. What had Morpheus shown me so far? Burned skeletons. Dead friends. Visions of demons and horrific hellscapes.

"What are you *really* afraid of?"

That was the question at the core of it all. I took a deep look inward and readied myself to face it. As the shadows I'd wrapped around that inner truth unraveled, Kelly let me have it.

"You fear the truth, and that all the people you burned that night—all two-thousand four-hundred twenty-eight of them—that they aren't even close to being the last lives you'll have to take. And you're afraid that I'm just the first of many friends you're going to lose on this path you're on."

Each sentence he spoke felt like another blow from a hammer. Each strike drove a stake deeper into my heart. And he didn't let up.

"You're terrified of accepting that there wasn't anything more you could've done to save me, not one damn thing, that you really were helpless, and no matter what call you made I was going to die. You're afraid because that means it could happen again to someone else. And it will."

Part of me wanted to cry, but I couldn't bring myself to do it. Not yet. I was too busy squeezing my eyes shut as if that would deafen me to Kelly's words, which I clearly needed to hear.

"But the deepest one? The one Morpheus has been showing you this whole time? What really scares you *isn't* that you're traumatized and broken . . . no."

He put a hand on my shoulder. A small gesture, a show of support as he carried me to the end of it.

"What really scares you is that you're okay. That you're already living with it. You're carrying on. And you're scared of what kind of man that makes you."

I looked the ghost of my friend in the eyes. "It makes me a monster, right? Like Black? That's what you're going to say. It means he and I really are the same."

Kelly's smiled a sad little smile and shook his head. "No. It means you're unbreakable. Whatever the fuck comes your way, you'll carry that weight. You talked about shackles chaining you to this life.

Well, guess what? You're not stuck in this life. This life is stuck with you. Because you can take it. The only thing you and Black have in common is that neither of you will give up. Unstoppable force, and an immovable object."

He gave me time. It was a solid five count where neither of us said anything more, the only sound was that gray wind blowing around us. Then, as if he felt the need to write a period at the end of this discussion, he clapped me on the shoulder and slowly backed away.

"For what it's worth, I forgive you," he said.

I couldn't help but laugh.

"That's nice but seeing as how you're just a figment of my imagination, and this entire conversation is just a Morpheus hallucination in my head, you're only a piece of my mind talking to myself."

Kelly's smile grew wider, and he began to fade away like smoke in the wind. "Yeah, maybe. But even if you're right about that, isn't that more important?"

It took a second for me to get what he'd just said. Then the ghost was gone. And so was I. The very nowhere place around me pulled away until I was not even a body in a place, until I was nothing but a thought. From somewhere, somewhere far away, I heard Kelly's voice one last time.

"So . . . you just gonna lay there bleeding? Or you gonna stand?"

Air filled my lungs in a sudden gasp. Warmth surged back through my veins quick as a whipcrack. I lay chest down in a puddle of my own blood and had to fight to draw myself up to my knees. Then it took every ounce of will to get one foot on the deck. By the time I'd gotten to my feet, it was from strength I didn't feel. When I took that first shaky step forward, I immediately fell back down to a knee.

Blood came up in a bad cough, and I gritted my teeth through the pain.

I could take it.

I *would* take it.

I forced myself up.

"Standing . . ." I said through red-stained lips. My breaths came ragged. Each one like a small jolt of life to keep me going. "Alright, Kelly, this last dance is for you."

The warmth of the burning helicopter was still behind me. Mr. Black walked away from me towards the Morpheus Engine. I could see that, once more, the core was exposed. Those iridescent green rods were painful to look at, their brightness searing into my mind more than my eyes. For some reason no nightmares invaded my thoughts yet. I wondered if that was just because I was so close to death's door.

Another painful cough sent blood down my chin.

"Stand, damn it!" I said to myself.

I swallowed down the coppery taste of blood in my throat and retrieved my last two Kick injectors from my pocket. The adrenaline mixture was meant to keep the nightmares at bay, now I was using it to barter with the reaper for just a few more moments. I stuck one of the autoinjectors into my thigh and pumped its content into the muscle.

The effects were instant. My pupils narrowed to pinpricks. My upper lip pulled back from my teeth in a defiant snarl. With one hand clamped over my side to keep my guts from falling out, I exploded with energy and ran at Black from behind. I then stabbed my last injector into the side of his neck. I thumbed the plunger, and he howled in surprise. He threw an elbow over his shoulder, which caught me in the nose and sent me sprawling backwards.

My idea had been simple. Damien Black was nothing more than the conjured nightmares of Adrian Rasp given form, so maybe, just maybe, I could bring a piece of the original man back.

Black plucked the needle from his neck and whirled around. Locks of his rain-soaked hair ran down in his face and his eyes had gone wild with rage. But he didn't attack immediately. There was just a second of hesitation. One hand went to his temple and, somehow, I knew whatever was left of Adrian Rasp was fighting to claw himself to the surface. He was wrestling for the steering wheel with the demon who'd been in control for years. Just as quickly, Adrian seemed to lose that fight.

Black screamed like he was possessed. Smoke from the burning wreckage blocked him from view for a second. Then he was there, leaping through the dark cloud, wild-eyed and full of rage. All semblance of humanity in his eyes was gone. This was death incarnate with blade in hand.

Too little time to dodge. Too weak and slow to parry.

One of Kelly's final words came back to me.

You can take it.

I reached forward and used my own hand as a shield to stop the point from going through my eye. His knife sank through my palm, passed between the small bones and tendons, and lit every single one of the nerve endings on fire as the tip came out the back.

The only reason his knife didn't immediately pierce my throat was that he'd been crippled down to a lone arm. Still, he pressed down with his one good hand and leaned all his body weight on me. I pushed back with everything I had. The dagger tip wandered away from my throat and drew a red line up my cheek, slicing through my face like a scalpel.

"That's it, *West.*"

He hissed the S in my name, a mad viper eager for the kill.

"Don't just give up now. Everyone I've *ever* killed let me take them so easy."

He accented every word with another heave of his weight upon the blade. The knife tip hovered by my eye. I felt the last of my strength fading away. Any second now it would be gone entirely, and he'd finish plunging his knife into my skull.

His maniacal smile returned, so I stabbed my thumb into his ruined shoulder. At the same time, he ripped his blade not back, but up, splitting my hand from palm to knuckle. Our screams echoed as one. Black flipped the knife into a reverse grip and lifted it high to plunge it into my chest as he straddled atop me.

"Cole!" a voice shouted from across the ring of fire.

We both looked. There was Tag. A slug trail of blood followed from where he'd crawled to his sub-nosed .44 revolver, the very one that Black had so carelessly discarded. The very one Black had used to so heartlessly kill our friend.

Tag aimed with a pale and shaking hand. Black had spent one of the revolver's rounds at the airport, one at the foundry, one at Home Site, and two more here. That left one chambered bullet remaining.

BANG!

I'll never know if Tag was aiming for it, or if the shot went wide, but that heavy magnum round struck Black's knife right as it stabbed down. I shielded my face into the crook of one arm and the blade exploded into a dozen crystalline shards. Black was not so protected. Rain had told me that obsidian was sharp on a microscopic level, and a dozen razor fragments had just recoiled into his face. It was like someone had shredded his neck and the side of his head with birdshot. He howled in seemingly slow motion as the black-glass shrapnel pelted deep into his face. One fragment sliced across the corner of his mouth and opened a grisly smile all the way to the ear.

I felt the moment stretch. It was like I'd stepped into the eye of the storm. Chaos all around me, but a stillness at the very center where I lay. My own heartbeat thumped in my ears.

Ba-bum.

Ba-bum.

My mangled hand pressed to my side where blood gently gushed against my ruined palm. Flames from a puddle of burning helicopter fuel near my side lazily licked at me. For once in a long while, I wasn't afraid of that fire.

I was looking past its surface at what lay beneath the flame: the other knife Black had dropped into the burning puddle was *still* there. The special one.

Ignoring all reason, blocking out all pain, I plunged my good hand into the fire. I pulled the knife from the flames and the fire coiled itself from dagger tip all the way to my wrist. It was as if that volcanic glass remembered what it was like to be forged in the earth's furnace, remembered and was eager to burn hot once more.

Black saw it. But there was a flicker behind his eyes, and I knew that the ghost of Adrian Rasp had managed to slow Black's hand for just a second. Just one.

There it was. That one moment, the one opening I would ever get. I thrust at his chest and his hand blurred as it moved to catch it.

Thanks to Adrian, Black was just that one second too slow.

The obsidian knife, coated in flame, sank halfway down its length into Black's chest. Sharpened obsidian passed through flesh and cracked through breastbone. The burning marble handle, and all the stolen souls allegedly frozen within its stone, seared my palm. But still I gripped it tighter.

You can take it.

Black's blood poured from the wound and sizzled against the hot knife. More of it painted his teeth red and flowed down his bottom lip as he reared his head back in a long scream that went unheard to my ears.

Black's hand pushed back against the knife in defiance as he glared at me, but in the stretched span of a single passing breath I felt his strength slip away. Mine wasn't far behind, but it would last long enough. His eyes looked everywhere but at the blade. He refused to see it. He was afraid to.

"What's the matter?" I asked as he fought to keep the knife from going deeper. "Scared?"

He stumbled backwards off of me, and I let it pull me back onto my own feet. Black kept staring at me, looking bewildered. Then he finally looked at the knife jutting from his heart. Both of his hands fell to his sides as he gave up against the death blow. Then, he smiled at me with crimson teeth and a bloody sliced open mouth. I could see every tooth to his cheekbone. That psychotic grin chilled me to my soul. His empty eyes glittered as if he were getting the last laugh after all.

"West . . ." he hissed, "that dark heart of yours? You'll carry it with you forever."

I buried the rest of the knife's length into his heart.

"I'm learning to carry a lot of things."

I twisted the handle and cracked the blade off. A bolt of lightning shattered the sky at the same time, as if God himself reveled in this monster's death. Black took a few steps back on trembling legs as his fingers fumbled at the blade, but like a key broken off in a lock, there was nothing to be done.

I threw the broken off marble handle to the ground and spat a mouthful of blood in his face. Those soulless eyes of his rolled back into his skull. Black's arms outstretched in an unholy stigmata pose, and his body plummeted over the edge of the dam to the watery grave awaiting below.

Knowing I had maybe mere seconds before my mortal coil followed suit, I limped to the Morpheus Engine. My legs finally gave out as I grabbed the remote. With a trembling hand, I powered the machine down, then rested my head against its cold metallic hull.

I looked out to the blood-red sky. One last bolt of lightning flashed and for a split-second I glimpsed that devil in metal from the nightmare world. The dark tyrant from that painful place filled the sky and reached for my soul, but then just as quickly the vision ended. The hell painted sky slowly vanished like an evaporating mirage, only to be replaced by gray skies. The fire raining down turned back to mere water, and I welcomed the chill upon my face. I let the rain fall upon me, and felt it wash all the blood away. The blood, the pain, and the fear.

Sunlight broke through the rain clouds, and I spotted blue sky beyond the gray. I smiled as the last bit of life the Kick needle granted me faded away. That blank nowhere place was calling me back. This time, I met it unafraid.

EPILOGUE

I

It took two full minutes for Vaun's chest to stop heaving and his heart rate to slow its gallop. By then the maintenance worker turned Krueger had long since bled out and grown cold near Vaun's feet. Half of Vaun's broken cane jutted out the side of the Krueger's neck. The last of his blood had gone out in a rhythmic spurt that stopped the second his heart did. Vaun gripped the other half of his broken walking cane and gave himself a knowing nod.

Disabled, not incapable.

Something crashed into the utility closet, and Vaun exploded up onto his feet. He flipped the jagged stick around in his hand like a knife, ready to go to work once more.

Except it was Dante trotting around the corner. Vaun blew out a shaky breath and let the hulking mastiff nuzzle his hand. Vaun allowed Dante to lead the way back to the lobby. There was a moment as they walked the hallways when Dante barked at the three dead Kruegers as if to see if Vaun appreciated his handiwork.

"Good dog," he said.

Dante *whuffed* in response.

When they reached the lobby, Vaun nearly shed a tear in gratitude. The security shutters had indeed lowered into place after all. None of Legion's army of Kruegers had made it onto the

Vancouver streets. Whatever damage Black's flyover had done was minimal compared to what would've happened if they'd all gotten loose.

II

My heart flatlined for over four minutes, brought back from death's door for the second time in my life by a shock to the heart. That, and many, many pints of blood. Of course, I only learned this after I woke up in the hospital some days later. A few of the nurses looked like they'd seen a ghost. Judging by some of their expressions, they must've placed some substantial bets on me biting it and were less than enthused I'd pulled through.

I'd expected Tag or Billy to be in the room when I woke. Their absence only meant one thing; none of us had walked away from this mission unscathed, and they were most likely still in beds of their own. Madison was there, though, and her expression spoke volumes.

Eyes rimmed red, had she been crying?

Her black pantsuit and white blouse—usually nothing less than immaculate—looked worn and soiled. Her vigil had been ongoing for some time.

"The tan blazer complements your hair more," I said.

She fought against the smirk, but I caught it at the corner of her mouth.

"I didn't know if I'd have to go to your funeral from here." There was a flicker of pain when she said it. She'd really thought I wasn't going to make it. Well, considering my level of absolute fucking agony, and despite the copious amounts of morphine running through my blood, I guess that made sense.

I took a long time working up to it, but I finally addressed one of the biggest elephants in the room.

"So . . . you being here, does that mean we're done hiding? Hiding whatever this is?"

"Oh, Captain, what makes you think I'm not just here to study and monitor the only living person to take such a high Morpheus dosage?"

She gently placed her hand on my arm, and I laughed, which hurt like hell. Each chuckle made me painfully aware of each and every stitch I had knitting me together. I reached for her hand and held it for a moment. Something about dying twice in a week will make a man brave enough to quit being so chickenshit about what he really feels for someone.

"Look, our boss is dead," I said. "And without Director Rourke, Black Spear is, well, it's history. It's over. The way I see it, fraternization isn't exactly a concern anymore."

She squeezed my hand and her lips pursed. "Was that really the only thing in the way for you? Company policy?"

"Maybe I'm just coming to terms with being damaged goods. And I'm hoping you can accept that, too. Since I'm about to be unemployed, I should free up some time to work on a few things."

Madison pulled away from me. That little action scared me deeply, which was saying something considering everything I'd gone through. Maybe the painkillers were breaking down some inhibitions that should've stayed intact. As it turned out, I was misreading the situation.

"About that, you have another visitor. I played gatekeeper as much as I could under the pretense of running tests on how your notoriously thick skull was doing, but they're getting pretty insistent."

I think my ears perked up like a dog. "Is it Tag or Billy? Are they-?"

"Hey, hey, there he is! Our hero's awake!" said a voice that one hundred percent did not belong to one of my squad mates. Walther Sloan pushed his way into what should have been a very private room.

He swaggered in as if he and I were lifelong drinking buddies.

Madison mouthed an apology, which I dismissed with a shake of the head as I donned my most convincing of fake smiles.

"What's a legitimate Deputy Director like yourself slumming it in the room of a nonexistent unknown such as myself?"

Sloan approached my bedside, slowing just for a beat as he passed a mirror to coif his hair, then gestured to Madison. "Doctor Archer, I presume? Mind if I have the room with your amazing mine canary here for a minute?"

She pretended to finish jotting down notes on a clipboard, gave Sloan a curt nod and left. Sloan took her chair and slouched into it deep. The CIA honcho craned his neck to watch Madison from behind as she exited.

"Ooh wee, little firecracker that one is, huh? Bounce a nickel off it."

"What do you want?"

Sloan adjusted his jacket and did a rapid drumbeat on his thighs with his palms. "Straight to business, that's fine. Lot of excitement going on right now. And you, Mister Unknown, could find yourself in some prime, Grade-A, *choice* center stage coming out of this."

My head was spinning, and not just from the anesthesia.

"Sir—Sloan? Whatever. What the hell are you talking about?"

"Opportunity, West. Plain and simple. See, Vancouver was an international embarrassment. Heads will fucking *roll* for that fuck up. Thing is? It's not our embarrassment. That's on the Canucks up north. Alain Virieux's going to be manning an empty post in the Yukon until Judgment Day after this. But, thanks to us, it wasn't the total disaster it could've been. You and me. It was us two who warned people something was going down. And, I might add, a few of those cameras that kept rolling got some shots of yours truly fighting the good fight. A picture says a thousand words, West."

If I didn't have more stitches in me than Frankenstein's monster and a hand that had been split in half a few days ago, I would've leapt off the cot and clocked him right there. 'Opportunity' he said. They'd had to wash the blood out of Vancouver by the gallons, and

Sloan saw that as a way to pave his own road to position.

"Here's the bottom line," Sloan said. "Word on the street is I'm on the short list for the *big* seat. Director. As soon as Mr. Rourke's casket gets lowered into the ground, Black Spear's finished. I mean, let's be honest, it's already been on the way out. A man like me could always use a man like you in his corner, and face facts you're not ready to hang that gun belt up just yet, are you? You and me, we have our tickets made. While there could never be anything as public as a press junket, I can promise you some face-to-face and handshakes with very important people, and we'll have some off the record conversations on how the two of us fucking saved Vancouver, eh?"

My stomach churned.

"You said 'the two of us,'" I said. "Maybe I lost more blood than I thought, but if I recall correctly both Captain Vaun and Director Goode had a hand in our pyrrhic victory."

The corner of Sloan's lip twitched. He took a second to fix his tie before continuing. "Vaun was one of Mr. Rourke's true believer zealots, and he'll cling to Black Spear's corpse until he gets gangrene. And Goode? That stunted fuck's department is going to be absorbed into the Agency along with any leftover Spear operators before the next election. Face it. I'm your lifeline."

There it was. The purpose of Sloan's little bedside call. He wanted me to kiss the ring, because he was fast-tracked for the throne. Of course, that seemed dependent on me backing his claim when it came time to seek credit for saving the day. He gave me a smile that would've made a crocodile uncomfortable.

"I'm offering longevity here, West. You think the director's seat is the goal post? Come on, I'm talking political office. I'm talking the whole enchilada and a seat that hasn't seen the likes of *real* warriors since Eisenhower or Teddy goddamn Roosevelt."

I felt like telling him to go fuck himself. Burning the bridge between us didn't feel adequate. I felt like pouring a metric fuck ton of gasoline on it and incinerating its last atom. Before I had a chance to strike the match in my head, another knock sounded at the door.

"Hate to interrupt," Vaun said with a signature half-smile.

"As a matter of fact, *ex*-Captain, Cerberus Squad's better leader and I were just—"

Vaun took the insult in stride and instead slapped a document into Sloan's chest. He walked right on past him and stopped next to me.

"Doing alright, brother?"

"Better now," I muttered.

Sloan's composure slipped as he feverishly read the paper. "What the fuck is this? Black Spear's done, you don't have the authority to—"

"That seal and header at the top of the page?" Vaun said, tapping the paper as condescendingly as possible. "Looks like a bald eagle holding some leaves and a couple arrows? Says 'Seal of the President of the United States'? Probably disagrees with you."

A sudden bead of sweat dripped from Sloan's temple to his cheek.

"That 'stunted fuck' Goode had a very convincing conversation with POTUS. Black Spear's not going away anytime soon," said Vaun, much less politely than before. "Oh, that's my only copy and it *is* eyes only, so I'm going to need that back. Thanks."

He jerked the document from Sloan's hands.

"On behalf of Black Spear's director, we appreciate your cooperation, Mister Sloan."

Sloan stared daggers at Vaun, then somehow dug deep into that smarmy political toolbox he was prepping and plastered on the fakest smile I'd ever seen. "New director, hmm? He have a name?"

Vaun did not return the smile, though his expression remained genial. "That's above your paygrade. Sir."

His smile unwavering, Sloan leaned in close.

"Trust me when I say you'd rather have me as a friend than an enemy," he said. "We're all on the same side here. Play it how you want. Whoever your new boss is, he doesn't have the pull Mr. Rourke did. Just a matter of time before you come into the fold and work for me anyway. I can play the long game."

Sloan patted Vaun on the shoulder and turned on his heels. "I haven't survived this long in Washington playing anything but, son."

Vaun waited until the door latched shut before speaking again.

"Gonna have to keep an eye on that one," Vaun said with a click of his tongue. "I don't think he likes us very much."

Job security was a comforting thing. Once more I remembered Kelly's words. I wasn't stuck in this life, it was stuck with me. Because I could hold the line and would not yield. I would do everything I could, for as long as I could. If Black Spear was here to stay, then by God so was I. The person who'd thought walking away was an option didn't even exist anymore.

"So . . ." I said, drawing it out as I waited for Vaun to turn back around and look at me. "Who is the new director?"

Vaun slowly faced me, the renewed executive charter held square between his hands.

"You're looking at him. And it's *Mister* Vaun."

III

The Brittle Woman had been broken.

That's what they whispered within Legion's highest circle now. Holt was certain of it. Rinx had been at her side through the entirety of her emergency surgery to save her hand, and replace her hip, and at that same time he reached out through her vast network of Branded. Those loyal to *her* above all else. With them, she could manipulate the narrative and silence those who would view the fallout of Vancouver as an opportunity to cement their own standing in the hierarchy. The whole world was becoming aware of Legion, and now they all knew to fear them.

Footage of the world's highest intelligence representatives tearing each other limb from limb circulated in the news for weeks. That was terror which would not dissipate so easily.

Backlash from the Vancouver fiasco could be used to their advantage. What irked Holt, what truly wormed under her skin like an annoying tick, was that such a miserable oaf as Carl goddamned Tannhauser had gotten the better of her. The man had been personally dispatched by Rinx in a manner which Holt surmised could only be personal, and personal matters tend to get sloppy. Which was precisely why the SD card Tannhauser had swallowed had gone unnoticed. Unseen by Rinx, and yet discovered later during the autopsy. An autopsy that wouldn't have been necessary had he simply been the victim of a mugging in an alley, but when a corpse has nearly every bone in its body broken it tends to raise questions.

She'd scolded Rinx about that, the withering stare she'd given him when news of the SD card surfaced could've melted steel. Already some sources called it 'The Tannhauser Dossier'. It didn't matter that their own people were perfectly placed at various levels of government and in various federal agencies, it didn't matter that those insiders could obfuscate, redact, and sabotage the files to protect Legion's other projects underway. Black Spear had assuredly gotten to the Tannhauser Dossier first.

Various of her safe havens were compromised. Her identity was exposed and known bank accounts frozen, millions in assets seized by INTERPOL. Pain flared across Holt's shattered hand at the thought. The money could be recovered. Money was nothing to her. They printed more of it every day, and with a simple keystroke it could be erased or doubled. It was the damage to her reputation that she found unforgivable.

She refused to dignify Carl Tannhauser's final insult with any more thought. Instead, she focused on how Legion had still won.

While the Morpheus Engine may have been lost to them, plenty else was still theirs. Such as the research they'd taken from the Basement. They now knew *how* one could mold the mind like clay. To turn one like Adrian Rasp into Damien Black. Secrets such as that could be instrumental in future endeavors. A process that could be replicated a dozen times. A hundred. Through the Darkheart research, they would birth a new generation of Demons and Immortals. Utterly void of anything but loyalty to *them*. Living, breathing, deadly weapons with but one purpose. To serve.

Still, there were some who would disagree with Holt that this was a victory. They might even be so bold as to try to take action against her in reprisal for the loss of their organization's anonymity.

Let them try.

She'd had to remove her signet ring and wore it on a white gold chain for now. She touched the skull-adorned band at the thought, quickly removing that irrational fear that somehow she had lost it. But it was there. Dangling from her neck so delicately. A more childish person would draw a connection between the tenuous hold one has on power and how it could become the very noose one hangs from.

Holt was no child. Power was hers and hers alone by right, and her lifetime of enduring agony only proved that she could survive and recover any fall. Even this. For now, she would plan. She would prepare. All the pawns positioned before she made the next move, and all could be done from the comfort of this seaside estate retreat she kept ever ready. She'd never actually needed it before, but life was full of firsts.

Every morning Rinx wheeled her out to the balcony overlooking the white beach below. And she would sit there, thinking. The waves gently rolling onto the sands were meant to calm some of her fury. It kept it contained, but only just. The sound of the tide coming in and out was like a metronome to her. Focus. That was what she was here for. Not peace. *Never* peace.

The next time she returned to speak with the others of her tier, it would be when she felt ready. She refused to let them see her injured. They would *not* see her defeated. When next they looked upon her face, they would remember why it was she, and she alone, who was called Lady Death. Why hers was the ring honored with the skull and not a snake nor bull nor spider. They would remember why-

"Ma'am."

It never ceased to amuse Holt how a man as titanic as Rinx could speak so softly when addressing her.

"Dorian, dear," she said, tilting her voice as much as she could away from sounding annoyed, "you don't need to inform me of whatever bloody dish the kitchen's prepared before every meal. They can send the tray up all the same as long as it doesn't require fork and knife."

When she was met with silence, she pursed her lips and looked over her shoulder at her Praetorian. The man looked deeply troubled. His velvet bowler cap was held in his hands, and he couldn't draw his eyes from the ground. Those massive shoulders of his sank, and Holt knew it could only mean one thing. Unwelcome news.

"It's not that, ma'am," he said. "You've been summoned. By *him*."

This was the most impossibly unwelcome news. Holt being called like she was some mongrel pup had a clear purpose. She was meant to be paraded before them all, and answer in her current state. Not at her choosing, not when she had recovered. Not when her Branded had been given instructions.

"Dorian, there are a few things I'd like to get in order first. When are we expected to meet him?"

Rinx's eyes finally left the floor, full of apology, and met hers.

"Ma'am, there's a car waiting."

She turned and looked past him, through the large portrait windows that lined the wall of her coastal escape, to the driveway past. There was the vehicle, with twelve grim-faced men in suits waiting for her. Though they didn't wear them, Holt knew their masks were just inside their jackets. Immortals. All of them. But these did not belong to her.

"Well then," she said, placing her hands upon her lap and signaling Rinx to begin pushing her, "we'd best not keep him waiting. He's not one to ask twice."

"No, ma'am."

Rinx wheeled her to the driveway.

Lady Margot Holt was nothing less than a matriarch within their organization. Her name had been one of such reverence, such influence, long before she'd claimed her seat of power within Legion. Her shadowed throne at their highest table. She shared that table with five others, and yet someone still had to sit at the head of that table. That someone was not a patient individual.

She was Lady Death, and she was terrified.

IV

It looked like Vaun was transitioning well into his new role as director. Whatever had happened to him in the months he'd gone missing after the Warmaker case, they had been nothing if not humbling. As I sat across from his desk in the newly furnished office of our newly black-budgeted building, I noted the change in him. No longer was he the dishonored captain bitter by being sidelined. Instead, here was the leader. The *true* leader I had always known him to be. Darren Rourke left some gargantuan loafers behind, and I wasn't naïve enough to say Vaun would fill them, but I knew he would find a way to cobble a pair all his own.

Take, for instance, Black Spear's director inviting me into his office to share a cup of coffee. Can't say I'd ever imagine his predecessor extending such an invitation my way.

"Surprised Kara Mason didn't fight you for this seat," I said as I took a sip from my mug.

Vaun stirred a single teaspoon's worth of sugar into his own. "You clearly don't know Kara if you think she'd want this. She belongs on the frontline and—unlike me—she has two good legs, which she can use to kick someone's ass at twice the rate I could."

I nodded, seeing the obviousness of his statement.

Vaun shrugged. "She only ever accepted the position of Rourke's assistant and bodyguard out of respect for him. And an obligation. Now that Black's gone, I suppose she considers that debt paid."

Vaun was always deliberate with his choice of words. Words held meaning, something he was very careful with.

"You said 'gone,'" I noted. "Not dead."

His empty expression answered my rhetorical statement.

"They didn't pull a body out from the dam, did they?"

He placed his mug on the desktop, palms encircling it as if its warmth might ease some of the pain with which he spoke. "No, they did not. It doesn't necessarily mean anything, though. A few million gallons of water crashing down upon a corpse could make it difficult to wash ashore. Or, it could've been swept down the river and out the inlet to the bay before we'd even gotten on scene to fish it out. Hell, Cole, if he was alive, I imagine Legion would be hungry to punish him even more than you."

Yeah, fat chance of that.

"You think I'm being paranoid."

Vaun sighed, then used his thumb to flip something into the air to me. I caught it one-handed without looking. It was the .45 Hades round I'd let him hold. The one promised for Black.

"I think there aren't many people who walk away from getting shot in the neck and stabbed in the heart," said Vaun. "I also think, given the circumstances, you won't feel closure until you see a body."

"I think I would need closure even if a nuke had gone off at his feet."

Vaun snorted, then picked his cup up and drank. "Now *you're* starting to sound like Rourke."

"Maybe I just see the value in his pragmatism now."

"Pragmatic, he was. Organized, however, now that may not have been his strong suit."

Before I could ask, Vaun reached into a desk drawer and pulled out a classified folder. He slid it towards me.

"I've been looking for this since POTUS signed the charter. Director Goode assisted me in accessing Rourke's ghost drive. Had a treasure trove of files he'd secluded there and nowhere else. It's not everything, but . . ."

He slid a short stack of papers to me. There were plenty of stamps and disclaimers on the letterhead regarding its classification.

"After a lot of searching, one weapons schematic for a Morpheus Engine prototype."

"Hot damn," I said as I began to scan the pages. "Would've been nice to have this cheat sheet before."

"I came across something weird while looking it over."

"Define weird. Pickle flavored ice cream weird or *our* weird?"

"We've been using 'Morpheus' to refer to both the engine itself and the strange metal that powers it."

"A diesel engine runs off diesel fuel. What's your point?"

"The designers referred to the metal differently. Just flip to page thirty-two. Check the section I highlighted for you."

I thumbed through the pages and began to read the section out loud. "Proposed device to use ambient levels of energy to incapacitate enemy forces, bla bla bla, powerful hallucinations can lead to cardiac arrest in individuals or complete disruption of organizations, yada yada yada. We already know this. The dispersal device will require forging the core from . . . whoa."

The next sentence stopped me in my tracks. I looked to Vaun, who nodded at me to continue reading aloud.

"It will require forging the fuel rods from the entirety of our remaining supply of the fourth substance."

Vaun let me stew in my seat for a breath before asking, "You have the same two questions I have?"

"Yeah. They said 'remaining', so if the engine was made out of what was left, where'd the rest go?"

"The other question scares me more," Vaun said, slowly pulling the papers off the desk before placing them once more in the drawer. "If Morpheus is the fourth substance, then what do the other three do?"

ᐯ

My fingertips fumbled at my tie. The doctors said that fine motor skills in my hand would take time to come back, and that I should be grateful they didn't have to amputate it entirely. Good luck getting me to accept that silver lining any time soon. It would be a long road of recovery before I felt ready to hold a gun or knife again.

Today, the insurmountable challenge took the form of a goddamn double Windsor with my non-dominant hand. I'd been having a rough go of it for the past ten minutes, and this latest failure made attempt number six. I had to fight the urge to take my bad arm out of the sling and re-attempt the knot with a mangled hand for assistance.

"Let me," grunted Tag.

He was a patchwork of wounds himself. Over the past week he'd taken multiple shots to the vest from his own .44, and that's not mentioning the knives Black stuck him with on two separate occasions. If any of the injuries pained him as he fixed my tie for me, he didn't let it show. I was surprised at how nimble his apish hands were.

He finished, gave me a firm pat on the shoulder, and went to adjust his own knot. I took a glance in the mirror.

"Thanks."

"Sure."

I spent a moment looking at my reflection. The black suit and tie were tailored, clean, and pressed. It was just a damn shame I was in such poor condition comparatively. The jacket hid a majority of the grisly wounds Black had inflicted upon me, the worst of them being where he'd opened me up from hip to shoulder. That's not the cut I was looking at, though. It was the cut he'd dragged across my cheek in that final embrace. A fanatic terrorist on my first mission had graced me with a worse one across the opposite eye, but the cut upon my cheek bothered me.

It would scar. And then, every time I saw a mirror, I'd remember *him*. Every morning shave. Every reflective window I passed by. Every still body of water I decided to gaze into. Every. Damn. Time. The grisly laceration that had nearly bisected me diagonally could be hidden under a shirt, but the one upon my face would be impossible to ignore.

"You two ready?" asked Vaun from the doorway. "It's time."

I nodded, and the three of us walked outside. Billy waited there. Like us, injured. He wore large sunglasses to hide his black eyes, and tape across the bridge of his nose where an Immortal's fist had broken it. He did his best to disguise his slouch as just part of his typical relaxed nature, but I knew he couldn't stand up straight lest he pop the stitches keeping his stomach inside his abdominal cavity.

We all hurt. We all experienced pain. But there wasn't a doctor on earth that would've kept us away from this. Because what we were about to do was going to hurt a hell of a lot worse.

Kara Mason and Burt Galleon joined us. The six of us took our positions. Together, we lifted Daniel Kelly's coffin.

A bagpipe started playing a dirge, which tried to pull my heart from my chest. The tune made me want to double over onto the ground and fall apart. But I wouldn't. For him, I would stand. For him, I could keep walking. We all would. There was something about the sorrowful music that made my eyes heavy. It scythed through any resolve I possessed. Any restraint. Earlier, I'd refused to let myself cry any tears. 'Not yet,' I'd told myself.

They came now, no shame at all in them.

On the other side of the coffin, I saw that Tag silently wept as well. There was no need to hide them. No need to wipe them away. Billy's sunglasses masked his eyes, but there was no mistaking the wet marks on either purpled cheek.

I'd been so busy looking at my guys, I hadn't bothered to see those who were in attendance. There were so many. Some I recognized, others I didn't. But it was the number that wrenched harder sobs from me. It was then that I knew these were all the people Kelly had either saved or served with. All of them. They'd all come. One look at Vaun, and he corroborated it with a solemn nod.

As we drew closer to where my friend, my brother, would lay eternal it finally dawned on me. Today Daniel Kelly wouldn't be remembered as a ghost. To the crowd in attendance, to those who had *truly* known him, he was no nameless assassin. He was a hero. And would be honored as one. The truth of that, which I thought he would be denied even in death, only brought forth more tears from my eyes. These, at least, were bittersweet.

If any in attendance thought it strange that our motley group, collectively damaged as we were, were the ones bearing his casket, they didn't show it. Every step closer to Kelly's final resting place felt like a mile. I tried with all my might to stay grounded. I wanted to be focused on being present, to remain in the moment, and not be pulled away by my thoughts. My dreads for tomorrow, my regrets from yesterday, they all tried to sink their hooks in and pull me away.

Instead, it was the good memories that drew me from the present. My first day meeting Kelly and learning his name only after we'd finished beating each other. Or how he'd been the first one to willingly show me around, showed me my locker, gave me my new uniform. It was only mere hours after that first day that he'd saved my life for the first time—far from the last—by pushing me out of a bullet's path. The men of Cerberus Squad were my brothers, but Kelly was the first who'd openly chosen to be my friend.

By the time I pulled myself free from my memories, and fought off the haze I'd drifted to, the casket was about to be lowered. There was a beat where it seemed as if nobody wanted the next part to come. Before it could, Tag abruptly made his way to the side of the casket and wrenched it open.

"I'm sorry," he said simply.

A few in attendance held their breath, concern raised by what the big man was doing, but this was by its very nature an irregular ceremony.

"The boatman might try to charge you a coin, but that was never your way, was it?" he said, and from the back of his belt Tag drew his snub-nosed revolver. His treasured .44 magnum. There was fresh pain in his eyes as he placed the weapon in our fallen comrade's hands. "You make him to take you, brother."

Both of Tag's eyes were bottomless pits that drowned with guilt. The only thing I wanted to do in that moment was pull him from those waters, but I knew this was a moment he needed to fare through on his own.

"I hope it serves you well on the other side," Tag said, and he gave the hand cannon a final pat.

A second later, he lowered the lid back into place with a grunt. Moments passed. The bagpipe's dirge continued. Our friend's casket descended into the earth. Things continued in a blur. Kelly's history was a sordid one, to say the least, and far too complicated to allow for speeches of remembrance. Eventually the bagpipe's song ended, and just our small crowd stood vigil in the rain before an open grave. One by one, the guests in attendance rose from their seats to depart. Some approached to toss a handful of dirt upon the casket. I noticed a few retired admirals and generals among them.

The light drizzle picked up to a heavier downpour and hurried most others to say their goodbyes. I became a sentinel before his grave, unwilling to move. There was a hole in the world, and it was right there in front of me. The second I finished saying goodbye and left, I'd be forced to truly accept and live with the hole in my life where my friend had once been. So instead, I stood fast in the rain as others left.

Before long, it was down to just four of us. The Cerberus Squad, alone and together again at last. I couldn't say how long we waited there together. A minute, an hour. It all felt the same. The four of us resembled statues. Still. Silent. Nothing spoken yet feelings mirrored as one all the same. These were things words wouldn't have captured, anyway.

Vaun was the first to fidget. It would've been easy to blame it on his bad leg, but I figured he was still wrestling with some shame over being elsewhere when Kelly died. When it finally won out, he gave a simple nod, grabbed a handful of dirt, and cast it down upon the casket. We all acknowledged his departure without judgment and continued our watch.

Tag was next to go. The big man hissed like a hydraulic machine as he eased down to a knee, his knife and bullet wounds screaming anew, and tossed his handful in. Tag was ever the quiet one, but there was something in his silence now that screamed of a different kind of pain. It was his own gun that had taken Kelly's life, and he hadn't even been there. That knowledge cut him in a way he might not ever heal from. Tag said something about us meeting Vaun and Mason somewhere. There was an offer to share drinks and stories, I replied with an ambiguous grunt straight out of Tag's own playbook.

The irony of that made Tag almost smile before he walked away.

Then, it was just me and Billy. A crack of thunder broke open the sky and the downpour transformed into a hard deluge. The water pelting me from head to toe seemed to gradually wash away the foul sadness, until once more all I felt was that tension burning off of Billy. We'd talked it over back at Pike Site, but that hatchet was far from buried. With the day's battle done and all manner of ill intentions thwarted at the moment, there was nothing left to distract us. We were forced to once more take stock of the bad blood between us.

I'd learned to forgive myself—at least partially—when Black had nearly killed me, but being forgiven at least partially by Billy was another matter.

"Billy," I finally managed to say, "I just wanted to—"

"Save it, Captain."

He pushed his sunglasses back up the bridge of his nose, quickly threw some dirt at the grave, and left without another word. I told myself that everyone grieved differently, but that was a bitter pill to swallow regardless of its truth.

"Give him time," someone said.

I turned back to see Kelly's ghost standing on the other side of the grave from me. The image was faint, almost like a developing photo but in reverse. I tried to rationalize it as residual Morpheus exposure finally wearing off, but I'd seen enough to think maybe it was just an honest to God ghost in front of me.

I rendered a salute. It was slow, very slow, and when my bladed hand brushed my forehead, Kelly rendered his own in kind. I held mine for what seemed like forever. Then, when I was finally ready, I lowered the salute just as slowly as I'd raised it. My hand once more passed across my line of sight, but this time when I finished the motion Kelly was gone.

There was only me, alone again, standing amidst the storm. I knelt down, clutched a handful of dirt, and cast it into the grave.

"Goodbye, my friend."

VI

I kept thinking about what's ahead. The wars to come, the many graves yet to be filled, and the threats to be faced. The sheer scale of the unknown looming ahead was staggering. Vaun's revelation about the Morpheus metal and the remaining secret substances was nothing less than a four-knuckled haymaker to the gut. There was so much more out there, and all of it potentially worse than what we'd already faced.

This was the burden Kelly said I was charged with. Not a curse, but a responsibility. I knew in my heart that Kelly was far from the last friend I would lose traveling this road, and that my gun belt had more than a few notches left to add. But I would face it all, unyielding, unflinching. No matter how hard it got, no matter the cost, I would keep going.

You can take it.

I headed to my private quarters, fully intending on crashing until the world made more sense. Which was probably never.

Something caught my attention the second I flipped on the light. There, stuck into the center of my desk in the corner of my room. Eight inches of sharpened obsidian stabbed into my desktop, and a burned marble handle next to it. Last time I saw this particular piece of volcanic glass, I'd just broken it off in Black's chest and watched it fall off a cliff.

All along its gleaming black edge were the brownish stains of long dried blood.

Too many questions sprouted. Nobody should have access to the room. Nobody. Did the bastard survive like I thought, or did one of Legion's other creatures pluck it from his corpse and leave it as a message for me? Either way, the message was clear. This wasn't over.

My hand went to my pocket and found the .45 round Vaun had

returned to me. It wasn't just a bullet anymore. It was a promise, one that would remain unbroken. I didn't know what awaited me down this road, but I knew I would stand strong before it. I was good with that, and with that final resolve I at last laid my weary head down for a proper sleep.

For the first time in many months, no nightmares haunted my dreams.

ACKNOWLEDGMENTS

In 2021, *FNG* introduced readers to Cole West. A couple years, three total novels, and some very fun short stories later, and one thing is true for Cole as much as it is me: no mission is ever completed alone. There's a reason I decided to call this series *Black Spear* and not *Cole West*. Even if one guy inevitably has to take the point, he can't do it without plenty of people backing his play and supporting in their unique ways. So here's to the team that helped get me this far! My name might be in big letters on the cover, but the content within the pages would be worth far less without your contributions.

Thank you to the whole Acorn Publishing team for taking Cole and *Black Spear* from a mere idea in my head and a Word Document on my desktop, and turning it into the award-winning series it is now.

A special heartfelt thanks to my wonderful editor, Laura, for taking said Word Documents and helping me elevate them into what they are now. Your support and guiding wisdom has made me a better writer, and I will be forever in your debt for it.

The Morpheus Engine is assuredly a creation of fiction, but I cannot overlook thanking both Mr. Brandon Wagner and Mr. Buford Mitchell of the U.S. Army's Maneuver Support Center of

Excellence. I was a student of theirs in 2024, and their expertise in nuclear weapons and radiological hazards was nothing less than encyclopedic. You gentlemen are truly the shepherds of legacy knowledge, may you both continue providing it to future generations of warfighters and ensure nothing gets lost by the bureaucracy of publication updates.

I've been fascinated with obsidian for some time, and am forever grateful to my friend Mr. Patrick Antuzzi providing me a mere glimpse into the wealth of knowledge he has. Your passion for your craft is no small thing, and though you've assured me it's okay I still have a twinge of regret that I've taken a smidgeon of that passion and used it to craft a truly monstrous character. Mr. Black and his obsidian daggers are better off from having your insights!

To the best friend, partner, wife, and cheerleader a guy could ever dream of having: thank you for being a fixed point of inspiration and motivation I could always count on. You've raised our children on your own when I've been deployed, a task that most days is arguably more challenging than negotiating with extreme terrorists. And yet, against all odds, I've returned to an intact home and (mostly) well-behaved children every time. Even with that impossible task, you've still encouraged me at every step. Best of all, you've never let me *stop* taking those steps and you've always kept me moving forward. You're the best, babe.

Lastly, to the readers. The ones who reached out to tell me that my writing mattered to them, that it was real, and that they felt something whether it was from the thrills, the chills, the snark, or the sadness. To the ones who have been right there alongside Cole from his first days and now to these darkest ones yet. The ones who went out of their way to tell me a character resonated with them regardless of if it was Cole West, Daniel Kelly, or even big dumb Dante. I love writing because it's so much fun, and if something on the page has made you smile wide then clearly I'm writing something right.

ABOUT THE AUTHOR

Born and raised in California, Benjamin Spada has had a lifelong passion for storytelling. A dedicated taco aficionado and self-described "Professor of Batmanology," he has made a career in the United States Marine Corps. He has been a martial arts instructor and a section leader in the Wounded Warrior Battalion for our nation's wounded, ill, and injured. Also, he has served overseas to help train our foreign military allies in defense against chemical, biological, and nuclear weapons. Despite these grim assignments, he has carried on with equal amounts of sarcasm and stoicism.

When out of uniform, Benjamin is an avid sci-fi and horror movie fan, tattoo collector, comic enthusiast, and two-time holder of the platinum trophy in The Elder Scrolls V: Skyrim. Benjamin lives with his wife and their four daughters, in Oceanside, California.

Project Darkheart is the third novel in his award-winning Black Spear series.